I0652716

CRIMINAL DEFENSE
REDEMPTION

ALICE J. HARRIS-WOOD

NEWMAN SPRINGS PUBLISHING
320 Broad Street
Red Bank, NJ 07701

First originally published by Newman Springs Publishing 2023

ISBN 978-1-68498-422-0 (Paperback)
ISBN 978-1-68498-420-6 (Digital)

Printed in the United States of America

IN LOVING MEMORY of all my family members who have long passed away. Family was very important to them. Their gene of loving the family, instead of the criminal gene, has been passed down to the current generation.

INTRODUCTION

CRIMINALS ARE AMONG us all, but Lola was a criminal by way of genetic defect. She was born to be a criminal, and only her family history would set her free from going to jail for a long time or maybe for life.

Lola was desperate and she needed to reveal the crimes of her forefathers to avoid going to jail. This is a story about love, revenge, murder, racketeering, prostitution, and many other crimes that were committed by the Harrison family dating back to the early 1900s.

Each generation were career criminals but loved that lifestyle. Lola never tried to be anything but a criminal until she found herself sitting in a dark, smelly jail cell. The past had caught up with her. She was the first of the entire family of criminals to land in a jail holding cell.

The Harrison family, throughout the years, had to overcome many challenges to survive. Each generation changed how they handled criminal activities and passed the wealth and knowledge to the next generation. Along with the wealth, they passed the criminal genes. Each generation loved that life.

As the family history was passed down to the next generations and as the family members fell in love and got married, the color of the family changed. This family never showed any signs of being prejudice and in fact did not even think about color. It was only a problem when outsiders became aware that this was an interracial family made up of black and white family members.

The Harrison family endured many ups and downs but always landed on their feet. At the end, the family came to Lola's defense, starting with the forefathers. This story is all about a family of criminals and how they came together to save Lola.

Alice Harris Wood is the youngest of thirteen children whose parents were from Littleton, North Carolina. Her father and mother and uncles and aunts did whatever it took to survive. If it meant being a criminal, that is how they lived. Many of the fictional characters and events came from actual family criminal behaviors. The Harrison families were true survivors. None of them ever went to jail, not even Lola.

THE HARRISON FAMILY
A Generation of Criminals

CHAPTER 1

*T*HIS IS A *dark place, the voices are loud, and it is cold and dirty. How did I allow myself to become part of this? Does anyone care? I hope no one touches me. If they do, I will scream, but will any-*one hear? Deep down inside of me, I know my life has been wrong, but am I responsible, or was it in my genes?* Lola's conversation with herself caused tears to flow down her pretty cream-color, small, smooth face. Her hair was without any shape, but it was still pretty, even though it needed a good shampooing.

Lola sat quietly in the corner on the floor hoping that the love of her life would come and rescue her. She waited and waited, and no one came. "Did anyone care?" she said to herself. She could hear different names being called but not hers. Lola knew that to survive, she had to save herself. At that moment, she relaxed and accepted the fact that this was the holding cell for the jail. Her next move would be leaving to go up to the Big House (jail).

I must understand my past in order to defend my future, thought Lola, *Who can I turn to, who knows the past? How did I become a gangster, and a madam, and a drug kingpin all in one body and end up in jail and maybe for life? Oh, I know the past because of what my grandparents left behind.*

Lola looked up from her small space in the cell, and there was a tall, good-looking young man who looked like he just stepped out of a magazine. His body was that of an athlete, and she could smell

3

his cologne that lightly covering his body. His light-golden skin and bedroom eyes made him a very handsome man. As he was kneeling down toward her, Lola thought, *Is he the one? He is a black man, but I believe he is the right man for me.*

"Are you Miss Lola?" asked the man softly.

"Yes," replied Lola, "and are you my prince who has come to rescue me?"

"Rescue, I don't know, but defend you, yes. You are accused of racketeering, drug selling, prostitution, and illegal liquor sales, and etc."

With his head low, Ted spoke in a very low voice so that others could not hear him. "This is my first case with such heavy charges. I am a specialist in traffic violations and was forced to handle this case for my boss. My boss is a good friend of your Uncle Nick, and he was asked to get you out of this mess at any cost.

"Then congratulations, you are a winner on your first criminal case. I got it all figured out. Just listen to my story and follow my lead. I come from good stock. Redd's children did not produce any dummies. You go and come back with a tape recorder and I will tell my story and the court will be understanding,"

"I have a tape recorder with me," said Ted. "Start from the beginning."

"Redd was my grandfather. He was an Irishman from Harrisonville, NC," said Lola.

Sitting in this dark corner, not wanting anyone to touch me, and smelling bad odors brought back memories of my family's past which created a hot fire in my chest that only the truth could put out. The bootlegging, speakeasies, the ladies of the night, and the reputation of not giving a damn, was all turning around in her head.

She took a deep breath and decided if she could explain her ancestry to this man and the court than an angel from heaven would descend upon her and raise her up from this hellhole and lead her on to live a righteous life. This was all that she had that she could hold on to.

"I believed it all started around early 1900s when my grandfather was a teenager. They called him Redd because he had red skin with dark curly black hair. He was Irish. My father would say, 'My father was the Godfather of the South, and he was a genius, and I loved him. He was my role model. When I grow up, I want to be just like him.'

"My father got his wish because he was a chip off the old block. He was the Godfather of the South, South Harrisonville County."

"'Do not drop any of that corn or the husk because we need it all. I have two types of moonshine to make, one for the blacks and one for the whites. This farm is a moneymaker, not a money loser. I pay good wages for a good day's work. If you cannot work, you will be replaced now and not tomorrow. Therefore, keep pushing and keep working,' said Redd as he looked over his workers.

"'Redd, the moonshine orders are coming in faster than we can make the liquor,' said his foreman.

"'Keep the orders coming we can build more stills. Call Harry and tell him to get over here, now. He needs to set up three more stills.'

"According to my father, Redd was a fair man who migrated here from the old country and believed in a day's work for a day's pay. If you could not do the work, then you were out of here. Deep in the swamp the stills were laid out and organized like tombstones in a graveyard. One side produced the mild stuff that was made from corn, and the other side produced the hellfire that was said to put hair on your chest. It was made from the corn husk."

"Redd said to his operator, 'I do not care if the blacks buy the hell fire. If they got the money, then we got the time to sell. Money is money I don't give a damn where it comes from. White power, black power, but green power is the only power that counts to me.'

"As the sun went down, many of the white men from the area would visit 'Redd's Do Drop Inn' and chill out from a long hard day's work. 'Welcome, have a good time, but do not start anything, or there will be two hits. I will hit you, and you will hit the floor,' said

Redd. Redd was a big man, about 6'10" and smart and he practiced what he preached.

"Do Drop Inn was a place for men only, but one day Redd was informed that Jumbo, a competitor, started having white women in his place serving men their drinks. This did not set well with Redd, so he decided to have black women serve drinks and cook food. This brought his regulars back but the competition did not stop trying to steal Redd's customers. Therefore, Redd decided to put an end to all of this nonsense.

"Redd said to his operator, 'Get me my shot gun and my black horse and five guys. This bastard is dead meat tonight. I am sick of this shit. I have given him many opportunities to leave my business alone, and now it is time to take action. I will buy him out or put him out.'

"It was raining hard, but Redd did not care. He was on a mission to put this sucker out of business tonight. The six of them rode for over an hour to Jumbo's spot. Redd went in with his backup behind him and his shotgun ready to fire. He walked right over to Jumbo and said in a soft voice, 'Jumbo, you have two options. You can leave and give your place to me or go six feet under. Which one you choose makes no difference to me. This place belongs to me tonight.'

"Jumbo knew of Redd's reputation and looked him dead in the eyes then lowered his head and, without looking up, walked out. Redd yelled out, "Let the good times roll. Fiddler, play some music, and you women push the tables back and grab a man, and let's dance. The moonshine is on me tonight!'

"Redd, on his way home with his men, were ambushed by Jumbo and his gang. Redd's horse was shot from under him, but he was able to hide in the woods. The other men were all slaughtered. Redd waited until the hunt for him was over and headed home. As the sun was coming up he stumbled into the kitchen and passed out on the floor.

"When he woke up, he said, 'As God is my witness, my family and I will never be defeated again by any man. We might be down but we will never be out.'

"'Rita,' he said, who was his wife, 'I want a breakfast fit for a king. For as of this day, I am the King. The Moonshine King, the only go to guy, without me nothings will move or happen.

"Rita quickly got his breakfast together and called their two sons to come and eat.

"Nate and Nick, who were twins, came to the table as if it was time for a new lesson in life. They were right it was a lesson on life that would be their family code that was to be adhered to at any cost.

"'Okay,' said Redd, 'this is the first day of us building an empire and to let our customers and clients know that we are open for business and we are the business.'

"Redd took a deep breath and looked around, nodding his head, and after a few minutes, yelled, 'I will not be undersold. I will do to others before they do to me. I will never be defeated [I might be down but not out]. I will do whatever it takes to keep my family safe and to feed them. I will kill to keep the family name intact for future generations. I will never be scared to die.

"'Boys, finish your meal for we have some business to take care of today,' said Redd.

"'What kind of business, Pop?' said Nick, looking concerned as he was the oldest of the two boy by one minute.

"'All I am going to tell you at this point is that you will not be disappointed.'

"Redd, Nick, and Nate saddled up their horses and off they went heading towards Jumbo's bar. Redd had in his saddle bags everything he needed to accomplish his mission. The boys still did not know the mission but it was understood that someone was not going to be happy in a few hours.

"The bar was closed because it did not open until late afternoon. Redd knew this and it was part of his plan. He did not want anyone but Jumbo to get hurt. He just wanted to eliminate Jumbo as a competitor and make him pay for the killing of his six men. His plan was a two-part plan. First burn down the bar, then find Jumbo, and kill him for killing his men.

"When they got to the bar, Redd handed Nick and Nate several bottles of kerosene with a flaming rag hanging from the top. 'Throw the bottles, boys, throw them now!' Redd yelled. They threw the bottles and the wood building went up in flames.

"Jumbo was inside and came running out shouting, 'I will kill you, Irish trash.'

"This really set Redd off. 'I will make sure that you will not have to see this trash ever again. You poor, white scumbag,' said Redd, with a look on his face that would have scared God. He rode right up to Jumbo and put his shotgun up against his head and pulled the trigger. Redd said in a voice that sounded like a priest, 'One more sinner going straight to hell!'

"Before the dust had settled over this situation, Redd took the bodies of his six men to the sheriff's office and said what had happened earlier.

"'I will take care of everything. You know you are my best friend. I will always have your back. You have taken care of this town and all that comes in contact with you. We here in Harrisonville respected your father and that is why this town is named after your family. You are our largest employer. I am your partner and so is this town,' said the sheriff.

"Redd's mind was always turning, trying to come up with new ways to make money and keep control in his hands. That day he was back talking and encouraging his workers to work harder and longer or someone else will replace you. 'Work harder, work longer, or you will be replaced!' Redd yelled.

"Rita called the family together for dinner. Redd had dreamed about his plans for building an empire of business enterprises, some legal and some not legal. The legal ones he would use to shelter the illegal businesses. At dinner he laid out his entire plan for expansion.

"As Redd started speaking, Nick and Nate glanced back and forward toward each other. They knew that his plans were well thought out and that they were to play a major part.

"Okay, boys,' said Redd, 'this is the plan. I will lay the whole organization out along with the system. My first cousin who lives in

Upstate PA has suddenly died. He was an only child and his parents died about ten years ago. He had bird seeds for a brain. He owned about 175 acres of farm, forest, and swampland. Can you believe all that to an idiot who was just a waste of meat?'

"Nick said, 'How did he die? Why didn't we know about this cousin?'

"Well, boys, the reason you did not know about him, was that he was not worth talking about. The farm was being run by a friend who was stealing everything from him. So I stopped that. I visited my cousin last summer for a few days and had him to do two things. I knew what needed to be done so I did it. He made a Will leaving everything to his beloved first cousin who grew up with him like a brother. You know that was a lie. Next, I became his power of attorney.'

"'Well, Pop,' the boys said at the same time, 'does this story have an interesting ending?'

"'Yes, because I caused it to have a great ending. Later I found out that he had a $100,000 paid up whole life insurance policy, which was purchased by his parents when he was baby. I made myself the sole beneficiary. It was a pity that the breaks on his truck failed, and he ran into a tree and was thrown out of the truck.

"'Oh my,' said, Nick.

"'Unbelievable,' said Nate.

"Little did they know that Redd had his cousin killed.

"'The police called and told me that he died. My cousin is in heaven. He was a dummy, but he never hurt anyone,' said Redd as he closed his eyes and said a short prayer.

"Speaking like a priest, Redd said, 'This man is going straight to heaven, and that is a fact.'

"'Now that we have more land and more money we can start our building of the empire that will be passed down for other generations. To start with, I want to send Nate to Georgia to work the land and the area,' Pop spoke like a general in the army.

"'You will find a woman and make her your wife. Make sure that you do love her and she is pretty. Have lots of children. By doing this, everyone will see you as a family man with many business ties.

"'Your main crop will be corn. In the swamp, you will set up your stills. You will open up several bars that are legal and sell our moonshine. I will handle the distribution of the moonshine to other parts of Georgia. You will find the drivers and I will guarantee the delivery. If trouble finds you, take care of it, but inform me before you kill anyone.

"'In your bars, hire fast women and offer good hometown cooking and music and keep the music going with dancing. It should be nonstop all night until the sun comes up. Have several guards at the door to throw out rough people. If the peace officers come, pay them off and give them a bottle of our best moonshine,' said Redd, as he started to stand up.

"'Keep an eye on the money! Have your wife in charge of the finances. Make an example out of someone who you know is stealing from you. This can be done in several ways. One cut off their hand or just kill them. Whatever happens you have to maintain your laws and your order.

"'If it appears that you are having a problem with the peace officers, send your wife over to charm them and to settle the problems,' Redd said with a deep conviction that this was the right course to take.'"

Lola stopped talking and was having a hard time keeping the family ancestry history going. Lola said remembering what her father would say about her mother, "What his Georgia Peach wanted, she got." She was thinking about her father's saying as she surveyed this gorgeous creature. Ted was great looking with smooth light-brown skin and pretty brown bedroom eyes. The aroma coming from his clothes was sending her straight to the bedroom. His eyes reminded her of her brother.

"Oh my," said Lola in a low, soft voice.

"What was that you said, Miss Lola?," Ted said, looking totally involved.

"I was thinking about something my father would say about my mother," said Lola.

"Lola, let's continue with your defense because what you have given me so far will not even get you a reduced sentence," replied Ted.

"It was told to me that Redd had even bigger and better plans for Nick," said Lola.

"Redd turned to Nick, who was the youngest of the twins, and said, 'You are a lot like me. I know it is in the genes. You think things through, you take action, and you will deliver. In this business, having all those attributes will make for an important man in this competitive field of business. Therefore, I have laid the ground work for you but all the small details of how to accomplish your mission will be up to you.' Redd, sounded like the good father giving his son some advice on how to make an honest living.

"'I have some very important friends in Philadelphia and New York. I have sent word that you will be there by the end of the month. They will provide you with two row homes in South Philly. You will take the money that I will give you and renovate the buildings by tearing down the adjoining walls. This will allow for a larger home. The home will have two basements, eight bedrooms, two kitchens, two bathrooms, one large living room, and one large dining room.' Redd spoke as if he had a list written in his brain.

"'You will put bars up at all the windows. This will keep the peace officers out until you can close down your activities,' said Redd.

"'I guess you want me to decide what activities will be going on at my home,' said Nick.

"'Yes and no,' replied Redd. 'My friends will teach you the business. Do not, under any circumstances, get married or fall in love. That will truly be your downfall. A woman in this business is a liability that will be hard to overcome. As you get further into the business, you will understand.' Redd spoke these word like a man who had been there and done that.

"Rita was a woman that he married to help raise his two boys. But he did not love her like a lover, only as a partner raising children, cleaning, and cooking. She did love him and was willing to settle for that small part of him.

"Redd's first wife name was named Nina. She was tall, thin, silky, smooth, creamy skin, with long dark-brown thick hair. No matter where she went, all heads would turn. She was beautiful from head to toe. She knew she was blessed with many of the benefits of beauty that most people could only dream about.

"Nina was very smart and at an early age decided what road she would travel in life. Her road consisted of having men to adore her with money. She learned the business from an older girl who was about twenty-two years old who saw the potential in Nina. She took one look at her and became Nina's good friend. Her name was Candee, and she had total control over her new young friend Nina, who was sixteen years old.

"'I want, more than anything, to use my gifts that God has given me to make men happy and, at the same time, become very wealthy,' Nina spoke these words to Candee as she was laying out Nina's future.

"'To begin with,' said Candee, 'all types of men are going to try to claim you. Do not let that happen. If you do, your chosen career will be over.

"'You must be sure this is what you want,' said Candee in a very directing voice. 'Never have sex with any customers. That is never acceptable in the business that we are going to introduce to this county.'

"'How do I start?' said Nina.

"'Tell your parents that you have a job in the next county,' said Candee.

"'I do not have any parents or any relatives but have always wished for a family of my own one day,' revealed Nina.

"'Well, you can start by calling me Candee, how's that?' said Candee as she smiled.

"'I have foster parents who will be happy to know that I am leaving. They were friends of my parents and took me in and gave me a place to live,' said Nina as she looked hopeful about her future.

"'I have dreamed of starting this business. I have most of the details worked out. Money will not be an issue because I have a boyfriend that just loves me. In fact, he wants to marry me but I am scared,' said Candee.

"'My friend's name is Buddy. He is a good looking guy. He has never been married. I would be the first. Becoming the first Mrs. Buddy and the wife of a true criminal sounds like a good future. Buddy is involved in many activities, but I act as though I do not know. I did some research on him and found out he is the boss in Harrisonville County. He is worth millions,' said Candee, spoken like an authority figure.

"'He once told me he had a business partner named Redd. They grew up together like brothers. Redd and Buddy has been friends since the age of sixteen. I have never seen this Redd character, but from what Buddy told me, he is someone worth knowing,' implied Candee.

"'Well, I would like to meet someone nice one day, but for now, I just want to get our business off the ground,' said Nina.

"'Okay, let's see, I will ask Buddy to give me one of his buildings for our saloon. We will open up late and stay open until day break. We will sell food that is cooked by the blacks in the area. They are the only ones in this county that can cook. Their cooking is so good that men will be asking us to sell them food to take home. Our clients will be men and women. We will also sell corn liquor supplied by Redd and his gang. The music will be played by the blacks because they know how to get it going. The singers can be white or black as long as they can sing and the customers can dance,' said Candee.

"'I have a few ideas,' said Nina. 'In a totally different area of the building, maybe the basement, we can have a special place for men and be women who what to get together to socialize. I can run that part of the business. I will charge the men by the hour for the room and pay the women per client. This part of the business will be open twenty-four hours and every day of the week.' Looking very innocent, Nina added, 'Is there a name for this type of business, Candee?'

"Yes, a gentlemen's basement," replied Candee in a joking way.

"Great, that is what we will call my area of expertise, The Gentlemen's Basement,' said Nina.

"'I will call my business Candee's Palace,' said Candee in a sweet, low, sexy voice.

"'I will get in touch with Buddy and run our plans past him. I know he will like the idea and will also be extending the services that we plan to provide. He thinks big and goes big with everything,' said Candee.

"Buddy had several businesses. They included farming—produce and livestock—rental properties, rooming homes, speakeasies, moonshine producing, gambling, banking, and insurance. Buddy grew up the hard way, fending for himself, because his father was killed robbing a bank. His mother gave him away after the death of his father to a childless preacher and his wife. When Buddy got the chance, he stole the church offering and took off. He was on his way to anywhere except that town.

"He landed in Harrisonville and met Redd. Redd's genes for criminal activities matched up with Buddy's perfectly, and they were friends instantly. Redd's experience from the old country made him the perfect partner in crime.

"Their empire all started with the introduction of making outstanding corn liquor that could be produced quickly without losing its quality. As times changed, they changed and they got involved in legal businesses that were profitable but at the same time concealed their true vocation. That is being professional gangsters."

Ted asked the jail attendant if he could have a private room to interview his client. As they were walking to the room, Ted walked slightly behind Nina. He started looking at her feet. He could see her toes in the flip-flops that she was wearing that her feet were well kept. Her toes were manicured with a bright-red polish that matched her lips and accented the shape and beauty of her feet.

As his eyes rolled upward, he noticed that her legs were perfect in shape and size. The short skirt she was wearing could only be worn by her. Anyone else would have destroyed the design. Ted thought to himself, *There must be a God that made such a beautiful creature.*

Lola's waist was just the right size to whole tight as a lover would to make love with her. Her breasts were small but sweet to look at. She was wearing a spaghetti-strapped top with a low-cut front.

Ted tried to stop himself from looking at Lola but was unable to control his eyes. His eyes wandered up to her neck, and that was when he stopped walking behind her and rushed up to open the door.

"After you, lovely lady," said Ted, spoken like a gentleman.

"Lola, your family history is getting very interesting, and I want to hear more," said Ted.

"Okay, there is plenty more to tell. This family of mine never gave me a chance in life to be an honest working person. It *is* really not their fault, for it is all about the genes," said Lola as she started sitting in the cushioned chair.

"Candee sent word to Buddy that she wanted to see him and it was all about business. Buddy knew that Redd was his best friend and partner and that all business must be discussed among the three of them.

"'I love Candee,' said Buddy.

"'Hopefully one day she will marry me. She has everything a man like me needs, but she changes the subject every time I come close to talking about future plans with her,' said Buddy with a sad look on his face.

"'Well, my friend, I will never fall in love. I love the single life. Having a different woman every night and loving it. Marriage will never work for me. I do not want someone asking me questions, like where are you going, when will you be back, and that suit does not look good on you. To hell with married life, I love this life, and it cannot get any better than this. Trust me, friend, we are better off single,' said Redd, spoken like a true friend.

"Buddy had a key to Candee's home, and he opened the door, and Redd and Buddy just walked right in. Walking in without being announced made Buddy feel like a husband. This gave him a pleasant feeling about his relationship with Candee.

"The two gals were sitting on the sofa having a drink when the men entered. 'This is my cousin Nina. She will be staying with me until she gets her own place, okay, boys?' said Candee in a low, sexy voice.

"The two men looked like school boys that just saw their first look at a woman's body. Their feet were frozen to the floor. No words were able to be formed because their jaws were shut tight and locked. Candee kept yelling Buddy's name, but he did not respond. Finally, Nina got up and went towards Redd and kissed him on his lips. At that point he came back astonished and shocked.

"Everything Redd had said about not falling in love was gone. He was in love at the sight of this beautiful woman. 'You are gorgeous, you are gorgeous, you are gorgeous,' said Redd, with no control of his words.

"'Redd, Redd, Redd, snap out of it, pull yourself together,' said Candee.

"'Guys, come and sit down and have a strong drink,' said Candee in a strong, commanding voice.

"'To start with, this is my cousin, and she is a beauty. She is young but willing to learn the business,' said, Candee.

"After taking a few sips of his drinks, Buddy said, 'What do you mean by learning the business?'

"'I have been with you for many years. Long before you became rich with influence. Your banking operation, insurance business, and the gambling enterprises have survived because of the long hours and hard work that I have devoted to the business. It is my time to open up a new business of my own with my cousin. I have many of the details worked out. I will start small and expand in a few years,' said Candee in a demanding-sounding voice.

"'So tell me what you want, my love,' said Buddy.

"'To begin with, you can see that Nina is beautiful. With her beauty and my business knowledge, we can get it right the first time. What is needed is a nice looking big building in town. We want it to be accessible to customers who are walking or riding. I like to open a saloon. It will be called Candee's Palace. I will serve alcohol, food, music, and dancing. It will be like a New York City club but located in Harrisonville. It will be glamorous with pretty girls serving the drinks and food. The music will be live with a band and singers. The customers can dance or sit and enjoy the music,' said Candee, looking very calculating.

"'In the basement, Nina will be dressed like a porcelain doll baby. Part of the basement will be for men who want to socialize with a beautiful woman like Nina. She will run that business. Located in the basement will be another business that will help to expand your current business like poker games. Even though the basement is illegal, there should not be much of a problem because of your influence with top-elected officials and the local law enforcement. Many of them will also be patrons of the Gentlemen's Basement,' said Candee.

"'If we have room, there can also be a number writing business for your bookies,' said Candee, looking business like. 'As you can see, I have been thinking about this a long time, and Nina came into my life and gave me hope, excitement, and energy to take on such a big project,' Candee added, spoken like a professional businesswoman.

"'Yes, it is obvious that this is what you want. It is also what I want for you. We can work out the details later, but there is one thing I would want from you. Let's go into the other room. This is between you and me,' said Buddy.

"Candee did not know what to expect, so she just followed Buddy into the other room without any hesitation.

"Redd looked at Nina and walked right up to her without blinking his eyes. 'I do not believe I am saying this, but you will be my wife. I cannot help myself, but no other woman has ever turned me on like you. I just met you for the first time. It is also the first time I met your cousin. Buddy talks about her all the time. I think if she asked him to go straight and be honest, he would do just that. I could never understand his love for this woman, but now I understand,' said Redd, with a very sober face.

"Nina looked at Redd and felt the same way, love at first sight. *I do not want a short romance before I tie the knot*, thought Nina. *Therefore, I will have him wine and dine me for a while or until I am twenty-one*, she mused further as she analyzed the situation.

"*Redd's beautiful curly black hair and red face made him look out-standing. He was dressed splendidly from neck to his feet. He was a tall slender man with a good speaking voice*, thought Nina. *He could have been anything in this world if he wanted it. But Redd chose to be a gangster*, she thought to herself as she looked him up and down in a girlish demeanor.

"'Nina, do you think I can meet your family soon?' said Redd.

"Oh, you do move quickly. Well, you see, Redd, Candee is all I have, and you met her tonight,' said Nina. 'Therefore, we can skip the family thing and go to dinner soon, okay?' said Nina.

"*That sounds like a lady who knows what she wants and how to get it*, thought Redd.

"'We will go to the finest place to dine in this state. That is my country club,' said Redd with great joy.

"'What should I wear to the club, Redd? You know I am just a small-town country gal,' said Nina, looking naive.

"'You will look good in anything, but if it will make you happy, then we will go shopping for all new clothes for an all new you. I will be the envy of every man in this county. One day I will be pleased to announce that you are my fiancée,' said Redd.

"Redd went home but Buddy stayed with Candee that night. Buddy could not get Candee out of his mind, for he had tunnel vision. All he could see and think about was Candee.

"The next day Buddy got busy making plans for the wedding with Candee. First he sent for all his staff. The business was really one business. That business of making money from any source. His staff was his lawyer, his accountant, and Candee, his manager.

"'Candee and I are going to get married in two months. I want to invite all the state and local politicians, law enforcement captains that are on our payroll plus local residents and friends. Whatever number it comes to is okay with us. We want this to be the wedding of the century. Do you understand?' implied Buddy.

"Next on Buddy's list was Candee's new business. 'Candee has come up with a great idea, which is to start a club called Candee's Palace. We need a location that is easy to get to, in which anyone who wants to come can walk or ride. I have a building that I won in a poker game just outside of town. It is the old Miller Mansion. It is located on a hill with plenty of space and land for parking and other activities for our patrons. Candee, maybe it should be called Miller Hill!' shouted Buddy.

"Smiling and looking quite pleased, Candee said, 'Sounds good to me. Let's go with it.'

"'Buddy, can we have the wedding at the country club?' said Candee.

"'This is why I love you, we think alike. That is just what I was going to suggest to you,' said Buddy smiling.

"Buddy was a good manager. The whole town was involved in getting Miller Hill ready for its grand opening for New Year's Eve and at the same time preparing the guest list, the food, and all the other things that go into planning a wedding. This was a great time for Harrisonville. There was plenty of excitement in the air. People were buzzing around happy with the feeling of nothing but joy was on its way."

"Did they get married, Buddy and Candee?" asked Ted.

"Yes, and it was everything that Candee could have dreamed," replied Lola.

"Buddy and Redd were part owners of the club with 55 percent. Redd believed that it would not be good for business if the membership knew they were owners," said Lola.

"*The bank*, as it was called, lent money to clients that could not borrow money from a government regulated bank. Their clients came from all over the county. Some were well-educated who needed money for a start-up business. On the other hand, some just needed it to make it to the next payday. Whatever the situation was, the bank would lend the money with a high interest rate. In some cases, it was as high as 60 percent—60 percent if they did not have any assets to use as collateral," said Lola.

"A payment with interest had to be made every week or Candee would send her collector to get the payment. The uncollected interest was added to the principle and when the balance was over a certain amount, an insurance policy would be taken out on the client with Candee as the beneficiary," Lola looked concerned as she spoke.

"Did they ever collect on the insurance policies?" asked Ted.

"Sure, all the time," said Lola. "This was a group of people that you did not want to owe them anything." Then she added with certainty, "If you did, you either paid up or died."

"'The swamp land on Redd's farm was the graveyard for poor souls who could not pay. After about a year of being missing, Candee would stake a claim and the adjustor who was on their payroll would submit the claim to the insurance company, and Candee would get paid,' confessed Lola.

"Getting back to the country club's ownership and how the two friends became partners. Redd was very good at poker, and the owner of the club was a regular at his weekend poker games. To play in these games, you had to buy in with at least two thousand dollars. The owner lost a lot of money playing poker and always thought he could win his money back. Without realizing it he was borrowing from Redd's bank. Because he wanted large sums, his country club had to be put up as collateral. He was making his payments on time, but the business slowed down, and he had a problem with his cash flow. He started missing payments and that was not a good thing to do.

"So Candee told the boys, 'We need to become his partners. Let him be the front man, but we will control the money and the business.' At first the owner did not like the idea, but he realized it was not worth dying for his country club. That is just what would happen, he would have been lying in the Swamp of Poor Souls," said Lola.

"The old plantation on the hill was the center of attention for Harrisonville. Unemployment in this town was very low. The only people that were not working was little kids and real old people. The plantation new name was Miller Hill, it needed a lot of work, but Buddy and Redd did not care for it was for their two lovely women.

"'Miller Hill was not always a happy place. It was almost destroyed by the Union soldiers during the war but was purchased later by a plantation owner in the area. He worked the farm but after the slaves were freed he could not afford to keep them or the plantation. He had two children and a wife who he loved. As he sat next to his fireplace with very little to eat but drinking whisky and getting more and more depressed, he took his shot gun and killed his whole family and then himself while they were sleeping in their beds. He left a note stating that he could not bear the fact that they were going to be put out on the street by the bank because the mortgage was a year behind,' said Lola in a low and sober voice.

"After many, many years of sitting abandoned, the boys purchased it from the bank for almost nothing. The bank just wanted to get rid of it," said Lola.

"The boys felt good and alive again. They were both in love, and nothing could stop them now," said Lola.

"Redd said, 'Before we do anything, let's set up a production plan and management plan so that we will be the greatest place in the state to eat, drink, gamble, and have fun with the ladies.'

"'Okay,' said Buddy. 'Candee, you and Nina work with our accountant to develop a plan for money and how it will be implemented.'

"'Yes, we will, my love, said Candee. 'First I need to call a meeting with our friends in high places to let them know and understand that we need their cooperation and help to make Miller Hill a complete success. I will make it perfectly clear that they will be well compensated for their services,' said Candee.

"Candee was all business and, most of the time, had a pleasant pretty smile on her face. But it was also known by all that knew her that her nickname was the Smiling Assassin. She would smile and be nice and then order you to be killed without you even knowing what she was going to do.

"She was also loved by all that met her. She was a very gracious lady. Only a handful of her closest associates knew the true Candee, and that is how she wanted it and lived," said Lola.

"The plans for Miller Hill called for a large porch with two large white columns. One on each side of the door as you entered the front door. The windows in the front would start at the top of the first floor and ended a few inches from the floor. The plans called for two huge windows on each side.

"As you entered the front, there was to be a massive foyer with a gold and glass chandelier. The chandelier was to be imported from France. Candee wanted everything to remind the guests that this was a palace and it was a special place to be happy and have fun.

"'Miller Hill would be rocking and rolling every day of the week. It would have something for everyone. The ladies would enjoy the shows and dancing along with the great food. If they had never been to Philadelphia or New York City, this would be a good substitute. The drinks would be served in fancy glasses and the waiters would be men with good service skills. Once inside, whatever you wanted Miller Hill provide. No request would be too small or too big,' said Candee as she got excited by her own words.

"'Okay, team, I want you to remember, customers come first. They are the reason for our business and not the cause of it,' said Candee as she smiled with total delight.

"'This is the plan. As you enter the foyer, you will be able to look up and see areas that gentlemen can take their wives or girlfriends or just a group of friends for dinner and drinks. As your eyes descend down, you will see a beautiful stage. In front of the stage at night would be a massive dance floor. Next will be small tables for two to four people to eat, drink, and be merry. Being happy is the name of the game. Happy people spend a lot of money. Do you understand, team?' said Candee.

"'I want everyone to leave except Frank, who is the accountant and financial manager,' said Candee. 'Besides the nightclub, there will be other enterprises. The basement is the total length of this mansion. Therefore, Buddy, Redd, and I want it utilized to the fullest. To do that, we are moving the bank, poker room, and bookie operation into the basement. There will also be an area of rooms for men who want the company of a beautiful lady. Frank, I want you to work with Nina to help set up the basement. It will be called the Gentlemen's Basement. It will look as elegant as the upper level or better for our customers,' said Candee.

"'A false wall will be designed to hide the basement door, just in case some of those religious nuts try to expose us. This area will be for existing customers who do not want anyone to know that they are patronizing the basement. It will have a bar and a dining area. Nina will run the Gentlemen's Basement, and I will run Miller Hill. How does that sound, Frank?' said Candee.

"'When will we be up and running?' asked Frank.

"'Buddy wants it to be ready for business New Year's Eve,' said Candee. 'Therefore, we have four months to get everything in shape. How's that sound?'

"'I believe it can be done, my lady,' replied Frank.

"Frank would do anything for Candee for he also loved her but was never able to express it because he knew Buddy would have killed him," quietly said Lola as if Buddy might hear her.

"All the plans had been set in motion, and everything was on schedule for Miller Hill and religious groups had joined with other agitators to prohibit the sale of liquor by the federal government. The prohibition of liquor seemed sure to be passed, and it was passed," said Lola.

"An emergency meeting was called for all the local officials and state lawmakers who were on the payroll to come together to work out a plan to keep the town from going belly up. They met at Redd's place because it was far away from everything. The agitators did not know where Redd lived," said Lola.

"Did they solve the problem? "asked Ted.

"Well, solved the problem, depending on how you see it," said Lola.

"This is how it when down. Redd's family came from the old country which was Ireland. His ancestors were the best bootleggers in that country. In fact, that is why they came to America because they were chased out of Ireland because of all their criminal activities. They were on the verge of being hung. They landed in Harrisonville and because of contagious disease like the whooping cough, his mother died soon after they got to Harrisonville," said Lola.

"Redd was smart and a quick learner. Therefore, he was able to set-up stills and start selling moonshine. His buddies, the lawmakers and local law enforcers decided they would ride it out with him until prohibition was overturned," said Lola.

"What about Miller Hill?" asked Ted.

"Miller Hill opened up on New Year's Eve as scheduled, with the local law officers as the security. Harrisonville felt that rest of the country did not know them and they did not know the rest of the country. They believed that they had a right to work and make money for the town and feed their families," said Lola as she raised her voice.

"Miller Hill was rocking and rolling with Redd's moonshine every night. The band, piano, and singers were bringing customers from not just this county but from other states. The food was the best food throughout the south. The Gentlemen's Basement had a waiting list to get in. You waited upstairs until someone came and got you. One man left and another man came in," said Lola.

"The bank, the poker room, bookie parlor, and rooms for special visitors with lovely ladies were the hottest attractions throughout the South. Things were going very well and the money was rolling in. Redd was selling moonshine in almost every state on the east coast. Redd and Buddy were on top of the world. Nothing could stop them now," said Lola.

"This went on big for several years until prohibition was appealed. Then things got even better. Nina was now almost twenty-one years old, and she was truly in love with Redd," said Lola. "So she decided it was time to be Redd's fiancé as he had predicted when she was only sixteen years old," said Lola, with tears in her eyes.

"'That night will be the night that I will have Redd propose to me,' thought Nina. 'How will I do it? Should I get him drunk and just tell him in the morning that after we made love, I said yes to his marriage proposal? Oh, I know, I will put on the same dress that he first saw me in with my bright-red lipstick. Then when he comes through the door, I will walk up to him and kiss him on the forehead, and he will understand that I am ready—ready to marry him,' Niña said to herself.

"Redd slowly opened the door and peeked in for he was always surprised about something that Nina had done or was doing. Before he could get his head past the doorway, Nina grabbed and pulled him in and said, 'I am ready to get married, are you?'

"'Yes!' said Redd. 'Let's go to Elkton, Maryland, tonight. That is where many of the famous celebrities go to get hooked up right away without any hassle or questions asked,' informed Redd.

"Nina replied, 'That sounds wonderful to me.'

"Nina threw a few things in her little red travel bag, and off they went to get married. Nina left a note for Candee, stating that the time has come for her to be made an honest woman. 'Redd and I are on our way to Elkton, Maryland, to be married. I will see you in a few days. Love, Nina.'

"Maryland turned out to be a long way off. Therefore, they stopped at a motel for the night. In that little red bag, Nina had a bottle of champagne with cheese and crackers. 'This was a night for making love and being loved,' thought Nina."

CHAPTER 2

"THAT NIGHT THEY made love like two teenagers who were stealing a small piece of time that could never be repeated like that night. The next day they went to breakfast with just smiles of joy on their faces and not saying much to each other. They did not have to talk because they understood other's deepest thoughts," said Lola.

"Walking down the streets of Elkton, Nina said with joy, 'There, over there is where I want to get married. It looks like us.'

"'You are right,' replied Redd. 'A small white building, with a white picket fence that looked like something out of a fairy tale, and that is how I feel, Nina,' said Redd.

"Nina read the sign which said, 'Wedding Chapel. All are welcome.'

"As Nina and Redd walked in, they were greeted by a semifat lady with red, rosy cheeks. 'I love couples like you two, who are looking to be married for the rest of their lives,' said the lady. 'My name is Kate, and I do it all. Are you ready to get married today?'

"Without hesitation, the two lovers said yes at the same time."

"Kate said, 'It will cost you $50, and if you want the full treatment, then it will be an extra $50.'

"Nina replied, 'What does the full treatment consist of?'

"'Well, lovebirds, my husband of forty years will play two songs, one before the service and one after the service. You can pick the songs from our book. It also includes 50 percent off a meal at the diner across the street. You will also receive a ticket for free parking in the lot where you are parked. How does that sound, lovebirds?' said Kate.

"'Well, give us the ticket for the parking and the music, and you can have the meal ticket. I will be taking my wife to the airport for a honeymoon in the Bahamas. My friend is making the plans as we are speaking,' said Redd.

"In the motel while Nina was sleeping, Redd placed a call to Buddy and told him that they were going to Elkton, Maryland, to get married in the morning. He asked him to make plans for them to fly to the Bahamas for their honeymoon for two weeks," said Lola.

Lola looked up at Ted and thought to herself, *Wouldn't a two-week honeymoon with this hunk be just wonderful?*

"Lola and I could get a lot done with a two-week honeymoon," said Ted to himself.

"How did the wedding turn out?" asked Ted.

"Just wonderful," replied Lola.

"Sure did and they had no problem getting to the Bahamas," stated Lola.

"Redd had planned to go to the Bahamas to meet with some associated about bring some ladies and some entertainers to Miller Hill. Therefore, he could combine business with pleasure," said Lola.

"In the Bahamas, business was conducted differently than in the States. Everyone wanted a piece of the action," said Lola.

"Nina understood Redd's desire to get some ladies and entertainers for Miller Hill. Therefore, he wanted Nina to draw the associates in with him using her charm," said Lola.

"Nina said, 'I have a plan. We will have a very outstanding dinner dance with all the most influential important people in the area. Let's show them how rich we are and how we party. I will purchase a very expensive dress from one of their most exclusive stores in the area. When asked, I will tell the clerk that it is a party for very exclusive group of people. The word will spread quickly, and everyone who is someone will want to be invited.'

"'We will have the hall set up like Miller Hill. It will have a stage for the band and singers, a dance floor, and small tables for two to four people. All the waiters will be the best in the business with good manners. Everything will be free. Anything that is requested will be provided,' said Redd.

"'My plan is to open up a Miller Hill in the Bahamas that Americans can take advantage of. It will be a totally legal operation. I have been tipped off by my friends in high places that the Feds are planning to audit our books. They are trying to get Buddy and me for tax evasion. Therefore, I want to hide my money here in the Bahamas, and maybe we will have to leave the States and live here,' said Redd.

"'I will live anywhere with you, Redd,' replied Nina. 'You are my man for life,' Nina continued on saying that it sounded like a great plan to her, and she loves the beaches and warm weather. 'The only thing that I have always wanted was a family. A house full of children is that okay with you, Redd, my love?' said Nina.

"Redd replied, 'I came from a family that was full of love. My father did whatever he could to provide a home and food for his wife and child. In the old country of Ireland, a man took care of his family, and that is what my father did for us.'

"Oh. Redd, you have made me very happy and I want to get started on our family as soon as possible.

"Redd and Nina decided to extend their stay for an extra few weeks so that they could plan the greatest party the Bahamas had ever hosted. Nina was in charge of the total planning for this event. She wanted only the best of everything. Cost was not an issue with Nina.

"She considered it an investment.

"The menu was made up of only American foods. She sent for her chef in the States, and he brought his entire crew of cooks and waiters. The chef was black and so was the crew. Next she scheduled the performers to come on the day before the party so that they could rehearse with the local popular band.

"When she finished, the only thing that was needed was for her to develop a guest list. Therefore, she asked the head housekeeper in the hotel to help her with the list. The head housekeeper knew all the important people in all of the Bahamas and adjacent islands. Nina left that up to Tanya the hotel's head housekeeper.

"Buddy job was to find a fantastic building that could hold around five hundred people. Buddy was thinking about the future. The building that was going to be used for the party would be the new Miller Hill, but this new location would need a new name. Therefore, he wanted Nina's opinion on the name.

"There were several buildings that he looked at but was not satisfied, and he was starting to get depressed. Just at that moment his guide, Lyle said, 'I know what you want, a place that makes the guests feel good and will return often to have a good time.'

"'That's right, my friend,' replied Redd.

"Lyle was a very good-looking businessman who had a dream of his own but did not have the money to make his dream come true. But with Redd as his backer, it would be possible. Lyle, the businessman, told Redd about his dream which included an outside stage that was designed with the look of the entertainment area of the Roman Empire. The guests would surround the stage but slightly elevated. Everything would be outside with a covering to block out the sun or rain. The location would be on the beach.

"'It would have bars and eating areas everywhere. Waiters, who would serve the drinks and food,' said Lyle, with a big smile on his face. 'We would use waitresses, pretty young ones in grass skirts. A big fence would surround the Palace. Only rich guests would be able to patronize this paradise. Flowers and plants with many colors would be used to decorate the total area. Live small animals such as beautiful birds will be in cages to present the flavor of the Bahamas,' said Lyle.

"Redd's eyes opened wide, and he said, 'Stop. I got it. My party will be on the beach. I love your idea, and I know Nina will love it also. Do you know an artist that can put the ideas down on a canvas?'

"Lyle, replied, 'Yes, I have already designed a layout. All I needed was a partner with money. A temporary stage and setup can be put into place in three weeks, tops.'

"'Oh, that is wonderful,' replied Redd. 'Nina's birthday is in three weeks, and she will be twenty-one years old. It will be her party,' said Redd. 'When we met, I thought she was twenty-one, but I was in love with her the moment I saw her. Nothing is too good for my love for Nina,' said Redd.

"Redd took a second look at Lyle and realized that Lyle was a gangster just like him.

"Nina loved the plans but did not know the party would be for her. She was working so hard getting her part accomplished. Redd sent word to Buddy and Candee telling them about the future plans and asking them to come to Nina's party. 'It is to be a surprise. Do not breathe a word to her,' said Redd.

"The day finally came for the party, and a big banner was hung, 'Welcome to Nina's Birthday Party, the Biggest and Best Party on Land.' As Nina approached the extremely large pavilion with a multilevel structure, she almost fainted for she was truly surprised. She was turning twenty-one, and it was the best day of her entire life. No one but Redd had ever loved her as much as a mother could love her child.

"'Oh my, how wonderful!' shouted Nina. She grabbed Redd and kissed him and hugged him, and it appeared that she could not stop herself from hugging and kissing. Finally, Candee approached and said, 'Times up, let's get it on, let's party!'

"The band started playing happy birthday, and the guests began singing. Redd got up on stage with Nina. 'This is Nina's day, and she is the love of my life. Join me in helping my wife have a birthday celebration that will be remembered by her and everyone here for many years to come. Let's toast to my wife.'

"Candee jumped up on stage and said, 'Nina is my cousin, and I will make the toast to Nina and then to the newlyweds for their union has been blessed by God. To Nina, may all your days be blessed, and may God bless both of you with a long life of happiness. Okay, let's party.'

"The sky opened with hundreds of balloons falling from the beautiful sky and the band playing with popular songs from the

States. The singers were gorgeous looking colored singers dressed to impress. She got the crowd up on their feet. People were dancing at their seats, on the dance floor and some even jumped on top of the tables. It was a site to see.

"Her selections along with common American hors d'oeuvres, and waitresses were sashaying around the tables waiting on everyone with complete joy.

"It was like old times at Miller Hill in Harrisonville. Buddy and Candee were having a great time, but Buddy knew that the good times were going to come to an end soon in the near future. Therefore, he shouted out, 'Let the good times roll!'

"The sun was coming up when the last guest left. Buddy, Candee, Nina, and Redd sat at the bar just laughing and reminiscing about when they first met each other.

"Buddy recalled the day he met Redd. Buddy said, 'We were both teenagers with a future in crime. The first person I met when I entered Harrisonville was Redd. I was a runaway from some old religious nutty family. I could not take going to church every Sunday and that Bible Study two days per week. It was killing me inside.'

"Redd said, 'My parents were great. They were true blue criminals. They were chased out of the old country Ireland when I was about ten. He was a bootlegger, loan shark, and had many other professions. My father was a real family man and believed in taking care of his wife and child. I am an only child and my mother died of whooping cough disease at the age of twenty-nine. When she died my father's love of life left also.'

"'He continued to practice his profession here in Harrisonville and at the same time established himself as a real trustworthy businessman. He started his own bank, his own bar, his own gambling parlor, and his own gentlemen and ladies gathering place. Pop did not put up with anyone crossing him. He found ways to solve the problem. He wanted and taught me the business at an early age. I did not have any other future professional dreams but to be a criminal,' said Redd.

"Nina and Candee both agreed that their stories were too sad to talk about at this time but here would be plenty of time for story telling in the future.

"The party was over and it was a big hit. That night Redd and Nina made love over and over again. It was like this was their last great time together.

"The next day Buddy caught up with Redd and told him they needed to talk. Over breakfast, Buddy gave Redd the bad news.

"Redd, said, 'Buddy, I would not come home if I were you. The Feds are looking for you. One of your trusted team members was a rat. I believe I can get out of it but you and Nina are in serious trouble.'

"'They think the club and Miller Hill are totally legit and all they want is for Candee and me to pay our back taxes. They have you down for bootlegging, racketeering, murder, prostitution, and you name it. They know you are there but cannot touch you. Please do not come home. Make this paradise your home. Please, Redd, you know I love you like a brother,' he spoke to Redd with tears in his eyes.

"'Buddy, I am making plans to start a club here in the Bahamas. The man that controls everything on this island helped with getting Nina's party together. His name is Lyle. Lyle is a criminal but we need him. He wants to be a partner in my new business venture,' said Redd.

"'Be careful with this, Lyle. People on this island are not loyal. They just want to be rich and important,' replied, Buddy.

"'Look, there is Lyle coming to our table. I will introduce him to all of you,' said Redd.

"'Good morning, Lyle,' said Redd. 'Thanks for helping me with my wife's party. It was more than I had hoped for. This is my lovely wife, Nina, her beautiful cousin Candee and her husband, Buddy, who is my best friend and partner.'

"'Do your friends know of our future plans?' said Lyle.

"'No, not yet,' replied Redd.

"'How about meeting today on the beach about 1:00 for a beach party?' asked Lyle.

"'That sounds great,' said Candee. 'Nina and I love the beach and the ocean. We should have been born fish but were born something else.'

"After Lyle left, Redd said, 'I will not go back to the States. It would be crazy for me to even think about returning. Nina and I will make a life for us right here in paradise,' replied Redd.

"At 1:00 all the players were on the beach. Lyle was the last to arrive. It was obvious that he thought he was in the driver's seat with these dumb Americans. But he did not know that they were professional criminals. They had already figured him out. All they had to do is come up with a plan that would allow them to use his influence to get things moving.

"Lyle had his replica of his design for his lifelong dream of an outside paradise set-up for the Americans. He also provided project gross revenue and cost.

"Nina and Candee said, 'Let's get wet first, eat and drink before we start talking about business.' Redd and Buddy agreed. This was also their way of slowing Lyle down for he needed their money for this venture.

"Lyle did not get into the ocean or eat or drink anything. He just sat and waited for them. After a couple of hours, Buddy said, 'Okay, let's talk.'

"Lyle said his bid for their support for his project. The replica was very detailed with multilevels that were designed for a full day of entertainment with beauty surrounding the compound. It consisted of five bars, five hundred tables, a large stage in the center, and three swimming pools. One pool for the family, one for adults only and one for the general public and several bathhouses for changing located on the grounds of the compound. A high private fence would enclose the whole area. Food would be served all day with a large selection. The waitresses would be local pretty girls.

"After explaining the compound, Lyle said, 'Now is time to talk turkey like you American would say. What is needed is about one million to set up compound and about $500,000 to purchase food and other merchandise. With a total startup cost of around 1.5 million.'

"'That's a lot of money,' replied Buddy. 'Maybe we could start small and add on as time goes on. Do you know what the estimated gross receipts would be on a weekly, monthly and yearly basis?'

"'Yes,' replied Lyle. 'My accountant is well known for his ability to apply past and future outcomes in the vacation industry and how it is going to grow because of increased incomes in the US. The US workers along with other countries will be looking for vacation locations to take the families. The Bahamas with be able to fulfill that need.'

"Buddy responded with confidence, 'This is a lovely spot. A person could just lose themselves here.'

"'Count me in,' said Redd.

"'Me too,' responded Buddy.

"The wives just looked at each other and said, "It sounds like a good plan, okay."

"Buddy and Redd agreed to give Lyle small installments of money to get things going. The first installment was to be for permits and blueprints. But first they wanted a contract with a real lawyer drawn up as to the nature and the agreement of the partnership. The ownership was to remain in the hands of Buddy and Redd with Lyle receiving a percentage of the net income.

"Buddy and Candee returned home. They were interested in finding out who was the rat that went to the Feds about their business dealings. Candee was considered a real lady but very few people knew her real personality. She was determined to find the mole.

"She called for her accountant because he normally knew everything that was going on. Frank entered the room and started talking, 'Candee, I searched a long time to find and tried to figure out who the rat was. It finally came to me. It was our state congressman who has been indicted for corruption. My sources tell me that he struck a deal with the government about Harrisonville's illegal businesses in order to avoid jail time. They are to just give him probation.'

"'Well, you know what to do,' replied Candee. 'That testimony will never take place. Make it look like a natural death. Without his testimony, they will have to drop all charges against Redd and Nina. Then they can come home where they belong. Oh, don't tell Buddy about this conversation or who the rat was.'

"The housekeeper who worked for the senator was on Candee's payroll. Frank told her to put rat poisoning in the senator's dinner dessert. The senator was over weigh and very unhealthy and loved to eat rich desserts. That night, the senator had his last supper. He died about an hour after eating while he was reading a book. No one suspected anything was wrong with the way he died because he looked like he was ready to keel over at any moment.

"After giving Lyle the money for the permits and architect, Redd waited a few weeks before asking Lyle for an update on the statist of the permits. Redd and Nina were having a great time in the Bahamas but they did miss their friends and home.

"Redd received a telegram from Buddy stating, 'If you like to come home everything is okay because the senator was the mole and he died suddenly and all charges on Nina and you have been dropped.'

"Redd was overjoyed. As they sat eating dinner that evening Redd said to Nina, 'I have some very good news to tell you. The senator was the mole and he suddenly dropped dead. All charges have been dropped against us. If we want to go home after we get the resort up and going, we can.'

"Nina replied, 'That is great news and I have some better news to tell you. I am pregnant and the baby will be due around your birthday.'

"'This is one of the happiest days of my life because the happiest day was the day I saw you,' replied Redd.

"The next day Redd decided to find Lyle so that he could get some updates on the status of the resort project. He did not know exactly where Lyle lived but as mayor, the sheriff's office would be able to help him. Redd wanted the baby to be born in Harrisonville and not the Bahamas.

"Redd entered the sheriff's office stating, 'I need to know where the mayor lives because I have some business to talk over with him.'

"Just then, Redd looked up at the wall and saw a large photo of a well-dressed distinguished older gentleman. On the bottom it gave his name and title mayor.

"Redd said, 'I guess that is a picture of your mayor from past years.'

"'No,' said the officer, 'he is still living and is still the mayor.'

"Redd reach in his pocket and pulled out a picture that was taken of Lyle and him the night of Nina's party. 'Well, do you know this man in the picture with me?' replied Redd.

"'Yes,' said the officer that is the mayor's younger brother who is a bum and is always trying to make a fast buck. He lives at the mansion with the mayor's wife and family. The mayor raised him like a son when their parents died years ago.

"'Where can I find the mansion?' asked Redd.

"Redd's face became redder and he was bursting with anger. As he walked out the door he said, 'With God as my witness, Lyle will never find another sucker.'

"Redd was extremely upset. He patted his under arm to make sure his little Sue was with him. That is what he called his pistol that was strapped to his shoulder under his arm at all times. When he got dressed for the day, Sue was always part of his wardrobe.

"As he walked down the sandy street and listening to the sound of the ocean he started thinking about the first person he killed. He had promised himself that after killing his father's murderer he would never kill anyone himself again.

"As he walked, he thought to himself, 'I was sixteen when I killed the man who killed my father. After Mom died, his pop put all his energy into his business operations. One night a man broke into their home to rob the family. Pop woke up to get a drink of water. At that time, he encountered the intruder who was his brother-in-law. The brother-in-law pulled a gun and shot Pop. I was given a small pistol for my birthday and Sue was used for the first time that night. Those loud noises woke me up and I grabbed my gun and walked into the room just as Pop was falling to the floor. Without speaking or thinking I just shot my uncle. Two men were dead because of money.'

"'Harrisonville said I was a hero for trying to defend my father. Earlier that day, my uncle had asked Pop for a loan and he refused because he knew it was for drugs. Pop hated drugs and was totally against selling them to anyone, even to the colored people,' thought Redd.

"Finally, Redd was standing in front of the mansion with sand inside his shoes. He took off his shoes and shook out the sand. Once again he patted Sue, knocked on the door and no one answered. Therefore, he started around the back. The sound of the ocean was beautiful and the light breeze on his face was perfect.

"Thinking to himself, 'This a perfect day for dying and today Lyle will die. No one is going to scam me and get away with it.'

"In the backyard, Lyle was sitting on the beach, drinking a margarita all by himself. Redd approached him like a gentleman. 'Hello, partner,' said Redd. 'Where have you been?'

"'Looking for you,' replied Lyle.

"'I am here. Do you have the permits yet and the architect's plans for the resort yet?' asked Redd.

"'Well, I ran into a small cash problem. It is going to cost a little more,' said Lyle.

"'How much more?' asked Redd.

"'Another ten thousand will seal the deal,' replied Lyle.

"'I decided to scrap the plan and go back home. Therefore, I'd like to have my money back,' said Redd.

"Lyle stood up quickly like a big man with power and said, 'You Yankee bastard! All of you come to our island looking to get rich off of us dumb islanders. No money, no permits, and no resort. So get lost. Go home you and that bitch of a wife!' yelled Lyle.

"'You called my wife a bitch. My bitch Sue will be your bitch!" roared Redd.

"No one was around, the warm light breeze appeared to stop and the sounds of the island had ceased. Redd took out Sue and shot Lyle in the head. He put Sue back in her resting spot and slowly walked away.

"When he returned to the hotel he told Nina to pack her things. Redd ordered a small plane to fly them to Miami. Nina looked concerned about packing up her things and leaving quickly like two gypsies stealing away in the middle of the night. But it was not night it was the middle of the day.

"'Redd,' said Nina, 'I am just going to leave everything. I have more of these things at home.' Redd did not reply and that was a signal for Nina to just keep moving quickly to get herself together.

"As Nina was gathering the little bit of clothes she planned to take, she knew it was not the time to ask any questions. Therefore, she made a mental list of all the things that could have happened that would cause Redd to want to leave this beautiful paradise in such a short notice.

"Understanding Redd, Nina only had one thing on her list. Murder, who did he murder? Nina was aware that Lyle had received a down payment for the resort that was being planned and that Redd was concerned about the progress and his money. Redd lived by a few rules, which were, do not mess with my woman, my money or me. If you crossed him, then your life would end quickly without much conversation.

"'Nina,' said Redd, 'that Lyle was a liar, and he stole my money. I took care of him. Plus, he called you a name, and you know what happened next.'

"Nina looked at Redd, and he knew he did not have to say anything else and that she was all in.

Lyle's body was not discovered until very late that night. Lyle's family was not liked by the servants or the residents of the area. They were living large while most of the workers were poor and starving. This family was stealing all the money that was supposed to go to the people. They controlled all levels of the government. All the servants were questioned and none of them gave up any information that could help them pin point the murderer.

"In fact, the mayor was not told that Redd had left quickly or that Lyle and Redd had a business relationship. After a short investigation the mayor decided that one of Lyle's girlfriends or his low life associates killed him. The mayor closed the case.

"As they flew back to the States, Redd thought to himself, 'I am who I am and it is what it is. I will just move on to the next part of my life, which is, my new wife that I love more than life itself.'

"The small plane landed in Miami, and Buddy and Candee were waiting for them. Buddy with a big smile on his face said, 'We are happy you are home. Things have not been the same without you two.' Candee seconded it with hugs and kisses.

"Buddy had a limo waiting for them, and they drove off to the hotel but stopped first to eat. Buddy said to Redd, 'With all our criminal activities God was still providing for us. That God must have a plan but whatever it was would not be revealed in our lifetime. 'What makes you say such a thing?' said Redd.

"'Well, my friend," said Buddy, 'as you know, all charges against you have been dropped because that fat weasel of a senator died suddenly. The case against you was based on his testimony. Without him they had no case so they had to drop the charges. That was God's hand that send him packing and cause the charges to be dropped. Next, my tax problems were solved. Nina and I only had to pay back taxes on the income from the Palace. We are now solid, honest taxpayers according to the government.'

"As they were eating, Candee thought to herself, Buddy does not know the real story and that is good. He has tunnel vision. It never occurred to him that God had nothing to do with the Senator's death and it was my hand that took care of the problem. I guess in this case I have earned my nickname that was given to me by my true friend Frank, the Smiling Assassin. Oh boy how I love that name. thought Candee as she quietly ate the meal with a smile.

"The next day they drove back to Harrisonville and Redd and Buddy discussed plans for their businesses at all levels. Because of the Feds, they wanted to find a way to move away from some of their business activities.

"Redd said, 'Whatever we do; we are not getting involved in drugs. Drugs harm too many people and destroy families. Drugs will lead to the destruction of our country and I don't want to be a part of that.' Buddy agreed and so did the ladies.

"Redd continued, we have the loan business which is good. How is that shaping up, Candee?'

"'Well, I had to use in a few cases alternative methods in order to get clients to pay. But I have a new system for paying. I call it the back-up plan,' said Candee.

"'How well is the back up working?' asked Redd.

"'In fact, it is the best plan that I have ever created. Frank worked with me and he has developed a good way of getting paid without roughing up clients,' said Candee.

"'It all involves insurance; in fact, it is life insurance. Frank has a friend who is an insurance broker and with his help we are able to buy life insurance policies through various life insurance companies,' said Candee.

"'Well, I will give you a brief outline as to how it works and if you would like us to make some changes it can be done,' said Candee.

"'In order for us to make a loan to a client, they must agree to take out a life insurance policy. Loans start at $100,000 with the usual interest rate. Interest and principal are paid weekly. If they miss a payment the interest due becomes part of the principal. As you know that has always been part of the system. What is new is the insurance. All policies start at $100,000 with one of the four of us being the beneficiary on a client's policy.

"'If a client misses a payment and his balance is catching up with the face value of the insurance, we lay out his options. We have many plans for our clients that do not involve any force. In almost every case, the back payments are paid. We don't break legs or do any bodily harm. We just have them die of a heart attack. We want to keep them alive for the small loans are our bread and butter. We want them to keep coming back for additional loans. They are our customers. There are other small details but this is the big picture.

Also, we don't pay taxes on life insurance,' said Candee with a big smile on her face.

"'Buddy what about the gaming operation?' asked Redd.

"It is alive and well. Nothing has changed except, the sheriff is a regular as are some of the officers. They love the Gentlemen's Basement and the liquor. Their favorite is our local brew, moonshine. It's cheap and good. Best kept secret in the south, said Buddy.

"'How is our country club?' asked Nina. Buddy and Candee looked at each other, and then Buddy said, 'That is a problem. Mitchell, our partner is complaining that his business has dropped because of the Palace and his only customers are old farts who just want to golf. His dining and catering side of the business might have to close. He blames us for the decline of his family business which has serviced the community for over sixty years.'

"'Mitchell has been very depressed and looks like he needs to be on medication. The word is out that his young beautiful wife has left him and the bank is going to foreclose on the club and his home,' said Candee.

"'We cannot give him any more money,' said Redd.

"'Do we have an insurance policy on him?' asked Nina.

"'Yes, we do, it is for $200,000, and Buddy is the beneficiary,' replied Candee.

"'Should we get rid of him before he does something stupid?' asked Redd.

"'Yes,' said Candee.

"'Make it happen soon,' replied Buddy.

"By the middle of the week they were all home. Everything was back to normal.

"Redd was making and selling his moonshine as fast as his workers could produce the corn. The stills were running day and night. Sales and production were up.

"Candee and Frank were both working closely together. Frank loved Candee but could not let her know about his feelings for her. He knew if Buddy found out, one of them would have to die. They ran the Bank very well as professionals with no serious problems. The clients understood Candee, and Frank were not the kind of people you would want to cross.

"Nina was running her Gentleman's Club with an increase in demand.

"Buddy was very concerned about Mitchell and decided to have him taken care of the next day. Buddy decided to pay Mitchell a visit to just make sure it was necessary. As Buddy approached the front door, Mitchell opened the door with a shot gun in his hand, shouting, 'You dirty bastard, you destroyed my life and my business. I hope you go to hell!' Without much warning, he shot Buddy in the head and then put the gun up to his chin and took his life. What a day, what a day," said Lola.

"Buddy was Mitchell's beneficiary but Candee was the contingent beneficiary. Candee also had $200,000 policy on Buddy. Candee collected on both policies. Candee became very sick for about a few months. She could not keep any thing down. Everyone believed it was because of Buddy's death," said Lola.

"Redd was so upset he appeared to have gone mad. At Buddy's funeral Redd was asked to say a few words. Redd looked into the faces of the people who had come to see Buddy for the last time. 'Buddy was my friend since we were sixteen years old,' said Redd. 'He lived the life that God had mapped out for him. At age twenty-nine he was taken away. May God have mercy on his soul. Thank you all for coming.'

"Redd shut down all their businesses. It was hard for him to even get out of the bed. Nina tried to encourage him to keep up his strength and eat," said Lola.

"Candee was feeling so bad, that she thought she was also dying. Finally, Nina convinced her to go to her doctor. After the exam, the doctor came into the room and said, 'You are not dying. You are pregnant.'

"Candee could not believe it. She kept shouting, 'Me, me, me! I lost Buddy, but God has given me a baby. Thank you! Thank you!' shouted Candee.

"Ted, Nina was happy for Candee she knew that having children would not happen for her. Nina is a diabetic and getting pregnant would most likely kill her. She went to many doctors looking for help but all of them gave the same prognosis," said Lola.

Ted looked at Lola's lips and thought they were perfect. Even without lip gloss or lip stick they had a natural light pink. Her nose was shaped like a perfect mold on her face. She is beautiful, thinking to himself as he tried to concentrate on Lola's words.

"Redd, with everything shut down, decided to reorganize which included a review of all businesses and how they are run. He wanted everything to be legal. Redd wanted a future for his wife and family that was without crime," said Lola.

"Redd did not know that Nina was told not to have children because of her diabetes. Nina made a decision to get pregnant and have a family like Candee," said Lola.

"Redd reorganized and shut down everything but the Palace and the Gentlemen's Basement. The Palace was a place that he could have fun and enjoy himself and relax," said Lola.

"With Buddy out of the picture, Frank was encouraged to confess his love to Candee," said Lola.

"As Frank was taking Candee home from the doctor's office, he said the following, 'Candee, I have loved you from the day I set eyes on you but you and Buddy looked like a couple that God had blessed. I want to marry you and raise your child as my own. Do you think that is possible?'

"Frank, only if you take me away from all this criminal activity today. I want my baby to live an honest life. Work for an honest day's pay. I don't want him to worry about an enemy walking up to my baby and shooting him in the head. God has given me a chance to live a Christian life. Will you change your ways and become a born-again Christian?' asked Candee.

"'Yes,' responded Frank, 'I was hoping that we could leave and start over. We should say good bye to our friends and not tell anyone where we are going. In fact, I do not know where we are going. We have plenty of money and can live a good life with each other no matter where we call home. I could open up my own accounting firm and you could work with me if you want.'

"Candee, replied, 'Let's go for it.'

CHAPTER 3

"CANDEE RUSHED TO find Nina and tell her the news. As she approached the house, the front door was open and Candee went in yelling, 'Nina! Nina!' As she ran through the rooms, there was no sign of Nina. Finally, as she passed the bathroom, that is where she found Nina," stated Lola.

"Nina was crying because she wanted to get pregnant but there was the health situation that might keep her from having the baby or living long enough to raise the baby. Nina was pregnant and now she would have to make a decision about whether to try to have the baby. Candee or Redd did not know about her health, and she decided not to tell them. She believed if she told them about her health they would try to get her to terminate the pregnancy," stated Lola.

"Nina said, 'I am pregnant. I just left the doctor's office.'

"'That's good, right?' responded Candee.

"'Yes,' replied Nina, 'but I don't know if Redd will want a family this soon after Buddy's death.'

"'I guarantee you that he will be extremely happy about being a father,' said Candee.

"'Nina, call Redd and have him to come home,' said Candee.

"Redd came home and Frank and Nina wanted their best friends to hear their good news first," said Lola.

"'We are leaving Harrisonville right now. Here are the deeds to all our real estate. I have signed everything over to both of you.

I want my baby to live a normal life. Frank and I are going to get married. This is Buddy's baby, but Frank will be his father. We love the two of you but we want to leave this town and this life behind us,' said Candee.

"'Now, Nina,' said Candee, 'it is your turn.'

"Nina looked straight into Redd's eyes and said, 'I am pregnant with twins.'

"Redd shouted, 'Wonderful!'

"'Our babies will hopefully meet up with each other one day. That is very good news for all of us. New family members and new beginnings,' said Frank.

"'Well, we are off, hitting the road to nowhere. If you ever need us put an ad in the N.C Journal. We will have it delivered to us no matter where we live. Use Harris as the code,' said Candee.

"As the months flew by Nina was totally bed ridden. She would not allow the doctor to tell Redd about her condition. The doctor informed Nina that she had a less than 50 percent of survival during the delivery of the babies," said Lola.

"All during that time Candee and Frank never tried to contact Nina or Redd. Their names were never mentioned. That part of their past was gone forever," said Lola.

"Your past is never gone. It is with you all your life and it will show up in future generations. I truly believe that about the past. We can't change the past but we can learn a valuable lesson from it," said Ted.

"On the day Nina went into labor, she had to have a C-section, and she died on the delivery table," said Lola.

"She died," said Ted with a surprised and stunned look on his face. "She never got to see the babies?" asked Ted.

"Coming out of the delivery room, Redd stopped the doctor, stating, 'How is my wife and the babies?'

"'Sorry, she did not make it. We only gave her less than a 50 percent chance of surviving the delivery,' informed the doctor. 'The babies are very healthy. With all her problems, she did take good care of the babies.'

"'What do you mean with all her medical problems?' asked Redd.

"'Your wife did not tell you even at the end?' responded the doctor.

"'Tell me what!' said Redd.

"'She is a diabetic, and she was told not to ever get pregnant because she might not survive the delivery. She was strong and if it had only been one baby her chances would have been better. Her heart and kidneys failed her and caused a heart attack,' said the doctor.

"Redd looked down at Nina and said, "I will never love any woman like I loved you. The short time we were together was wonderful and I am thankful. Goodbye my love, with tears flowing down his face as he covered her face with the white sheets and walked out.

"As he looked into the nursery he saw the two babies. Two boys that looked just like Nina both with black curly hair and beautiful. What should I call them? I want them to have their mother's initials, thinking to himself.

"'Nickolas and Nathan, that's it, and your mother will be proud of the two of you someday,' he talked out loud to himself.

"Coming home from the Palace and not having Nina with him made Redd withdraw from his friends. The day the babies were picked up Redd had no idea how to care for the two identical twins that were given to him by God to be a parent.

"Therefore, the nurse at the hospital gave him the name of an older lady whose husband had died and her children were grown and she needed something to keep her busy," said Lola.

"It was the answer to his prayers for this lady took good care of the boys. Redd sent them to a private school because he wanted the best for the two of them.

"Redd kept the moonshine business going and the Palace and the Gentlemen's Basement. Many of the big shots hung out at Redd's place. All three businesses were alive and well. Business was better than ever. Redd was one of the best repeated clients at the Gentlemen's

Basement. He had all kinds of liquor but loved his moonshine," said Lola.

"The women were running after Redd but he only wanted one thing from them. That was to make love with them as if it was Nina. Some of the women realized this but thought he might fall in love with them. But that never happened," said Lola.

"One night Redd came home from the Palace and Ida, the house keeper, was lying on the kitchen floor. She was dead. The doctors said she died of a heart attack. The boys were older, around 8 years old. The boys were big enough to help around the house and the farm. Redd had dreams for them. He wanted them to go to college and become honest business men. He also, wanted them to understand how to protect and take care of their business," said Lola.

"With all that was going on with Redd, he needed help. Shortly after Ida died a little young gal about nineteen years old knocked on his door, stating, 'I am looking for work, I just moved here last week and the operator at the boarding home in town said that you might need some help with the kids and housekeeping,' said the young gal.

"Redd looked her over and thought to himself, She was cute but not his Nina.

"After a few seconds, Redd said, 'Come in and let's talk.' Rita started working that day and Redd liked her a lot but she was not Nina," said Lola.

"Rita and Redd became an item. Folks sometime referred to her as Mrs. Redd. And she would reply, 'Not yet.'

"One day out of the blue, Redd came home early, stating, 'Rita, I need to talk to you. I am getting older, and the boys are men, and I need a wife. Will you marry me?'

"Rita, looking shocked, said, 'Yes!'

"Rita knew her marriage to Redd was not going to be the same as it was when he had Nina, but she was ready to settle for second place. Rita was at least hoping for a big wedding but Redd wanted to just go to the Justice of the Peace and get married so that is what happened," said Lola.

"As the years passed by, the boys were getting older and they started hanging around with Redd. They would listen and hang on to every word he spoke. They loved their father and wanted to be just like him. He had learned over the years to be a fair man but if you crossed him, you would pay the price," said Lola.

"The boys were smart in every way, that is, street smart and book smart. They learned how to work the farm and how to manage the Palace very quickly. In fact, they had some ideas to run pass Redd. When it came time for them to go off to college, Redd was happy but sad at the same time. He loved the boys and would miss having them around, but at the same time he wanted them to get a quality education. They both got scholarships to the same university and off they went," said Lola.

"Lola, did they ever try to contact Candee to let them know that Nina had died?" asked Ted.

"No, Redd said that he wanted to let them have a clean break from the past."

"So all those years passed, and he never heard from them again," said Ted.

"That's right, never again. Candee and Frank were only in their late twenties and had plenty of time to change their life and to start over again," said Lola.

"After the boys went away to college, what did Redd do?" asked Ted.

"Redd got totally involved with the Palace and his moonshine sales. Moonshine was very popular in the south. It was cheap and easy to get. Redd did not pay any taxes or fees connected to the moonshine. With the blue laws in some of the Northern states moonshine at Sunday speakeasies was very profitable even in the South," said Lola.

"The twins were very popular at the college. They were popular for several reasons. They were making and selling moonshine in the woods near the school and having poker games on Saturday night. They were very smart and both were majoring in business. These subjects and the material came very easy to them. In fact, they were in the top 5 percent of their class," said Lola.

"Even some of the staff at the college became regular customers. Because they were very good looking, the gals were chasing after them. They had the charm and looks of Nina and the business sense of Redd. They were not running these businesses because they needed the money but because they saw opportunity and it was in the genes.

"The boys informed their father about their business activities and Redd told him to stop making the moonshine and that he would make deliveries in suitcases once a month. Redd did not want them to get caught making the liquor and get kicked out of school," said Lola.

"Nick and Nate were so good at selling the moonshine that Redd wanted to expand in other colleges. During spring breaks the twins would sell to Greek fraternities for their houses and beach parties. The distribution system that was set-up was well organized with colleges in the south and the north as far as New York," said Lola.

"By the time we graduate, we will have plenty of money to go legit," said Nick.

"'Our future partners are chemistry majors and have shown me figures that suggest that bio-fuels will be the thing of the future. We are only in our early twenties and if we start now developing out product the bio-fuel market will be ours. Pop's generation did whatever they had to do to make it. Now it is our turn to do it our way,' said Nick.

"'Nick and Nate were alike in many ways but also different in many ways. Nick wanted to go legit on the other hand Nate secretly loved the criminal life. That life style gave him power and influence over others,' said Lola.

"Not long after graduation they returned home and worked the college operation from the farm, but they could not grow enough corn to keep up with demand. So Nick called on his chemistry friend to develop an additive to put in the liquor in order to increase the supply. The friend came up with an additive which proved to be wonderful. Production was back on track," said Lola.

"Rita worked hard taking care of the house and cooking for Redd and the boys. Redd was spending most of his time at the Palace especially the Gentlemen's Basement. Rita was not getting attention. Many people wondered why she stayed with Redd. Deep down inside she loved him and was willing to do anything to just be with him," said Lola.

"The moonshine competitor that Redd killed was Rita's oldest brother. Rita never knew her brother for he left home a few years after she was born. They were fifteen years' difference in their ages. She never told anyone that he was her brother. Her brother was looked upon by the community as the lower class in Harrisonville. She had status, money and influence which she thought was enough," said Lola.

"Thinking to herself, Rita said, 'I have cleaned this house, cooked his meals, and raised his boys and what do I have to show for all these years. Now he has killed my brother.'

"Rita quietly drank a few glasses of moonshine and sat in the dark living room waiting for Redd to come home. The longer she sat the more she drank," said Lola.

"Rita fell asleep and when she woke up Redd was in the bed fast asleep. She picked up Sue, his hand gun, walk right over to him, and point the gun to his head, stating, 'Nina is gone, and now you can go with her.' One shot to the head killed him. Then she put Sue under her chin and pulled the trigger. And that was the end of that generation of criminals," said Lola.

"Oh my, oh my." Looking stunned, Ted was lost for words.

"Nick and Nate closed down the Palace for the night and came home. As they entered the house they could smell the strange odor of death in the air. The house was completely dark and totally calm and quiet," said Lola.

"Walking slowly through the house they called out for Rita and Redd but no one responded. Finally, they turned on the lights in Redd's bedroom and there they were, lying in pools of blood. Their faces were not recognizable. It was like looking at two monsters," said Lola.

"Nick, call the sheriff!" said Nate.

"When the sheriff got to the house, he could not believe what he saw. 'Do you know why she killed Redd?' said the sheriff.

"There are no notes or indication that they were arguing," said Nick.

"'Well, boys, this is a tragedy and a devastating loss for Harrisonville. Nothing will ever be the same,' said the sheriff.

"'What should we do, Sheriff?' said Nate.

"'Gather up everything that you want and any papers that are important. After you have secured your things, set the house on fire. It is better for the community to remember these two as a loving couple. I will make a statement that they died in the fire and could not get out,' said the sheriff.

"Within about an hour the two boys had cleared the house of its entire valuables and set the house on fire," said Lola.

"'Nate,' said Nick, 'Pop had plans for us, but I have my own plans. I want to go legit. We have plenty of money and we are the heirs of all his assets. He also has an insurance policy for $2,000,000 with the two of us as the beneficiaries. I also would like to try my hand at law school. I would like to have my own law firm someday.'

"Nick continued, 'My chemistry friends have convinced me that bio-fuels will be a cleaner and better alternative in the future to oil. We are young and have time to invest in this alternative fuel. Our corn supply can be divided into feed for livestock, consumption, and biofuel.'

"'Nick, I like living on the edge and it is in my genes. I am going to stay on here at Harrisonville and continue running the Palace. Nothing is forever, and Pop's generation is now gone, and we have to be strong and stay focused,' said Nate.

"'Let's split up his estate. You take the Palace, and I will take the farm. Any other real estate we will sell to the locals,' said Nick.

"On the farm Nick and his chemistry friends designed and built a large complex with state of the art labs. In the labs they developed better quality corn and fertilizers which enabled them to grow the crops faster. At the same time, Nick enrolled in the local university's law school.

"Nick's new life was going very well. He was an outstanding law student and entrepreneur. Using corn as a bio-fuel caused big concerns with producers and sellers of oil. Nick in the back of his head always remembered his father's plans about building an empire of businesses. Nick realized that growing corn for biofuel would be the key component of his future empire," said Lola.

"Nate was busy reorganizing the banking system, gaming hall, and the Palace in order to modernize their systems. He loved criminal activities. It was in his genes. But before he reopened in full force, he wanted to have a memorial for his father and Rita. Nick felt that there should be closure on the old generation so that the new generation could start over without any regrets," said Lola.

"The memorial was held at the Palace. Many politicians, law officers, and friends attended. Frank and Candee did not come. Nick and Nate had heard stories about Frank and Candee but had never met them. Nick found a note written by Candee stating, if you ever need us. Put an ad in the NC Journal and we will come. "Nick put the ad in but they did not show up," said Lola.

"At the memorial, Nick and Nate spoke. Nick said the following: 'My mother Nina and my father were in love. My mother died, having my brother and me in the name of love. My father loved her from the first time he saw her. Now they are together. May God have mercy on their souls.'

"Nick and Nate knew what Rita did and her name was not mentioned at the memorial. No pictures of her were displayed. All the pictures were of Nina and Grandpa," said Lola.

"When the memorial was over everyone was invited to the opening of the new Palace in fact the name had changed to Palace Grande. A big banner was across the entrance was stating 'Nina and Redd you will be missed,'" said Lola.

"As you walked in, a live band and singers were getting it on. All the tables were decorated with pretty flowers, just like if Nina and Candee had fixed the tables.

"A waiter greeted everyone at the door and escorted them to a table. A different set of waiters took your drink order which was on the house. A third set of waiters walked around with Hors d'oeuvres. After almost all the tables were filled, a long row of all types of foods were uncovered. A dance floor was designed to hold a great number of dancers at the same time. Nate had remodeled the whole building. Even the Gentlemen's Basement was grander," said Lola.

"Nate and Nick were sitting at the bar and a tall, beautiful young lady walked through the door. She had long coal-black hair, skin that was the color of pure cream, and bright green eyes. She was dressed in a slim red dress that curved with her body. She looked like she just stepped out of *Vogue* magazine," said Lola.

"Nate could not take his eyes off her. She stopped, looked around and then headed straight for the bar. As she approached, Nate started sweating and taking deep breaths. It took her a long time to make it to the bar because she moved very slowly as if she was auditioning for a part in a movie. This beauty had all the right moves. It was obvious that she was a professional at whatever it was that she did. At some point she was standing in front of Nate," said Lola.

"'Hello, boys,' she said, 'you look like twins. Double trouble I see. I have been traveling all night and most of the day. How about buying a lady a drink? Make that a margarita.' Sipping on her drink, she asked, this appears to be a nice place to work. Do you know if they are hiring?'

"Nate without hesitating said, 'Yes.'

"Nick said, 'Wait, what are your skills?'

"'Guys, I can do everything. I can dance, sing, play the piano, bartend, and wait on customers. I am the complete package,' she said confidently.

"'Well,' said Nick, 'those are the easy things. Can you cook?'

"'Sir, I told you I can do everything. Cooking is my middle name,' she responded, smiling.

"'Okay, dance with me. I have dreamed for a gal who can do everything,' said Nate.

"Touching her body was like touching an angel that just fell out of the sky from heaven as they slow danced to Etta James song 'At Last,' thought Nate. As they were dancing, Nate said, 'What is your name?'

"'My name is Zola,' she responded.

"'That sounds like music to my ears,' said Nate.

"Zola and Nate are my parents, they are criminals of the second generation," said Lola.

"Zola was from New Orleans. She was part French and part Black. She was considered creole. She looked white but was not 100 percent. Many of her family members on her mother side were dark skin blacks. She never tried to act white she was just herself," said Lola.

"After dancing, Nick wanted to see her sing and play the piano. Without hesitation, he jumped on the baby grand and shouted, "Let's roll!"

"After a few notes she started singing Fats Domino's song 'Blueberry Hill.' Everyone that could get up started dancing. The whole Palace Grande was singing with her. If they could not get on the dance floor, they stood on top of the tables. When the song was over they yelled for more. It seemed as if she played all night, she was enjoying herself. She played and sang her favorites, which appeared to be everyone else's favorites also. 'I'm in love again. I'm walkin', walking to New Orleans, and ain't it a shame.' Zola all by herself brought boogie woogie to a little country town like Harrisonville. That was my mother, the Gal that could do everything," said Lola.

"Nick looked at Nate and shook his head for he knew his brother would be okay, and walked out," said Lola.

"Zola went home with Nate and claimed him for herself that night. She was nineteen years old but looked and acted older and Nate was twenty-six years old. They both loved each other. Within a few weeks they were married.

"Zola was from New Orleans and wanted to bring her home town to Harrisonville. Nate wanted to reorganize and it was the right time to make the changes. Zola's layout included an outside component during spring and summer with barbecue being cooked outside in a large pit, clams on the half shell, corn on cob, greens, all types of salads, and a large bar. Tables with umbrellas would surround the live band and singers.

"Inside, would be several bars with beautiful decorated tables with a deejay. On the inside, the tables would be beautifully decorated with waiters to take the orders with a full menu. Zola had suggested that they be opened just Friday, Saturday, and Sunday. This way they would have the rest of the week for planning and relaxation.

"In the plans, Zola wanted a large swimming pool so that the whole family could enjoy the Palace Grande. Nate loved the plans. Within a short period of time they were up and running. Zola was the major entertainment attraction on Saturday night. She played the piano, sang, and danced to the local band. She was a big hit on and off the stage.

"Zola knew that as some point she would have to tell Nate that she was not totally white. She did not know how he would feel. So she decided not to tell right away."

Ted looked a Lola and said, "You are not white."

"No, not totally," replied Lola.

CHAPTER 4

"MY GRANDMOTHER ON my mother's side was black and we have a rainbow of colors in our family which makes it a fun family to be associated with. We have never tried to past for white. We marry people that we love and not because of the color of their skin. My mother said it was the color of a person's heart that counts and not the color of their skin," said Lola.

"That is the only reason a person should marry, for love. My grandparents married for love. Their love for each other is what got them through the hard times so that they could enjoy the good times. That is what I want for my wife and me one day," said Ted.

"The Gentlemen's Basement and the gambling hall was opened every night. That area was remodeled, and it had its own adult exercise room and swimming pool, bar, and, restaurant. It was totally separate from the rest of the complex. After a few years, Zola decided, they should add a few amusements for the kids. The surrounding area put up hotels to accommodate outside visitors. Harrisonville had become a vacation spot for couples and families.

"Back in New Orleans, my grandparents controlled the whole area. They controlled all the drugs, liquor sales, gambling, and prostitution activities. They were people that you did not want to cross. If you did you would end up in The Swamp.

"People feared them. They even had the police force and government official on their payroll. Visitors to New Orleans could eat, drink, gamble, dance and have a good time. New Orleans is where Zola learned how to do almost everything.

"Singing and playing the piano came natural for her. On the weekends she would visit The Hill her parents' club and entertained the customers. One night at the club my mother was high off of marijuana and just finished playing and singing. She was on her way home and a man grabbed her and tried to rape her. She pulled out a knife and stabbed him over and over. With blood all over herself, she went back to the club. Her parents cleaned her up and gave her money and a ticket out of town and that is how she ended up in Harrisonville.

"The man she killed was a police officer. Being the type of business people they were, her father thought it would be better for her to leave and let the murder go unsolved. One of the workers at the club heard the conversation between my grandparents and my mother and decided to blackmail my grandparents. Well he ended up in The Swamp.

"Previous years my grandparents were in a drug war with two other drug cartels. The Brotherhood of NO and the Blood Brothers who controlled most of the wards but they were uneducated and did not understand how to stay in business. The Brotherhood was a white cartel and the Blood Brothers were black. They were always having wars and coming to my grandparents for help.

"In many cases it was for large sums of money. The cartel would have to give something as a guarantee in case the repayment was late or not repaid. Territory or customers were the most common forms of repayment. With the ongoing cartel wars and the loans, these two cartels were put out of business and my grandparents moved in and took over. They controlled everything.

"Any small business in the area had to buy insurance from them. This insurance allowed them to operate without fear of being robbed or the police harassing their business. Every month a collector would stop by the business and pick-up the cash. All fees were the same.

"My grandparents were professional gangsters they owned the police department, most of the clubs and bars, rooming houses, and controlled horse racing track, and gaming tables for poker. My grandfather was the best when it came to playing poker. In fact, that is how he acquired his first bar, playing poker. He won the club from a lady who had relocated to New Orleans from Philadelphia. She was good but did not know that he was a card shark who did not like losing. Winning the club was the beginning of his building of his criminal empire. After that acquiring other establishments and buying influence became easy.

"Therefore, my mother grew up in an environment of lawlessness and crime. Nate did not know much about my mother, but he loved her and her background would not have made any difference.

"Mom and Dad had been married about two years when she became pregnant. Mom knew it was time to tell Dad that she was part black. Her ability to cook came from her mother's side of the family. As a small child, she was taught how to cook food the New Orleans style. Zola became an outstanding cook.

"One night when the Palace Grande was closed, she cooked a fantastic dinner and got dressed in her sexiest dress and waited for Nate to come home. Her mom had always told me, that the way to a man's heart was his stomach.

"Zola heard Nate coming and she rushed to the door. 'Hello, honey,' said Zola. 'I have several treats for you tonight.'

"Nate looked at her and smiled. 'I surrender, and I know I am all yours tonight. So let's eat, it smells great,' said Nate.

"'Nate,' said Zola, 'I have a few things to tell you. First, my parents are not legit business people. I don't know how to say this, so I will just tell it like it is. They are gangsters. They control all of New Orleans and beyond. I am part black; my mother is what they called creole, half French and half black. Next I am pregnant with twins.' She looked relieved as she looked Nate straight in his eyes.

"Nate was not surprised about her background but overwhelmed with joy about the babies. 'Nina, oh, I mean, Zola, my twin brother as you know is a lawyer. He looked into your background years ago before we got married. I know all about your mother and father. I also know why you landed in Harrisonville. Nick said that the two families were a perfect fit. Family partners in crime and our babies will be beautiful, just like their mother,' said Nate.

"Nick heard about the good news and wanted to tell them in person how happy he was for the two of them. The next day he stopped by for dinner and it was a wonderful dinner. Louisiana-style chicken, rice and beans, collard greens, and sweet potatoes. Zola was right, she was an excellent cook.

"Holding up a glass of red wine, Nick said, 'You two are my best friends; I will always be there for you.'

"At that point, Nate said, 'We want you to be the God Father of the twins. You are living a legit life and in our business, life can be short. Therefore, we want you to raise our kids if anything happens to us. Can we count on you?'

"Without hesitation, Nick said, 'Thank you, it will be a pleasure. I will always look out for them whether you are alive or have passed on.'

Ted said to Lola, "Your defense is very creditable. I believe we have a slam dunk defense. Tomorrow you will go before the judge and he will ask you how you plead. You will say not guilty. Then I will say not guilty because of mental disease, mental defect, and extreme family criminal environment. They produced a life style that was considered normal in her family. If your mother's family was anything like your father's family. You will be off the hook. Tomorrow is a big day. Try to get some sleep. Court starts a nine, and I will be on time. I will ask if you can be released on your own recognizance. This is your first offense and you should be released with a small bail. I know the prosecutor. He is fair. He is an old man and I heard some stories about his parents that question his early life growing up in a family that has a bad family background. This might help our case."

Lola walked into court looking very stunning. Her hair was pulled up, and even though she had very little makeup on, she was still beautiful. With tears in her eyes, she said, "Not guilty."

Ted said to the judge the reason behind her not guilty plea. The prosecutor was shocked by the reason and just remained silent for a few minutes. To Ted's surprise, the prosecutor agreed to release her with a small bail.

Ted said to Lola, "Do you know the prosecutor?"

"No, but maybe he knows my family," responded Lola.

"He has always been fair, but not that fair," said Ted.

When Lola got home, Ted came in and said, "Okay, let's get back to your defense."

Lola had no problem getting back to her defense.

"My Uncle Nick's life was full of excitement. His farm and bio-lab was shaping up very well. He had developed several types of special corn. None of the types used much water but produced quicker with larger crops. 25 percent of the corn harvest was for consumption, 35 percent for feed, and 40 percent for biofuels. The farm in Upstate PA was used strictly for biofuels," said Lola.

"One day as he sat on his big porch in Harrisonville, a well-dressed man drove up in a limo and asked to speak to Nick. 'I am Nick,' he responded.

"'The waste from your biolab is contaminating the soil and water in the PA area. You will have to stop your experiments and production,' said the man.

"'Who are you?' asked Nick.

"'I represent groups of individuals that are in the oil business. We'd like to buy your farm. We have purchased almost all the facilities that are producing biofuels. Here's my card. Call me when you are ready to talk,' said the man. 'Harry Jones, Special Services—888-235-9080.'

"'Sorry, but I am not selling,' said Nick.

"'You will,' responded the man.

"Nick realized that his biofuels were driving the price of oil down. He had received a nice letter from the EPA praising him for his dedication with respect to the environment. All his testing were within the guidelines of the EPA.

"Nick worked hard every day trying not to become a criminal like the environment that he was raised in. But this situation might cause him to lose control.

"Nick called Nate and told him what was going on. Nate said, 'Nick, I am coming to PA with a few of my best helpers, and we will guard the farm.'

"When they arrived, workers told them that some men had come by and told them 'to leave for they might find themselves in the ashes.' Nate patted his shoulder to see if his father's gun was still there. Sue was reliable. If he needed her, she was ready for action.

"That night the men worked shifts to keep an eye on the lab and corn fields. Nick said to Nate, 'Maybe you should sell the farm. It is not worth anyone getting hurt. Tomorrow we can go put a complaint in with the local police department. If they do not help, we can call the state police, okay?'

"That next morning the boys went to the police office and said to them the situation. Nick pulled out the man's business card. 'Special Services,' said the sheriff. 'We will see how special he is when I lock him up for terroristic threats.'

"Nick called Mr. Jones, and he set up a meeting for that Friday. What Mr. Jones did not know was that the sheriff would be at the meeting. The meeting took place, and the boys told Mr. Jones under no circumstances were they selling the farm. The sheriff reminded Mr. Jones that this was their final answer.

Ted asked, "Did anything ever happen to the farm, Lola?"

"Not right away, but it became a problem later," responded Lola.

"That Mr. Jones had the law officers on his side, that day at the farm was a sham to make it look like things were going to be okay. But every week, Nick was getting something in the mail from the county about some made up violation. On various occasions a township inspector would come out and complained about something. Nick was getting tired of the harassment and called Nate.

"'Nate,' said Nick, 'let's sell everything in PA and Harrisonville and move out of state.'

"'Zola is pregnant with twins, and I don't know if she wants to move at this moment. I will ask her,' said Nate.

"Zola was seven and a half months pregnant but was still working hard at the Palace Grande. That night Nate said to Zola, 'Nick wants to sell everything and move out of state and start over. It sounds like a good idea. It is all up to you,' said Nate.

"'I believe it will be the best thing for all of us, twins included,' responded Zola.

"'I have only one request. I want to move back to New Orleans,' said Zola.

"'That sounds good to me and I know it will be fine with Nick,' responded Nate.

"'When my brother and I were born, my Uncle Nick said we were the prettiest babies that he had ever seen. Basically that is how our family and friends felt also,' said Lola.

"I looked white but my brother took after my mother's ancestors. He was light brown with black hair that he cut very short, tall and with brown eyes," said Lola.

"Both boys understood their father's plans for them but they had their own plans. Nick said to Nate, 'I want to practice law, get married, have a bunch of children, live on a boathouse, and make honest money. We are millionaires. Why put ourselves through this horror every day?'

"Nate lowered his head and said, 'It is in my blood. It was in our grandfather, our father, and now, I have a wife and in-laws who can never get enough power, influence, or money to be satisfied. Sorry brother, but that is the way the cookie crumbled."

"Nick opened up a law office and Nate joined forces with Eddie and Ella his in-laws. Together they were untouchable," said Lola.

"New Orleans was Sin City. Nick opened up his law office in the heart of downtown. He made up his mind that he would interview potential clients and if he believed they were innocent he would represent them. That sounded good until a great looking lady walked into his office. Nick could not take his eyes off of her.

"As Nick was standing up to greet her, he felt that before she gave her story as to why she needed a lawyer, she was guilty. He could see it in her beautiful bright blue eyes.

"'My name is Eva Johns and the police told me I need a good lawyer,' she said.

"'Start from the beginning and tell me your story,' responded Nick.

"'My boyfriend who was really my sugar daddy was beating me up and I felt like he was going to kill me. So I reached over and grabbed his gun off the night stand and shot him three times. This happened last night. The police took pictures of me. I went to the hospital and the doctor said I have bruised ribs, a concussion, and bruises on my hips,' said Eva.

"'What is the name of the deceased?' asked Nick.

"'His name is Eddie,' responded Eva.

"'The Eddie who is the most powerful man in New Orleans,' said Nick.

"'Yes, that is my sugar daddy,' responded Eva.

"'Let's go get a drink at my place,' said Nick.

"When they got to Nick's apartment, Eva started crying, stating, 'I don't know how I got myself mixed up in such a mess. I am a college graduate student working on a paper about underworld crime bosses. I had to play the part in order to get the story,' said Eva.

"About a year ago, I went to the club knowing that he would be there. It was known that he was a sucker for young, good looking women. For some reason, his wife always turned the other way and acted like business as normal. Nothing seen to bother her and as time went by we became lovers. He trusted me with many of his secret dealings,' said Eva.

"'I don't know if I will be able to take your case. Eddie is my twin brother's father-in-law. They are partners. But there is a law firm down the street that is very good and they have a reputation of getting good results in cases like yours. I will call them in the morning for you. For now, why don't you go into my bedroom and get a good night's sleep. We can talk more in the morning,' said Nick.

"The next morning Eva was up early and was making breakfast. 'Good morning, Nick,' said Eva. 'I feel better today. I hope that law firm takes my case. I have very little money but will work to pay them,' said Eva.

"'I will help you,' responded Nick. He did not truly believe her story but he could not determine what she was hiding. Nick called Stevenson Law Firm and spoke to Mr. Stevenson. He had read about Eddie's death in the local newspaper.

"Stevenson wanted Nick to bring her over that afternoon. Nick was feeling very good and found himself attracted to Eva. He loved the way she walked, her hair, her body and the way she talked. Eva was also attracted to Nick.

"Mr. Stevenson said to Nick, 'You are from Harrisonville, NC, I understand. My parents lived there for several years but moved to New Orleans before I was born. That was long before your time.'

"'Yes, I was born in Harrisonville,' responded Nick.

"'What brings you to New Orleans?' asked Mr. Stevenson.

"'My twin brother's in-laws live here. In fact, Eddie was my brother's father-in-law,' said Nick.

"'Well, that complicated things and I want you to leave and don't tell anyone that you came here with Eva. Her defense will be between her and her legal team,' responded Mr. Stevenson.

"As Nick was leaving he was thinking to himself. 'I think this lawyer knows something about my family that he is hiding from me. Maybe he does not want to embarrass me in front of Eva or maybe it is personal,' thought Nick.

"'Eva, I can get you off but you will have to tell me the truth. Not some of the truth but all of it,' said Mr. Stevenson.

"'My father worked for Eddie and Ella as their bookkeeper. One day when I was only a teenager my father went missing. Later his body was found in the swamp. My mother died with a broken heart. Before she died, she told me that Eddie's daughter left town because she killed a police officer. My father found out about the murder and was blackmailing Eddie and he had him killed. When I went away to college, I changed my name and vowed to get revenge for my father's murder and my mother's broken heart,' said Eva.

"'You know that Ella is not going to let this go. She will get to you. She is worse than Eddie. She is the mastermind behind their operations. She calls all the shots,' said Mr. Stevenson.

"'I played my part very well and Eddie allowed me to be part of his daily business transactions. I have photo copies of drug transactions with clients, prostitution records with customer's names, and all the names of judges, elected officials, and law enforcement. I am an undercover agent with the FBI. Please do not blow my cover. Don't allow Nick to know who I am. I believe he is honest but his brother and the rest of the family are gangsters. I know Eddie and Ella have murdered many people including my father who was their bookkeeper.

"'My father as their bookkeeper kept secret records of Eddie's everyday activities. It is in the form of a diary. My mother did not know about these records. I found them by accident. After my mother died, I was having some renovation work done because I was planning on selling the homestead. I discovered a false wall in the bathroom and when I knocked it open, I found the diary. Even the FBI doesn't know what I have. I told them that I was onto something but it was a work in progress,' said Eva.

"'Eddie paid off all my college loans. In my senior year, I was recruited by the FBI and I asked to be assigned to New Orleans because I understood the people and the mentality of the culture.

"'I have been working this case for three years. Do not tell the prosecutor this story. He is in Eddie's book. We will have to get the FBI involved,' said Eva.

"'What a story but I have something to show you. This is my FBI badge. I am with the FBI. When you landed in my office, I knew it might be the big break I was looking for,' said Mr. Stevenson.

"'What's next?' asked Eva.

"'That depends on what the diary and your records prove,' said Mr. Stevenson.

"'Okay, why was Eddie beating on you?' asked Mr. Stevenson.

"'He went to my apartment when I was not home. He pays the rent therefore he has a key. I forgot and left a picture of my mother and father lying on my bed. That is how he figured out who I really was. The daughter of the man he killed,' said Eva.

"'He was sitting in the living room in the dark with a drink in his hand when I entered the apartment. As I entered the doorway, he yelled out you fucking bitch! I knew it was over. He asked me to verify who I really was and I told him. I also told him he was under arrest and that I was an FBI agent. He took his fist and socked me in the face and started kicking me around. He was shouting you will never live to see me go to jail you bitch! After a few minutes of his abuse, I looked on the end table and realized he had left his gun sitting there. With both eyes almost shut. I reached over and grabbed his gun and shot him several times in the head. And that is how it happened.'

"'Did you tell anyone else about what really happened?' asked Mr. Stevenson.

"'No,' responded Eva.

"'Good, if you do, we will both be dead before the sun sets today. Let's get the records and take them to the bank and put them in my safety deposit box. I will give you a key in case something happens to me,' said Mr. Stevenson.

"'After they got the records, Eva called Nick and asked him if she could stay with him for a while,' said Lola.

"'Oh boy, what a story. Let's see Nick is your uncle, okay?' asked Ted.

"That's right and much later he married Eva. So she became my aunt. The FBI had the case transferred out of state. They knew that many of the officials in Louisiana were corrupt and could not be trusted," said Lola.

"'Nate and Zola were not in any of my records. They have only recently moved to New Orleans. Lucky for them, that they were still living in Harrisonville when most of the corruption was taking place,' said Eva."

CHAPTER 5

"'NATE AND HIS wife dodged bullets here but that family has been under investigation for many years. During the time the father Buddy was living, he was indicted for murder but the main witness who was a state senator died suddenly. Charges were dropped and the case was closed. But that family has a long history of illegal activities. That generation is gone but the next generation was trained to be just like the parents. Nick is the only honest one to ever be born in that bloodline. Even the great-grandfather had criminal genes,' said Mr. Stevenson.

"Ella was so upset over Eddie's being murdered by this little bitch that she put a contract out on her. Ella did not know that the FBI was involved. She called in her big guns to find out more about Eva," said Lola.

"'I want her investigated,' said Ella as she spoke to the chief of police. 'I do not have a good feeling about her. She's got more going for her then just a pretty face. If I have anything to do with it, that face will not be pretty much longer. You have her finger prints, put them through the system and see what comes up.'

"'Ella, I put her finger prints in the system and it said classified. Something is wrong, she is working for some government agency,' said Chief Wise.

"'Do you have any connections in DC that could find out who she is?' asked Ella.

"'I have one associate, but she would want to be paid a lot of money. At least $10,000 would be her asking price. If she got caught, it would mean jail time for her. Plus, I want $5,000 for my services. Everything must be in cash,' said the chief.

"'Get the information and I will pay your fees,' said Ella.

"Ella called in her circle of associates and explained the situation. 'Nate and Zola, I want you to get out of the business. We are in for some hard times to come. I don't know all the details but it is not good. You are not involved in our business here in New Orleans and I want my grandchildren to grow up with a father and mother who are respected by the community for good works. So this is your last day of being involved with my enterprises,' said Ella.

"Zola was more like her mother then her father. She and Nate agreed to leave the business but both had plans to return one day," said Lola.

"Lola, Nate and Zola were your mother and father, and they were truly corrupt parents," said Ted.

"Yes, now you are beginning to understand my defense," responded Lola.

"The FBI came and kept a low profile because they wanted to get the biggies at the top of the corruption ring. They started with Chief Wise. Agent Stevenson was given a team and he selected Eva to be part of the team," said Lola.

"Chief Wise, if you cooperate with the FBI, you will be given full immunity and will be allowed to retire with a full pension. Do you understand that this situation is serious?" said Agent Stevenson.

Without hesitation, the chief said, "You will have my complete cooperation."

"The chief was very greedy man and wanted the $5,000 that was agreed upon with Ella. That day he went to see Ella and gave her an envelope with a detailed report on Eva. Even the changing of her name and her family history was included," said Lola.

"Chief Wise understood Ella's mentality, as he entered the club, he pulled out his gun. 'Ella, here is the information you wanted, now give me my money,' said the chief.

"She handed the chief an envelope with the money, and after he took it, he pointed his gun at Ella, saying, 'I read the report. Eva is an FBI agent. This is the end of our relationship. Don't try to contact me about anything. I will be testifying for the FBI on your massive organization. You can expect to go to jail for life. I suggest that you leave the States today or be arrested tomorrow. They have all the proof necessary to lock you up. Eva kept a diary and has her father's detailed records. I was told this by a close associate. Leave now before it is too late.'

"Ella sat quietly by herself and started talking out loud. 'I will not die in jail. I will die on my own terms. First I need to tell Zola where all my money is located. The Feds will take all the nightclubs and houses but they will not get my cash!'

"'Next, I will send the information to Zola in the mail, and after that, I will write my own obituary. In my obituary I will give honor to my mother who was black. My father and mother loved each other until they died. Eddie and I loved our families and helped them when they needed it,' said Ella as she outlined her course of actions out loud.

"'After I finish my paperwork, I will call my hairdresser. I want my hair, my makeup, fingernails, and toenails to look fantastic. I will put on my dress for the wake. Without telling anyone anything, after dinner I will have my favorite cup of tea and lace it with arsenic. I will lie in my bed and look like a porcelain doll baby when they find me,' thought Ella.

"Her hair was done, nails painted and make-up was perfect and after eating her favorite meal she had her tea. That was the end of Eddie and Ella. My mother and father were standing by to take over," said Lola.

"Did anyone go to jail?" asked Ted.

"Oh yes, the FBI took the corruption case out of state. The next day Ella's body was found by the maid. A large group of FBI agents decended on New Orleans and broke down into small groups. The FBI was determined to send a message that the days of deep rooted corruption was over.

"Every crook that was listed in Eva's notes and her father's records were rounded up. There were so many, that they had to take them to a special location for arraignment. Based on who they were; some were given limited immunity. This corruption case lasted for about five years. The FBI had a 100 percent conviction rate," said Lola.

"Eva became friends with Mr. Stevenson and one night at dinner he said, 'My family has a strange past also. As of tonight, I want you to call me Eric. My father divorced my mother when I was four years old for another woman that he was in love with.'

"'I was born in Harrisonville, NC and they lived in Harrisonville. After the divorce, my mother moved to New Orleans for a new start. As a kid growing up my father never visited me or my mother. He would send child support on time and on my birthday and Christmas a card with a large sum of money enclosed.'

"'My mother changed my last name, and her last name back to her maiden name.

"'The return address for my father was a town in California. In fact, he owned a large vineyard in southern California. My father and his wife were multi-millionaires. I went to visit them but never told my mother. I stopped in to visit their winery and taste their wines. His wife name was Candee and his name was Frank. Located on the vineyard was a large bed and breakfast. I spend two nights there and Candee and Frank paid a lot of attention to me but I could not bring myself to tell them who I was,' said Eric.

"'They were living in California for a reason, and I didn't want to cause them harm by bringing back their past. In those few days we became good friends and I promised to stay in touch with them. That was the last time I saw them. My cards and money continued to come. My father paid my tuition for all my schooling even law school. I was hoping that he would come to my graduation ceremonies but that did not happen. While at the vineyard I took plenty of pictures. One strange thing that struck me was that they never talked about their family. Therefore, I didn't talk about my family,' said Eric.

"'Yesterday I got a telegram from my father's lawyer to call him right away. There was a family emergency. I called and he gave me the bad news. Candee and my father were both killed in a car accident by a drunk driver. I needed to come to California as soon as possible. I will be leaving in the morning and will be there until I settle my father's affairs,' said Eric.

"'Would you like for me to go with you Eric?' asked Eva.

"'No, this something I need to do on my own,' said Eric.

"Now that the New Orleans corruption cases were over, my mother and father were kept busy raising my brother and me. We were cute kids and my Uncle Nick gave my brother a nickname. His nickname was Toto. How he came up with that name always puzzled me. My brother's real name was Kevin. His nickname stuck with him and everyone called him Toto," said Lola.

"We lived just outside of New Orleans in a big white house located on 35 acres. The house was huge with seven bedrooms, five bathrooms, large living room, large kitchen, breakfast room, formal dining room and a large wrap around porch. The basement had three levels. My father called it a split level basement. The backyard had a swimming pool, playground, picnic grove, bar, and a large pavilion for barbecue. My father loved his old country club in Harrisonville. It was missed by my mother and father. Because he wanted to be back in the business in some fashion, he turned the back yard into a country club. He named it Harrisonville Country Club," said Lola.

"Every Friday, Saturday, and Sunday afternoon our country club was jumping. All the neighbors that wanted to party came to our home. My mother and her cousins would cook all day on Thursday for the weekend. At our home we had a farm with all kinds of animals. If they were cooking chickens, she would go get a half dozen of chickens and kill them. Her cousins would help her prepare the chickens and all the side dishes and desserts. It was wonderful to see my parents enjoying themselves," said Lola.

"From Friday to Sunday guests at the club were white and black. Spook Jackson, who lived on the farm next door, was a regular. He could play the piano by ear. Toto would sit with him and watch

CRIMINAL DEFENSE: REDEMPTION

him play and sing. My mother was also good at playing by ear and singing. I guess I was a chip off the old block because I also had my mother's talents," said Lola.

"My father loved to drink, mostly beer, but he also made moonshine that was the favorite drink. The guests did not have to buy any food but was expected to bring Papa some beer. If the beer ran out, the guests understood that they needed go get some more.

"My mother's cousin opened up a bar with a restaurant in town. He asked my mother to work for him. She worked only on Sunday nights, singing her favorite songs. The patrons loved her. Toto was very talented and Mom would take Toto with her. He could dance, sing, and play the piano and it got the crowd going. He was only about 7 years old but was cute as a button. She made him a tux of all white silk with a black bowtie, white top hat and white patent leather shoes. He was cool. His stage was the counter top of the bar," said Lola.

"Whatever happened to Eric, Lola?" asked Ted.

"Eric flew out the next day to California and went straight to the vineyard. To his surprise, there was another relative that greeted him at the door. He said, 'You must be Eric, my older brother.'

"'I am Eric but who did you say you were,' responded Eric.

"'Your brother,' replied the man.

"'My name is Robert,' said his brother.

"'I just found out about you today. They kept you a secret,' replied Robert.

"'They kept both of us a secret,' said Eric.

"'Our parent's law firm is going to read the will and a letter addressed to both of us,' said Robert.

"'May I have everyone's attention? The order of business today is to read a letter in private to Wright's two sons. After that the will can be read, said the executor. But before I get started I'd like to say a few words about my true friends Frank and Candee,' said the executor.

"I was the first person that they met when they landed in California some thirty years ago. I helped them with the purchasing of the vineyard. They employed many workers and gave them fair wages. On birthdays and holidays all employees were given bonuses. They were active members of our church. I know they had a past but we have a forgiving savior in Jesus Christ. Frank and Candee were born again Christians. They were loved by all that knew them, thank you,' said the executor.

"'I want to tell you two that your parents were my best friends. I don't know what is in this letter. Therefore, I am going to leave the room while you two read the letter together. This letter is for you only. What you read in the letter must stay in this room. That is what your parents wanted. They needed to tell you something so that you didn't make the same mistakes that they made. Candee told me that she didn't want that life for you two. So read the letter and let me know when you are done,' said the executor.

"'After this is over, let's go somewhere, so we can talk, said Eric'

"'That's okay with me,' responded Robert. 'My brother, call me Bobby.'

"Eric was given the letter and he started reading,

To my two sons,

We are very proud of the two of you. We have followed both careers. Eric is a respected lawyer with his own firm. Bobby is a federal prosecutor in the state of California. He has successfully prosecuted many cases and won. He has never lost a case.

Candee and I have a past that we are not proud of. We were criminals as young adults. We had a few options but we chose the worst ones. We became very wealthy off of other people's misery. Over the past thirty years we have lived everyday trying to make others' lives better. We believe God has forgiven us. May God bless both of you?

We pray that the two of you become best friends. We know we robbed the two of you of many years of joy you could have experienced together. Because of our horrible past, we did not want your life affected by our sins. Now that we have crossed over, it is time for the two of you to form a bond that will allow you to grow spiritually and mentally.

Don't go back and try to reconstruct our past. It will only depress you. Take your inheritance and move forward. Your inheritance is all honest money. We gave away the bad money years ago, to the church and the poor.

We have loved both of you always.

Your Mom and Dad

"'What do you think Eric?' said Bobby.

"'My emotions are mixed. I have always loved him, even at a distance. You were fortunate to have a mother and a father all your life. My mother was a good mother so I am blessed with those memories. I did come to California and looked them up. I stayed at their bed and breakfast. They were so nice to me that I did not have the heart to tell them who I was. I was supposed to stay in touch but I felt that there was a reason for their absence from my life. I realized it was not me but them. I also went to Harrisonville and asked around about them. Many of the old timers remembered them and told me some wild stories. I checked some of the court records but there was not much available. Based on the interviews with the older residents, our parents were gangsters. I would just like to let it go. What happened in Harrisonville should die in Harrisonville,' said Eric.

"'I agree and I would like for you to know that they knew who you were. I found a picture years ago of you at your high school graduation. Dad kept it in his bible. I asked my mother who was the boy in the picture and she said, someone that you will love and get to know some day,' said Bobby.

"'I believe they decided years ago that their past was not going to interfere with our lives. They left all their best friends behind and never looked back or returned,' said Eric.

"As the executor read the will, it was amazing how much wealth they had accumulated throughout the years. "The Wrights left $5,000 per person to everyone who is currently working for them. A college fund will be set-up for migrant worker's children to go to college.

"The church will receive 10 percent of their total assets. The administrative staff are to receive $100,000 each. The balance will be divided between our two sons, Eric and Robert. Please use your gifts wisely to better your lives and that of others. That is what your parents wanted for you,' said the executor.

"'In conclusion, Frank and Candee wanted to be cremated and don't want to have any type of memorial. They want their ashes to be sprinkled around the graves of their best friends from Harrisonville. They are Buddy Miller, Redd Harrison, and Nina Harrison. I believe they are all in the same graveyard," said the executor.

"'If it is okay with you, we can work and do everything together,' said Eric.

"'That sounds like a good plan,' responded Bobby.

"'Let's write out a plan of what we need to do. Since we are both lawyers we can do all our legal work. The plan should include selling all of their assets and then dividing them up between us. We should give out all the money gifts to their staff and workers as soon as possible,' said Eric.

"Bobby looked at Eric and said, 'I believe they are the last of their generation including their close friends. Maybe we should have the minister to come to the house and say a prayer blessing them and their friends,' said Bobby.

"Eric looked like he wanted to cry. His sadness spilled over into Bobby and they both sat down and the tears rolled down their weary faces. 'Let's go and get something to eat. We need to keep up our strength and health because we have a tough job ahead of us,' said Bobby.

"As they were cleaning out their parent's papers, Eric found a file box that was locked. 'I wonder what's in this box? If it is locked then it must be important,' said Eric.

"It took a lot of effort to get the box opened. It had Bobby's birth certificate. Bobby kept staring at the paper and then he dropped it on the floor, stating, 'My whole life has been a lie. Oh my, what a lie. They should have told me. I would have understood.'

"Eric picked up the paper and realized that Buddy Miller was Bobby's biological father and Frank had adopted him at birth. 'Bobby get over it. What difference does it make that you didn't come from Frank's blood line? You were loved and received the best education possible. You are the attorney general for the state of California. When we are born. We have no say as to who will nurture and raise us. It is God's will as to what path he set for us to follow. They might have been scumbags in their early lives, but became better people after God showed them the way. Forgive them, the same way I did many years ago,' said Eric.

"'You are right, let's move on to Harrisonville to spread their ashes,' said Bobby.

"Eva and Nick were seeing each other often and had fallen in loved. My father wanted to know more about his family's history. He felt that if they had children, it would be important to understand and know your family. He knew the best place to start was Harrisonville," said Lola.

"'Do you want me to go to Harrisonville with you?' asked Eva.

"'Yes, I just want closure on that generation. They were a group of friends that functioned like a family of criminals. I'd like to see their graves and say a prayer for their souls. Maybe my brother and Zola will go with us,' said Nick.

"Nate and Zola did not really want to go back to Harrisonville but he knew it would make his brother happy. Within a few weeks they were off to Harrisonville. Even though my brother and I were babies, they took us with them," said Lola.

"As they approached the grave site, they saw Mr. Stevenson from New Orleans standing in front of my grandparents' headstones. Beside him was another man that Nick recognized as the state attorney general for the state of Louisiana.

"'Oh my,' said Nick. 'Our past will not let go of us. I hope they are not trying to pin anything on us. Please God let it be for something good and not bad,' he begged silently to himself with his head bowed.

"'Hello, Eric, your telegram said for you to come to California but here you are in Harrisonville. I know you were born in Harrisonville but why are you standing over Nick and Nate's parent's grave?' asked Eva.

"'You are right. I did go to California. I will be going back in the morning. This is my brother Bobby. We are following our parents' wishes to sprinkle their ashes over their best friend's graves. They are Buddy and Candee Miller, Nina and Redd Harrison,' said Eric.

"Nate just stood there and suddenly took a few steps back. 'Your parents knew them?' asked Nate.

"Bobby spoke up and said, 'They were their best friends and partners here in Harrisonville.'

"'Wow, we came here for closure on that generation and met up by fate with descendants of the same generation,' said Nick.

"'Let's spread the ashes and say a prayer. Maybe your family will join us for a bite to eat. This way we can help each other to find closure,' said Eric.

"'God forgive them for all their sins. Amen,' said Nick.

"'After today, this will be my last time I will meet with your families on a social or professional level. As you know, I am the state attorney for the state of California. In the future, we might meet again but it will not be social,' said Bobby.

"'You Harrison boys were born and raised in Harrisonville. Tell us how it was growing up with these two families of friends. Don't hold back anything. I want to hear the good and the bad, okay,' he said, looking very serious as he ordered his lunch.

"'As kids, we observed many of their activities. One thing good about our conversation is that they are dead and their crimes went to the grave with them. I would like for you Bobby to give Nate and me full immunity from any legal actions for information given to you about this family of organized gangsters. Full immunity at all levels, criminal or civil actions,' said Nick.

"'We want protection for all our assets. Even though they were criminals, we have lived an honest adult life. We should not have to pay for their crimes,' said Nate.

"'If you write out a contract giving us full immunity and all the items I have mentioned, we can all sign it and tonight in your hotel room I will give you all the information that will enable you to find answers to closed cases,' said Nick.

"That night they met Bobby in the hotel room. The contract was reviewed by Nate and Nick. After a few more negotiations on different issues, the immunity was agreed upon and signed on the state Attorney's General's letter head," said Lola.

"'Nina, Candee, Redd, Buddy, and Frank were all friends whose friendship was sealed with a long history of crime that started as young kids. They were a group of criminals who functioned like a family,' said Nick.

"'Before you get started I want you to know that this is being recorded, understood,' said Eric.

"'Yes, we understand,' responded Nate.

"'To begin with, this family of criminals were just kids when they started their careers as gangsters. What we are about to tell you was witnessed by us, Nate and Nick Harrison. Other accounts were told to us by one of them to us, or overheard, or we took part in the criminal acts,' said Nick.

"'Redd, our father came here with our grandparents from Ireland. They were forced to leave because of being bootleggers and were about to go to jail. They had money and purchased a farm. They raised corn for consumption, animals, and moonshine. Business was going very well. His brother-in-law who was a drunk came to our home late one night after my grandmother had passed away to rob my grandfather. In the process he woke up and was killed by his brother-in-law. Redd grabbed his handgun who he called Sue and shot him. That was the first person he killed at age sixteen. The local police liked the Harrison family and just wrote it off as self-defense. When we were about twenty-two years old, just out of college, our father executed a bootlegger competitor named Jumbo. Shot him up close in the head. We both witness this event. They had a gambling hall, prostitution business in which most of the town big shots patronized often. I know this for a fact because we were regular non-paying customers,' said Nick.

"'Our mother, Nina, ran the prostitution business, she called it the Gentlemen's Basement. Most of the women were flown into Harrisonville from foreign countries for the purpose of prostitution. Their biggest reward was living in the States. Nina was extremely beautiful and was very sweet. She was loved by all that met her. She would never hurt anyone. Even if someone could not pay their bill in full at the end of the month she would let them slide,' said Nate.

"'One day I was looking through some papers and saw plans and blueprints for a resort in the Bahamas. I asked my father about the plans and he said, "Do unto others before they do unto you. I had a partner in the Bahamas name Lyle and he stole from me a lot of money. Later I found out he was the mayor's baby brother and a crook. He refused to refund my money so I killed him and left the Bahamas. That was the end of my Bahamas dream."

"'I am not sure how many people my father killed but there are many buried in the farm's swamp. Candee was very good looking, also. She was everything you could ask for in a lady. She had a secret personality. People that worked for her or knew her well nicknamed her the Smiling Assassin. She ran The Bank. It was used for loan sharking. Say a client owed a large sum and was far behind in their payments. She would have Frank to have an insurance policy taken out on that person and after about 6 months or more, she would have the client killed and would collect on the policy. All the members of this family group of criminals were horrifying but she was the worst,' said Nate.

"'Buddy and Redd were teenagers when they teamed up to pursue their career as criminals together. Based on the stories they told us, they were instant friends and were born to be criminals. Their motto was Friends to the End. Sure enough that how they ended their lives as criminals who were friends at the end,' said Nick.

"'Buddy was the business CEO. He kept abreast of all the incoming money and all the payouts. He conducted weekly meetings to determine if changes needed to take place. He determined whether or not to purchase real estate or how to get it free. He loved the word free. Buddy would go to the tax sales in the county and buy up tax liens. He was not liked by some of Harrison County residence because his overreaching of tax liens. If a resident approached him with anger about his buying of liens, he would say, pay your taxes, or your home will be my home. He turned the homes into rentals and the businesses he would build them up and when he was legally able, he would sell the business for a profit,' said Nick.

CHAPTER 6

"**B**UDDY WAS NOT a killer that was Redd's department. Buddy was all business and money. Buddy would have you beat up by one of his goons. If you didn't come around to his way of thinking, he would inform Redd and the situation would be solved. Buddy was killed by an associate and Redd took over everything. He was doing a good job but hung out every night very late. Redd was murdered by Rita our stepmother. We took everything of value out of the house and with the sheriff's blessings we burned the house down with the two dead bodies inside. One thing we discovered was Buddy's journal. It had a log of all the incoming money and payout that took place daily. That senator who was indicted on Federal charges that was given total immunity to testify against Redd's indictment on many charges was poisoned by Frank on Candee's orders.

"'They used rat poison which is hard to detect,' said Nate.

"'The journal listed all the important people that were on the payroll. Some names have a line drawn through them. That signified that these people were eliminated. The senator's name was in the book with a line through his name. I have the book but would like to keep it for a while. It is like an insurance policy in many ways,' said Nick.

"'Oh my,' said Bobby, 'our parents were awful people. Growing up, they hid their past well from me. It was hard for them to even kill an insect. They loved both of us boys and did not want anything to interfere in our lives as honest adults. They did a good job. I feel that was their small way of easing the pain of the past. On holidays I would hear my mother crying and my father talking to her. He would hold her for hours while they played religious hymns. They never got over the past but continued to live the best they knew how. I believe that is what's next for all of us.

"'Here is the tape; this family group of criminals is gone. Their sins died with them. Keep the tape and keep it safe. You never know when it might come in handy. I often tell young people; you know where you been but you don't know where you are going. It was nice meeting you two guys and maybe in the future we will meet up again on a happier occasion,' said Bobby.

"Lola, did they ever get together again?" asked Ted.

"No, Bobby resigned as the state attorney general and married his childhood sweetheart. My father received a post card from him years ago sent from Paris, France. That was the end of their relationship. Because of his family history, it was believed that he felt he was the wrong person for that position.

"Nick built a beautiful boathouse on the river here in New Orleans. He now works as a legal aid helping poor people get justice. I understand he works for free. Last year there was a big write up in the local paper about his success stories. He also sponsors a full four-year scholarship to one student with outstanding grades and good citizenship. He is around but does not get involved with our family," said Lola.

"My mother, Zola, loved working for her cousin and my father loved his country club. My mother was only twenty-one when she married my father and he was thirty-six. The age difference didn't matter at first but after we were born, she wanted more than just being a Sunday afternoon singer.

"She did not want any more children. She would tell her family and friends two was enough.

"Zola did get pregnant and I had the cutest little baby sister, her name Janet. She looked like an angel. In fact, Mom called her Angel.

Toto and I were three years old when Janet was born, and Mom was spending more and more time at her cousin's restaurant and bar. She was not just working, she was having fun with the customers, especially the men," said Lola.

"During the week, Mom would go out partying with her girlfriends. Pop opened up a liquor store down by the harbor. He worked long hours even after the store had closed. Sometimes he would get home after two o'clock in the morning. He didn't need the money but just wanted to be in the loop. He wanted to work and be an honest husband and father.

"Mom on the other hand felt that Papa was getting too old for her and she started meeting up with guys her age. She would invite them to Papa's country club. They would come with beer and eat and drink all evening and into the early morning," said Lola.

"Some of Mom's girlfriends were very outgoing and would flirt with Papa. 'Keep your fucking hands off my man. I have had three babies for him, and he belongs to me!' Mom would shout.

"The girlfriends would back off, but Papa would get drunk and pursue them, stating, 'You look so good. You look like angels from heaven,' spoken like a player.

"Mom walked up to Papa and cracked him in the head with anything she could find. Sometimes it would be a bottle, dinner plate, or whatever," said Lola.

"Papa was trying very hard to be an honest man. His country club on the weekends was his way of filling in that desire for criminal activity. Mom on the other hand didn't give a damn. She missed her parents and her enjoyment of singing every night. One night Mom skipped out on Papa while he was at his liquor store working late. She left us with a teenager. Mom had turned on the iron to press a dress. She went out of Harrison County to get an abortion. She forgot to turn the iron off and the house went up in flames," said Lola.

"Karen the babysitter got my brother and me out but forgot about Janet until she turned around looking at the burning house. Yelling at the top of her voice, she yelled, "There is one more!"

"By that time it was too late to try to save Janet. Janet was only three years old and had a very short life," said Lola with her eyes tearing up.

"'Do you know where Mrs. Harrison is Karen?' asked the fire marshal.

"'Not exactly, she said she was going to visit a friend in the next county. She left a phone number. She told me she would be home very late,' said Karen.

"Papa was called and was told to come home now for there was a family emergency. As he drove up he could smell smoke and see the flames. 'Oh no, not my home, not my family, God, please save them and keep them safe,' he said to himself as the fire chief stopped him from going too close.

"'What about my family, are my kids and wife safe?' he asked.

"'Nate, do you know where your wife is?' ask the chief.

"'She is supposed to be home with the kids,' responded Nate.

"'Well, she isn't,' said the chief.

'The whole yard was full with family, neighbors, and onlookers. My cousin Amy came up to my father and said, 'Come with me, Nate. We need to talk to you.'

"'Where are the kids?' asked Nate.

"'They took them to the hospital to check them out,' she responded.

"'The fire was out and only the smell of smoke and burnt wood filled the night air. My sister was the cutest little girl who was full of joy and life,' said Lola as tears flowed down her lovely cheeks.

"Nate said, screaming to the top of his lungs over and over again, 'My god! Why Janet?' Finally he remembered he had two other children and a wife. 'Where is the rest of my family?' asked Nate.

"The chief responded, 'We took the children to the hospital just for a routine checkup. Janet is there also.'

"'Where is my wife?' ask Nate.

"'We were hoping you could tell us,' responded the chief.

"'She was home when I left to go to my store. She did not have any plans to go out tonight that she shared with me,' said Nate.

"'The babysitter told us that she only said she would be home late,' said the chief.

"The sun was rising as Zola was almost home. The air was full of strange smells. The smell of death was the most obvious smell which was mixed with a smoky hard nose burning odor. Zola started coughing as she approached her home.

"'Oh, oh, what happened to my home? Where are my children?' asked Zola. As she got out of her red Cadillac, her cousin approached.

"'There has been a terrible tragedy. Come home with me, and I will explain everything to you,' said the cousin.

"Her cousin Barbara fixed her a cup of tea. 'First of all, the children are at the hospital for a checkup. They are okay. Nate is there with them. You look awful, Zola. You take one of my sleeping pills and Nate will talk to you later,' said Barbara.

"Barbara called the hospital to speak to Nate and told him that Zola was at her home sleeping and she didn't know anything about Janet. 'That is your job to tell her,' said Barbara.

"Sometime late in the evening, Zola woke up, and my brother and I were sitting on the bed. Nate was sitting in the chair. 'The doctor had given him a sedative for he was about to go out of his mind,' said Lola.

"'Where is Janet?' asked Zola.

"Barbara responded, 'With God.'

"Zola looked at my father and us children and started yelling, 'No! No! No! Not my baby!'

"My mother's crying was out of control, so they sent us to the next room to be with cousin Barbara," said Lola.

"'Zola, you know I love you. We will get through these hard days so that we can live on and enjoy our children. But I need you to tell me the truth. I might not forgive you today but I will in the future,' said Nate.

"'Nate, I went out of the county to get an abortion. I didn't want any more children. Three is enough. I left them with a reliable babysitter. I don't understand why our home caught on fire and burned down,' said Zola.

"Zola saw Nate's face turn beet red, and he looked like fire was coming out of his head. At this moment, he was his father's son. He even looked like Redd. Zola realized that nothing would ever be the same.

"Zola fell back into the bed, thinking to herself, 'I have lost Janet, and now I have lost Nate. What is left for me in this world? My parents are gone and now my family.'

"With a tears dropping from his chin, Nate stood up over Zola, stating the following: 'I have loved you from the day I saw you. I have watched you coming and going out with single girlfriends. As long as you came home to me at night, it was okay. But this is unacceptable. As of this moment we will be husband and wife but nothing will never be the same. One last thing, was this my baby?'

"With her eyes closed, Zola responded, 'Yes.'

"Nick moved Nate and his family into his boathouse on the river. He understood the whole situation from all sides. He felt that the calming waves of the water would help Zola recover from her sorrows faster. A nurse was hired to take care of her because she had a nervous breakdown after finding out the cause of the fire was her fault. According to the fire chief, the iron was left on with it sitting flat down on the board," said Lola.

"After a few months, Mom got up from her bed and said to the nurse, 'You are no longer needed. I will take care of my husband and children.'

"My father had a new home rebuilt right on the same spot of the original home. We continued to live with my Uncle Nick until the new home was ready. He enjoyed us living with him.

"Uncle Nick was always the most honest of all my relatives. He worked hard while in law school and graduated number one in his class. He was also president of his senior undergraduate class at Harvard. As a small child, I wanted to be honest and a good civic minded resident of Louisiana. But that never happened. Our home was rebuilt and we move back home to Vinton," said Lola.

"My father allowed my mother's cousins to run the liquor store while my mother and father hung out at the racetrack. They were at home at the track and appeared to had forgotten about Janet. This racetrack had secret areas inside that were known only to special people. My mother and father were considered special people. Mom was a good flirt, so she decided to ask their friend, the owner, if she could open a gentlemen's room for very special clients," said Lola.

"'If you allow me to run the room, it will enhance your other activities such as your secret poker room and the after hour's liquor sales. I have lots of experience because I was in charge of this business in Harrisonville for many years. In Harrisonville it was called the Gentlemen's Basement,' said Zola.

"Without much thought, Lenny the owner said, 'Sounds good to me. I will set-up the business but after it is making a profit, you will have to pay all the expenses and give me 65 percent of all profits from all sources.

"'This will be your business and your responsibility for activities, legal and questionable.'

"'It will not take me long to start making a profit. We have friends in New Orleans that will deliver the liquor well below wholesale prices. My husband and I will bring in our associates from Harrisonville and New Orleans who are the top professionals in this line of business,' said Zola.

"'The racetrack became a full service operation. The poker room, after hours speak easy, and prostitutes for clients that wanted to have a good time were provided by Nate and Zola.

"The racetrack owner was known to be a crook. During a big purse race, management would fix the race so that a 75 to 1 horse would win over much better horses. This way the owner and his friends would have a big payday," said Lola.

"Lola, next week, I will be receiving from the prosecutor's office all his discovery information. He will want our information also. But I have to be careful not to give away our defense. I believe we are halfway home. Because of personal reasons, I will be stepping down as your attorney after we finish with your story. I will be assisting the new attorney. I have talked it over with my boss and he feels that I should step down. You will not be going to jail. I guarantee the verdict will be one that will be in your favor," said Ted.

Lola looked at Ted, and for the first time, she could see love in his eyes. *Who is this Ted?* Lola thought to herself. *He is my lawyer. He is tall and handsome. Maybe I should interview him. No, I will wait until the trial is over. He might think I am trying to hit on him. We have a good relationship, and I do not want to destroy it by acting like a classless bitch.*

"Okay, Lola, tell me about the business and anything spectacular that happened to them while working at the track," stated Ted.

"Yes, my mother kept getting pregnant every twelve months," said Lola.

"Well, I thought the twins were her only children," responded Ted.

"We are her only living children. She ended up having six full term babies. After delivery they would live a few hours or for a few days and die before coming home. Her first dead baby had a big knock on his head. It was a boy and she named him Henry. Zola said she hit herself on the end of a table at the track. But I witnessed her and my father fighting. She hit him in the head with a tire iron and was running away from him and tripped.

"This took place at home and an ambulance was called and the police came too. Mama told them that he was drunk and fell down the steps. Papa seconded the lie.

"She always started the arguments. Most of the time it was because she would over hear Papa making a pass at a woman. His favorite line was, you look so good, and in fact you look like an angel that just fell from heaven. That was all she needed to hear and she would get off on him. Fire would be coming from her eyes. Her favorite statement was that I have had babies for you and your son of bitch trying to give everything away to another woman. You old fart.

"The next baby had an enlarged heart. Mainly because of Mama's poor diet, which included drinking and smoking. This baby lasted a full day. It was a boy and he was named James. The next baby she was a girl, her name Susan, and Mama had to have a cesarean section because the cord was wrapped around the baby's neck. The baby died, and Mama was depressed for a while.

"When she got pregnant, Papa would question whether he was the father. That would set her off. She would start drinking and when she was nasty drunk would just go right up to him with whatever was in her hands and start hitting him. Papa would never fight back. But he did try to protect himself. Every time she would hit him it was to his head. She would call the ambulance and tell the police some made up story and he would go along with it.

"It was about two years before she had the fourth baby. This baby was born with a skin over its face and suffocated. It was a boy and only lived a few minutes after birth. His name was John. The fifth baby was a girl and she was turned upside down and Mama had to have a second cesarean section. She died the next day because her weak heart could not handle the trauma.

"The last baby was born dead and it was a boy and she named him Enough Harrison. Mama had gained a little weight but still had sex appeal. I was about eleven years old and stayed home from school because I was sick. Papa was at the track and Mama stayed home with me. I was in the bed and one of Papa's friends from the track stopped by.

"His name was John. He was my father's best friend. I could hear them talking in the kitchen but they did not see me. As I was listening, it was obvious that they were lovers. Mama was trying to figure out how to get rid of Papa," said Lola.

"John looked at her and said, 'Just hit him in the head with a baseball bat and tell the cops it was self-defense.'

"Mama said, 'Oh no, I could never kill him. He is the father of my children. He has loved me even with all my bad habits. We have been through a lot of ups and downs. I will just divorce him,' Mama said.

"So that was the plan. As John was driving home, his brakes on his truck stuck and the wheel froze as he was trying to turn the corner leading up to his street. His truck struck a pole and he was killed instantly. He died that day, and so did Mama's heart," said Lola.

"Instead of being depressed she decided to get back into action with her cooking, singing, dancing and piano playing at the special room at the track," said Lola.

"Nate, I am going to purchase a baby grand piano for the bar area at the track, set up a New Orleans style restaurant, and have live music on Friday, Saturday, and Sunday afternoon. It will be called Zola's Lounge," said Zola.

"'Maybe Toto can play the piano, sing and dance with you on Sunday afternoon. He loves music and is very talented in many areas. Just like his mother,' said Nate.

"Toto's real name was Kevin, but he was given this nickname by my mother because he loved to dance on his toes when he heard music. Therefore, she named him Toto. Plus, she loved the name because she said it sounded like a name for a gangster. She was right, the name was perfect, and he became a gangster, "said Lola.

"'As the owner of the track, Zola, I am very pleased with your innovations which will increase our numbers for the poker room and at the same time provide an extra incentive for customers to come often,' responded Hank."

CHAPTER 7

"**M**AMA WORKED DAY and night getting the restaurant set-up. She ordered the piano and got local talent to play for her on the weekends. Toto was featured on Sunday afternoon. We were eleven and a half when we were both introduced to the world of criminal activity. Toto was in the entertainment part and I worked in the kitchen. We were both tall and looked older than our age. We loved the business. We both wanted to learn everything about running the business. At the time we did not know it was mostly illegal," said Lola.

"Opening night came and the people were pouring in. The room held 250 people and the line was all the way out to the race track area. It now cost $5 just to get inside. Mama did two shows per night and only one show on Sunday afternoon. People waited at the door. If someone left, then someone could come in. That is how packed it was.

"Mama would open up with Blue Berry Hill and the room would go wild. After she was singing and playing, Scooby Johnson a local would keep them going with the saxophone, New Orleans style. Even though I was young I helped keep the food flowing. Mama would come in the kitchen when she could to check on things. At 2:00 a.m. the Zola's Lounge was closed and the special people were allowed to stay. After 2:00 a.m. the after hour bar would be opened along with the Gentlemen's Basement.

"Behind the bar, they sold Cuban cigars that were smuggled in from Cuba. Also, any type of dope could be purchased. Clients had an ID number. Without your number, you could not purchase any cigars or drugs," said Lola.

"Toto was featured for Sunday afternoon. He was the afternoon sensation. It cost $6 to get in on Sunday for the show. Toto would come out on stage in his white tux with tails. He was good looking. He had brown skin, tall, and looking much older than he was. Soon as he walked out the room burst into a thunder of clapping. The band would play a song that he could tap dance to and he just took off like Sammy Davis Jr. Next he went to the piano and would hit a few notes and then start playing and singing rock and roll songs that the room loved. That was Toto, the great entertainer," said Lola.

"Everything was going wonderful. Mama and Papa were getting along better and she was not beating on him anymore. Papa was a big gambler and had lost large amounts of money betting on the horses and playing poker. He did not tell Mama because she would have been furious. Therefore, he decided to go to tax office and buy up homes that were up for tax sale. These homes would become rental homes. Good money was coming from the business. With 40 percent net profit it made them very rich. Zola did not allow Papa to handle any of this money. She knew that he had become a gambler and did not want their money to be used for gambling. She was thinking ahead for their children's future education which included college and beyond," said Lola.

"Papa took the money he had left from his inheritance and invested into real estate. He became the main buyer at the tax sales. In fact, sometimes he was the only buyer. He became the go to person for rentals in and around town. His water front properties were very popular. He turned them into condos.

"In some circles, he was a hated man. His business practices were very rough and questionable in many situations. I was with Papa when a man came up to him and said fuck you Nate. You took my brother's home. One day you will get yours. Papa just looked at him and said, I hope your taxes are paid up, because your home will be next. I just put my head down in shame," said Lola.

"When clients received credit in order to play poker and were behind in paying off their debt, Papa would hire collectors to go get his money. I had heard stories about my grandfather Redd and his criminal mind and activities. It was becoming obvious that my father was more like his father than Nick. But when it came to Zola, he was a gentle as a kitty cat. Papa would tell the collectors not to come back empty handed. If they want to settle out with me, I will meet with them. In most cases the client knew it was either the money or their life. Papa had a solution to that problem. They would have to make him beneficiary to any insurance policy and prove that payments were being made. Or if it was a large sum of money, they were required to sign over their deed to their homes to him. He did not care if the client was male or female, blind, cripple, or crazy. He wanted his money. At the end he got paid," said Lola.

"'Nate, soon we will have enough money saved that we can send our two bright children to any university in the States. Just like you and Nick. Toto and Lola both wanted to get a degree in business and I told them not to stop there to go for their MBA's. I want them to work and earn an honest living. This life is all we know. Maybe if our parents had kept us away from this life, things might have been different but it is what it is. We cannot go back it is too late for us,' said Zola.

"Zola and Nate understood that paying your taxes at all levels was important and they hired the best accountant to handle their business. He paid all their taxes on time and they trusted him completely. Mama decided that she wanted a bigger home on the river and did not want a mortgage. She had planned to pay with cash. Our old home they planned to rent out. The home on the river was priced at $1.1 million. It was beautiful. Just close your eyes and anything you could dream of was in this home. Mama wrote a check for the deposit which was 20 percent of the selling price. After a few weeks, the bank notified them that their check bounced and my parents were horrified," said Lola.

"'Nate, there must be a mistake. Did you spend all our money?' asked Zola.

"'No, I never touched any of it. I have enough in my saving to buy your dream home. I will call Gary our accountant and see what happened to the money. Gary will have the answer. Gary does not manage my money, I do it myself. Remember, I do have a degree in business,' said Nate.

"Zola was extremely upset. She had worked hard for her money by not going on big expensive vacations. She did not want to wait for the next day. That night she went to Gary's home to talk to him about the bad check. She knocked on the door several times real hard. No one answered and it appeared that they had left. All the furniture was gone. She turned the door handle and it opened. As she walked in she knew he had stolen all of their money.

"The next day, Mama went to the bank, and there was only $100 in the account. Gary had forged her signature on several checks over a three-month period until he wiped out the account. Gary skipped town with his family," said Lola.

"'Nate, we cannot let him get away with our money. We will have to hunt him down and get our money back. My parents had a private eye who was very good. I will call him and ask him to take our case. When he finds him, he will give it back or he will never live to spend it,' said Zola.

"The next day, Mama called Bruce and gave him all the details. 'Bruce, he took $1.9 million from my account. I want every penny back. If he has it in the bank, take him to the bank and get it. Return him to his home, tie up him and his wife and burn their home down with them in it. Do not harm their children. Do it when the kids are at school. You need to, wait until the time is right. But get the job done. Your pay day will be $100,000. I know I can depend on you. My parents believed in you, and you are the best,' said Zola.

"That night Mama poured herself a big glass of whisky on the rocks and sat in the family room in the dark. When Papa came home he saw Mama sitting in the dark with her drink. At that moment, he could see her mother's personality in Zola. The fun loving young gal he met years ago was gone. All was left was an almost thirty-year-old woman who was out to get even with her thief," said Lola.

"It took about a week for Bruce to find Gary. He was so dumb. He went to New Orleans, Zola's hometown. Anything that happened to him would go unnoticed. Murder was common in New Orleans. Stealing from Zola is the last person he should have stolen from.

"Within two weeks, Zola received a cashier's check from Bruce. He had recovered all the money. When he returned, Bruce filled her in on the details. 'He did not have a wife or children. He lived by himself. He is dead. I burned him up in the house. I made it look like an accident. He was an outsider and no one would care. But he did tell me that he was made to take the money by an old man with a Caribbean accent who appeared to be from the Bahamas or from that area. He also said that the man was going to kill me and hunt down and kill my sisters and brother if I did not steal the money,' said Bruce.

"Mama became very concerned. She told Nate the story and he knew exactly who it was. 'Zola, we might be in trouble, this old man is the brother of the conman that my father killed in the Bahamas before Nick and I were born. He must have figured it out that it was my father who killed his brother. Even though Papa is dead, he wants revenge. I do not think he wants to physically harm us but we must find him. My father lived by his words. Do unto others before they do unto you,' said Nate.

"'Where do we start?' asked Zola.

"'I have some old papers of my father's. Maybe I can get a name from them,' responded Nate.

"The next morning, Nate called Uncle Nick," said Lola.

"'Nick, I need you to come for a visit. A very troubling situation has surfaced from the past that involves us. Please come as soon as possible,' said Nate.

"'New Orleans is only a two-hour drive to Vinton. I will leave after breakfast,' Nick said to Eva, who now was living with him.

"'I will go with you. Maybe I can help in some small way,' replied Eva.

"'I wonder what from the past could cause concerns for us today. My brother wants me to bring pictures or papers that I might have of my parents and their friends. I have plenty pictures and papers. The pictures were all dated and the people were named. My mother did that because she wanted her boys to understand the past so that we would have a good life without criminal activities. My parents were born criminals. A psychologist would say that criminals are not born but are made. Sorry, that is not the case with my parents. My grandparents were criminals, my parents were criminals, and my brother is a criminal. I pray to God that my nephew and niece grow up to be good citizens,' said Nick.

"The next morning Nick and Eva arrived with boxes and papers. Some of the papers, no one had ever looked at until now. We were asked to go into the family room while the adults sat and had coffee in the kitchen with the boxes. We could hear everything. As we listened, it became known to us that our family has a dark, sinister past," said Lola.

*****

"What is this?" said Eva. She held up a small blue notebook that was covered with mold and pages that were sticking together. "I think this is your father's confession book." Eva took a thin knife and carefully separated the pages. She began to read the first page.

"I have kept a record of all my criminal activity. One day after my generation is long gone. The authorities will be able to solve murders and other crimes that have gone unsolved for many years. This is my way of asking God to forgive me for taking this path in life, submitted by Redd Harrison."

"The dates and times of the murders are recorded and the circumstances that led up to the murders. This book needs to be turned over to the FBI," said Eva.

"That might be true, but for now we need to find the name of this old man who wants to harm us. I believe his name is here somewhere, okay?" said Nick.

"Redd's first murder was his uncle who killed his father while trying to rob him. His second was a competitor who beat him up and killed some of his workers. The next was his cousin for his land and insurance money. The last was Lyle from the Bahamas who was the mayor's baby brother. This is it, jackpot, his name is Lyle! All we have to do is find out the name of the mayor during that time. After that we can develop a plan to stop this man who is trying to get revenge after all these years," said Eva.

*****

"The next day I was looking at the pictures of my grandparents. They were good looking people. Their friends were also good looking. In order to make a living in their line of business, they were very smart people. It is a shame that it was not developed differently like the Rockefeller's," said Lola.

*****

As the adults sat in kitchen were looking through papers, Nick said, "Let's hire Bruce to find him, but he is not to approach him, just let us know where he is. Bruce can find a needle in a haystack."

"That sounds good but you are not going to harm him. If you do you will be just like your parents," said Eva.

"Let's have a drink," said Zola.

No one said anything, so Zola poured herself a big glass of wine.

"We need a plan. After he finds the old man and then what and who will go to talk to him without being aggressive?" said Nick.

All eyes turned to Nick; he was the lawyer and could give the old man some legal reasons to leave the children of Redd alone.

Without hesitating, Nick said, "Okay."

Bruce was hired and was told only to report back to Nick the old man's location. It took Bruce longer than normal to find the man but he did. Bruce had gotten a picture from the Bahamas of their former mayor. The man was staying in New Orleans and was spotted at the bank talking to the bank manager about the money the accountant had deposited in the bank a few months ago. The old man did not know that the accountant was dead. All he knew was that the money had been deposited into the bank with both of their names on the account.

"The account was closed out a few months ago and all the money was withdrawn?" asked the old man.

Hearing that news, the old man knew that this family of criminals was on to him and that he would be lucky to get away with his life. Bruce followed the man back to his hotel and called Nick.

"Nick, the old man is staying at The Fish Bone Hotel of New Orleans. I am in the lobby. Do you want me to stay here until you get to the hotel?" asked Bruce.

"Yes, I will come now. How did you find him?" asked Nick.

"He was at the bank, trying to withdraw the money and found out it was gone," responded Bruce.

"Oh Nick, he is in the lobby with his suit case. It looks like he is getting out of town," said Bruce.

"Follow him. Do not let him out of your sight," responded Nick.

The old man when to the airport where he had a ticket back to the Bahamas and Bruce called Nick. "He is on his way home. The Harrison name must have scared him, especially since all the money was gone. Maybe he figured he should get out now before he loses not only the money but his life," said Bruce.

*****

"Nick was happy to hear the news but he did not know that Bruce had murdered the accountant. He did know that murder was part of his duties when he worked for Zola's parents," said Lola.

*****

"Thank goodness that's over. Maybe know we can plan our wedding," said Eva.

Nate knew something was wrong with Zola but could not figure it out. She was drinking very heavy and working long hours at the track. My father did not want her to have any more pregnancies so he went and got fixed. He did not tell Zola. He thought it would upset her.

My father made sure that she got her dream home. He was hoping this would change her back to the woman he knew who loved life and was happy to be alive. But the new home did nothing for my mother.

Nick always wanted to have a wife and children and now he had the perfect woman who wanted to be called Mrs. Nicholas Young Harrison. He had waited a long time for Eva. Eva no longer worked for the FBI. With money not an issue, she planned the wedding with very little help from a wedding planner.

It was a beautiful spring night as Eva and Nick sat on the deck of his boathouse making plans for the future. She put her head on his shoulder and closed her eyes. He leaned over and kissed her forehead. "Nothing will ever come between us. Our marriage will be blessed by God. I would like to get married in a church," said Nick.

"Oh, I was hoping that we would get married in my church. I pay my tithes every month. My mother will be looking down on us with her blessings. God knows your goodness and so do I," said Eva.

Just then there was a loud knocking at the front door. It was Zola. "Can I stay with you because Nate might kill me!" yelled Zola.

"What's going on?" asked Eva.

"I am pregnant," she responded.

"That is wonderful," responded Nick and Eva.

"No, it's not!" yelling and screaming like a wild woman, said Zola.

"Tonight I told Nate I was pregnant and he flipped out and was calling me all kinds of names. He said I was a fucking bitch. He said I was just like my mother and maybe I should do all of us a favor and comment suicide like my mother. I ran out the house and came straight here," said Zola.

"I don't understand, why he was he so upset to that point?" asked Nick.

"He had himself fixed about a year ago and did not tell me. This baby is not his," said Zola.

"Oh no, I think it is time for a drink," said Nick.

"A drink, I need more than a drink, I need an abortion," said Zola.

"Come with me and I am going to run the water so that you can take a hot bath. We will figure all of this out tomorrow," said Eva.

The next morning Zola got up early and appeared to be ready to leave. "Good morning, family. I had a good night sleep. The best I have had in years. I thought about my past and what I need to do for my future. The first thing is to look at the truth. I will never be happy if I do not accept the truth about my parents and how I have been living my life," said Zola.

"My parents lived a life as professional criminals. They loved me but provided their type of life style for me. To begin with my grandmother was a black woman who was a performer in France and she married a Frenchmen and had six children, two boys and four girls. My mother was the baby girl. She was also talented. She was an entertainer and that is how she met my father. He was selling moonshine in the parking lot of the club she was performing. My father had big ideas for his future. It did not include working for an honest day's pay. He wanted to be in charge of any criminal activity in the area. He was twenty-two and my mother was twenty. As time went on, they got married shortly after they met. They both wanted the same things and one thing was to make big money.

"My father was a good card player and won a lot of money playing poker. In fact, that is how he got his first juke joint. He won it in a card game from one of the local businessmen. He called it the Pico's Junction. He turned it into a place where you could, drink, eat, smoke Cuban cigars, enjoy the company of fast women, and purchase whatever type of drugs your heart desired. That was Pico Junction and that was my parents.

"At some point they became the major players in the drug culture of New Orleans. With law enforcement on their payroll they became the go to people. My mother was a very pretty, talented lady. She always carried herself like a lady. But she was vicious on the inside. She was far more dangerous than my father. There is no way of determining how many people she killed or had killed but no one crossed her. She did not believe in second chances.

"My father followed her lead and was a willing partner in all her decisions. He killed his share of violators. My mother did not get pregnant with me until later in life. I was delivered by cesarean section, but the doctor told her she needed to have an operation to stop the bleeding. Because of the operation, she would not be able to have any more children. That is when she allowed my father to start seeing and visiting the fast women of the club.

"My next confession is about me. I have decided to change my ways and become a different person. How I will accomplish this, I do not know at this point. But it will happen. Eva has a law enforcement background and I am asking her not to report what I am about to say to the law. I will spend the rest of my life helping others and want a second chance," said Zola.

"We agree," said Eva and Nick.

"When I was nineteen, I killed a cop who was trying to rape me and my parents sent me out of town and I landed in Harrisonville, NC. That is where I met Nick and Nate. My accountant who stole my life savings was murdered on my orders. I have sold all kinds of drugs, was a madam in my own house of prostitution and a few other things like gaming and a loan sharking and my own private bank. In order to survive with all my baggage, I started drinking very heavily. I did not do drugs but it was not easy with my guilt about Janet, my baby dying in the fire that was my fault. I abused my body by getting pregnant every year and only to lose the baby at the end of the 9 months. Some of these babies did not belong to Nate but he never knew. Please do not tell him. I have been to hell and know I need to find a way to get to heaven one day.

"This is my confession. I will be leaving shortly to go stay with my great aunt who is my grandmother's sister who is seventy-six years old but in good health. She will help me sort things out and help me find myself. She is a devout Christian woman. She lives in Lynnville, Alabama and is waiting for my arrival. She told me to leave the kids with their father because he needed to learn how to be a real man.

"Please give Nate this note and maybe someday our paths will meet again under better circumstances. I wish you two the very best in your upcoming marriage. Take a look at the criminal history of this family and raise your future children to lead and live Christian life. I got to go but my children will always be on my heart and mine," said Zola.

As Nate read the note, tears ran down his eyes. The tears fell on the note and faded out some of Zola's words but they were now etched in his mine forever.

Nate wanted Nick to know what was in the note. "Dear love, I have let you down many times throughout the years. It is time that I leave and allow you and the children to live a life that is without a lost soul like me. Hopefully, I will be able to find myself and become a better person. Please do not attempt to look for me. I need to be able to rest my corrupt soul and reclaim my life. I have given it to the devil. I will always love you and the kids. I have to leave in order to save us all and with love in my heart, Zola," said Nate.

Nate slowly tore up the note, turned and walked out the house. It appeared he was in a daze. Nick caught up with him. "Nick how did all this happen to me and my family?" asked Nate.

"Well, Nate, do not blame yourself. It all started long before we were born. Criminal activity started with our grandparents or maybe great-grandparent. We were introduced to it at an early age but at some point we made our own decisions as to what we wanted," said Nick.

"I am leaving, Nick. Years ago when the babies were born, you and Eva became the godparents. At that time, we asked the two of you to take care of our children if were not able. Well, I am leaving and giving them to you. I will sign a paper giving you custody of

Toto and Lola. I am not worthy of raising children. I have a criminal mind. These children need someone they can depend on every day. I am going to get in my car and take off. Everything I have here I want to put in trust for them. I will send you a PO box address to mail the paper. Please do this for me. They deserve a chance in life. With me as their father it might not happen," said Nate.

The next day Nate gave both children a big hug and told them that their mother was gone away to get well. "She will be back some-day but until then your Uncle Nick is going to take care of you because I have to leave. Today you do not understand but one day you will understand. Your mother and I love you today, tomorrow, and forever," said Nate.

*****

"Nick got up early the next morning to try to convince Nate not to go but he was gone. The kids were now thirteen and Nick did not know that they were young criminals. This was the beginning of the third generation of criminals," said Lola.

"How did you feel without a mother or father?" asked Ted.

"It was a very low period in my brother's and my life. Because of our parent's lack of supervision, we were raising ourselves. I recall when Toto was about three years old and our parents were having a party at our home and he got into my mother's jug of homemade cough syrup. I can't say for sure but I believed Toto was born an alco-holic. Even I love to drink. My mother loved wine and beer and she must have been drinking when she was pregnant with us.

"That night Toto had passed out. Mom came into the room to check on us. Toto was shooting a stream of pee straight up in the air. She took one look at him and knew what had happened. I had a few slips and was very dizzy but not out. Toto was out. I told her that we were coughing and needed the syrup. She was not happy. She did not know that Toto was stealing sips of her wine and beer whenever she left it unattended. Sometimes he would steal the drinks of their guest. Toto didn't care whose drink it was. He wanted it and he got it," said Lola.

"Drinking to him was like having a bottle of milk. Toto was very smart, good looking, great athlete, and tall for his age, and light brown skin with bedroom eyes. That was my brother and I love him. As he got older, he was very popular among his circle of friends. I remember in fourth grade seeing him on the playground. He was selling cigarettes that he stole from my father to the older kids or anyone with the money. He did not need money but it was the excitement of doing it that was pleasing to him. He smoked and drank and wanted company," said Lola.

"Toto loved sports and started playing little league, running track, basketball, and tennis. He was good at all of them. He was the only kid on any of these teams that was drunk the night before and was the most valuable player the next day," said Lola.

"Eva started planning her wedding and it was to take place in the fall of the next year. Meanwhile, I was having my problems. I saw what Toto was doing and decided to stay straight and not drink or smoke. I needed to watch out for Toto. Uncle Nick believed that we were good kids. After Eva and Uncle Nick got married, they purchased a big nice home in New Orleans. We all moved from the boathouse to the new home. In the new home we had our own living quarters. It consisted of two bedrooms, an activity room, two bathrooms, and a small kitchen.

"My uncle and Eva were very wealthy but worked every day to help others. My Uncle had his own law firm for low income residents and Eva was his office manager. Sometimes they would represent important people. They work long hours during the week. Therefore, once again we were raising ourselves," said, Lola.

"I took up music and dance in high school and excelled quickly with my talent. My great-grand mother, grand-mother, and mother were entertainers and that is what I wanted. I was always the lead performer in all the musicals at school.

"Toto decided to stick with football which he did not start playing until the coach discovered him during gym in his freshmen year of high school. Being a smart businessman, he knew he could find more clients on the football field then on the playground," said Lola.

"Toto your position is wide receiver. You are an athlete. You are quick, smart with your moves, and can figure out how to catch the ball and be aggressive. There are other positions you could play but that is what I need this year," said the coach.

"Toto, thinking to his self, in this position, I have to be sober but I can sell wine to the defense. They will be awesome. They will be feared. We will win the state championship for the next four years.

"My uncle and Eva were at all our events and were very proud of us. We got good grades and were always on the honor roll. Something was happening to Toto that was uncontrollable. Even I was becoming different," said Lola.

"Our special section of the house was becoming very popular with the teenagers in town. At first we would ask our uncle if we could have some friends over. This was the beginning of our decision to follow the family tradition of being professional criminals. We came up with reasons to have a party. Our uncle never said no. They loved us and we were nice kids. We had chores at home and were popular at school. Even the teachers liked us. We were model students," said Lola.

"With the parties we needed booze. So my brother would find a bum and give him a few dollars with a list of alcohol to purchase. Toto and his friends would wait in parking lot at the local diner to make the exchange. I started wearing makeup and keeping myself pretty. The guys loved me but I was not interested. I wanted to wait for the man of my dreams. But Toto was completely opposite. He would have sex with anyone. He would often state, I don't care if they are blind, cripple or crazy. A woman is a woman and that is how he lived his life. On the edge of danger," said Lola.

"Toto decided to start inviting adults to our weekly parties. My uncle and Eva would also come to make sure there was enough food. I loved to play the piano and sing and Toto was good at playing by ear, singing, and dancing. One of my parent's best friends, Spook

Jackson, would stop by often and play his sax. The Blues was on every Saturday night.

Eva wanted us to enjoy the house and moved our Saturday night parties into their main ballroom. This was the beginning of opening of a whole different can of worms," said Lola.

"Did your parents ever try to contact you or your brother?" asked Ted.

"They sent birthday and Christmas cards with gifts," responded Lola.

"Having Saturday-night parties turned into a regular thing, and the neighborhood became standard guests. Spook Jackson and Slap the Hog along with Toto and I were the main entertainers. Spook played the sax and Slap the Hog played the piano. I danced and sung jazz songs. Toto did it all but he loved women and liquor.

"Consuming, buying, and selling liquor was Toto's main objective in high school. As a member of the team he played wide receiver and understood to be good at that position, he had to be sober. He also realized that the offensive and defensive line would be fearless with a little help from the bottle. Therefore, before each game, Toto would sell moonshine that he learned to make from people like Spook. Spook was his partner in name only. Spook was well aware of what Toto was capable of doing.

"Toto's liquor business got so big that he recruited me to work with him. Spook owned several acres of land and that is where Toto set-up his stills. The moonshine sales had a special target market. This market was mainly teenagers and college students.

"The football team's coach knew what Toto was doing but turned his head as long as the Silver Knights were undefeated. The defense was so good that their opponents looked defeated as they entered the football field. The team practiced hard and played the game even harder. During half-time the coach and the offensive and defensive linesmen would take a shot of corn liquor. When they entered the field, the score would be so lopsided in their favor that they would just go through the motions."

CHAPTER 8

"TOTO'S YOUNG YEARS were where he learned to be a professional criminal. Professional because he was smart, and understood how to work with people, compassionate and could figure out how to solve issues and come up with great solutions. His first real test was on the football field. A team from up North wanted to play the Silver knights because of their reputation. This northern team also had a reputation. They had been undefeated for two seasons and had become nationally known. The news stations had featured them several times on TV. When asked how they became so good. The coach would reply, hard work with reliable dedicated players," said Lola.

"Toto said to the coach, 'I want this team to feel welcomed. I would like to have an early afternoon party for them. The menu will be barbecue ribs and chicken, corn on the cob, potato salad, greens, and baked beans. I will serve punch, soda, and water with homemade peach cobbler. This way we can get to know this fearless team before we play them."

"'Good,' said the Coach, 'but no funny stuff in the punch.'

"Without responding, Toto just smiled.

"My uncle and aunt were so happy that they were reaching out to this team of minority players. They felt good about how we were being raised.

"This northern team was made up of a bunch of city slickers. They were just a few steps away from being criminals. Toto had done his research on this team and the coach. He discovered that they came from a part of the city that was infested with gangs. Many of them were former gang members. These kids were ordered by the courts to join a sport or activity in their school while on probation or go into a detention facility. Knowing this information, Toto decided to put his best moonshine in a special punch bowl. The team captain was told about the special bowl and the word spread among his team like a wildfire. It did not matter if the Silver Nights drank this punch because it was like lemonade to them. If they came out to play sober, they would lose all their games. Drunk is the only way they played," said Lola.

"The teams ate and drank everything. Nothing was left. Everyone had a good time. When the sun was going down, everyone was invited into the Ballroom to finish off the party. Toto got on the piano and started playing and I sang the best R&B songs that were popular at that time. The party was on and so was the game.

"Toto said to me, 'May they eat, drink, and be happy because tomorrow they will be losers.'

"Sure enough, they were losers. Not just losers but shut out. Score was 21 to 0. What an embarrassment. I felt bad for this team and now the Silver Knights were featured on the evening news for shutting this northern team down. That is how Toto plays the criminal game. Study your enemy and then design a winning game plan.

"Toto lay in bed that evening with a big smile on his face. He knew he had out slicked the city slickers. 'I am the greatest!' Toto shouted over and over again. 'Tomorrow will bring new opportunities and challenges and I am ready for them all,' said Toto out loud.

"On Monday morning, I was sick and my aunt suggested that I stay home from school. God must have been on Toto's side because the school called the house and I answered the phone," said Lola.

"Mrs. Harrison this is the school nurse. Toto has a small bottle of something that smells like it has liquor in it. He said it is your home made version of cough syrup. He was caught with it in his history class. If that is true, he needs to give me a note telling me how often and how much to give him during the day," said the nurse.

"Yes, ever thing he told you was right. I gave him my home-made cough syrup because he did not want to miss school. He has had perfect attendance every year since kindergarten and did not want to mess up his record," said Lola.

'We were doing great and our liquor sales were growing and getting larger. In fact, a few friends of Toto's were hired to help with the making of the moonshine. After football season was over, Toto and I had to find other places to sell our liquor. It did not take long. We started attending the Friday night dances at our school and other nearby high schools. We doubled our supply and would sell out before the dance was over.

"Toto was tested once again. He was still a freshman but a wise one. At one of the dances at our school, Maria who was very popular with Toto and some of the other guys loved to dance. She was just the right partner for Toto. He was not just a lover but a dancer too. At this dance he offered Maria some moonshine and she gladly accepted. She was a good looking gal but no one but her cousin knew she was epileptic. She drank the liquor straight down and within seconds started having a seizure. She was yelling, 'Demo, Demo!'" said Lola.

"'I am Demo, I am Demo!' yelled Toto.

"Everyone was scared and Toto got a cold glass of water and threw in Maria's face. She stopped shaking and all her seizure activity stopped. After that Toto was known as Demo. The word traveled quickly and that was his new nick name. Demo was a better name then Toto," said Lola.

"After what happened to Maria, Demo focused his sales at school and on Saturday nights in the Ballroom. Summer had arrived and Demo and I were honor roll students entering into the tenth grade. That summer was unbelievable. Every day was full of excitement. Ladies of all age loved Demo and men of all ages loved me. Demo engaged in liquor and women but I just loved to look good and be nice but no sex.

"My uncle and aunt felt that something was going on but could not put their fingers on it. Every good thing has to come to an end at some point. The end was near when the cleaning lady who was a wino approached Demo for sex. She was about sixty years old but thought she was still a looker. Two years ago, she was hit by a car on the major highway in town and my uncle handled her case. Because she was drunk crossing the street when she got hit, she did not get much money. In the accident, she lost her leg. Her name was Maggie.

"My uncle felt sorry for her and invited her to live with them and become the head housekeeper. She not only was the head housekeeper but the head of the house drunks. Demo, thought it would be cool to have sex with a one legged woman," said Lola.

"Maggie knew no one was home and would not take no for an answer. It did not take much for Demo to comply. As they were going at it and unaware that my Uncle and Aunt had come home and were looking for Demo. After calling and looking, they decided to check into Maggie's quarters. As they entered her living room there were Demo and Maggie rolling all over the floor.

"My aunt screamed and fainted. It was a sight to see. Maggie was asked to leave and Demo was under house arrest. This did not stop Demo, his summer was just beginning," said Lola.

"'Lola, we will be sixteen in a few weeks and will be able to get our driver's licenses. Hopefully Uncle Nick will buy us a car,' said Demo.

"If you watch yourself and keep a low profile, maybe he will. Because of our criminal genes, he wants to make sure we live an honest life. Sorry Uncle, it is too late. We are criminals and loving it," responded Lola.

"My uncle gave us driver's lessons because he felt that everyone should know how to drive even if they did not have anything to drive. We needed licenses in case of an emergency.

"One hot summer early evening some of our buddies wanted to go roller skating but no one had any transportation. My uncle and aunt were out of town and were scheduled to return in the morning," said Lola.

"'I know, I will use my uncle's Mercedes, and he will never know it. We need some liquor to take with us. I will ask Maggie to go get us some booze from Blank's Liquor Store. I will have to buy her a pint of wine. She is an old fool but a good fuck,' said Demo.

"Nick and Eva were beginning to realize what they were raising and decided to get some professional help. They had planned to take us to a child therapist on Monday morning when they returned home," said Lola.

"We had a good time at the skating rink. We sat in the car after skating and drank our liquor. Demo was in no shape to drive so Ken offered to drive. He was drunker than Demo, so I was the driver. I was also drunk.

"We were almost home when I passed out. The car ran up on our neighbor's lawn and landed in her living room. No one was hurt but we were all passed out. The local newspaper came and took pictures. This town had never had anyone's car end up in someone's living room. The Headlines read, Teenagers, drunk and all underage landed in their neighbor's living room after a night of drinking," said Lola.

"The cops took us to the hospital to check us out. It was hard to tell who was driving because no one was behind the wheel. Police asked but we could not remember. I was so scared that my pants were soaking wet. Demo was cool. He had a story, he told the truth.

"His truth was that we all stole the car. That was his truth; he stole the car and dragged us along. My uncle was very upset and the first thing on Monday morning we were sitting in the therapist's office," said Lola.

"The therapist was given a complete history of the Harrison Family and after talking to us alone without my uncle, she said, "I will see all of you in four weeks and I will have a report which will outline the problems and a plan to rehabilitate these two teenagers. During summer vacation, they should be in a summer camp. One that builds values such as learning to improve on a sport or learning a sport or learning a foreign language," she said.

"That night my uncle wrote out a contract that he read to us and required us to sign. He did not know that Demo and I were alcoholics. He soon found out the hard way," said Lola.

"'This is your contract,' said Uncle Nick:

1. I will keep my room clean.
2. I will do my own laundry.
3. I will help with the yard work.
4. I will attend a summer camp.
5. I will give up all access to any money or allowances.
6. I will not have any company or Saturday-night parties.

Lola Harrison _____
Kevin Harrison _____

"Just to be on the safe side, my uncle removed all liquor so that we did not have our Saturday night parties for the neighborhood. Money was never an issue but this caused a serious problem for us. We were alcoholics and loved to smoke cigarettes and without any money we were doomed," said Lola.

"Demo got in touch with Spook Jackson and asked him to start up the stills.

"'I have a few bucks saved for hard times and this is the time to reinvest. We need to start right away. Lola and I will be at a summer camp during the day but in the evening we will be able to help. I will work on developing clients at the camp. Most of the campers are from our high school and they will be ready for some refreshments,' said Demo.

"This was a camp for teenagers who were interested in learning a foreign language. We enrolled in two classes, Spanish and French. Demo figured we would be exposed to more kids who would become clients," said Lola.

She added, "Yes, he was right. Demo was a born salesman along with his other gifts. Not only was he selling to the campers he was selling to selected staff. He knew who to sell to. He was back in business and I loved it. Our criminal empire started at camp."

Johnny the camp nerd bumped into Demo. "Oh excuse me, you are Demo Harrison. I have seen you at school. You are a cool guy. I have watched you operate. I run a small operation at school but nothing like yours. I deal with black market cigarettes and Cuban cigars. To get to the point, I can be a big asset to you in helping you grow your business into a larger business. You have the looks and the business brains in order for us to move forward. I'm not scared of no one or nothing," said Johnny.

"My uncle in New Orleans has many connections. Even law enforcement is on his payroll. He is a left over from the last big mobster boss who was killed years ago and his wife commented suicide in order to keep from going to jail, and maybe for life. If we join forces, I will take care of any rough stuff. That was my Uncle's job before he became the boss. How about it do we have a deal?" asked Johnny.

"Well, just a few questions, did this old boss have a daughter, if so what was her name?" responded Demo.

"Yes, I believe her name was Zola or something like that," said Johnny.

"That's interesting, okay we have a deal. After camp, let's get together at my house, my uncle will love you because you look honest and have the looks of a good citizen," said Demo.

"That's what makes me good at what I do. My looks are an asset and do not give me away," said Johnny.

"That evening Johnny came to dinner and my uncle and aunt just loved him. All three of us were A students. We were all the bright lights of the school. Success was our final destination in life. Little did they know that being great criminals was our final destination," said Lola.

"Lola, you do remember that I am not the lead lawyer on your case, only the assistant. Based on what you have told me; this case is more than about you. It is about a long line of criminals from way back. Your case is going to solve many unsolved cases. The FBI will have to come in at some point. We will ask for total immunity for you and any family members that are still alive. How does that sound?" asked Ted.

"That sounds good, but with what I have told you so far, how are my chances of getting off?" asked Lola.

"If what you told me holds up, this is a slam dunk. The court will not know what hit them," responded Ted.

"Okay, let's get back because the good stuff is about to start," said Lola.

Ted looked at Lola and realized she was the woman of his dreams, if he could get her off and she became an honest lady. I believed after this was over she would be a new person, Ted thought to himself.

"Ted, there is a lot more. Demo and I developed our own network of criminal activity. It did not take long. By the time we were entering college we had a team assembled that were experts in their special chosen careers. Johnny handled all the merchandise deliveries. Henry was the bookkeeper and accountant. Leroy was the enforcer. Spook was in charge of growing the corn on his twenty-five-acre farm that was used in the making of the corn liquor. Stump was responsible for distribution and management of his clients. Lola and I over looked the total operation, made adjustments as needed, and kept the law off our backs. All decisions were made by Demo and me. We were the owners and they were the staff. Demo made it quite clear that we were the bosses.

"With Johnny as part of our operation, we were able to add the black market cigarettes. My uncle and aunt started to be concerned about us. All summer during camp we were selling to the campers and many of the young adults who were college students. Henry was a freshman in college who was a camp counselor. He spoke several languages and was here from France on a student visa. He needed money for college and his off campus apartment. He was perfect for the organization. Instead of an apartment we rented him a large older home with five acres and a basement. This became our headquarters" explained Lola.

CHAPTER 9

"LEROY WAS THE leader of one of the biggest gangs in town. He was excellent in his role because he was good at roughing people up and he also had his own group. This was the management team for our organization. All we needed was a name. The Redd's after my grandfather who would have been proud of us," said Lola.

"How did Demo and you know how to put together a criminal organization of this magnitude? You were just kids, high school kids," said Ted.

"We had help," responded Lola.

"When my uncle took custody of us, we moved off his boathouse and into a big home. One day my brother and I were playing in the basement and ran across some boxes that were labeled Redd & Nina Harrison, Candee and Buddy, Frank. We recognized our grandparent's names but the other names did not mean much. As we opened all the boxes it was like reliving history. These boxes told the whole story. My grandfather would be the narrator. His words were just popping off the pages.

"Someone had put them in order as much as possible by dates beginning in the early 1900s. It was my uncle because he was the lawyer in the family. These boxes had tape recordings, journals, diaries, deeds, pictures, and basic notebooks. Their account had made an organizational chart listing everyone's title. His ledger included things like how much money was being collected daily, weekly, monthly, and yearly. The records were excellent.

"The pictures were labeled with names, places, and dates. We figured that my grandmother was the picture lady. There was also another set of boxes labeled Zola's family, FBI. We weren't going to open it, but we needed to know both sides of the family. We were only about twelve at the time but were very aggressive and smart. Every Saturday and Sunday afternoon we would go to the basement to play. We even had our games set-up like we were playing but we were reading every scrap of paper and we also listened to the tapes that were made by the State Attorney General's office about our grandparents and their associates.

"That is when Demo and I decided that it would be more exciting to be criminals than to work in an office from nine to five," said Lola.

"Everything we needed to know was in those boxes. It was a road map of how to become a criminal and be good at it. They were good. But at the end they died. Well, no one will live forever. Maybe we should all just do what makes us happy. For Demo and me criminal life is our only life. It makes us happy. Both parents skipped out on us and my wonderful uncle was left to raise us two criminals," said Lola.

"Have you ever thought about your future of being an honest person or what else you could do to make your life complete and happy?" asked Ted.

"Reading my grandmother's diary, it was obvious that she was truly in love with my grandfather from the first time they met. She wanted to have a family so badly that she disregarded the doctor's advice which was not to get pregnant. Her health was bad and with her diabetes it could be fatal. As you know it was. I would like to be in love like that and have a large family. I would like to give something back to the community. In college I majored in science with most of my courses in chemistry. I would like to go back to school and get a PhD in chemistry and open my laboratory someday. At twenty-four, I am still young enough to start over," said Lola.

"When we get you off from all of these charges, maybe you will have shot at all your dreams. When did your uncle and aunt finally discover your criminal activities? "asked Ted.

"The summer of us going into our senior year in high school is when it finally hit them in the face. They first discovered that Demo was a juvenile alcoholic. Demo never drank during the week but on Friday evening he was ready for action. He would mix moonshine with coke and walked around all night with a glass of coke in his hand. This continued all weekend. Our grades were outstanding in school which threw them off. Demo had many years of drinking and he was able to drink without getting drunk," said Lola.

"One Saturday night Demo and his buddies from the neighborhood went roller skating in a town about ten miles away. By this time my uncle had purchased a car for both of us. They were used cars but nice. I had a black Chevy Impala and Demo's car was a red Ford Crown Victoria convertible. The guys in the town where the skating rink was located, and had sent word to Demo and his friends that they were not welcome in their town and talking to their girls. Demo believed he was invincible and no one could hurt him or do harm. He had his organization behind him. After skating was over, they had a dance and that is when Demo got a wake-up call.

'Demo was a tall good looking black guy. A great dancer and he had his booze with him in his coke bottle. His buddies also had booze in a bottle. As the music got good and Demo started showing off this dancing abilities, the girls were lining up and would not dance with no one but Demo. It was Demo's show, just like old times with his mother," said Lola.

"The guys from the town started gathering in small groups and were eyeing down the outsiders. One of the leaders came up to Demo and said," you should clear out now while you can go home with both of your eyes."

"His buddies were not fighters they were want-to-be players. Many of them had never been in a fight. They were Demo's social friends and best customers. All during the dance Demo and his friends were the only ones the girls would dance with. If they could not get Demo they would take one of his friends. After the dance was over and Demo and his buddies were leaving with a few girls, the action started. Demo was in the back seat with his girl and his three buddies were standing outside the car. A local gang with tire irons and baseball bats charged at them. Without much notice this buddies were on the ground. The gang was kicking them and yelling, 'Go back to Squaresville you fucking hicks. Leave our girls alone. If you come back, we'll kill you!'

"They pulled Demo out the car and beat up on him. Next they smashed up the car. Even the roof was almost missing. The only thing that saved them that night from more torture, one of the workers at the skating rink called the police. The police took all of them to the hospital. My uncle was called," said Lola.

"Mr. Harrison, this is the Laurence Police Department. We have your nephew here at the police station along with his three friends. They were in a fight with a local gang. They were beaten up very badly but they will survive. We took them to the hospital and got them medical attention. They have many cuts that required stitches. They were intoxicated and had liquor on them. They need an adult to pick them up or they will have to go to jail. Your nephew's car was totaled," said the officer.

"My uncle called the other boys parents and had them to pick up their kids. My uncle was totally shocked. He did not know what to do. He knew after Demo had stolen his car and wrecked it several years ago that Demo had some problems. But without any other altercations over the years, he believed that going to camp that summer had cured him," said Lola.

"Demo looked awful. He had cuts all over his forehead, broken jaw, and bruised ribs. His eyes were both shut tight. I almost did not recognize my brother. The car was totaled. It was a pile of junk," said Lola.

"'The next day my uncle and aunt sat both of us down. Please tell us what is going on. We love you now and forever. We are family and want to help,' said Uncle Nick.

"Demo and I had already decided to tell the truth, with a few things left out," said Lola.

"'We are both alcoholics. If I had been sober and just went to skate and dance none of this would have happened. Trust me; this will not happen ever again. We want to go to AA for juvenile alcoholics. After last night, I escaped death and don't want to go down that path again. We have been alcoholics for many years. It all started with our parents and the fact that liquor was always around. When we had a cold, Mom would give us her homemade cough syrup. It was made out of corn liquor. We learned to love it and would steal it whenever we could. They never caught on to us,' said Demo.

"'Okay, that's the plan. When you recover from last night, you two will start your program. I will set it up for you two,' responded Uncle Nick.

"While Demo was recovering from wake-up call, I took over the organization. I had a different way of operating. Leroy came to me and wanted to sell drugs in our market. In my grandfather's papers it was clear that drugs were prohibited. He believed that they harmed kids, families, and destroyed lives. Demo and I believed the same. I told Leroy that would be his decision and his business because I did not want anything to do with drugs. He started selling the next day," said Lola.

"In my grandparent's papers they had spoken about the different services they offered clients. The gambling and Gentleman's Basement were very appealing to me. Many college students needed money for college and this would be a good way to earn it. Many of them were giving it away for free so now it was time to make it payoff.

"I decided to call it Zola's Room. There was an outstanding description of the Gentlemen's Basement, therefore I copied Zola's Room after the Gentlemen's Basement. The rental house basement was just right for it. The dining room and living room I turned into poker rooms. Poker is very popular on college campuses. I believe where there is a need or want someone will eventually fill that need. I was the right person," said Lola.

"It took Demo all summer to recover from his injuries. He would ask me how things were going and I would respond, just great!

I wanted to surprise him. Money was never our motivation. We had money, it was power, influence, control, and to grow-up and be just like our grandparents. That is what did it for us. The other members of our organization needed the money. We never allowed them to know that we were wealthy. Demo and I believed if they knew, they might resent us," said Lola.

"Demo recovered just in time to go back to school. It was our senior year and we wanted to graduate in a dead heat for number one in our class. Demo was the class president all four years and I was the vice president all four years. He was perfect for that job. He was truly a leader. He could have been a leader in any occupation," said Lola.

Demo was back playing football. He was a wide receiver. He never drank while playing for he wanted to be the best with a great offensive line to work with him. The team was undefeated three years. The moonshine he sold the defense made them play like animals. In fact, their nickname was the Animals.

"Just before school started, Demo dropped by the house which was now called Off Campus. Demo's eyes opened wide as he entered the house. He yelled, 'This is wonderful, what a place! Students can come here to relax and have fun without fear of getting locked up. Great name Off Campus,' said Demo.

"I'm glad you like it," responded Lola.

"Did Demo and you stay out of trouble with the law during your senior year?" asked Ted.

"As long as we were going to our AA meeting we were somewhat okay. I could see some changes in Demo but I was not able figure it out. He would always speak at AA and tell it all. He had found another place to take over," said Lola.

"'My name is Kevin Harrison but my friends call me Demo. Demo sounds better than Kevin. It is more fitting for a teenage alcoholic. I have been an alcoholic before I was potty-trained. It started with my Mother giving me her homemade cough syrup. I enjoyed faking a cough so that I could get the cough syrup which was made with moonshine. After that I would just help myself to it when my parents were not around. Later it got so controlling that I took it to school and drank it in the bathroom during the changing of the classes.

"'I got caught just once at school. But that did not stop me. Later I stole my wonderful uncle's car and destroyed it by running into a house and landing in the front living room. I was drunk. I was a drunk. I believe God was on my side, for I should have been dead with all that alcohol in my system for all those young years. Maybe God is saving me for something bigger. Who knows, I am still alive and well. Let's end my talk with Amazing Grace,' said Demo.

"Are you faking this entire AA stuff or you playing it straight?" responded Lola.

"'I am not sure. The words just come out of my mouth,' said Demo.

"It was at that moment that I knew Demo would not be a criminal all his life. This was just getting ready for something bigger. What, when, where, and how he would change might be revealed someday," said Lola.

"The football team went undefeated our senior year and most of the team were seniors. The coach knew that a team like this only comes along once in a life time and the Demos of the world were rare. The state championship was on the radio. My uncle Nick invited the neighbors over on a first come basis to listen to the game in the ball room while we went to the game.

"The Silver Knights won by 3 points. 15 to 12, a field goal was kicked with ten seconds left on the clock. Demo had delivered 2 touchdowns. The field goal was kicked by his buddy in crime, the kicker," said Lola.

"Did you two stop drinking and get ready for college?" asked Ted.

"We slowed down a little but we were still drunks. As I look back, I believe it might have been because we missed our parents. The organization was going good and I decided to start giving out my own student loans. I remembered reading in my grandparent's papers that they had a bank. This bank's function was to loan money at high interest rates. Our student clients did not qualify for traditional bank loans and most of them just wanted some extra pocket change.

"Henry, the bookkeeper, ran the bank. He would receive 60 percent of all interest collected. Henry was good at his job and decided to major in accounting. He was getting plenty of experience from The Redd's, said Lola.

"Did your parents come to your high school graduation?" asked Ted.

"No," said Lola.

"That's it, just no?" responded Ted.

"Let's move on," said Lola.

"Demo and I were named co-valedictorians of the graduating class. After the ceremony we went to several parties. Everyone wanted us at their party, even their parents. We were wasted. I was driving my black Chevy Impala and Demo said, 'Let's rob Tony's Liquor Store.'

"Everyone agreed and that is what we did. We took a hammer and knocked out the front window display and took all the display liquor and then stepped inside and stole all the best stuff. Off we went to our headquarters. Before we got a half block down the road, Officer Jones put on his siren and pulled us over. As he pulled up and Demo put a bottle of Chevis Regal out and offered Officer Jones a drink," said Lola.

"'Get out of the car and all of you get into my car,' said Officer Jones.

"It was late, about 2:00 a.m. My uncle knew we would be home late because of all the parties. He did throw the book at us before we when out partying," said Lola.

"'No drinking or smoking dope. If you get into trouble and get picked up by the cops, don't call me. We are done with that nonsense. We managed to get the two of you through school alive and now you need to act like adults. Remember don't call me,' said Nick.

"I told Officer Jones not to call my uncle but he did anyway," said Lola.

"'This is Officer Jones, I just picked up a bunch of drunken kids and two belong to you. They robbed Tony's Liquor Store. Do you want to come and get yours? They are not 18 years old yet,' said the officer.

"'You got them, you keep them. I will see you in the morning,' responded Nick.

"Spending a night in jail with a bunch of drunken kids and bums was awful. It was smelly and wet. This should have been a wakeup call for me but it wasn't," said Lola.

"As my uncle Nick walked into the police station and was escorted to the holding cell where all of us were, it was obvious that he was disgusted by the look on his face.

"I have been there for the two of you all your life. I was in the hospital when you were born. I have loved you before your mother gave birth to both of you. I do not understand why you two are the way you are. It must be in the genes.

"'It could be a family curse. Only God knows. I still love you and will fight for your life to live it as an honest, productive citizen of this great country,' said Nick.

"Demo and I looked at each other in shame but I could see that Demo was truly upset with himself. I just did not understand how upset he was with his life," said Lola.

"Lola, I am going back to AA and this time I plan to live up to my commitment to stay sober. I feel good when I am sober. I cannot blame my alcohol condition on anyone but myself. It might have started with Mom but it has to end with me. From this day on I want to be called by my birth name Kevin. Kevin sounds like a name for a nice young man who wants something in life,' said Demo.

"Like my parents, I liked the power and the ability to control others. It was totally a gene thing. That summer was the beginning of a new life for me. Kevin was still my partner but in name only. I was always out and he stuck around the house working in the garden and helping anywhere there was a need.

'My focus was mainly on the business and getting organized the way I had dreamed. I was proud of being a young entrepreneur. Kevin was at the point where he wanted to stay away from any place that involved alcohol. I had also stopped drinking but still loved the business.

"I added a few improvements. We now had a menu that included; chicken wings, hot dogs, chili, chips, nonalcohol drinks, and moonshine. I hired a few waitresses who wore uniforms that looked like a swim suits.

"A cook, a bouncer, bartender, a gal to run the Gentlemen's Basement, and poker dealers who worked Friday evening until 3:00 a.m., Saturday from 6:00 p.m. to 3:00 a.m., and Sunday 3:00 p.m. until 11:00 p.m. We were closed Monday–Thursday. I wanted the students to study on those days and go to classes.

"That summer business got so busy that we had to issue membership cards. The cards cost $5. It was good until you finished college. I also had a couple parking lot attendants. The cars were directed into the woods. I now employed about twenty young people," said Lola.

"Things were going great until I caught Leroy selling dope in the parking lot of the club.

"Leroy, you agreed not to sell here at the Club. This is my business that dope is your business. Sell it on the streets or anywhere but not here!" yelled Lola.

"Leroy took one look at Lola and said, 'I will sell any fucking place I want to sell, madam!'

Lola had her bouncer with her and he had a gun. "Look here, dirtbag, you heard Lola, stop selling and leave and do not return!" said her bouncer.

"Our business relationship is over, don't come around anymore," said Lola.

"It was a few days before we started college. My uncle and aunt wanted to take Kevin and me out for dinner to celebrate our graduation. My uncle was very proud of us because Kevin was in AA and I did not appear to be getting into any trouble all summer. My uncle thought that both of us had been reborn and were now honest adults," said Lola.

"I have something to tell you Lola. I want you to understand that I love you but I will be going to a different college. This way we will learn to be independent. I have been accepted into UCLA and will be leaving tomorrow. I need my space. I need to find out if I have what it takes to be my own person. I hope you understand," said Kevin.

It was hard at first not having Kevin around but after a few weeks at the local university I was back to my old self. That is studying and managing the Off Campus Club.

"I decided to major in business because it would fit right in with my club. In school I met Ricky and we started hanging out together. He was also a business major. At first I did not want to let him know that I was the owner of the Off Campus Club because I felt it would ruin our relationship. Ricky already knew, for he was a steady customer of Kevin's in high school, even though he went to a different school. Ricky said he never met my brother but would buy his moonshine, and cigarettes, and dope from Leroy," said Lola.

"Ricky was very handsome and fun to be around. We were spending a great deal of time together. Therefore, I decided to move out of my uncle's home and move into the Club. My uncle did not know this rented house was a college nightclub. My uncle and aunt were busy traveling and enjoying themselves now that we were grown. They believed it was their time," said Lola.

"I did not see or hear from Kevin until Thanksgiving. He told the family he needed time to develop a new life. My uncle invited many family members, mostly on my grandmother's side. As I told you before, my great grandmother was black and while performing in France fell in love with a Frenchman and married him.

The ballroom was full and my cousins were happy to be invited for dinner. We have never tried to keep it a secret that our family was of mixed heritage. Most people in the area knew it. It was never an issue with my uncle and aunt or our friends or in their professional life.

"Ricky entered the ballroom with me and it was decorated beyond belief. A perfect Christmas tree, red and white poinsettias inside and out and all five tables set like something from better homes and gardens. Ricky was totally impressed. As he looked around he noticed that the blacks outnumbered the white guests. At that point he did not say anything. Kevin had not arrived yet. As we were escorted to our table I could see from the look on his face that something was wrong. But I could not figure it out. Our family had many black and white friends. The color of their skin was not important; it was what was in their heart," said Lola.

"At our table was my uncle and aunt, Mr. Stevenson and his girlfriend, Uncle Nick's first cousin and her husband and Ricky and me, and a seat reserved for Kevin. Kevin was coming in from California and was expected to be a little late. When Kevin walked into the ballroom, everyone stood up and clapped. He was still very handsome. His skin was a little tan from the California sun, slim and tall, and had a great smile. I grabbed him and took him to our table," said Lola.

"Ricky, this is my twin brother Kevin," said Lola with a big proud smile on her face.

Ricky stood up and said, "This is a black family and all these black people are your relatives. I have been dating a black girl. I will be a laughing stock among all my friends."

"He left and just walked out of my life that day and even transferred to another university out of state the next semester. I never saw or heard from him again," said Lola.

With or without Ricky we had a great dinner and evening. After dinner, Kevin got on the baby grand piano and sang and played some popular songs. Many of the cousins were very talented and wanted to play their instruments or sing or dance. My aunt decided we would have talent night. She made up a list of the guests that wanted to perform and she introduced them. There were solos, family groups, musicians, and dancers. It was a lot of fun.

"Even through most of the guests were drinking wine or beer. Kevin only had ice tea. I followed his lead and drank ice tea all night," said Lola.

"What a Thanksgiving. How did you feel about Ricky after he exposed his racism?" asked Ted.

"I was very hurt. He was my very first boyfriend. I had dreamed it would be like my grandmother and grandfather, the way they felt the first time they set eyes on each other," said Lola.

"Kevin was going to leave Sunday night to go back to school therefore my uncle wanted to have a private talk with the two of us. Kevin and I did not know what the talk was going to be about but we knew it was serious," said Lola.

"Your grandparents were loving people who believed in taking care of their children and families. Before you were born, they set-up a trust fund for their grandchildren. It was to be divided equally among all the grandchildren and dispersed at age twenty-two. Eva and I have not been blessed with any children and you two are the only grandchildren from Redd and Nina. When you graduate from college an account will be set-up in each of your names. It will be a large sum. Please use it wisely and for a good cause," said Nick.

"With Ricky gone from my life. I was depressed for about a week, until I met up with my older cousin Belle who was about sixty-five. Let go to lunch and catch up on old times," I said.

"Without Ricky, I feel lost. I just want to turn over and die," I told my cousin.

"'Girl you better straighten up and fly straight. That situation is a dead cat on a line. If my mother was alive she would say, let the hair go with the hide. You can't put your life in the hands of a man. You need to put your hands in the hands of the man who parted the sea. He will take care of you. Come to church on Sunday and let him help,' said my cousin Belle.

"As I lay in bed, I remembered my parents and how in love they were in the early years. What happened to them that made them two lost souls? Maybe if God had been invited into their lives, things would have turned out very differently. I hope where ever they are that they are happy and healthy. May God bless them and keep them safe until they return to us. This was my prayer that night," said Lola.

"My cousin was right, I needed to stop feeling depressed and get back into the swing of things again. I decided not to fall in love with anyone unless I interviewed them first. I would tell them that I was black. If they got through that comment, then we could go on with getting more involved."

CHAPTER 10

" $\mathbf{B}$ ACK IN SCHOOL, I got deeply involved with the school work and the Off Campus Café. I decided it needed a new look and a new owner. I was now twenty-one, and next year, my trust fund would be coming. I decided to buy the Café House. It looked run down on the outside but was nice on the inside. I had done a lot of work that the owner did not know about. The owner lived out of state and never bothered to check on his investment. I never asked him to fix anything. My offer was to buy the house as is. I had money saved from all the years from being in business. I put the money in a hidden safe in a false wall in my bedroom. Kevin had given me his share before he went off to college.

"For a few weeks, I sat down and jotted downs some ideas. I wanted to expand and include more services. The Bank was my little pet project. I made a contract for my clients. If they fell behind on their loan payments and were unable to catch-up, they would have to work it off at the Off Campus Café until the debt was paid. If they did not pay or work off the debt my debt collector would visit the client. I used an old friend of my grandparents' name Bruce from New Orleans who was good at scaring and collecting. Bruce was expensive and wanted to be paid monthly even if he did not have to collect. Bruce had his own organization. I informed Bruce that I could not have students borrowing from The Bank and not planning on paying The Bank back. He had my approval to do whatever it took to get justice but do not kill anyone or maim them for life, he agreed," said Lola.

"I purchased the house and my uncle and aunt were very proud of me. I told them that I was starting an Off Campus Café for college students and needed my trust fund monies to make the necessary improvements. I said to them that I would be acquiring all the necessary licenses and permits to operate a restaurant, dance hall, and over twenty-one bars that served beer and wine only. I got the permits for the improvements and necessary licenses for the restaurant and dance hall. I had no plans on giving up the Gentlemen's Basement, gambling, The Bank, or serving moonshine. It was too profitable.

"My improvements included an addition to the building which would be my living space, new siding, a swimming pool with cabanas, and a complete renovation of the gambling room, restaurant, kitchen, dance hall, and Gentlemen's Basement," said Lola.

"My uncle loaned me the money until my trust fund kicked in. Everything was going great. The students were having fun and it was the place to go to on the weekends. I graduated from college with a business major and Kevin graduated also. My graduation was first so my uncle and aunt came to my graduation. We flew out to UCLA for Kevin's graduation. He was the valedictorian of his class with a major in theology. It was announced that Kevin would be entering into advanced training to become a Catholic priest. Boy was I shocked and my Uncle was completely overcome with joy. I looked at him, and I could see tears flowing from his eyes. Eva was crying like a new born baby. I could not help from crying. Kevin was born a criminal and alcoholic. I believed it was AA and my uncle and aunt's love that helped turn his life around. He was a good example for the whole family as to how a person can change his life if given a little help and lots of love," said Lola.

'If I get out of this mess I will promise God, I will change my life. How do you think my chances are after hearing the family story?" asked Lola.

"Well, young lady, your legal team is the best and I think your chances are very good. We are going to put in a plea of not guilty by mental disease and mental defect. Your trial will start in 30 days. Remember, I am now the assistant to the lead attorney. The lead attorney is an old friend of your father. He was informed about the situation and has agreed to represent you. He has said that you should have a chance for a new beginning. He believes that your family history has set you up for a life in crime. He will be flying in within a few days. He has a lot of work to do and will need you and your uncle's help," said Ted.

"Let's take a break and go out for dinner," said Ted.

"Okay if you don't mind eating with a colored gal. Give me a few minutes to take a shower and change my clothes," said Lola.

Ted might be the man of my dreams. It took me all these years and all the things that I have done to find him. I wonder if he feels the same way about me. If I get out of this mess, I will devote my life to living clean. I would like to find my parents, and I pray that they are okay, thought Lola as she took a hot shower.

"I am in love with Lola," said Ted to himself. *She deserves a second chance for happiness. I have loved her from the first time I set eyes on her in that jail cell. She was gorgeous then and she is more gorgeous now. I feel like Redd when he first set eyes on Nina. I understand Redd's feeling that evening. I would like to say the same words to Lola that Redd said to Nina. That is, I want to marry you someday,* thought Ted.

As Ted was looking around the room, he saw a picture of Nina and Redd on their wedding day. He was surprised to see that Lola looked just like Nina. Both were beautiful and at that moment Ted knew that fate has brought the two of them together. After the trial he decided he would ask Lola to marry him.

"I am ready," said Lola.

"Let's drive to New Orleans and have some real fun. On the way you can tell me how you ended up in a holding cell in jail," said Ted.

"Remember Leroy, the gang leader that I caught selling dope at the club and I had my bouncer to put him out. He turned him in for a lesser charge of manslaughter. Leroy killed a man and before he when to court, wanted to plea down to a lesser charge. Leroy said he killed the man in self-defense. The prosecutor said no. Leroy told him that he could give him some information about an organization call Redd's Club that was doing illegal business in all areas. Selling and dealing with kids and underage college students. Therefore, the prosecutor went for the deal. It was a Saturday night and the Club was jammed. All the gambling tables were full. The liquor was flowing and the music was going strong. The Gentlemen's Basement had a waiting list. In walked ten police officers and shut us down and asked for me by name. I did not want any extra trouble so I came forward. I had just got out of the shower and had to put on some clothes. My hair was a mess but at that point I did not care. I just did not want anyone to get hurt.

"They had an arrest warrant and they read me my rights. Sitting on the floor of the cell I began to wonder how I develop this lifestyle of being a criminal. Then it came to me that I was born into a family of criminals and it was in my genes. Then you walked in and I took one look at you and I knew I was going to have a second chance at a new life like Kevin," said Lola.

That night in New Orleans Lola and Ted had dinner and went dancing at a jazz club. It got late and they decided to spend the night.

As they were booking a room at the hotel, Ted said, "One room with a king-size bed, and we are Ted Burch and Lola Burch."

That night they made love, and Lola was finally happy even if it was going to be for a short time. She now had the love of a man who totally loved her and not for the color of her skin.

The next day after breakfast they drove back home and Lola and Ted were ready to finalized Lola's criminal defense. Within a short period of time, they arrived home. As Nick pulled up a second car followed him.

"This is Mr. Robert Wright. He will be the lead attorney on your case. He understands the situation. He was the State District Attorney for California for many years. He has the experience and the knowledge and has influence to win your case," said Nick.

"Your criminal defense is not guilty because of mental disease and mental defect. This was caused by growing up in a family that used criminal activity as a way to make a living. That environment caused you to become a criminal. As a young child you were an alcoholic and once an alcoholic always an alcoholic. You attended AA for juveniles. You had multiples relapses and had to return to AA. We have the documentation from your doctor.

"You and your brother made and sold moonshine in high school and college. As a young child, you developed a system that helped to run the organization from day to day. Leroy who is a witness for the prosecutor will help us. He will be asked to describe how well organized The Redd Gang was functioning. Without knowing it, he will help win our case. The jurors will fall in love with this beautiful young girl who was abused, raised in such a deep-rooted criminal family.

"Next I will need to make a list of the entire living family member who was involved in criminal activity. They will be on the witness list.

'I have a few smoking guns. Most defense lawyers normally only have one but we have several. We need to locate your mother and father. I have their social security numbers. I will have them run to see if they have worked or filed taxes. We should be able to locate them that way. If not, we will go to your mother's aunt in Alabama and interview her to see if she can help us. We will find them. They owe it to you to return in response to your criminal defense," said Mr. Wright.

"I have the Harrison family information in Redd's notes, Nina's diary, financial records, list of all murders, list all names of law enforcement officers that were on the payroll. We also have Zola's family's financial records and history which was compiled by the FBI," said Nick.

"We will ask for total immunity for everyone in your family. With total immunity no one can come back and file civil lawsuits against the family. In return, we will give them information necessary so they are able to solve old cases, including murder. I believe they will go for it. After all, this is your first offense. You would get off with a light sentence if convicted," said Mr. Wright.

"Let's make a list of what we have. Tomorrow to can present it to the prosecutor," said Nick.

"We won't tell what we have. We will tell him what we can do for him. After he agrees to full immunity in writing we will give him the list of family members that will need. Then we will turn over our papers. We will make copies of all papers," said Mr. Wright.

"I have a recording from Lola about the family criminal activity that will also verify the papers," said Ted.

"How did Lola know the family history?" asked Mr. Wright.

"My brother and I found our grandparent's papers in my uncle's basement. We modeled our businesses after the information that we attained by reading the papers. My uncle never knew that we found these papers," said Lola.

"I am going to ask that the total immunity apply to anyone who testifies on your behalf. The information that we can give them goes back many years and will solve many cold cases. The law enforcement will look very good in the public eye," said Mr. Wright.

"When do we go to court?" asked Lola.

"Since I am the new lead attorney we have been given additional time. Court will start in three weeks. That will give us time to send out subpoenas and get the immunity issues confirmed in writing," said Mr. Wright.

"We will also need to send what we have along with our witness list to the District Attorney's Office. They in return will send us their evidence," added Mr. Wright.

"Nick what I will need is the address of my list of witnesses which will include your brother and his wife, and your nephew. Johnny Jones [employee of Off Campus Café] Henry Bryant [employee of Off Campus Café], Eva Harrison [Lola's aunt], and Bruce Carson [the longtime friend of the family] will all be on the list," said Ted.

"I need all the witnesses here next week so that we can go over their testimony. I do not want any surprises," said Mr. Wright.

"Get the subpoenas and I will have the addresses ready in a few days. They will show-up or go to jail. This is my niece's life at stake and this is their small contribution in helping to give her a fresh beginning," said Nick.

"Mr. Wright are you any related to Candee and Frank Wright?" asked Lola.

"Yes, they were my parents. I was raised in California and after their death; I learned that they were criminals. As young adults they were criminal partners with your grandparents. Most of what I know came from your two uncles and information that was left or found in their belongings after they died. I moved to France and got married. I agreed to return and help you because it was the only right thing to do. My parents got a second chance and now I want you also to have a second chance. I feel like family, so for now on, I want to be called Bobby."

"Are we going to have any trouble with the district attorney's office? Every time I see him, he looks like he is ready to say something but doesn't know how," said Nick.

"I have gotten that feeling also. He keeps looking at me as if he has seen a ghost from the past," said Lola.

"Maybe he has, maybe his past is catching up with him. Time will tell," said Bobby.

Lola did not go back to live at the Off Campus Café. Ted offered to let her stay at his place. She just wanted time away from all that life and have a chance to search for what she wanted. Lola went to visit her great aunt who was her grandmother's baby sister in Alabama. She did not tell her she was coming. She had not seen her for over fifteen years. Aunt Lulu had moved away from New Orleans as a young bride when she married a local preacher.

"Alabama was much different than New Orleans; most of the area was still country. After asking questions and getting directions Lola finally arrived at her Aunt's home. The house was a big white classic farm house with a large church down the road. The farm had horses, cows, goats, pigs, chickens, and a beautiful golden retriever. As she stepped out of my car, the golden retriever greeted her.

"Hello gorgeous, what is your name?" asked Lola to the dog.

Lola knocked on the front door and no one answered. She saw that there was mail in the mail box. To make sure she was at the right place, she looked at the address on the mail. It said Lulu Brown.

Thinking to herself, she said, That's right, that's my aunt.

On the door was a plaque that said, "Sunshine, Laughter, and Friends Are Always Welcome." This made Lola feel good and wanted. She sat on the porch with the good dog by her chair, and she fell asleep.

Lola was dreaming about her life with her mother. Her mother loved to sing, dance, play the piano, and cook. "God had giving her many gifts and she enjoyed using them. Having black blood in her was never a liability for Mom. In fact, she believed it was an asset. Her gifts were inherited from her grandmother who was a black woman who loved life. How my grandmother became a criminal was puzzling to me. It must have been learned," dreamt Lola as she slept.

"Wake up, young lady. I hope you have enjoyed your nap. Do I know you?" asked Aunt Lulu.

"Yes, I am Lola Harrison. My mother is Zola," she said.

"You look just like Nina. It is as if she was reincarnated. It is so wonderful to see you after all these years. I see you have already met Brandon. He is a very good judge of character. Therefore, you have passed his test. Why are you here?" asked Aunt Lulu.

"It is a long story, but I needed time to sort out my life. I have many criminal charges against me. I will be going to court in a few weeks. I was hoping being out here in God's Country for a few days might help," said Lola.

"Your mother is living here. She is a different person then you knew when you were 12 years old. She has changed her life. She does not drink, do drugs, or smoke. She is a member of my church and the music director. The community loves her. She used her money to build a new church for the people of this neighborhood. She started a food bank and shelter for the poor. She works everyday trying to improve the lives of others. With God's help she is doing a good job," said Aunt Lulu.

"She goes to church?" replied Lola.

"Not only does she go to church but she has been taking piano and organ lessons and plays the music every Sunday," said Aunt Lulu.

"Where is she now?" asked Lola.

"Working, working at the church and food bank," replied Aunt Lulu.

"She will be coming home shortly," said Aunt Lulu.

At that moment a car pulled up and it was Zola. She was still beautiful. With her was a young boy. He looked like Kevin. Zola walked in and was greeted by her aunt in the foyer.

"Lola is here. I have told her about your new life but it is your responsibility to explain to her about your leaving and why. Derek will also need to be explained. Tell her the truth and let her decide what your relationship will be in the future. As you know she is in trouble with the law. She knows that you have been subpoenaed to testify on her behalf. This is your chance to make-up for years of lost love of your family," said Aunt Lulu.

As Zola walked into the living room, Lola ran over to her and started hugging her mother. "Mom! Mom! I love you and have missed you," said Lola.

Tears were flowing down from both of their eyes. It was so wonderful that Aunt Lulu was also crying. Derek looked up and said, "Who is this lady?"

"This is your sister. Her name is Lola," said Zola.

Good smells were coming from the kitchen. "Let's eat, and afterwards, we can talk," said Aunt Lulu.

The table was being set when Uncle Bert, who was Aunt Lulu's husband, was coming through the door. He was surprised to see Lola all grown up and looking just as beautiful as her mother.

"Well, let's eat and if can help you ladies in anyway please ask for my help," said Uncle Bert.

Sitting in the living room, Zola started speaking. "My life was a mess. It was a mess from the time I was born. My parents lived a criminal life. I was raised by criminals. That is all I ever knew. I left that life but not my children or husband. I needed my family to be set free from a life of crime. Derek is your brother. I was pregnant with him when I left New Orleans. He had been one of the joys of my life. I pray that you and Kevin will accept him. He needs your love. He does not know of my past. One day he can be told," said Zola.

"I knew that we would be together one day but I did not know it would be because of my problems. My lawyer feels that I have a good chance of being found not guilty. My family history of criminal activity is my defense. Criminal defense are the words that my lawyer is counting on that will set me free," said Lola.

"How is your brother?" asked Zola.

"You will be very proud of him. He entered the seminary. He is planning on being a priest. He had a bumpy beginning but with Uncle Nick's love and help, Kevin has turned his life around. He will be in court with Dad and other family members to testify on my behalf. You do know that everyone who testifies for the defense will be given total immunity. You will only be asked about the family and me as a child growing up," said Lola.

After a few days, Uncle Bert, Aunt Lulu, Lola, and Derek all packed their things to go to Louisiana for Lola's big day in court. They arrived early as requested by Mr. Wright.

Nick and Eva were glad to see the whole gang. This was the first time the family was going to be together. This had never happened before. Lola's problems with the law created a family for the first time. Kevin was going to arrive in two days and Nate would be arriving early in the morning.

Lulu was a good swimmer and could not wait to get into the pool. I have not been in a pool in many years. I can swim. As a young girl, I went swimming every day at 12 noon in the county pool located in the county park. The Red Cross gave lessons every summer, said Lulu.

Before you knew it everyone was in the pool having fun and acting as if it was going to be the last time they would be together. The cook made a meal that was southern style and they eat outside in the beautiful yard with a colorful perfect garden.

Kevin was concerned about his returning to Louisiana, so he paid a visit to his bishop.

"In a few days, I will have to make a journey which will lead me back home where the devil was with me for many years. I need to have the ability to rise above and fight off the devil so that I can help my twin sister. She has been lost for many years, but after this criminal complaint is resolved, I believe she will take a different path. After all we have a common bond that I plan to use to help guide her to God. Bishop I need your prayers to help me in my duty by God," explained Kevin.

"I will pray with you, but God will be your guide. This is God's plan for you. To make you an ambassador for God was his plan the day you were born. As an ambassador you will win in and out of court. For you it was like crawling into church on your knees like an alcoholic who had fallen into that bottomless pit of hell. God saved you for this day. He stood at the opening of the pit and refused to let you fall. Now you are with him," responded the Bishop.

Mr. Wright was up early on the morning for his meeting with the Harrison family. He knew he had to face this family and associates of criminals and develop a defense that the jurors could relate to and understand.

"Good morning, my name is Robert Wright. I am the lead attorney, and Ted Johnson is my assistant. With your help our criminal defense is going to win Lola a not guilty decision. I understand her defense and believe in her. She had no control over the ancestral history of criminals that was her family. I would first like to tell you that everyone who testifies on her behalf has been giving total immunity. This means that you cannot be charged for anything that is discovered in court through your testimony.

"Do not add anything about yourself that might connect you to any murders. Murder is not part of the immunity agreement. Answer the questions do not add anything. I have documentation that will help the law to solve several cold cases for your immunity. I will call your name from the list.

- Nick Harrison (uncle)
- Zola Harrison (mother)

- Nate Harrison (father)
- Kevin Harrison (brother)
- Eva Harrison (aunt)
- Spook Jackson (partner)
- Johnny Jones (employee)
- Bruce Carson (employee)
- Lulu Dupree (aunt)
- Bert Dupree (uncle)

"I also have a doctor to testify.

"Everyone here?" asked Bobby.

"No," said Nick. "Nate is not here. He is expected to be coming. I am sure he will be here for court."

"Are there any questions?" asked Bobby. "If not, this is the order I want you to enter the court room. I believe the prosecutor has something up his sleeve. Therefore, I want to set the tone for this case. Nate and Zola walk in together next Nick and Eva. Kevin, Spook, Johnny, and Bruce will walk in by themselves. Lulu and Bert will walk in last together."

"Go home and get a good night's sleep and have Father Kevin Harrison to pray for our success tomorrow and that maybe all your lives might change for the better," said Ted.

Ted looked over at Zola and said, "I feel you could use a friend. I have something I found out and I need to tell you and Bobby. Let's go over to my home and have a bite to eat, and I will tell the both of you. It might be good or it might be bad.

CHAPTER 11

TED ORDERED CHINESE food, and as they were eating, he said, "I hired an investigator to check into the prosecutor's background. I did this because he appeared to have more knowledge about the Harrison family than what was in the discovery reports. Yesterday, I received a report on the good prosecutor. It appears that he from Harrisonville, NC. He is the same age as Redd. The investigator asked around town and found out that his father was the sheriff during the time Mr. Harrison; Redd's father arrived in the area from Ireland. In fact, the sheriff was the one who lead the charge to chance the name of the town to Harrisonville after Redd's father died. The sheriff became good friends with Redd and his partner in crime. He was on Redd's payroll. His name is in the ledger that Bobby's father the accountant kept. Now you can see how important this information can be. How it can be used, I do not know how right now," said Ted.

The next day Nate was not at the courthouse. Zola entered first by herself. The rest of the group followed. They all sat together like one big happy family. The prosecutor kept looking as each one entered the courtroom. He did not know what Bobby and Ted had found out about him. In fact, he could have been on the witness list to tell the story about this family of criminals. His father was one of them.

The judge entered the courtroom and everyone was ordered to rise. Within a few minutes after sitting down Nate walked in. The prosecutor's face turned red. He knew he was going to lose this case. Nate knew the prosecutor because he lived in Harrisonville longer then Nick. His father, the sheriff, was the person who told the boys to burn down his father's home after he was murdered by Rita.

"I will now hear the opening statements. Mr. Wright you are first," said the judge.

"Excuse me, Judge, but can we have a side bar?" said the prosecutor.

"The defense has elected not to have any jurors and to let you decide if Lola is guilty. Can we go into your chambers for a short conference, Judge?" asked the prosecutor.

"After reviewing all the discovery information and the background of the witnesses, I have decided that the information supports Lola Harrison's claim of not guilty by mental defect and disease is true. I would like for her to seek therapy for her mental problems as part of the settlement. Also, she is not allowed to take part in any form of illegal activities," said the prosecutor.

"Call Miss Harrison in and see if she agrees and If so all charges will be dropped," said the Judge.

Lola entered the Judge's chambers slowly with her head bowed slightly. She knew this could be the end of her life. But for a brief moment, a small ray of hope passed before her. As she looked into the Judge's eyes she knew that God was on her side.

"Miss Harrison, all charges will be dropped if you agree to the following:

Seek therapy for your illness and never surround yourself or get involve with any criminal activity," said the judge.

"Yes, I agree. Thank you, Judge," said Lola.

"Don't thank me, thank the prosecutor. This is his last case, tomorrow he is retiring. I believe he will be moving back to a small town called Harrisonville in NC," said the judge.

Lola's eyes opened wide and just as she was about to say something, Ted put his hand on her shoulder and led her out of the Judge's chambers.

The judge came out and announced that all charges were dropped and court was adjourned. Everyone stood up and clapped. As Lola walked out with Ted by her side, friends, relatives, and spectators all lined up as Lola walked down the hall and congratulated her on her victory.

Lola looked at Ted and knew that this man was her savior. He had saved her from a life of shame and hopelessness. He was the man of her dreams. She felt just liked Nina when she saw Redd for the first time.

Was this history repeating itself? My life is still a mess. I first must get my life together before I hope to invite Ted to share it with me, thought Lola.

Nate and Kevin were staying at the same hotel but the rest of the family was at Nick's home. Nick said, "I want the family to have dinner at my place tonight. I have something to share with you."

Zola walked over to Nate and looked straight into his eyes and said, "You are still good-looking, and I still love you. I understand that you could never love me again after all that I put you through."

"You did put me through many years of misery but my love for you has never died. You are more beautiful today than the day I first laid eyes on you. I have missed you and still love you. You are still my wife. If you will have me, I'd like to come home," said Nate.

Tears were flowing down Zola's eyes, and she almost fainted when she heard the words I still love you.

"Nate, I have someone you need to meet. His name is Derek and he is your son. He is the baby I was carrying when I left Louisiana. Whatever you did to yourself it did not work. God has given us a chance to start over. Derek was sick as a baby and needed a blood transfusion. His blood type did not match mine therefore I called the man that I thought was his father and his was not a match. I called your doctor and he sent your blood type to Derek's doctor and it was a match. In fact, he told me you were the father. You and Derek have a very rare blood type. He looks just like you," said Zola.

"Where is he now? I want to meet my miracle son from God," said Nate.

"You will meet him tonight at dinner," said Zola.

"It is nice to have all the family here for dinner. Nina would have loved this moment. In remembrance of the relatives before us, will our priest, Kevin say the prayer?" asked Nick.

> Our Father in heaven, this family has taken a long route around the house of God. We are blessed by your forgiveness of all our sins. This meal represents all that is good. Keep us from evil and guide through the light that we will find peace in our belief in You. Amen.

"That was wonderful. What I would like is for each family member to tell a little bit about yourself because it has been many years since we have sat at a table for a meal," said Nick.

"I will go first," responded Aunt Lulu. I am the matriarch of the family. I am seventy-six years old and the youngest of fifteen children. As you can see I am black. My sister who was your great-grandmother married a Frenchman in France. They only had one child and from that marriage one granddaughter who is Zola. Even though some of you look white, we are black. We have been proud of our mixed heritage.

"I have always been in the church and can't remember not going to church. I married Bert at a young age and he became a minister. We never had any children but we have been blessed with a wonderful church, good family, and good friends. Thank you Lord," said Lulu.

"I like to say something. I am not related but would love to be part of this remarkable family. Lola has told me the family story based on the information she read in her grandfather's and grandmother's papers. After all you did survive. Not only did you survive you have become honest and caring," said Ted.

Nate was ready to take his turn. "I have been a criminal most of my life. After Zola and I parted, I found God. I used my money to open up a group home for seniors in West Virginia. These seniors do not have much but my staff and I take good care of them. I love my new profession and Zola has agreed to go back to West Virginia and work with me. We both feel good about each other and only want the very best for our children and family. Taking care of seniors is our calling and we will devote the rest of our lives doing just that," said Nate.

Turning to Lola, Ted said," Lola in plain words, will you marry me?"

"Yes," said Lola.

Everyone clapped and was happy for the two of them. This was truly the high point of the family dinner.

"Okay. Okay now it is my turn," said Zola. "I am black and proud of it. I marred a white man and he loves me. I have had some rough times but was blessed by God to be here for the good times. I am serving God now and not myself. I will serve him until my spirit passes up to God. I love my family."

"I am a priest but was once lost in sin. The devil had me, but God won the battle. God will always win the battle. I was the worst of all sinners. I have destroyed many lives. I pray that God has saved them," said Father Kevin.

"I'm next," said Eva. "I married into the family. I was an FBI agent investigating Zola's parents. I fell in love with Nick, and we are having a wonderful life together. That is all I need to say."

"After I speak, I want to tell the family my news. I have always loved the lord. I realized at an early age that crime was not for me. I did not have the stomach for that life style. It was in the genes, for I had to fight like an alcoholic every day to keep from following that road of crime. I understood what my niece and nephew were going through. Therefore, I loved them and told them so. I was devoted to them. Today will be a new chapter in Lola's life. My plan for her will develop all her gifts that have been given her. She is the one who brought all of us together. May God be with her always," said Nick.

Nick got up and pulled a white sheet off his replica of his dream palace. "This is the Harrison Paradise Club. Lola put her home up for sale and I purchased it. I got all the required licenses which included a liquor license. As you can see, it has a regulation size pool with cabanas. A bath house, eating areas, bar area, and fifty room hotels with tennis courts and a golf course which is what Redd and Buddy always dreamed about. I am giving it to Lola. She and Ted will be the owners. It will be their wedding present. Tomorrow is the grand opening of Harrison Paradise Club. I have hired all the staff and we are fully booked for the hotel. The penthouse is for Ted and Lola. The guests will start arriving at 11:00 a.m. The guests include local lawmakers who are paying their own way. No freebies are going to be given out at this club. Everyone pays their way. Congratulations on being the new owners of the Harrison Paradise Club," said Uncle Nick.

"Thanks, Uncle Nick," said Lola. "Thank you for sticking by me for all these years. You have always been positive in your approach to getting my brother and me through those difficult teenage years. We were blessed to have an uncle like you on our side," said Lola.

Everyone got up early to go to the club. Lola said she could not sleep because she was so excited. They had all planned to eat breakfast at the club together.

The Harrison Paradise Club was located on thirty acres with a large lake for boating and fishing. As you approached, the Club it looked like paradise. There were large columns as you entered the main building. The lobby of the hotel was fantastic. A huge glass chandelier hung from the ceiling and a winding staircase took you upstairs to the dining room or you could take the elevator. All the hotel rooms had kitchenettes with a wet bar for entertaining. On the thirty acres was a golf course with eighteen holes. The golf course was the prettiest in the state.

Lola could not believe this all belonged to her. She just stood there and looked. "This is where I would like to get married. The family is all here. Ted, let's get married this week. I want my family to be here for my wedding. Kevin can perform the service," said Lola.

The club was so beautiful that it did not need much or anything done to it. The family agreed and Kevin agreed to perform the wedding. A few friends were invited but it was mainly family.

It happened that Saturday and the weather was perfect. The wedding took place down by the lake. Lola looked more beautiful than words could express. Ted was the most handsome man there. Lola had lived a life as a criminal but developed into an honest, loving, and lovely young lady.

As the wedding music played and the bride walked down the carpeted path, everyone was crying. Kevin said, "Continue to cry, for they are not tears of sorrow but tears of joy. Amen."

INTRODUCTION

The Donovan Family
The Next Generation
of Criminals

TOM AND ALLIE truly believed that they were born criminals. The two of them were determined to live an honest life. Their earlier years were full of activities that would have landed others in jail. Tom had the support of a father who only wanted the best for his son. On the other hand, Allie was all by herself until a lawyer paved the way for her to start over.

Tom, facing his family's past, helped him overcome many challenges that would have caused others to just give in to being a criminal. Most of his life, he was led to believe, he was an only child. After his father died, he found out that he had a half-sister. Her name was Joni. Tom and Joni didn't know each other. Tom's search for his half-sister presented many roadblocks which were overcome with the help of Allie.

Allie grew up with daily challenges. She accepted the early years as a normal criminal way of life. The underworld of organized crime became her family until the court system gave her a second chance.

The second chance was laced with a dangerous life-style that was backed by the law. She was determined to come out on top every day.

Tom and Allie are good examples of two people who turned their lives around and at the same time worked hard to make lives better for others. They learned that heredity only plays a small part as to how we want to live. They used the family criminal genes as their defense during their young years but love of friends, family, and God kept them alive. They finally learned the God was their best defense and their future was in his hands.

This story is full of true events. Many of the events came from what Alice J. Harris-Wood experienced or was told to by family and friends. The author believes that we are in control of our life and not our genes. At the same time, we know where we've been but only God knows where we are going.

CHAPTER 12

"I DO NOT LIKE graveyards," said Tom Donovan to himself, as he approached his parent's headstone. He just wanted to be near them for he was an only child. Tom's father just died a few weeks ago and left everything to his son.

"Jesse Donovan, my father, was the sheriff of Harrisonville for over thirty years. The town's people loved him. He protected the residents of Harrisonville especially his best friend James Harrison," thought Tom.

As Tom was looking down at the headstone he pulled out a letter his father had written to him. It was to be opened after his death. "Jesse Donovan, my father, was the sheriff of Harrisonville for over thirty-seven years. The town's people loved him. He protected the residents of Harrisonville especially his best friend James Harrison," Tom thought it would be nice to read it out loud at the grave site.

Dear son,

I love you, and I am very proud of you and the profession you have chosen. Your hard work has paid off. As a retired district attorney for the state of Louisiana, this was an outstanding accomplishment for you.

I have lived the life I had chosen and enjoyed being in charge, that is, in charge of Harrisonville. I did my best for all the residents, even though I was working outside the law or performing my duties like a criminal.

I have helped many businesses in Harrisonville to become very profitable. Some were legal and some were illegal. Every business no matter how it functioned was good for Harrisonville's economy. In helping the businesses, I became very wealthy. Any monies that I received through illegal business was given away to help the poor in this town.

All my wealth belongs to you with one request. You have a half-sister. Her name is Joni. She is a good girl. I met her mother at The Palace working as a waitress. To make a long story short. We fell in love. Your mother knew about Laura but I took care of all three of them. Laura never told Joni anything about me as her father.

After Laura died, Joni's mother, I lost contact with her. They lived in Harrisonville and Laura and I continued to see each other until she died. She had a heart attack over ten years ago. When she died, so did I. I loved you, Laura, Joni and your mother.

I wanted to protect all of you from having to live in a town that might not be forgiving. The town did not care about me and Laura but they would have cared if a black woman and I had a baby. Laura looked white but she was black. To live and work in this town, she lived as a white woman who was the sheriff's mistress.

I need you to share my wealth and help Joni. She now lives in New Orleans and is involved with the head of the biggest gangster organization in that city. I do not know for sure what you can do but you are smart and have lots of experience dealing with these types of situations.

Joni does not know her mother was black. Therefore, if you believe it would make a difference in her life, I will leave it up to you to tell her. Use the information that I left you to help your sister to turn her life around. Remember, be careful as to how you use this information and who you share it with.

I have been a survivor and maybe a special survivor. Hopefully, Joni and you will find a way to become good friends and at the same time become survivors of many years of perpetual family criminal activities.

Good luck, and may God lead you in the correct path.

Love,
Dad

Tom just stood looking down at the letter. He was totally shocked at what he just read. "I have a sister!" My father only loved himself and his prestige of being *the sheriff*. He should have allowed Joni to be part of the family from the very beginning. "Now he wants her to be family in the end," thought Tom to himself.

As Tom was leaving the graveyard his mind was tossing around many ideas and scenarios that might be possible to bring Joni into the family. He decided that the best thing to do was to find her and do the right thing by her. Just like the Harrison family did for Lola when I was the prosecutor in her criminal case. Lola is the great-granddaughter of James Harrison. He recalled how divided the family was throughout the years but when it came to saving Lola, from going to jail, they all came together, even Redd in what he left behind.

"It is going to take a long time to go through all Dad's papers but I will do it. My sister, that I do not know, deserves a second chance and if she is willing, I will find a way to lead her in the right direction," thought Tom.

That night Tom tried to get a good night's sleep but couldn't, so he decided to just get up and go to New Orleans to find his sister. As he was driving he was starting to wonder what could be in the boxes of papers that his father left that might help his sister. He knew for years his father was a crooked law enforcement officer but no one was never able to find evidence of any wrong doings in his department.

The sun was coming up and Tom decided to stop at the next rest stop and get some sleep. Now he was sleepy and sleep is what he needed to face what was coming next.

Tom woke up around 10:00 a.m. and was ready to take off. So off he went. He drove all day with one mission, to find his sister. He also was thinking about whether to tell her about her heritage.

It was a Sunday morning and the highway was almost deserted.

Without any warning his tire blew out and his car was out of control. Finally, he was able to stop.

"Damn, I need some divine intervention to help me. I do not have a spare tire. This is my second flat within a few weeks," thought Tom.

At that point a red two-seater sports car pulled up. Behind the wheel was a beautiful blonde.

Tom always wore a cowboy hat that appeared to be made just for him.

"Hello, cowboy," said the blonde.

"You look like you need some help," she stated.

"I need more than help, I need a ride to the closest station," replied Tom.

"Get in and we will be there in ten minutes. It is just up the street. Where are you headed?" asked the blonde.

"Going to New Orleans to take care of some family business," stated Tom.

"We are only twenty miles away. Maybe you like to have something to eat while your tire is being fixed. By the way my name is Allie. There is a café with good food called Lawnside Inn," explained Allie.

"Okay, my name is Tom," he replied.

"Tom, everybody knows you. I worked under you for several years. I was even at your retirement party. With your custom cowboy hats, you cannot be missed. The department has not been the same since your retirement. Even I miss you," said Allie.

"You work in law enforcement?" asked Tom.

"Yes, I am an undercover FBI agent. That is why I drive this expensive car. It gives the appearance that I have plenty of money and influence with the right people. I have helped to put some big time gangsters in jail for a very long time," explained Allie.

Sitting in the café, Allie continued to talk to Tom. She was concerned about Tom for he was a great law enforcement officer. His integrity had been tested over and over for many years without him knowing that the system was watching him.

"Tom, I should not tell you this but your father was on the payroll of the biggest gangster organization in North Carolina, the Harrison family," explained Allie.

"Allie, you appear to be an honest person. So just to set the record straight, I left home shortly after high school graduation and went off to college. I did not want to live in a small country town all my life. I wanted more, and worked long, hard hours while studying in law school. In fact, I was number one in my graduating class.

"Whatever you know about my father, it died with him. His life is not my life. Let's move on and talk about other things. Thanks, for the information about me. It makes me feel good that my career counted for something with so many people," stated Tom.

"Have you lived in the New Orleans long?" asked Tom.

"The Big Easy is my home, and I have lived here all my life," responded Allie.

"I was a troubled teenager and was in and out of foster homes and juvenile detention centers until I was eighteen. My parents were both killed in a plane crash when I was three years old. I was taken in by my mother's parents, who wasted all my money from the insurance company to buy expensive cars and take exotic vacations. The only thing they gave me was room and board. By age 10 the money was gone and they told the state they were too old to care for me and that is how I ended up in foster care," stated Allie.

"Did you have any family that could have helped you?" asked Tom.

"No, not really. My mother has a twin sister who has been in and out of jail all her life. In fact, she has spent more time in jail then out. My father's brother has done well for himself. He and his wife tried to take me in but I was such a troubled girl, they were not able to deal with me and work. Both of them are school teachers," explained Allie.

"Well, that is an interesting story, my life is boring compared to yours," said Tom.

"I like to tell you the rest of my life story but your car is ready. I have to check in with my gangster friends before they start looking for me," explained Allie.

"When can we meet up again? I may need your help on a personal situation," explained Tom.

"When you get to New Orleans call me on this number: 856-555-9865. It is a secured line. I do not want anyone to know that I have met or even talked to you. My gangster friends would not be happy," explained Allie.

"The Big Easy is the nickname for New Orleans, and that is just what it is," thought Tom.

Tom decided to stay at a glamourous hotel. The Waldorf Wisteria which is known for its outstanding hospitality. Tom walked up to the clerk to check in but before he could say anything the clerk said, "Hello, Mr. Donovan. Welcome back to The Big Easy," said the clerk.

"Hello to you also," responded Tom.

Tom could not understand how a clerk knew him. I guess I was well known. I did solve many crimes as a law enforcement officer of the court and as fair. One thing that my father often said, you are only as good as the public sees you, thought Tom.

After settling in, Tom decided to go to the local police precinct to see if they could help him locate his sister. As he walked in all heads turned towards him. Tom was familiar with this precinct because it was one of the most popular hot spots in New Orleans for serious crimes.

The captain of the precinct was standing at the in-take desk as Tom approached.

"Hello, Tom, good to see you, I hope this is a friendly visit and not a professional one," said the captain.

"I am not sure what to call it, but I need your help. Can we go to your office?" asked Tom.

"Follow me," said the captain.

"I have a half-sister, and she lives somewhere here in New Orleans. She is involved with one of the biggest gangster organizations here in town. I need to locate her to introduce myself and help her get her life back on track," explained Tom.

"What is her name?" asked the Captain.

"Her name is Joni Basset," responded Tom.

"Do you know what she looks like? What color hair does she have? Has she used other names?" asked the captain.

"I don't know anything about her. My father died a few months ago and left a tell all letter and confessed of having a baby by one of residents of our town. He asked me to find her and share my inheritance with her. He said she was a troubled girl and lost contact with her after her mother passed away. She is between twenty-two and thirty years old. That is all I know now but I might know more later," stated Tom.

The captain checked his computer for her but her name was not in the system.

"She is not in the system, but she could be using a different name. Sometimes, criminals use IDs from dead people or make up names to cover their tracks," stated the Captain.

"Are there any other sources you can fall back on to help me?" asked Tom.

"Yes, only if you can provide a picture. We have a photo identification system that will allow us to do deeper searching," replied the captain.

Tom called Allie and asked her to dinner. He was very concerned about his sister and hoped Allie might be able to help him. He believed that the boxes of papers his father left might have pictures and other information that could be helpful.

"Allie, I have some family matters and I hope you might be able to help me. I have a half-sister who is here in New Orleans hanging out with the most dangerous gangsters in Louisiana. Her name is Joni Basset," explained Tom.

"No, that name does not ring a bell. The largest gangster group is the Irish Brotherhood. They have been around a long time; it is now in its third generation of family criminals. stated Allie.

"I have had plenty of dealings with them as a prosecutor. I put many of them in jail. The head person of the group has never been caught. We could not determine who was in charge. It appears there is a well-organized system to manage the Irish Brotherhood. They have several layers of leadership," explained Tom.

"We will find your sister. I hope she can be saved. How long has she been with them?" asked Allie.

"Her mother died shortly after she graduated from high school and she went to college in New Orleans. She could have joined The Brotherhood while in college, but I am not sure," explained Tom.

"With all the technology that we have available today, we will locate her. I have some suggestions but it will take time. Is there anything else I need to know that could help?" asked Allie.

"As you already know, my father was on the take with the Harrison crime family. I like to tell you about their relationship, just to clear the air," explained Tom.

CHAPTER 13

"MY FATHER TOLD me how it all began," said Tom.

"Both of them, Jesse Donovan and James Harrison, were friends from the same town in Ireland. They were born on the same day and because the parents were friends, they named them together, Jesse and James," explained Tom.

"One day Jesse came home without his coat and told his mother the teacher threw his coat in the trash. I believe this was the beginning of his training on how to survive," stated Tom.

"Jesse, we are going to your school to get your coat. That teacher will live to regret putting your coat in her trash can," stated James mother.

"Grandmother walked right into the classroom while the teacher was grading papers. No one was in the room but the teacher, Mom, and Jesse," explained Tom. "Jesse, today you will have your first lesson on how to handle your business when it is necessary," stated his mother.

"Good afternoon Mrs. Donovan. Is there something I can help you with?" asked the teacher.

"Yes, I understand you trashed my son's coat," stated Jesse's mother.

"Jesse's coat was torn and looked worse than a dust rag. Therefore, I trashed it, hoping you would replace it with something appropriate. Also, it was a few sizes too big," explained the teacher.

"I came to get his coat. You are going to go to the trash can, and get it, and take it home, and wash his coat. If you refuse, I will kick your ass! Do you understand me?" stated Jesse's mother in a very low, dangerous sounding voice.

The teacher was stunned and could not say anything but yes. Grandmother, in her long house dress and large handbag, stood up straight, and poked her chest out, and sashayed out the door without a smile on her face. Grandmother was not looking for trouble but was ready for it, if needed.

The next day when Jesse came home from school, he had a clean coat with a note from the teacher.

Dear Mrs. Donovan,

Sorry for the misunderstanding, please accept my apology. Jesse is a very sweet, nice, and good student. It is a pleasure to have him in my class.

Sincerely,
Miss Kelly

"Oh, what a story. Your grandmother was a tough lady. I would not want to mess with her. I bet no one ever did," said Allie.

"My father told me that his mother and father worked as a team. They had planned to leave Ireland because the law was about to lock them up. They both died before they were able to leave. My father was a teenager when he left his buddy, Jesse Harrison," explained Tom.

"My father, on many occasions, came home dirty and his clothes torn with cuts and bruises all over his face and body. My grandmother was the type of person that never wanted to be on a losing side. Therefore, she told James the following," stated Tom.

"If you get in a fight, you better come home a winner or I will give you a second beating," explained Grandmother.

"Jesse told his best buddy, James about his problem with his mother. Jesse and James decided to form their own gang with members that were having all kinds of problems with other kids.

In the basement of James's home, the Irish Brotherhood was born. The coleaders were Jesse and James," stated Tom.

"The brotherhood started with a few members and by the time Jesse and James were twelve years old, they had ten members. Members were just from their community. These members had been given titles. Jesse was the main leader, James shared the leadership, the rest of the group were called soldiers," explained Tom.

"Jesse and James considered themselves brothers and lived their lives like brothers. If you bothered one you had to deal with the other. As Jesse was walking home from school JD, the boldest and the most feared kid in town, jumped him. He beat him so hard that Jesse was knocked unconscious. Just as JD was about to give the final blow, James appeared hit him with his baseball bat on his legs," explained Tom.

"Did JD die?" asked Allie.

"No, but he was never the same. He would cross the street whenever James or Jesse came near him," responded Tom.

"One day, James stopped JD and asked him to be part of the brotherhood. JD was so delighted you would have thought he had hit the lottery. James felt that JD, as big as he was, would be the leader of the soldiers. James wanted to expand to include making money by being security in Mom-and-Pop stores in their community," said Tom.

"My father said he was about thirteen when his father asked him to invite his gang over for a group meeting. My grandfather and grandmother knew about the brotherhood and decided that they were going to make them part of their criminal organization," explained Tom.

"As the boys filed into the house like toy soldiers, my grandfather was smiling from ear to ear, for he knew he had a new supply of loyal recruits," explained Tom.

"How could they be security as kids?" asked Allie.

"It seems strange but they did it. JD, Jesse, and James were the security. They only worked Saturday's at first and as they got older they expanded to all week," explained Tom.

"Did they negotiate how much to be paid?" asked Allie.

"Yes and no. James told his parents about their money making idea and they were all in. Grandmother, decided that they were to be paid what other employees were paid per hour," said Tom.

"Some of the owners, tried to haggle over the money but Grandmother came out on top because she threatened to cut off their supply of moonshine if the boys were not paid what they were worth.

"Moonshine was a major part of the Mom and Pop store's income. No one was making moonshine in the area but the Donovan family. All moonshine making and sales came through the Donovan's," explained Tom.

"How many days a week were your father and James working?" asked Allie.

"They work every day after school until closing and all day on the weekends. Their main job was to look out and catch shoplifters. Shoplifters had to deal with James, Jesse, and JD," stated Tom.

"They started out with just three stores but ended up with all the little retailers in the community. The soldiers were now all working. My grandparents got 35 percent of everything. Their 35 percent was administrative cost or the cost of doing business, according to my grandparents. Jesse and James got 20 percent and the rest went to the soldiers. With all the soldiers working, Jesse and James job was to help collect the money for security work," explained Tom.

"If Jesse and James had a problem collecting the security money, then they would call in the enforcer, who was my grandfather. He had a gun strapped to his right ankle. If he needed to show it or use it he would," stated Tom.

"So the Irish Brotherhood started in Ireland," stated Allie.

"I don't think many people know that Irish Brotherhood started with two young kids. It sounds interesting and I would like to hear more.

Let's get some wine and go over to my home and continue this conversation," stated Allie.

As Tom and Allie sat on the sofa sipping wine, Tom restated his conversation about the Irish Brotherhood. Everything that he was telling her was told to him by his father.

"My grandfather's, nighttime dreams, is when he would come up with big ideas but never shared them with my grandmother until the sun went down the next day," explained Tom.

"Did he dream up a plan to expand his organization?" asked Allie.

"Yes, and it included the Brotherhood. In fact, his plan gave new life to his criminal organization. The plan was all in his head. My grandfather, Conor Donovan had an excellent memory. He could meet you one time and ten years later, remember your name without hesitating," explained Tom.

Conor had a no nonsense personality. If you crossed him, he would not react right away. He would retaliate on his time table. Sometimes it would take years for him to get even, but believe me he would get even. Because he was very short, about 5'1" and had a very pleasant smile on his face, people would misread him. They took his size and his smiling face as a form of weakness. Conor was not a weak man. He was just the opposite, cold blooded criminal who would do whatever he needed to do, to come out on top," explained Tom.

"Jesse, my father, was expected to be home by 11:00 p.m. anytime he was out socializing. He tested his father and came home after 1:00 a.m. one Saturday morning. According to my father, he thought he had got over on Conor. Conor did not say anything but was waiting for the right time to react. My father came home on time for several months but decided to hangout late on New Year's Eve. That was a mistake. The sun was coming up when my father who was seventeen years old came home.

To his surprise, all his clothes were thrown in the middle of the street.

"His father not only threw his clothes in the street but tore them to shreds. That was my grandfather and that is how he lived," stated Tom.

"What happened to your father after that?" asked Allie.

"He knew that this was the end of his father/son relationship and it was a message to leave and move on. My father had a good relationship with the captain of a ship that delivered moonshine and gin to the US once a month. He asked him if he could work for him. The captain knew Conor Donovan for he was his only moonshine client," explained Tom.

"What did the captain tell your father?" asked Allie.

"Young man, I would be glad to have you work for me because Conor Donovan is my best friend and as his son, he raised you to be a real man. That is what my business needs, real men. The next shipment will be leaving tomorrow. Will you be ready to go?" asked the captain.

"Yes, I am ready now. Do you have anything you might need me to do?" asked Jesse.

"Well, can you let your father know that his shipment needs to be loaded after dark because the law has been trying to catch me loading liquor. Even though some US states have banned liquor sales for years, the U.S. government is putting pressure on our government to help stop illegal liquor shipments. That damn Volstead Act, which enforced the US Eighteenth Amendment to the Constitution is trying stop us from making a living. Instead of slowing or stopping the flow, it is getting better," said the captain sternly.

"Speakeasies are popping up all over the South and North of the US. Every time one is shut down, two more open up the next day. Business is great and with your father's dedication to this industry it is only going to get better," explained the captain.

"Tom, do you know what happened at the meeting that your grandfather called with the Brotherhood? I would like to know more because it might help me find the top leaders of the organization," explained Allie.

"Grandfather started off explaining that all business organizations have to make changes from time to time in order to stay in business," explained Tom.

Then my grandfather stated, "My little soldiers, meet the big guys. As of today we will be one big happy family of criminals. Yes, we are criminals. You should know who you are so that you can be the best at your job.

"In my book, put you name and address and a person to contact if we need to. It appears that we have ten soldiers and five officers. This is a good number. It is easy to manage when slicing up territories into small units. We are now the Irish Brotherhood forever, understand," stated Conor Donovan.

"To get started, I have made a chart with the five officers and their territories. They can now select two soldiers that will work in each territory. The officers will also have other workers under them.

"Next, we will be making moonshine in large quantities and shipping 60 percent of it to America. My distributor is having problems with the government and needs some help from us. I have a friend who owns a shipping company and has agreed to ship our product to our distributor.

The law enforcement in this county is all in with us. We will be opening up several speakeasies. They are places that function like a club or bar but are illegal. They specialize in after hour selling of alcohol, gaming, and women.

They are popular in a New York City, mostly in a black neighborhood called Harlem. I heard a visitor say, USA is "flesh and bone dry," so we will give them a "dust cutter." Our best moonshine their money can buy.

"It has come to my attention; they have this new music called jazz. I went to Harlem last year to meet up with some potential distributors at a club called the Cotton Club." This black woman by the name of Josephine White was singing the jazz. I was told she just got back from Paris and while there, married a white man. She was flamboyant and put on an exotic performance. The audience went crazy.

Last night, as I was dreaming about my plans, I knew I had to have her or some other black Jazz players and singers to perform at my clubs. My speakeasies would not be complete without jazz. Then it came to me like an angel descending down from heaven. My stepson, who was my wife's son by her first marriage, married a black entertainer. Could it had been Josephine White? Sure enough, it was Josephine White," explained Conor.

Before Josephine White could leave the stage, Conor ran up on the stage and grabbed Josephine White by her hand.

"Josephine White, my name is Conor Donovan, your husband's stepfather. I need your help. Your performance was out of this world. It was the greatest performance I have ever seen," explained Conor.

"I know who you are. I saw pictures of my husband's family. He speaks very highly of you. He said as kids, his stepbrother had his back all the time. Your nickname is Little Dynamite. He told me after his mother gave Jesse a little pep talk, his life changed forever," explained Josephine White.

"Anything for my new family. I have been treated extremely good in foreign countries. Not like in the US, where I have to go outside to an outhouse to shit," said Josephine.

"Josephine White was married to your grandfather's stepson, right?" responded Allie.

"Yes, my grandmother was not Irish, she was French but learned to act like an Irish mafia bitch. Her son was just the opposite. When he got older he wanted to return to France and live with his father. Jerry's father owned the Paris LRN which sponsored all types of performers mainly from New York City's Harlem. He only picked the best performers to perform on his stage. Josephine White was performing at the LRN and Jerry, my uncle was working as a stage hand. That is when he fell in love with Josephine White.

"It was not a long courtship. They were married within a year and had a beautiful set of twin girls. Ella Lynn Basset and Ellen Laura Basset were identical but their personalities were completely different. Ella, became a mafia bitch just like her grandmother," explained Tom.

"Did your father ever meet his nieces?" asked Allie.

"No, but his nieces would send cards on mother's day, and on her birthday. Sometimes, according to my father a card would come at Christmas time. That was the only involvement they had with my grandparents," explained Tom.

"I don't know much about the two girls. Someone said that after the girls graduated from high school, they left France and went to America. I believe they settled in New Orleans," explained Tom.

"Basset would have been their maiden names. I wonder if they got married," asked Allie.

"Well, it is getting late and I should be getting back to my hotel. If you have time we can talk more tomorrow," said Tom.

"Tom, I will make time. I need to know more about the Irish Brotherhood. I believe we might be on to something. Your sister will be found. I can guarantee you, we will locate her. You might be disappointed in what we discover. So be ready for bad news," said Allie.

"Check out of the hotel and come stay with me. I have a spare bed room. This way we can pool all our resources and maybe solve a few mysteries," said Allie.

That night Tom decided to go home and check out the boxes his father left for him. *He believes that everything that is missing in Joni's and his life were in the boxes*, thought Tom.

The next morning, Tom checked out of the hotel and called Allie and told her his plans.

"Allie, I am going back home and go through the boxes my father left me. If I find something that will help you bring down the brotherhood, I will call you. Don't tell anyone about me or what we are doing. I think my father was a bigger player than just Harrisonville," explained Tom.

"Do you want me to come with you, Tom?" asked Allie.

"Yes, my house is big enough for the two of us. There are many boxes and we will be able to work day and night without any interruptions. Harrisonville is a small country town with a history of being the home of big time bootleggers, mainly the Harrison family. All their businesses were sold years ago by Nate and Nick Harrison. Those two just wanted to get a clean start. When their parents were living, the two boys who were twins, did not have a chance at living an honest life," explained Tom.

"Tom, this will give me a chance to finish telling you my sad story. You will be the first person who has heard my story from the very beginning. I was saved by people who cared and they made me feel special. I am a special survivor," stated Allie.

CHAPTER 14

TOM STARTED THINKING about what his father said about being careful with whom he shared his information. *I plan to share all the information in those boxes with Allie. I feel confident that she will be okay and will do everything possible to help me find my half sister*, thought Tom.

Tom picked Allie up and off they went to Harrisonville. "Tom, I have come a long way. As I stated before, I was in and out of foster homes. I was a criminal when I was very young.

"My grandparents sent me to foster care at age ten. The first family that I lived with were nice but they had two other foster kids. Wilbert and Wilma, were twins. The twins were 11 years old and were Special Education students. The foster parents were white and Wilbert and Wilma were black. The school system was mostly white.

"Every day Wilbert would get into fights with the white students. He was very good at fighting and lying. Wilbert was a very chubby kid, and short for his age. One day as I was eating my lunch, Wilbert snuck up on me and hit me hard with his book bag. I turned around and struck him so hard that I broke his jaw. Our foster mother was called. Wilbert, while waiting for the ambulance, he started telling his big lies," explained Allie with a little bitterness in her voice.

"Allie hit me and I did not do anything to her," stated Wilbert.

"He was black and his sister who was also a bad little fat bitch seconded the lie. Of course no one was going to dispute her because she would whip their asses. She was a mean little girl. I do not think she was a little girl. To me she was a grownup in a child's body.

"No one wanted to hear my side of the story. My foster parents, that night, took me to the police station and told them to call my caseworker," explained Allie. The caseworker said to my foster parents, "take Allie home and we will talk it over tomorrow."

"Tomorrow never came because the foster parents refused to take me home. They told the police about the fight and stated I was a danger to myself and others. That was the end of my first foster home," stated Allie with a pair of wet eyes.

"The next home was awful. The foster parents were a middle age white couple who were just one step away from welfare. All they wanted was the money. They told child protective service that they had jobs. Their job was ducking work. The house was dirty, smelly, and needed many repairs. In this home there were five of us children, four boys and me. I was scared of my foster parents.

"All they fed us was TV dinners if we were lucky while they cooked shrimp, steak, pork chops, and hamburgers for themselves. If they were given advance notice that the case manager was coming at dinner time, then they would make us help clean the house. This was the only time we got a good meal. The foster parents would serve us hamburgers with French fries and a dessert. None of us dared to open up to the case manager about the real situation," said Allie sounding like a little girl who was afraid to speak.

"Now I was going on twelve years old and was starting to mature. Ben the foster father started acting very strange around me. Sue, the wife finally got a job, Ben on many occasions stated that work was not in his vocabulary. Therefore, Ben was our care taker. Sue worked at night and did not get home until after 8:00 in the morning.

"Ben came into my bedroom one night and said he had something special for me. He climbed into my bed and tried to touch me in all the wrong places. After the last foster home, I knew I had to protect myself because the case manager was only collecting a paycheck. I had found a hammer in the storage room and hid it under my mattress.

"I was able to get away from Ben. I got out of the bed and pulled out the hammer and started swinging it all over. I could hear voices in the other bedroom. By now I was hysterical. Ben, and noises in the dark room were all driving me crazy. I just started swinging and pounding and when it was over Ben was dead," stated Allie.

"I told my story and they believed me. But the judge sent me to a juvenile detention center for one year and after the one year, I was to stay in a group home for emotionally disturbed juveniles until I was eighteen years old," stated Allie.

"Did things get better or worse?" asked Tom.

"The meals got better but the situation was not the kind of environment for a kid. In the detention center I met Leroy. Leroy was very nice to me. In fact, my only friend. He was about seventeen years old, and I was twelve years old but looked older.

"Leroy worked in the kitchen of the girl's campus, because he was considered an excellent inmate. Many of the guards were working with Leroy to help sell drugs inside the boys and girls detention center for the Brotherhood. Leroy said the following to me," explained Allie.

"You look like a very nice little lady who got a raw deal. I heard all about what happened to you. In here you need friends. Without friends what you endured was nothing as to what will happen to you in here," stated Leroy with a slick smile on his face.

"I don't understand, Mr. Leroy," responded Allie.

"Oh, I like that title, Mr. Leroy. It makes me feel special. I guess I am special. I have survived several years on my own. I am a special survivor or special criminal.

"Well, little lady, I will be getting out of here in thirty days. My gang will protect you. You need protection from the lesbians and guards. This place is a cesspool and it will consume the good and the bad," warned Leroy.

"What did you have to do for Leroy?" asked Tom.

"Collect his drug money and turn it over to one of the guards," responded Allie.

"Drug money!" responded Tom.

"Parents would put money into their children's money account and most of them use it to buy marijuana, or other drugs, or alcohol. Most of the guards got paid very well by Leroy. In some cases, Leroy's gang members, outside the detention center, would threaten to harm the guards' families if they did not team up with them.

"Drugs would come into the detention center three ways. One way was packages labeled as powdered eggs. Next was shipments of medication or just hand carried in by guards," explained Allie like a big-shot CEO.

"I can understand how drugs came in with powdered eggs and medications but hand carried in by the guards. Wow, what an operation!" stated Tom.

"Leroy was an exceptional intellectual in the area of criminal organizational operations. He got all his abilities and knowledge from his father who was a top soldier in the Brotherhood. His father was the first black soldier with the Brotherhood and later controlled all the black wards in New Orleans. He was a bad MF. He died the way he lived, with danger surrounding him from all sources," stated Allie.

"How did he die?" asked Tom.

"Leroy's father loved women and the women loved him. He started having an affair with a white woman who would not leave him alone.

Finally, he gave into her but his wife found out about him and this white woman.

"One night he was at a private jazz club with the white woman and his wife followed him to the club. She waited until he was somewhat drunk and went up to the both of them and shot them both in the head," explained Allie.

"What happened to Leroy's mother?" asked Tom.

"Nothing, she dropped the gun and walked out the front door. No one dimed her out. Mainly because she did the Brotherhood a favor and they in return protecting her," explained Allie.

"Do you know her name?" asked Tom.

"Yes, Lucille Wallace," responded Allie.

"I know her, I know her!" shouted Tom.

"She works as a community organizer in the black wards. I tried to get an interview with her about crime in the black neighborhoods, but she would not respond. I even went to her headquarters but was told she was out of town. Never could reach her," stated Tom.

"She got away with it because Malachi Wallace, Leroy's father was getting too big for his breeches, and the Brotherhood wanted him eliminated. Lucille took them both out," explained Allie.

"Working as Leroy's cashier in the detention center, one of guards warned me not to cross Leroy for he was just like his parents. He told me that Leroy was a mean MF that would eliminate me without blinking an eye. The guard also told me about Leroy's mother and father in order to insure that I would do as I was told," explained Allie.

"Okay, were you good at your job?" asked Tom.

"Yes, I was great. I have always loved to keep records and that is what I did for Leroy. It was hard to keep track of everything because there were over two thousand girls at our compound. I was going crazy trying to manage the money. Therefore, I had to come up with something that was practical and functional.

"The girls and boy's centers were like a college campus but with armed guards. So I said to Leroy, 'I need some recordkeeping books and some helpers. You are losing money by not having a better system.'

"I will get you all the help you need but if they steal from me, I will know because all of you will be watched," warned Leroy.

"How did they get the drugs to you and how did you distribute and collect the money?" asked Tom.

"It was unbelievable the poor system that existed but the upgraded system that I put in place worked great," stated Allie.

"Let's stop and get a quick bite to eat and we can talk more while we eat," stated Tom.

"You were just a kid and not even a teenager yet," responded Tom.

"You are right, but one day I decided to see if I could find some information about my parents because no one ever talked about them not even her brother or sister. When I went to work for the FBI, I found out that my Aunt Jeanie was my mother and I was born in prison.

At this point I realized it was not my fault that in my early years, I was a criminal and enjoyed it," explained Allie.

"Wow, this is deep!" exclaimed Tom.

"How is your meal?" asked Allie.

"Just as good as your story so far," responded Tom.

"My steak is brown on the outside and bloody on the inside just like my childhood. I did not know any better and was very happy being a criminal. It took many years for me to discover that being a criminal was in my genes until I was saved by an FBI agent," stated Allie.

"Well, my meal was good but It's time to get back on the road," explained Tom.

"We have been driving for over eight hours, and your story has got me wondering what stories lie ahead for me in those boxes that my father left behind. Therefore, let's just get a room or two rooms and get a good night's sleep. Tomorrow is a new day with more stories," stated Tom inquisitively.

"Okay, but we only need one room with two full size beds. I trust you and I feel you respect women. I feel safe around you," stated Allie.

In the middle of the night Allie was tossing and turning in her bed and decided Tom's body next to hers would give her great comfort. So without making any noise, she crawled into his bed and wrapped her arms around him. That was the beginning of a new life for both of them.

Tom woke up early and unwrapped himself from Allie. There was a coffee pot in the room so he made coffee for both of them.

Years ago, a friend once told Tom, when a woman selects you, then you know it is the right gal, thought Tom.

At that moment, Allie woke up and stated, "Good morning, cowboy."

"Good morning to you also. I hope you had a restful sleep," responded Tom.

"I sure did! With you next to me, it was like passing out in heaven," responded Allie.

"We are only a few hours from Harrisonville, so let's get some breakfast and hit the road," stated Tom.

"Okay, but I would like to continue telling you my story. It makes me feel better telling you the awful things that happened to me as a young girl growing up," explained Allie.

As they were leaving the hotel room, Tom realized that Allie was not just any normal woman. She was a strong woman who had been through more than one person should be forced to endure. With all of her past behind her, she was still beautiful, honest, and fun to be around. She had weathered the stormy days of her childhood and was now living every day to make things right for her own peace of mind.

"Waitress, I will have the breakfast special," stated Allie.

"That sounds like a winner. I will have the same thing," responded Tom.

"Tom, I am a believer in God, and he brings people together for a reason. We both are looking for something. I think we are looking for the door that was shut and now we have a chance to open the door so that we can enjoy the future," explained Allie.

"Allie, let's go back to the detention center. You were just a kid. Leroy gave you a lot of responsibility," stated Tom.

"I was considered very bright. I was always fascinated with numbers and recordkeeping. At school, I was the person in charge of organizing fundraisers with the teachers and parents. They loved how I was dedicated with whatever was planned. As time passed, Leroy was very impressed with my abilities at such a young age," explained Allie proudly.

"We only have a few hours left before we get to Harrisonville. My home is just the type of place that we can work and relax," explained Tom.

"Okay, continue with your outstanding accounts receivable plan," Tom responded jokingly.

"To begin with, the warden or director of the center was being paid by the Brotherhood to run the drug operation inside the centers. Some of the guards were soldiers of the Brotherhood. My job was to collect the money and give the buyer a colored ribbon. The color of the ribbon would tell the nurse in the doctor's office, what they ordered and that I had collected the money.

"No names were ever listed or the amount that was being collected. Prices were all told to me and I had to keep them in my head. I have a good memory. The girl inmates would go to the nurse's station and say their period was on and they needed some pads. Once in the nurse's station, they handed the nurse the ribbon and she would hand them the drugs.

"At some point, the colored ribbons would come back to me and I would just recycle them back into the system," explained Allie.

"Did you ever have any problems with the money?" asked Tom.

"My roommate stole a few ribbons from me while I was sleeping and my money came up short. I always counted my ribbons every night before I went to sleep and put them under my mattress. I told Leroy right away. Leroy had my roommate moved in with one of the most dangerous females who did not give a damn about anything. Her new roommate, when she turns 18 years old will be incarcerated with the adult women to serve a twenty-year term. She killed her father and mother because they would not give her any money for drugs," explained Allie.

"After Roni stole the ribbons, I decided that no more ribbons would be stolen. Therefore, I made a special belt and secured them around my waist at night," explained Allie.

"Did anything happen to Roni?" asked Tom.

"Yes, she was found dead the next morning. They claimed she had an asthma attack and died before she could receive medical attention," responded Allie.

"Did you ever feel that you could be replaced?" asked Tom.

"All the time. That is why I slept with the ribbons around my waist," responded Allie.

"How many females are we talking about at this facility?" asked Tom. "A lot, maybe over two thousand girls of all ages. This center was like a college campus with a gymnasium, dining room with a large kitchen, activity center with a library, and a large nurse and doctor office area. The head man in charge, lived on campus in a home that looked like a mansion," responded Allie.

"Leroy the scumbag, worked in the kitchen," responded Tom in an angry tone.

"That's right, Leroy worked in the kitchen," responded Allie.

"I always wore a T-shirt and underneath around my waist was a money bag. I decided that the money would be turned over every three hours to the head guard. If he was off duty, I was told to give it to his backup guard. When the money was turned over, they would give me a new money bag. This was an all-day thing.

"The guards would drop off the money bags at the back door of the mansion. The door, had a large opening for the money bags to be placed through. To cover myself, I made a quick count as to how many colors of each ribbon that were handed out per day and gave a written report to Leroy the next day. Leroy was very pleased with my recordkeeping system for he did not trust anyone, not even the head man in charge. It was like having a real job," explained Allie with pride.

CHAPTER 15

"**A**LLIE, THAT YEAR you spent at the detention center must have been hell," stated Tom.

"No, it was the best place I lived since my grandparents sent me to foster care. I had status and a few workers under me. If I wanted something special to eat, it was given to me. I was allowed to sit in the dining room with my posse. My posse consisted of 5 girls who were lesbians. They tried to hook up with me but I let them know that I liked males. That was the end of their trying to get friendly with me," stated Allie.

"What were your posse's jobs?" asked Tom.

"Each girl in my posse was to wear a special earring on the left side of their nose. This would let me know they were in my gang. Gang members would come and go because their time was up. Some of the girls worked at the nurse's station and some worked in the doctor's office doing intake and other paperwork. Some of the girls collected the ribbons and would tally how much money should be turned in that day. Their numbers and my records should have balanced out each day," explained Allie.

"As an FBI agent did you ever try to stop the flow of drugs in the detention centers?" asked Tom.

"No, because I am looking for the King Pin or the top players of the Brotherhood," responded Allie.

"Did you have any involvement in the male center that was just five miles away?" asked Tom.

"No, but I was told that they were bringing in big, big money per month with the male sector," stated Allie.

"We are only an hour away from Harrisonville. I am anxious to see what is in my father's boxes. Your story is a very powerful journey for such a young girl. I believe you were blessed to have survived such a life," stated Tom.

"I did my year at the center and was sent to a group home as ordered by the judge. Leroy found me in the group home and encouraged me to run away. I took his advice and was living at Leroy's place. My job now was to oversee the drug counting and recording of the drug money coming in daily.

"At Leroy's place, the girls wore swim suits so that if they tried to steal any money it would be detected quickly. I sat at a desk that was on a platform looking down on them. A surveillance system was inside and outside the home so that I could monitor what was going on all around me," explained Allie.

"We are here, home sweet home," stated Tom.

As Tom was pulling into the driveway, his housekeeper, Mary was standing at the door. "Welcome home, cowboy. You have a visitor. I tried to tell her to come back tomorrow after you returned home but she refused to leave. She has a gun and she told me if I tried calling you she would kill me," stated Mary in a trembling voice.

"Okay, young lady. No one needs to get hurt. Let's go inside and talk," responded Tom.

Allie was still in the car. She recognized the girl. It was Vonda, one of the enforcers for the Brotherhood. Allie lay flat down on the front seat of the car so that Vonda could not see her. Allie knew if Vonda saw her with Tom, she would kill both of them.

Vonda was a bad, bad piece of work, thought Allie.

This gal is too pretty to be holding a gun on anyone. With her looks and body, she could have been a model, thought Tom.

"You think you are all that, Mr. District Attorney, but I am here to let you know, to stay out of New Orleans. Nothing goes on in the Big Easy without the Brotherhood finding out. We have soldiers everywhere. Captain Wise called us shortly after you spoke to him at the precinct. So, you are looking for your half-sister. Well, stop looking, she does not want to be found. If I come back to Harrisonville, it will be to kill you," explained the gal.

She threw the housekeeper on the floor and walked out. Tom had never shot or killed anyone during his career as a law enforcement officer. His only involvement with criminals was in the courtroom. Now Tom felt that he might have to get a gun.

"Tom, that was Vonda. She is an enforcer with the Brotherhood. In fact, the best they have. She enforces the Brotherhood commands. If they command her to kill you, she will. She was in the detention center with me. She has known me almost all my life and will not hesitate to kill me if necessary. She once told me she killed Roni, my first roommate at the center," stated Allie.

"Allie, we have to do two things, find my half-sister and put the brotherhood out of business. When my father told me about my grandfather and his friend James Harrison, I was shocked. I did not let on to him that I was trying to hunt down the leader or leaders of the Brotherhood. I believe my father left his boxes to me, so that I could get justice for all the people who were hurt or killed by the Brotherhood. As you know, I was and always will be a law enforcement officer, it is in my genes," stated Tom.

"Let's get Mary home. She is a nervous wreck. Mary, I want you to stay home for a while. I will continue to pay you. I need you to keep a low profile and do not tell anyone about tonight. If you do, your family and you might be in danger," stated Tom.

That evening Allie and Tom sipped on a glass of wine while they stared at the boxes in the basement. Tom wanted to just dig right into the boxes but he was concerned as to what he might find out.

How did the Brotherhood find its way to New Orleans? Was Jesse Donovan and James Harrison involved together in New Orleans? thought Tom.

Allie looked at Tom and she could see that he was concerned about the information that was in the boxes. To set his mind at ease,

Allie stated the following, "Tom, you know I am a FBI agent. The information in the boxes should be given to the FBI but only after we check it all out. If you feel that some things should just go to the grave with your father, I will go along with your wishes."

Tom nodded and poured more wine into his empty glass. Allie moved closer to Tom and kissed him on the cheek. Tom wrapped his arms around Allie gave her a sweet kiss back.

"Allie, you are a very pretty lady and I believe for the first time, I am truly in love. In love with everything about you. I hope you feel the same way about me," stated Tom.

"Tom, I have been in love with you for many years. I believe it was your cowboy hat that made me notice you. But as the years went by working around you, I gave up on ever meeting you. You were so involved in your work. Having any romance in your life did not seem possible until I picked you up on that lonely highway heading to New Orleans," explained Allie.

"Do you believe in God, Tom?" asked Allie.

"Yes, and our meeting the way we met was God's plan," responded Tom.

"Okay, let's go to bed and continue working on God's plan," stated Allie jokingly.

The next morning, Allie got up before Tom and cooked breakfast. She made waffles, eggs, and bacon with a fresh pot of coffee. The smell was consuming the whole house. It had been a long time since Tom had woken up to this type of smell.

It was the smell of a woman making breakfast with love in her heart, thought Tom.

"You were wonderful in bed last night. I am glad you saved all your love for me. You made me feel so good that everything that I had endured growing up was wiped out. I feel that with you by my side, I can move on to what I need to do in order to be happy today, tomorrow, and in the future. Let's eat!" stated Allie.

"My family started out as bootleggers, and in my research, I discovered that the term 'bootlegger' came from the late 1800s, when trading with Native Americans, traders would hide flasks of illegal liquor in their boot tops," explained Tom.

"It will be very interesting to see if your father has any information about the bootlegging from way back in the day. Those boxes most likely will contain a lot of history," stated Allie.

"I noticed that the boxes have dates on them. Let's start with the oldest box. That Vonda person appeared to know my sister. At least we now know she is in New Orleans. We will take the Brotherhood down, just like the government took out Capone and he ended up in Alcatraz and died of syphilis contracted in one his whorehouses," explained Tom.

Tom carefully cut open the first box and was surprised to find weapons. They were not just any weapons but very old ones. They were all labeled. The box included a sub-machine gun labeled the Tommy gun, a Smith & Wesson Model 19, a Colt M1911A1, a Remington Model 870, and the final weapon, a Molotov cocktail bottle.

"Damn, look at this. A box full of old weapons with a hand written note from my father," stated Tom.

Dear son,

These are very valuable weapons. They all belonged to me. Now they belong to you.

Love,
Dad

"Wow, wow, wow!" shouted Tom.

"What's in the box, Tom?" asked Allie.

"I'll give you three guesses, and the last two don't count," responded Tom.

"I have no idea what is in the box," explained Allie.

"Look for yourself and tell me what you think," responded Tom.

"Unbelievable, guns and old ones at that," responded Allie.

"My father left this note but it does not tell me much. It only states that they belonged to him and now they belong to me," explained Tom.

"I plan to get the guns registered and appraised. Next, I will give them to you to turn over to the FBI. You can send the guns to the FBI lab. They can test them and see if they were ever used in the commitment of a crime. I need to know more about my father. I think he was a major player with the Brotherhood. He didn't just drop out of the Brotherhood once he came to America," explained Tom.

"You might be on to something. When was the last time you saw your father?" asked Allie.

"A year before he died, but I called him once a month to see how he was doing. I knew he was a bad apple and I didn't want to be around him. He would come to New Orleans a few times a year on business. He did not stay with me. He had a good friend that he stayed with while he was in New Orleans. He would stay a few weeks at a time. I often wondered what was the nature of his visits," stated Tom.

"After I ran away from the group home and ended up with Leroy, I wore a gun strapped to my ankle. I wore jeans all the time. Leroy gave me the gun. He often stated that it was better to be safe than sorry," explained Allie.

"Did you ever need to use a gun?" asked Tom.

"Yes, on many occasions, I would have to threaten the girl money counters with my gun and let them know I was in charge. I was a bad little gal. I learned it all from Leroy. But I never killed anyone until I was an undercover FBI agent," explained Allie.

"Oh, I hope it was in the line of duty," responded Tom.

"I was cleared by the FBI for the use of deadly force. Within hours, they sent me back on the street with the Brotherhood," explained Allie.

"You sound a little upset," responded Tom.

"Not really, for that was my job and its part of what is expected as a good undercover agent. I was back in the hell house as soon as possible," explained Allie.

"I am anxious about what might be in the next box. The first one was shocking. A box full of old guns. The guns must have been important to my father or he would not have kept them all these years. Maybe as we go through the boxes, the full story about what took place in Ireland, Harrisonville, and New Orleans might be revealed," explained Tom.

"I think we might need something a little stronger than your wine. How about getting a few bottles of Bourbon? I feel that these boxes are going to take on a life of its own. When that happens, you and I are going to need a good stiff drink in our glass," explained Allie.

"You should put on a scarf and pull your hair back. I have a pair of sunglasses you can use. If anyone recognizes you, your cover will be blown and we could get killed. The Brotherhood has eyes looking at me from every corner. They don't know you are here and that is the way we will keep it. Call your office at the FBI and tell the office you have a family emergency and will be gone for a few weeks. We can't trust anyone. The Brotherhood is embedded deeply with law enforcement. Especially here in Harrisonville," stated Tom.

"I'd like to go to a beauty supply store to get a wig. A dark color maybe a black wig. When you go to purchase the liquor, small talk the clerk and tell her your girlfriend is living with you at your father's house. That will be passed on to the right people as an update on you," stated Allie.

The next box was marked Personal. As Tom reached into the box, he grabbed a handful of smelly papers. It was the same smell that he smelled before as a little boy. Tom could not remember where, when, and under what circumstances he had come into contact with that smell. The smell was not a smell of a good memory but the smell of a memory that he had long forgotten and didn't want to remember.

"This is amazing! It's a box full of obituaries. Some are very old. Wow! My grandparent's obituaries are in this box. I hope I will be able to find more about those two criminals. All I know is what my father told me. Conor was Irish and Sally was French. Most of the time, he wanted to talk about how proud he was of the Brotherhood. Jesse Donovan and James Harrison, that met and started the Brotherhood in my grandparent's basement," stated Tom.

Both obituaries were short and to the point. Full name, parents, place of birth, date died, occupation, and children. Tom was surprised that the obituaries were so short and did not reveal much information. "Why don't you go to the store and get my wig? I will stay here and look through the obituaries. There might be something that will help us bring down the Brotherhood. Oh, don't forget the bourbon!" shouted Allie.

Allie grabbed a handful of obituaries, lay on the sofa, and started flipping through the papers. Then she started recognizing a few names. The obituaries were not family and friends but old gangsters from Harrisonville and New Orleans. Allie decided to make a list of names from the obituaries and to do some research as to how and where they died. She was hoping this might be the smoking gun she needed to find the leadership of the Brotherhood.

I need Tom to continue telling me his family story that started in Ireland. Knowing the past will help Tom and me to uncover and shut down the Brotherhood, thought Allie.

As Tom was walking through the door, Allie yelled out, "These are dead gangster obituaries. Your grandparents are in this box because they were gangsters. Your father was the record-keeper for the Brotherhood. The obituaries are all in order by dates. Inside are short notes as to how they died and under what circumstances."

"How did you figure that out?" asked Tom.

"I recognized a few old timers and looked at the handwritten notes. There were no notes on your grandparent's obituaries but they were the Brotherhood. I need you to tell me everything your father told you about his parents," stated Allie.

CHAPTER 16

"**A**S A KID growing up, I had to listen to my father's stories about his parents and their associates. He wanted his proud family past recorded in my memory so that nothing would be forgotten," explained Tom.

As we sat eating dinner, my father often stated, "Tom, I was born into a family of criminals and I am special, a special survivor. I remember everything, so now I am going to tell you the family story," stated Jesse Donovan.

"Conor, my father was a short mean man. If you crossed him, you were dead meat. He did not believe in second chances. He was also mean with me. My mother was much nicer than my father but just by a little bit. Both wanted me to take over the Brotherhood after they died," explained Jesse.

"Father, I am the Brotherhood. I started this group in the basement of our home," stated Jesse.

Without any warning, Conor slapped Jesse so hard he fell out of his chair and landed on the floor.

"You little crumb crusher, who do you think you are talking to me like that!" yelled Conor.

Jesse slowly got up and slipped back into his chair. He realized that the Brotherhood belonged to his parents and he was just a soldier. "James, JD, and from now on we will do as we are told or they will end up dead in a dry well," thought Jesse.

"My education ended the day I graduated from eighth grade. I loved school, but my father said he needed me to work on the farm. When he said the farm, he was actually talking about the making of moonshine. All my soldiers were working with the moonshine in some way. The security part of the business was handled by the adult soldiers. The production of moonshine had increased because the demand for corn liquor was very demanding among American consumers, mainly because of the US prohibition on alcohol," said Jesse to his son Tom.

"Tom, my father who was your grandfather came to me one day and told me that a newcomer by the name of Rocco was in town. This newcomer was interfering with his sales at his clubs. Rocco had opened up a club with a big bar and restaurant. Many of my father's longtime customers were now going over to Rocco's club. My father was not happy. While my father was in New York City on business, he went to club Harlem in order to get some fresh ideas. That is where he saw the black performer Josephine and heard Jazz for the first time. My father realized that Jazz and Josephine might be his secret weapon to put his competition out of business," explained Jesse.

"How did that work out?" asked Tom.

"It was okay at first. Customers came back and it was exciting to hear live black entertainers singing and playing the new music, jazz. The customers went crazy over the performances. Do Drop Inn was my father's best club. It was so popular that he was able to have a cover charge in order to get into the club. The club had a capacity for about two hundred customers. This club had three levels. The ground level is where my father added food, beer, and corn liquor. The middle level had a stage for the entertainers with small tables for food, beer, alcohol, and corn liquor. At this location, the basement was used for gambling and the company of fast women. Customers waited outside the front of the building until they were able to get in. As customers left, a few more were allowed in. It was the place to go on Friday night, Saturday, and Sunday." Do Drop Inn," was a hot place to be. It was hotter than the Fourth of July," stated Jesse.

"What happen to change things?" asked Tom.

"It took a few years before Noah's Ark, which was the name of Rocco's club to finally fold. That was not enough for my father. He wanted Rocco for leave his county for good. My father did not know that Rocco was part of the Italian mobsters who were trying to enter this Irish market.

"The Italians were more ruthless than my father's Brotherhood gang. They had fire power that my father had never seen before. Rocco paid my father a visit and told him that he wanted to buy him out. Rocco wanted all of my father's businesses, even his farm where he grew corn and made his famous moonshine. Rocco's taking over included complete control over the Brotherhood. Rocco insisted that he was going to be the main supplier of gin and moonshine that was sent to America," explained Jesse.

"As we sat many nights after dinner talking about the Rocco situation, my father was getting very upset and decided to do something about it," stated Jesse.

"Son, this Rocco person thinks I am just a push over but I will show him that Conor Donovan is the Brotherhood. I am the controller of all things in my county. I believe in one thing, that is, to do unto others before they do unto you," stated Conor.

"I sat straight up in my chair and leaned over to try to calm my father down, but he was in a different zone. This was a zone that I never witnessed in him before. The devil was surely taking over. As I looked at Conor, my father, I saw a different person that I had never known was sitting across the table." *Whatever he was planning was not going to end well for Rocco or my father*, thought Jesse.

"Father, what can I do to help make Rocco leave town?" asked Jesse.

"Go get your boy soldiers and bring them to me. I do have a plan, but I need some help from your little crumb crushers," explained Conor.

Jesse went and got James and together they found JD lying beside one of the stills. JD was drunk as a skunk for he was out like a light. Jesse and James knew for a long time that JD was hooked on moonshine but It never interfered with his work performance. James got a big pail of water and threw it in JD's face.

"Wake up, you big piece of shit. The Boss needs us and wants us to come now," stated James.

"Boys, I have a plan to get rid of that Italian grease meat ball but I need you do as you are told and keep it to yourself. If you tell anyone, you will surely go to jail for life!" yelled Conor.

"James, you take my best horse and deliver a message to Rocco. Tell him I have accepted his offer and to come over to my home so that we can go over the terms. James. You and JD stand at the porch door, and when he enters, hit him with the baseball bat in the head and knees. Then I will stab him over and over again until he is dead. Next we will wait until it is dark and take him back to "Noah's Ark." I will burn the building down with him in it. Everyone will think he left town because his business went belly up. Okay boys, let's go and get the job done," stated Conor.

Rocco was a gangster and he was always prepared. As Jesse approached Rocco's house, Jesse stopped short of the front step and started yelling out Rocco's name. Jesse and James were just sixteen years old but would be turning seventeen in a few months. They were very wise for their age. JD on the other hand was all muscle and big with no common sense and no brains.

"I'd like to talk to you Rocco. My father sent me. He wants to accept your offer but needs you to come over to our house to talk over the details," explained Jesse.

"Okay boy, let me get my hat and saddle up my best horse," responded Rocco.

Rocco's house was like a mansion compared to most of the houses in the county. It was a brick and wood frame house sitting on over a hundred acres. This was a real farm. It was not a farm for making moonshine. His farm had all kinds of animals, mainly horses and cattle.

"I understand you and your friend James started the Brotherhood while you were still in diapers," stated Rocco with a smile on his face.

"Yes, and my father took it away from us. We are now just workers at the farm, making corn liquor," replied Jesse.

"You sound angry and appear to be ready for some changes in your life," stated Rocco.

"I would like to do honest work and not have to look over my shoulder every moment. Especially with my father who is a lifelong criminal. My parents are a team. My mother, she is a pretty woman and loves being in the background. She is the one who comes up with how to implement my father's plans without going to jail. In other words, she is his legal advisor," responded Jesse.

"Jesse, you appear to be different than your father and I think you might have a future with me and my organization. If you ever find your way to America, look me up. I will be in New Orleans for a few years," explained Rocco.

"Thanks, I will remember your invite," stated Jesse.

As they started up the steps of Conor's porch, Jesse yelled, "Stop, Rocco!"

Rocco stopped and looked back a Jesse.

"What's going on, Jesse?" asked Rocco.

"You need to stop and come back to me. My father has two of his soldiers waiting to help take you out. He plans to kill you," explained Jesse.

"Jesse, I am not dying today or anytime soon. Your father's soldiers are in big trouble. You should go in first and tell your father that I have a gun and if I point it, I will fire it. I have a good aim and someone will die," explained Rocco.

As Jesse walked in, his father grabbed him by the collar. "What is going on you little crumb crusher and where is Rocco?" asked Conor.

"He is outside. He has a gun and plans to use it if you try any funny stuff. Father, he is not the type of person you would want to mess with. Rocco is more dangerous than any person I have ever met. He will not think twice about killing all of us. Make a deal with him and get revenge later, please father," Jesse.

"Okay, maybe you are right. I will sell him Do Drop Inn but only this one club. If he tries to take over everything, I will kill him. Go get him," explained Conor.

Conor gathered up James and JD and told them to hit Rocco as planned. Conor felt that Rocco had made a positive impression on Jesse in such a short period of time. Conor was not the type of a person to give up anything of value that he considered his. *Jesse believes Rocco is dangerous, but I put the D in dangerous*, thought Conor.

Rocco's personality taught him to be prepared for everything and trust no one. As he was approaching the steps of the porch, Rocco could smell fear in the air. The fear was the fear of others waiting to take him out.

Rocco was not concerned because he had met up with fear many times. Looking down at his belt he patted his gun like it was a special friend. Moving slowly up the steps he pulled his gun out and held it down by his side. As Jesse opened the door, JD stepped out with a baseball bat in his hand. Jesse saw JD with the bat and was surprised that his father was going with his original plan.

"No! No!" yelled Jesse as JD stepped out on the porch with the bat to subdue Rocco.

Rocco calmly raised his gun, pointed it at JD, and shot him in the head.

Jesse was yelling and crying. This was the first member of his Irish Brotherhood that died or even got hurt. He knew that his relationship with his father would never be the same. He was right. Jesse became a man in just a few minutes. He was not a little crumb crusher anymore as of this very moment.

When Conor saw what happened to JD, he raised his hands and surrendered. James ran out the back door and came around the front. James stood by Jesse's side and held him like a baby.

"James, we are survivors. You and I have lived like brothers. We are brother from different mothers. We are not only survivors but special survivors. Whatever comes our way we can handle it. Stay focused and let's do whatever Rocco wants us to do. Your father is living in the past. We are the future," explained Jesse.

Rocco got control of everything because of his gun. Conor was told what to do with JD's body. JD's body was thrown down a dry well. His parents reported him as missing. Jesse told JD's parents that he got a job on a cargo ship going to America. The search for JD came to an end, and so did the Irish Brotherhood.

"Okay, Conor, all your soldiers will now be working and answering to me. I will own the Do Drop Inn. You can keep everything else even your moonshine with one exception. I want 70 percent of all moonshine made and I need a minimum amount of gallons per week. The number of gallons you must produce will be determined later. If you don't agree to my terms, then I will just have to kill you. If that happens, then I will own everything, even your farm. Our agreement will state that if you die, I will own all your assets," stated Rocco.

"What about my wife?" asked Conor.

"Well, your wife is a good looking independent woman. I am sure she will find a man to take care of her. Maybe that man might be me," explained Rocco.

Conor was so upset he could not come up with any words to defend his wife or himself. He could only stare at this "Wop" who he hated.

"Stop talking about my wife. Let's stick to business. I will agree to all your terms," explained Conor.

Rocco reached in his pocket and pulled out a few papers. "This is an agreement of sale. I want it dated for today. I also need your wife to sign it. It appears she is on the deed," stated Rocco.

"She might not go along with it," said Conor.

"Well, if that is the case you both can go together, that is, straight to hell," explained Rocco.

Just then Vera Donovan walked in. She was surprised to see Rocco and her husband with Jesse and James. Slowly she looked across the room and saw a large puddle of blood. Without saying anything she backed away and sat down. She could smell death in the air and was hoping it was not human blood.

"Vera, that is JD's blood. He tried to kill me, so I shot him. Your husband and you are going to sign this agreement of sale. Everything is spelled out. He can fill you in with the details later. For now, I need your signature. If you do not sign it. You can go with JD, down that dry well. Do you understand?" stated Rocco.

"Yes, just give me those damn papers. You are the worst person I have ever met. I have done many bad things but to kill JD is awful. JD never did anything to anyone. If JD tried to kill you, he was just following orders. Most likely it was ordered by my husband. You should have killed my husband," stated Vera.

"Well, Miss Vera, one day I might and your suggestion may happen," explained Rocco.

CHAPTER 17

CONOR AND VERA sat in their living room, just looking at each other. Conor realized that Vera might not be the loyal wife and partner he believed her to be all these years. The statement she made to Rocco was hard for him to forget. "You should have killed my husband" was being repeated over and over in his head. Conor got up and went over to Vera and hit her with his fist. He hit her so hard that his knuckles left a dent on her face.

"You bitch, a wife is supposed to support her husband and not want him dead," stated Conor in a mean tone.

Vera sat straight up and looked at Conor from the corner of her eyes. Blood was pouring out of her nose like a pig who was knocked in the head before he was slaughtered. She carefully touched her nose and realized it was broken. As she made her way to the bathroom, Vera yelled out, "If you ever hit or touch me again, I will kill you! I have kept you out of jail and have worked to keep the Brotherhood strong. Our son is smarter than you. He is the one who came up with the idea of forming the Brotherhood. You took it away from him. Now it belongs to the Italians."

"That Wop will never control this county. This is my county and I have earned the right to be in charge. Rocco won today but I will win back everything and maybe more, the next time we meet," stated Conor firmly.

"All you know is how to talk tough. You are a little mean MF. You couldn't fight your way out of a brown paper bag. Even if your life dependent on it," shouting Vera.

"Our relationship is over. Get your shit and get out. I do not need you. I have Jesse and we will do just fine without you!" stated Conor, banging and shouting.

Vera was shocked to hear and see Conor out of control. Conor has always been very calm and calculating when he made decisions to react to any situation. As Conor's wife, Vera felt that she must get out while she only had a broken nose.

Large sums of money were hidden in several places in the house. When Vera heard Conor slamming the front door, she knew this would be the only time she could retaliate by taking all the money. With her bloody nose dripping, she gathered up the money, a few clothes, and left a note on the bed. The note stated, "BLOOD MONEY, YOU MF." Her note was covered with big drops of blood and off she went.

I'll go to Rocco's house. He is single and I was impressed over how he man handled Conor. I am upset over the killing of JD but the money helps me to get back on track and feel good about leaving Conor. JD was a young criminal and got caught trying to be a bad ass. He never learned that danger and death, the two D's, are only one step behind living. In this business, sometimes you give out the death sentence and sometime it's given to you. That is the life style of a criminal. Poor JD was not a special survivor; he was a little kid in a man's body, thought Vera.

Vera not only took all Conor's money but she took his horse, Lucky, that she believed he loved more than he loved her. Now she had the money and the horse.

The hell with Conor, thought Vera.

Rocco opened the door and Vera looked up and said, "I ran into a fist."

"You look like hell. Well, hell is forever but your bruises will go away. I have a friend who is a doctor. He takes care of my guys when they get hurt. You will feel much better in a few days. Believe me, you will feel better. What's in your big bag?" asked Rocco in a concerned voice.

"Clothes and money," responded Vera as she looked down at the bag.

"What happened to you?" asked Rocco.

"Can we talk about what happened tomorrow? It is complicated and I need a drink, a bath, and a good night's sleep," explained Vera as she closed her eyes.

The next morning, Vera was worried and restless. She did not know what Conor would do when he realized all the money was gone. Vera decided to hide the money. It was over a million dollars. She found a few lose floor boards in the hall closet. Vera stuffed the money under the floorboards, then she settled down and sipped on a cup of coffee.

"Good morning, Vera. How is your nose?" asked Rocco.

"Sore but I will live. Is your doctor coming soon?" asked Vera.

"Yes, he just pulled up in his buggy. Conor did a number on you. He was upset over what you said about him. He was embarrassed. Conor was shocked and lost for words. I think I would have felt the same way but I would not have pounded on your face," explained Rocco.

The doctor gave Rocco written instructions as to how to care for Vera. Vera was very protective over her looks and would not leave the mansion. She did not want anyone to see her. As she sat around for several weeks, doing nothing, she started having headaches. The headaches were so bad that she would cry for hours. Nothing she did help with the headaches.

Rocco called back the doctor. The doctor checked Vera for all kinds of possible causes but ruled out everything. He gave her a sedative but it did not help. The doctor recorded her physical health every other day because Rocco ordered him to come. Every time the doctor checked his notes from his last visit, her condition was getting worse.

"Vera, can you hear me asked the doctor?" asked the doctor.

Without speaking she nodded her head to imply yes.

"I'd like to go over a few things that you told me on my first visit. Okay. Conor and you were fighting and he hit you with his fist. Next, you came straight over here to Rocco's home. Rocco called me and I took care of your nose and gave you some pain medication. You got better and after a few weeks started having these headaches. Is that right?" asked the doctor.

Vera could not speak, so she nodded.

"Here is a pencil and pad for your answers. How many fingers do you see me showing you? Yes, three is the correct answer. Now I am going to stand across the room and I want you to tell me how many fingers you see?" asked the doctor.

Vera started writing her answer and without any warning, dropped the pencil. Her fingers froze up and her hands were in pain. Her mouth was twisted and her eyes had sailed up in the air. Her body was shaking all over like wild an animal trying to get out of a cage. Rocco and the doctor held her down, and in a few seconds, she stopped.

"She just had a seizure and a stroke followed. I believe she has a broken blood vessel in her brain. Headaches, stiff neck, slurred speech, seizure and lack of mobility in hands and limbs are signs of my diagnosis. If I am right, she only has about twenty-four hours to live. Maybe you should contact her son," said the doctor in a sorrowful tone.

Rocco ordered one of his ranch hands to go get Jesse. When Jesse got to Rocco's ranch he was surprised to see his mother sick, in bed and at Rocco's house. Jesse was told by his father, his mother left the two of them for another man. One look at his mother, Jesse knew the condition of her face was caused by his father. What he did not know was she only had less than twenty-four hours to live.

Jesse leaned down and kissed his mother on the forehead and told her he loved her. She smiled and asked him to come closer. Rocco left the room so that they could have a moment together.

It was hard for her to talk but she took a deep breath and was able give him a message. "Jesse, in the hall closet, under the floor board is a bag of money. It is your heritage. It belongs to you. Do not tell you father. He did this to me and will take the money for himself. Your father is a gambler and he would have lost it all playing cards, years ago. He does not know exactly how much I saved over the last twenty-plus years but I do. Take and use it for your future family and to help others," said Vera in a soft fading voice.

Jesse kissed her again and Vera closed her eyes and smiled. Jesse sat by her side holding her hand as she appeared to have fallen asleep. Vera opened her eyes and said, "Jesse this is going to be very hurtful but I must tell you. I am not your mother.

Conor is your father and your mother died at child birth. Conor got your mother pregnant but I did not know about the two of them. I found out the day she died. I took you in my arms and loved every moment. "I am your Mama. I love you, son. James and you were born on the same day but it was only by chance that I met his parents. They lived in our neighborhood. We became friends and decided on the names for the babies. I am not your mother, but I am your Mama," explained Vera as she drifted away.

Vera closed her eyes again. Jesse called out, "Mama, Mama!" She did not respond and Jesse realized that his mother was not asleep but had slipped away to be with God. She looked pain free and peaceful.

Yelling and crying Jesse called Rocco. "She's gone. My Mama is gone. It's all my father's fault. I hate him. He is a little piece of shit. First he took away my friend JD and now Mama!" yelled Jesse.

"Jesse, the first time I saw your mother, she was working at the "Do Drop Inn." She was a real lady and the customers loved her. I fell in love with her that day. She was married and I did not want her to know how I felt. Your mother knew how I felt because the meeting of our eyes told the whole story. Love at first sight," explained Rocco.

CHAPTER 18

"ROCCO, MY MAMA had my back in everything I did in and out of school. I often remember her setting my teacher straight when she threw my coat in the trash. The Brotherhood was started because of her. On several occasions, I would come home with cuts and bruises all over my body. My mother did not like that. She told me if it happened again she would give me a second beating. I told James and we got a few kids together in my basement and formed the Brotherhood," explained Jesse in a tell-all voice.

"What do you want to do? I will help with any arrangements. How do you plan to tell your father? If you want, I will tell him. Are there any other relatives that should be notified?" asked Rocco.

"Rocco, I need to tell you something. Forget it, I will tell you later," stated Jesse, with tears dripping down his face.

"I have a step-brother who lives in France. His name is Jerry Basset. It would be helpful if you could send him a telegram. In the telegram just tell his mother passed suddenly from a rare disease. He might come to her funeral, who knows," explained Jesse.

"We need an obituary," explained Rocco.

"What's in an obituary?" asked Jesse.

"The person's full name, parents, place of birth, date died, occupation, and children's names," explained Rocco with sorrow in his voice. "Well, ask Jerry those questions since he was born in France and has a mother and father. I only have a mama and piece of shit father," responded Jesse.

"I don't understand where all this anger is coming from. You need to get over it and get on with your life," responded Rocco.

"What information do I need from Jerry for Mama's obituary?" asked Jesse.

"Your Mama's full name, place of birth, and parents is all we need from Jerry," stated Rocco.

"Let's keep occupation out of the obituary," stated Jesse.

"No, include her occupation, even if she was a criminal. She was management. Just say, Vera worked many years as a dedicated manager of several restaurants mainly the Do Drop Inn," responded Rocco.

"You're right, I will move on but will never forget what he did to my mama," stated Jesse in an angry low tone.

"I will tell your father about Vera, but you will have to go home and face him with all the facts. By the way, Vera came with a large bag. I asked her what was in the bag. She stated, clothes and money. Everything in the bag belongs to you. She did not say how much money was in the bag but it should be enough to help you to be independent of your father. Do not tell him about the money. Conor would want it all," stated Rocco.

As Rocco was about to knock on Conor's door, Conor opened the door with his shot gun. "Oh, It's you, the town Wop. What do you want?" asked Conor.

"You are drunk! I have some bad news for you. Vera died from complications caused by the pounding you gave her. She died yester-day and your son is upset. So upset, he would like to kill you. When he comes home you should be scared. Her dying is not just about you; it is also about him. Give your relationship a fresh start. If you don't, I will step in and be your replacement," explained Rocco with a determined tone.

Jesse returned home late that evening after his father's set cur-few. His curfew was 11:00 p.m. Conor did not say anything because he felt it was the wrong time. Jesse was relieved by his father's silence.

At Vera's funeral, many people went up to the podium to speak highly about Vera. Jesse felt this was the right time to let the family and friends know that Vera was not his mother but his mama.

"I want to thank all of you for coming out to my mama's homecoming. Just a few minutes before she died, she gathered up enough air to tell me that she loves me and wanted me to know the truth. She felt that knowing the truth would definitely guide my future. She told me she was not my mother but my mama. My biological mother died in the hospital giving birth. My father is my father. He was left with the responsibility of taking care of this baby.

"Vera, my mama took me in her arms and raised me as if she had given birth. She loved me and I loved her. I don't know where I am going in life but I know where I've been. It's been a good life living in this county. But there will come a time when I will have to move on. Therefore, thanks for being in my life and thanks for coming," explained Jesse with sorrow in his voice.

Rocco was feeling down and depressed decided to let his lieutenant run all the businesses. That included, the moonshine, bars, gambling, gentleman clubs, and store security which were in full swing in the county. The only place he felt at peace was in his mansion where Vera died. After a few months of just getting by Rocco decided to go to America and take the Brotherhood with him. Rocco was not sure where he wanted to go, so he hung up a map and threw a dart at the map. He decided that where it stuck is where he would go. The dart landed smack in New Orleans. That was a great throw. *New Orleans, the Brotherhood, and me will never be the same*, thought Rocco.

Rocco could not leave until he got everything set-up for his lieutenants and to inform James that he would be running the organization. Rocco trusted James and felt he was the right person to leave in charge. James was always in the shadow of Jesse. He was never given a chance to show off what he could do. James had more energy than Jesse and was willing to take more chances. He was also brighter and better looking.

Jesse needed to get his mother's things. Especially the money she left for him. How would he get the money without Rocco knowing was a problem for Jesse? Jesse felt that he should tell James about the money and he would be happy for him. James was very good at coming up with creative plans.

"Okay, this is what we can do. First I am glad for you. Your mama saved for years and never took any vacations. She was looking out for you. Deep down in her heart she felt that things would change one day and she wanted to be prepared. She gave it to you so you keep it," stated James with an understanding tone.

"She did say to share the money with others to help them," responded Jesse.

"Let's get the money then we can decide how to spend or give it away," stated James.

"Do you have a plan?" asked Jesse.

"Yes, I'll throw it in the crawl space. It will depend on where the crawl space in the house is located. I will need you to ask the housekeeper about the crawl space and what area of the house does the crawl space cover. I hope the crawl space is at least in the hall closet area," stated Jesse.

"There's a good possibility that the bag of money will end up in the crawl space. If so, then we are well on our way in getting it," stated James.

That afternoon, Jesse went over to see Rocco hoping he was able to talk to the housekeeper. He got to Rocco's house around lunch time expecting lunch to be served. He was right. Lunch was about ready to be served. Rocco invited Jesse to stay for lunch.

As they were eating, one of the ranch hands came in and told Rocco there was an emergency in the stable. His favorite prize horse was sick. Rocco left the table and went directly to the stable.

"You are a good cook. I bet you have been cooking for many years. Have you been the housekeeper from the time Rocco arrived in this county?" asked Jesse.

"I am a leftover from the last owner who died. I have been employed in this house since I was 18 years old. Before me, my mother worked for the owner until she died. The owner asked me to take over and I did just that," stated Mary, the housekeeper with a proud look on her face.

"So you know all about this house? Does this house have a basement? If not, does it have a crawl space?" asked Jesse.

"Yes, I know all about this house. I have cooked and cleaned it for many years. It doesn't have a basement but it has a crawl space under the whole house," responded Mary in a voice of authority.

"You are a good cook. Thanks for the conversation. I must go and help Rocco," stated Jesse.

Phase one now completed, James can work on the next part of the plan to get the money. On his way to the stable, Jesse started thinking about his father. I need to leave town. I need to get away from my father. With this money, I can choose a different lifestyle. A life that is honest. Maybe I can become something in law enforcement since I understand the minds of criminals. I would have to start at the bottom and work my way up. Starting at the bottom sounds like a good place to start. I will ask Rocco if he has any honest friends in law enforcement, thought Jesse.

As Jesse was about to enter the stable, Conor came charging up on his horse. He looked like the devil but worse. "Where's my money? Does Rocco have it? I know your mother told you where it is!" shouted. Conor, with fire coming out of his mouth.

"Money! Money! What money are you talking about?" responded Jesse like a little schoolboy.

"When your mother left, she took all our savings. On the bed was a note. She came straight here. If Rocco has it, I know I will have to kill him in order to get the money!" shouted Conor in an angry tone.

"Money is all you are about. You killed Butch, Mama, and now you are talking about killing Rocco. Wishful thinking because you killing Rocco will never happen. He is too smart for you. If anyone is going to die it will be you," responded Jesse.

"Yes, Rocco has the money. He said it belongs to me. Mama told him to give it to me. It is my inheritance. Mama earned it and I am keeping it. If you want it, you will have to take it from Rocco. He is in charge of the money," stated Jesse with a sassy look on his face.

Conor got back on Lucky, his horse, stuck up his middle finger at Jesse, and rode off. Jesse went into the stable. "I'm here to help. What can I do?" asked Jesse with a look of relief on his face.

That evening, James and Jesse decided to hang out at the Do Drop Inn and drink moonshine. They felt like men, real men for the first time in their lives. The music was the best that the two of them had ever heard. It was Jazz with a pretty singer. She was white but she could sing. James wanted to meet her. "You better step right up before someone else," responded Jesse in a joking voice.

James was leaning on the bar and a soft touching hand tapped him on his shoulder. It was the singer, looking like an angel who had just descending down from heaven. "I saw you staring at me, I am here so you can get a good look. I hope seeing me close up is as good as far away. By the way my name is Zoe," stated the singer with a big smile on her face.

Zoe's hair was jet black. Her lips were a perfect shape with red lip stick. Her skin was a creamy light beige. Her sky blue eyes were the finishing touch that made her the prettiest gal in the county, thought James.

"Still staring at me, I see. Say something, like hello gorgeous," stated Zoe with a big smile on her face.

"I'll say it. Hello gorgeous!" responded Jesse.

"Thanks, but it is his turn," responded Zoe.

James guzzled down the rest of his moonshine and grabbed Zoe and kissed her on her ruby red lips and yelled out, "Hello, gorgeous!"

Just then Rocco walked in and was surprised to see Jesse and James.

He shouted out to the crowd, "Look here, Jesse/James are my outlaws. They were not born in the West but right here in your county. All drinks on the house. Let's party!"

Jesse returned home after curfew and realized that he was not going to get away with coming home late. In the middle of his street were his clothes. His father threw his clothes in the street. As Jesse picked them up, he dropped his clothes. They were all cut to shreds. Jesse understood that it was time for him to leave.

Jesse headed to Rocco's house. He needed to get the money, now.

Therefore, he found the outside door to the crawl space and crawled in. Once in, he saw the bag with the money hanging from the ceiling boards. He pulled on the bag and was able to shake it loose. As he was crawling out he noticed there were many wooden boxes. All but one box was not locked. Jesse opened a box and it was full of guns. Jesse took one of the guns, it was a Smith & Wesson Model 19.

Rocco will never miss this gun. If he does he will think one of his worker's took the gun. I have the money and the gun. Both will take care of me now and in the future. I will go to James's house and stay a few days until I figure out my next move. Maybe James can help me to move on, thought Jesse.

Jesse showed James the gun and the money. James did not want any of it. He only wanted his buddy to be happy and safe. Jesse made James take part of the money.

"You are in love and if it all works out, Zoe and you will get married and start a family. This money will be my gift to the both of you. I will be leaving for America tonight on a cargo ship carrying supplies, gin, and moonshine to America. Hopefully, you will join me one day and we will live a long happy life with our families," stated Jesse as the two friends hugged each other as if it was goodbye forever.

Zoe was only working in Ireland for a few weeks but James convinced her to stay and perform at the Do Drop Inn. Rocco was glad to have a regular performer even through Zoe was only working Thursday, Friday, Saturday, and Sunday. The customers loved her singing and she enjoyed performing.

James never heard from Jesse but he married Zoe. Within a years' time, they had started their family. James was blessed with a baby boy. He had dark hair and a red face.

"Let's name him Redd, Redd Harrison!" shouted James in high-pitch voice.

"Okay, it sounds like a name for a leader. I feel that we should try to get him to America one day. America is the land of opportunity. As Irishmen, we need to live where we are rewarded for our hard work. If you love the name Redd, then I love it also!" stated Zoe in a supportive tone.

CHAPTER 19

A
S A BABY, Redd's father was very proud of his son. James would take him over to Conor's farm and explain to Redd all that was going on. The smell of moonshine was embedded in his blood. When he started walking, he would pick the corn. Some of it he would try to eat or throw in the basket of picked corn.

Conor never forgot the situation with Rocco, Vera, and Jesse. It was consuming all his thoughts day and night. As time when on, he decided to go over to Rocco's and find out about his money. He made sure that he consumed plenty of moonshine. The moonshine would give him courage to stand up to this "Dago." It had been four plus years since Vera died and Jesse left for America.

Conor had lived up to his contract with Rocco. He did everything his contract required of him. Everything was going okay for Rocco but not for Conor. Conor was trying to wait for the right time and place to take Rocco out. One night Conor over did it with moonshine and got up enough courage to pay Rocco a visit.

"Where is my money! Where is my money!" said Conor, shouting and yelling like a crazy man at Rocco.

"What money?" asked Rocco.

"The money your bitch took the night she left," explained Conor as he stumbled on to the porch.

"I never saw the money but I knew about it. I didn't know how much was in the bag. Jesse took it with him to America. His mama wanted him to have it. It was his inheritance. Sorry, Conor, get over it," stated Rocco in a stern tone.

The next day, Rocco went to the sheriff's office and ordered him to lock Conor up for making moonshine, for distributing it in our county, and for overseas sales in America. The sheriff was on Rocco's payroll. The sheriff took one look at Rocco and asked, "Are you sure about this?"

"Yes, because he is about to start trouble for all of us," explained Rocco.

The next day, Conor returned to Rocco's house and ordered him to come outside like a man. Conor was still drunk. He pulled out his gun and fired over and over again but missed Rocco.

"The next time you draw a gun on me, make sure you hit your target. If you don't, I won't miss," stated Rocco.

The next day, the sheriff and his officers showed up at Conor's farm.

"We are here to break up your stills and to take you in. You are accused of making moonshine for distribution here and to sell in America. Come with us. Make it easy on yourself," stated the sheriff.

"I have lived here all my life. You know me. Can you cut me a break and come back tomorrow morning? I need time to get myself together and call Rocco," said Conor.

"Rocco is the one who told us to lock you up," responded the sheriff.

"That Wop!" responded Conor.

"Okay, tomorrow it is," responded the sheriff in a low voice.

That night Conor was ready to get his revenge. After Vera died, Rocco gave Conor his favorite horse "Lucky "back. Lucky was a special animal. He could smell Conor's body odor long before he came into the stable. As Conor walked into the stable, Lucky was waiting for him. Head up, shoulders back, and eyes were wide open just like a soldier ready to go into battle.

Conor ran his hand through Lucky's long silky mane and hugged him around his neck. I have nothing to live for and nothing to lose. Tonight, if I come out on top, I will regain my respect, my county, and all assets. I know that is a lot to regain in one night but it's time for me to get back what I lost a few years ago.

Conor sat down next to Lucky and filled ten bottles with moonshine. He was making Molotov cocktail bottles and filled the bottles with his best moonshine.

My bottles will light up his so called mansion. This is the strongest and best moonshine in the county. Over 100 proof and will burn a hole in your stomach if you try to drink it straight. Tonight Rocco will die and I will burn down his farm and claim everything belongs to me, thought Conor.

After filling the bottles, Conor decided to have a drink of his moonshine to celebrate his new beginning. Within a short period of time, Conor fell asleep. In the stable was a lantern that was lit. Conor rolled over and knocked the lantern over and the stable went up in flames. Lucky managed to get loose and drag Conor out by his shirt. The smoke had overcome Conor and he died.

The merchant ship that Jesse was working on, was scheduled to return in a few weeks. When the ship came in, James was waiting at the dock for Jesse. All the crew exited the ship. James did not see Jesse. The captain was approaching James, James stopped the captain. "Were is Jesse Harrison?" asked James.

"He quit," responded the captain.

"Quit!" shouted James.

"He only worked one way to America. His Mama dying did a number on him. I talked to him and gave him some fatherly advice. He listened and made a decision to move on. I was told, he was working in security, somewhere in New Orleans. That's all I know," explained the captain.

Rocco was at his club when he got the news that his farm was on fire. *I hope that little piece of shit Conor, didn't do anything stupid. This was the first time in months that I was totally relaxed. Now this, what's next?* thought Rocco.

The smell of dead animals and burning wood filled the air. Smoke was hanging around, low to the ground to let the bystanders know that the farm had come to an end. The smell of death was stronger than anything Rocco had ever inhaled. It was the smell of his horses who were defenseless against a fire that should have never happened.

Lucky was standing over Conor's dead body. He was making sounds that were sounds of sorrow. It was sad to see a horse acting like a close friend or relative grieving over the passing of a loved one. Lucky was not just a horse he was Conor's best friend.

Rocco stood beside Lucky and started talking to him as if he was human.

"Lucky, I know Conor saw you born but everyone has a beginning and an ending. Your day and my day will come but today belongs to Conor. He was a man whose life was full of danger. He was a man who was in love with fear. Having people fear him made him feel six feet tall. But we know he was short," explained Rocco to Lucky as both stood together.

Tonight is the end of the Donovan's bloodline in this county. The Donovan's, controlled everything for many years. The Brotherhood, was started by Jesse Donovan and James Harrison. Poor JD was the first to die because of Conor. Vera Donovan died with injuries caused by her husband. Jesse left with his inheritance for America to start a new life. Conor was a mean MF who had a big black heart. He died trying to get revenge. But revenge conquered him at the end. So I say good bye to the Donovan's whose son is special. It is my opinion, Jesse will be a special survivor, thought Rocco, as he hugged Lucky and took him home with him.

"Well, what a story," said Allie.

"I have just gotten started. Now you know how the Smith & Wesson Model 19 and my grandparent's obituary got in the boxes. My father saved them as reminders of the life he left behind," stated Tom.

"Look at this obituary. It is Rocco's. Do you know more about him?"

"My father shared many stories about Rocco and other gangsters with me. He kept the history of the gangs in his head. He knew just how each gangster lived and died. My father went to Louisiana when he was very young and James stayed in Ireland with his family. According to my father, James was the major supplier of corn liquor and Bourbon for organized crime bosses in Louisiana," explained Tom.

"How old was James Harrison when he came to America?" asked Allie.

"I'm not sure but he was married with his one son, Redd," explained Tom.

You said that James supplied moonshine and bourbon for the Louisiana crime bosses. He must have had an extensive organization in order to produce large amounts of liquor," responded Allie.

"James was a mastermind. He was a notorious gangster with an organization that was into everything. With Rocco still part of the organization, James's gang, eventually fell into the hands of the Italian Mafia. The Italian Mafia's headquarters was in New Orleans which was organized and controlled by Rocco, explained Tom.

"What was Rocco's full name?" asked Allie.

"His full name was Rocco Muscurelo but was known as the "Magus." He got this nickname because he could disappear and re-appear with ease. He was a member of a hereditary class of career criminals. Rocco gave rise to the Brotherhood in New Orleans," stated Tom, sounding like a historian.

"James was second in control in the county under Rocco. Other than moonshine, did he keep up with the other money making services at the clubs?" asked Allie.

"He not only maintained the other businesses but started his own club, which included gangs that reported directly to James. Each gang was allowed to defend their turf. Besides moonshine, the Brotherhood was now into narcotics, robbery, illegal gambling, prostitution, loan sharking, and political intimidation. This was James's secret dream, to make it big as a gangster.

My father would keep me up all night on the weekends. He would drink his moonshine and tell stories about his friend James and how proud he was of him. A small town country boy who made it big in the gangster world. Now I will share James story with you," explained Tom.

James looked around at his favorite club, the Do Drop Inn, and could not believe all of it was under his control. I have come a long way. The little school boy who help form the Brotherhood. It was created to protect Jesse and me from other bigger and stronger kids in the neighborhood. I needed something that was started by me, owned by me and run by me. Everything that my father started and Rocco is not my dreams. It was their dreams. I need my own dreams. "I got it!" shouted James. *I will start a country club on my farm that will serve Rum, Bourbon, and Moonshine. I could not have a successful business without moonshine*, thought James.

"James wife's name was Barbara but her nickname was Zoe. Zoe was very petite and very cute. She was only about 4'11". She had earned a reputation that followed her. The word was out, don't lie or cross Zoe, for she will surely kill you," explained Tom.

It was Zoe's birthday and James and his friends planned a surprise birthday party for Zoe. Zoe went out of the county on a shopping spree for her birthday with a couple of her girlfriends. The party went as planned. Zoe was totally surprised. The food was the best that money could buy. Anything a guest wanted James had at the party. A Jazz band from Louisiana known as "Big Dad's" (Browns Reliance Brass Band), which was the most well-known band among white ragtime bands.

This was also opening night for James's new country club called Lawnside Country Club. It was called Lawnside Country Club because all the barbecue ribs and chicken was cooked outside on the lawn. In fact, everything was done on a beautiful lawn. A stage was constructed for the entertainers with a liquor bar as you entered the gate. The guest list was made up of law makers, customers, family, and friends.

As the band played on, James got drunk and Zoe was even drunker. Zoe had given James a few warmings in the past about flirting with women. That night James forgot and grabbed a pretty young thing and stated "you look like an angel that just came down from heaven. What is your name sweetie"? asked James in a voice that was trying to act like a player.

"I heard that, you Irish MF. See how sweet this feels," said Zoe as she knocked him in the head with his best bottle of rum.

Everyone was stung. But the band played on. Big Daddy sang out "Don't mess with Zoe, no! No! No! Don't mess with Zoe, no! No! No! The band played on, and everyone started dancing. Then the band smoothly when into playing Happy Birthday to Zoe. Everyone was singing and happy. Zoe yelled out, "James might be a piece of shit tonight but I love him." And the band played on.

The next day, Zoe and James did not remember exactly what had happened and no one ever talked about it. People knew not to mess with Zoe. Zoe felt that her birthday was a big success but did not understand why James had a big lump on his head and a black eye. Sue the housekeeper was cleaning up from the party, so Zoe decided to ask her about her husband's lump on his head.

"Sue, what happened to James head?" asked Zoe.

"That lump is from the bottle of rum you used to knock him out. I know now not to mess with you. You are in a small package but you can land a big blow. Girl you are dynamite. Like the band said, "Don't mess with Zoe, no! No! No!" said Sue as walked away laughing so hard she almost passed out.

"Zoe, do you know how I got this big ass lump on my head and black eye?" asked James in tone that was looking for answers.

"No, James, maybe you walked into a door," responded Zoe in a joking manner.

CHAPTER 20

"ZOE I WILL be gone for a few days starting tomorrow. So, whatever you want me to do, it needs to get done today. I will be traveling throughout the county paying off workers, gamblers, and the law. I plan to give everyone a jar of my best moonshine. My best has the XXX. All my moonshine has a reputation of being the best. XXX tells the buyer that it has been triple-distilled. Some of the bootleggers use dangerous ways to make hooch.

"I make my liquor out of fresh grown corn. Some of those MF use barley, rye, and even fruit. I have used hog feed at some point if I didn't have enough corn to meet the demand for my moonshine and bourbon. These unscrupulous MF moonshiners need to be stopped. These dangerous bizarre ingredients (manure and sweet mash drawings from insects and rodents) that they are using can hurt the moonshine business. One of my soldiers got real sick off moonshine that his uncle gave him.

"My soldier later learned where it came from. He told me who it was. Tomorrow I will pay him a visit. All moonshine for sale in this county is made by my organization. He will be stopped.

"The heavy whiskey excise tax in America which is hated by the people has made our moonshine very popular. The third X on the bottle let's our customers know it is guaranteed and the jug contained some serious stuff," stated James in a serious tone.

"James, before you do pay this moonshiner a visit, I have something to tell you. It might help now and in the future. I was introduced a few years ago to Jake Hutch, he is a farmer who is a botanist. He was at my birthday party. He told me that he had finally discovered how to grow corn under any conditions. His new strain of corn is pest resistant. It is also fast growing. His uncle who is a gangster in Louisiana wants to hook up with your organization to grow and use this corn. Demand is off the charts in America for good moonshine and bourbon," explained Zoe.

"If what you are telling me is true, then I need to pay Sammy Coonan at visit.

"I plan to offer him a deal he and his gang can't refuse. His gang is the Irish Hill Gang. They have been cutting into our profits for many years with bad and dangerous moonshine. Conor just let them off the hook. I do not plan to let them destroy the moonshine business by making bad moonshine," said James with determination in his voice.

"What is your plan?" asked Zoe.

"I have a plan, that is all you need to know," explained James in a dangerous tone.

That afternoon, James went to see Sammy Coonan, the leader of the Irish Hill Gang. His plan was to extend his hand to Sammy and bring him into the Brotherhood. Sammy was an old man who was set in his ways but he had a son who was always looking to be part of the future. His son Mickey was ruthless and would do anything if it involved making big money. James had his posse hiding in the brushes in case he ran into trouble.

As James approached the porch. Mickey pointed a gun at his head and stated, "Stop! Why are you here, you piece of shit?" asked Mickey.

"I came to tell you to stop making that bad moonshine. It is making our customers sick and in some cases it has killed a few. So stop making it. I have a farmer who has developed a strain of corn that will grow in any condition and is bug resistant. It also grows quickly. I want to make you part of the Brotherhood. We have expanded into New Orleans and plan to go to New York City. If you are interested, I will get the corn and we can start growing corn right away on your farm. Therefore, you will not have to use animal manure which makes poor moonshine. I will give you a return of 25 percent of everything we sell here and in America. I will pay for the corn that you plant. It will be delivered every three months, are you in?" asked James who sounded like the boss.

"Yes, but my father will not like doing business with you. He is old and has no outlook for the future of our business. He only lives for today. He is the reason we sell bad moonshine. He has often stated, "Let them drink the shit, who gives a damn," said Mickey in a gangster tone.

"Well, I will leave it up to you to handle you father," stated James.

"I will handle him. Just wait here," said Mickey.

Mickey went into the house and saw his father in a drunken sleep. He took his gun and pointed it at the front of his father's head and pulled the trigger. Blood went everywhere. His mother entered the room to see what was going on. Without blinking an eye, she said, "may he go straight to hell. Hell is waiting for him." She turned around and went back into to the kitchen. That night she cooked a dinner that was fit for a king.

"I took care of my father, James, we are all in. I need your help with something," stated Mickey.

"Not a problem, what is it you need help with?" asked James.

"Help me throw my father down that dry well. No one will miss him. Everyone hated him. That includes Mama and me," stated Mickey with no sorrow in his voice.

James went back home and got a big glass of moonshine with lemonade. That was his favorite way of drinking his own brew. He could not believe Mickey killed his father.

Mickey is a very intimidating person. He will make an outstanding soldier if he can be controlled and if no one kills him first, thought James.

"Why are you drinking so early in the day, James?" asked Zoe.

"I saw a man get killed by his own son. I even helped the son get rid of the body. No one needs to die like that. Even if he is a piece of shit," explained James in an angry tone.

"What is the status of the Irish Hill Gang? That gang and the Brotherhood have never gotten along. They go back long before Rocco came to our county. Conor on several occasions tried to eliminate that gang but they somehow kept bouncing back. Just like weeds in your garden. Rocco would kill a few soldiers and think he had them on the run. Before the bodies were cold, the Irish Hill Gang pop back up. Stronger than ever," explained Zoe sounding very discouraged.

"Mickey has agreed to grow corn on his farm for the Brotherhood. He will be using the new corn seeds that you told me about. I have to talk to Jake Hutch. Why does that name sounds like someone I should know?" asked James.

"His father was the famous gangster, Sammy, Irish Red Neck Sam, in Louisiana who stole several thousand dollars' worth of liquor. He was the hijacker of hijackers until he was killed by Jim Mendini," explained Zoe.

"How do you know so much about the Hutch family?" asked James.

"He was my mother's first cousin. I come from several generation of criminals. That is why I was able to fit right into your family. I am not a criminal but it is hard sometimes to stay straight. I feel that I am a survivor of many generations of criminals. It is in my genes. That is my defense. I am a survivor, a special survivor," explained Zoe.

"Why don't you come and go with me to talk to the Hutches. They are your family. Is that why they approached you at the party, instead of coming directly to me?" asked James.

"They are family but I do not really know them. After my father and mother passed away, I lost touch with that side of the family. I will go with you. They are nice and smart people from what my mother told me," explained Zoe.

"Hello, Zoe, and this is your wonderful, good looking husband, I presume," stated Jake.

"Yes, this is James Harrison. I told him about the corn and he would like to see the corn and have you to grow the corn on your farm and our farm," explained Zoe.

"Welcome, James. I believe I have the answer to your supply problem. This corn is not good for human consumption but makes a great tasting corn liquor and bourbon. I have been working on this strain for several years. I have planted one acre at a time and discovered that the turnover time for this corn is every thirty days. Every part of the corn can be used. Based on what part of the corn is used, will determine the quality of the liquor. I made some moonshine and bourbon for you to taste. Let's go inside and have a drink," stated Jake sounding like a gracious host.

"The last time I saw you Jake, was at my mother's funeral. My mother talked about her educated cousin. She said you worked hard and put yourself through school. She was very proud of you and your family," explained Zoe.

"We are educated but education alone does not put money in your pocket, food on your table, a roof over your head, or clothes on your back. I found out that everyone needs a hustle. My hustle is growing corn for liquor. My uncle in New Orleans needs moonshine and bourbon. He said the Brotherhood, with my corn would be able to make large quantities of liquor. It is my understanding that you have an organization that grows corn, turns it into liquor, distributes throughout the county and to New Orleans docks.

When the liquor gets to the New Orleans docks, my uncle's soldiers are there to get your shipped liquor. Shipments of liquor are coming in slowly because of a shortage of corn. With my corn, the supply chain will be consistent and reliable," explained Jake with his head held high as if he was talking to his team of workers.

"What is your uncle's name?" asked James.

"His street name is The Czar, but Rocco Muscurelo is his name," responded Jake.

"Wow, that is my boss. Now I understand why he told you to hook up with the Brotherhood," responded James as he shook his head slightly up and down.

"Zoe, did you know that Rocco was related to you?" asked James.

"No, Rocco is not in my mother's bloodline, stated Zoe.

"So he comes from the other side of your family, your father," responded James with amazement.

"James, you see why I am all messed up. Both sides of my family come with layers of several generations of criminals. That is why I did not have a problem hitting James over the head with that bottle of bourbon. It was in my blood. I didn't think before hitting him. I just did it," explained Zoe with a schoolgirl smile on her face.

"That's how I got this big lump on my head and this black eye. It came from you, bitch. The next time you hit me with anything, you better kill me. You survived this round but next time you will not be so lucky. Don't you ever embarrass me in front of anyone again!" stated James in a tone that would have scared the devil.

"Okay, you two love birds, let's get back to business," stated Jake.

"Did The Czar work out any details with you?" asked James.

"The Czar said that you know the business and your business associates think very highly of you. Therefore, you are in charge of all the decisions and everything that goes with the liquor-making business," explained Jake.

"Moonshine is very easy to make but the bourbon takes a little longer. What I need is a plan for growing the corn, making the liquor, shipping the liquor to America, and selling it in my clubs and bars. It is also sold throughout the county. I will work out a plan and a time table with Zoe. She is good at planning, along with hitting me in the head," stated James with a grin on his face from ear to ear.

CHAPTER 21

"WHEN ROCCO WENT to New Orleans, his number one goal was to bring all the little gangs together under one leader. He settled in New Orleans with his best well-trained soldiers from the Brotherhood. He got his street name as the Czar because he was able to bring his Mafia experience to the city. The Brotherhood, which is the Mafia, became the dominant criminal organization in New Orleans. I work for Rocco. He inherited the businesses from his family. The family established a monopoly in illegal gambling, narcotics, rum business, bourbon, moonshine, speakeasies, and gentlemen's clubs. Now Rocco is the absolute ruler of the underworld in New Orleans," explained Jake.

"Does he have control over the New Orleans Police Department?" asked James.

"Yes, the Louisiana's governor is involved with Rocco's Mafia. The governor is the main reason; Rocco's Brotherhood became the dominant criminal organization in New Orleans. Muscurelo family with Rocco at the helm makes him the head man in charge of the underworld of New Orleans," explained Jake.

"We will have a plan for operating here in our county as soon as possible. I believe it should be somewhat like what Rocco is doing in New Orleans. If we operate on the same premise as the Czar, then most of our operating plans can be up and running very soon. We do have a few small gangs in this county that will have to be dealt with but it will not be an issue. The only thing that I would like to add is rooming houses and loan sharking. These two things will add value to our organization," explained Zoe.

"The two of us will start getting the gangs under control. The Brotherhood will control everything in this county. We will be establishing ourselves as the dominant criminal organization in this county. We won't take no for answer from the smaller gangs. I will put out the word that all gangs are to meet at my farm on Saturday, that is two days from now. If they do not show up. Then they will be eliminated," stated James in a determined tone.

Zoe suggested that we should have a big party to show off our wealth and strength. She wanted it to be better than her birthday party. It was to be held at the Lawnside Country Club. Most of the gangs owned small bars. Zoe wanted them to experience for themselves, the opportunities that would open up for them under their leadership.

Jazz was new for everyone in Ireland but the Brotherhood would be the first to establish it as the main focus of entertainment in county. Because the county was located on a thriving major sea port that was controlled by the Brotherhood, this county was on target to be first entertainment center for "ratty" music—that is, bands that improvised jazz.

The MacBride family were the only gang that did not come to the party/meeting. James was upset because the MacBride family controlled large amounts of narcotics. James wanted the MacBride family narcotic ring to bring its territories under him.

Harry MacBride, had complete control of his family of gangsters. He ordered no one was to go to the party. At the party, Zoe served all types of hors d'oeuvres which she had seen in the cooking section of the paper. The jazz band was made up of the best creole band from New Orleans. The women and men were dressed to impress. A dance floor was constructed and the guest were enjoying the music but no one was dancing. Zoe got up and yelled out, "You might be old but you are not cold, so get up and let's kick it out."

Within seconds, the dance floor was packed. Everyone was having a good time. The music sent everyone crazy. The barbecue ribs, chicken, ham, sweet potatoes, greens, potato salad was cooked by a creole cook and staff. The food was delicious.

"Okay, it time to start getting down to business. This meeting is now called to order. The fact that you are here tells me you want to come in with the Brotherhood. Many of you don't even know how the Brotherhood got started. Let me give you a brief history of the Brotherhood."

"It was started by Jesse Donovan and James Harrison in the basement of Jesse's family's house. These two kids had a vision. That was to protect themselves and at the same time make money. They were having trouble with kids in the neighborhood and recruited other kids as soldiers to form a gang to protect each other.

"Jesse's parents who crossed over a few years ago, found out about the brotherhood and took over. They not only took over but kept the name of the gang, the Brotherhood. I am the Brotherhood here in this county. With all of you joining me, we can take out business to the next level.

"The next level will establish us as a criminal monopoly which will include illegal gambling, narcotics, rum business, bourbon, moonshine, speakeasies, gentlemen's clubs, and a bank for lending money to customers. All of us will make plenty of money. I will not accept any one in this county doing business on their own. If you are not with us, then you are against us. With a large organization we can branch out into other counties. Once we branch out, we will be able to control all of Ireland. Maybe we will be able to change the name from Ireland to the Brotherhood," stated James in a commanding tone.

"James, can I speak to you in private?" said a man that James did not know.

"Okay, but make it quick. I have to shore-up my support for expanding my organization. My wife is working the crowd for commitments in writing. She also has a map of all the gang's territories. Everyone will pledge their support and loyalty. A loyal soldier is always ready to die for the organization and will never be a snitch," stated James.

"My name is Eddie Acosta. I am an Italian gangster from Chicago. I left Chicago because my boss was going to jail for a long time, maybe for life. They got him for violation of the Volstead Act. I am not a snitch. So, I left town before the Feds caught up with me. I ended up here and working for Harry MacBride. The MacBride family is small time. They would not last one day in Chicago. The MacBride family is making plans to take you out. I know that you were trained by the "Czar" who is the biggest boss in New Orleans. I want to join your organization. With a few soldiers, I can get rid of your problem," explained Eddie in a gangster tone of voice.

"How does MacBride plan to kill me?" asked James.

"I do not know but he plans to do it," responded Eddie.

"Well, if you want to join me, then take out MacBride and bring me his head. That will let me know you are an enforcer," responded James.

"It will take some planning because his soldiers, most of them are his sons. He has three sons and they are mean, dangerous, and very intimidating," explained Eddie.

"When you take him out, his sons will have to go with him. They are not going to let anyone live who they believe had anything to do with the killing of their father," responded James.

"Okay, the four of them must go. I will need some help. I have a few buddies in New Orleans that owe me a few favors. One is my girlfriend, she is cold blooded and you would not want to mess with her. It will take time to gather them all up. I will need to go back to New Orleans to get them. I will see you in a few weeks," stated Eddie with an expressionless face.

Just as the party was about to end. Joey, James's best soldier came tearing through the crowd looking for James. Joey looked like a man who had found the devil and was scared of dying.

"James, something awful has happened. The MacBride family set fire to the Do Drop Inn. Our bar is gone. They burned it down to the ground. Everyone was able to get out with just minor injuries.

They gave me a message to give you. *"We will never do business with any of the Brotherhood. The Brotherhood killed our cousin, JD. Now we plan to take out the Brotherhood. The war is on."*

"How did they find out JD was dead? It was rumored that he run off to America," stated James.

"One of your former soldiers went to work for the MacBride family because of what happen to JD. He told them how Rocco shot him and he was thrown down a dry well on Conor's farm. They found the well and sure enough, JD was at the bottom," explained Eddie.

"Are you related to that bunch?" asked James.

"No, I'm a Wop, not Irish trash!" shouted Eddie.

James decided to wait until the next day to deal with the MacBride family. He felt that he needed a plan to take the father and his sons out all at the same time. As he lay in his bed, James decided to have them locked up by his buddie the sheriff who was on his payroll. If they tried to challenge the sheriff and his officers, they were to take them out.

The next day James told Eddie his plan. Eddie told James to let them stay in jail until his gang came. Have the Judge to hold them without bail.

"What is your girlfriends name?" asked James.

"Her name is Ella. Ella Basset, she is French but knows how to kill. She is young but knows how to take out a target without blinking an eye. After she does her job, I will be sending her back to New Orleans. She is too valuable to lose," stated Eddie.

The sheriff locked up the MacBride family without any trouble. The sheriff felt it was too easy, no resistance, no cursing, and no yelling. They all went peacefully. The next day the MacBrides pleaded not guilty and were ready to post bail. They were biting at the bit go after the Brotherhood. The judge denied bail. The MacBrides left the courtroom screaming and yelling. The judge stated that MacBride's were a menace to the town because of the alleged burning down of the "Do Drop Inn." That was the judge's favorite hangout spot. The judge was pissed off.

Eddie quickly left for New Orleans hoping to return with at least five guys and his girlfriend Ella. Eddie felt, if he got rid of the MacBride family with no complications, then one day he could return to New Orleans as the Boss after Rocco steps down or gets killed.

"Eddie, my love," cried out Ella. Things have not been the same since you left. I love you more today than the day I met you. I hope you plan to stay here in New Orleans. The organization needs you and I need you," said Ella with love in her eyes.

"Ella, I am here on a mission. I need you and maybe five other soldiers to help with a small problem in this large seaport county in Ireland. The Brotherhood is having trouble with a family of gang misfits. They need to be taken out. I need your help. You are a young lady with great promise with the organization. Hopefully, one day you and I will control all of New Orleans. We need to do this thing in order to move up in the organization. Rocco needs to know that the Brotherhood will remain strong even after he is gone. We are strong and together the Brotherhood will live forever," explained Eddie with certainty in his voice.

"Eddie, if I help you, then you need to do something for me," stated Ella.

"What is it Ella?" responded Eddie.

"You need to marry me before we go to Ireland. I want to be your wife even if it is just for one day. It will be worth it. This situation in Ireland might go against us. If it does, I would have been happy for a day," stated Ella in a commanding tone.

"I love you. Having you as my wife will be the best thing that has ever happened to me," explained Eddie.

"I need to tell you something. First of all, you know a lot about me but I must tell you something that might make a difference," explained Ella.

"What is your something, Ella?" asked Eddie.

"I am not white. My mother is black. My father is white and they are retired, living in France. My twin sister and I left France to move to the *land of opportunity* which is America the week after we graduated from school. We both loved New Orleans but she was forced to leave because of her profession," stated Ella.

"Young lady, your color does not matter to me. Love is color blind, patient, understanding, and everlasting. I love you today, tomorrow, and forever. Pack your little red bag. We are going to my judge in the morning to get hitched. Tomorrow, you will be under new management. I will have papers on you!" shouted Eddie.

CHAPTER 22

"DO YOU THINK your father ever met the twin sister?" asked Allie.

"I am not sure but maybe Laura was the twin sister," responded Tom.

"Did you say she was working as a waitress when your father met her?" asked Allie.

"Yes, and the twin sister's name was Ella and they were mixed," responded Tom.

"Let's take a look at the obituaries in this box. This box also has some written notes. These notes are in the form of a diary. It looks like your father has left a lot of information about his life and everyone he was involved with. Oh no, information about JD, Sammy Cooan (the Irish Hill Gang), Mickey (Sammy's son), Jake Hutch (Zoe's cousin who developed the new strain of corn), Rocco (the New Orleans mafia boss), and Eddie and Ella Acosta (died in New Orleans).

"Let's stop working and have something to eat. I'm a good cook. I love steak when cooked medium rare. I will cook the steaks and you can make the salad," explained Allie with her eyes wide opened.

"Allie, I would like to hear more about your growing up as a kid but first I would like to see what my father has to say. I am hoping that his leftovers help me find my sister. She is in New Orleans, we know that because of the Brotherhood enforcer who paid us a visit. I plan to get a gun for protection," explained Tom.

"You don't need a gun. I have a hand gun and a shotgun. That is enough fire power for both of us," explained Allie who appeared to be ready. What does it say in his diary?" asked Tom with a half-smile on his face.

"Well, the beginning is just the same as what you told me so far. There are stories about your grandfather and grandmother and how they died. It also mentions that your grandmother was not his mother but his mama," explained Allie, sounding like a teacher of high school students.

"Does his diary mention me?" asked Tom.

"No, not yet. It is in the order of dates. But your father's birth certificate is here. Wow! Conor was your father and your mother was Cora Cooan. She was Sammy Cooan's daughter. That is why he hated your family. Mickey is your uncle. Mickey killed your grandfather who was your mother's father. I wonder if Jesse new that Sammy Cooan was also his grandfather," stated Allie as she sipped on her bourbon.

"It appears that I was born into a family of criminals. This is very depressing. I think I need some bourbon on the rocks," responded Tom with a turned down mouth.

"This is interesting. Harry MacBride's Family were all murdered. It tells everything in great details. You sure you want to hear it?" asked Allie.

"Yes, start from the beginning," responded Tom.

Ella Basset was now Ella Acosta. Mr. and Mrs. Eddie Acosta. The next day they left to travel to Ireland with four other soldiers to take out the MacBride family. Ella was very pretty but was a vicious gangster queen. She was young but had learned how to take care of business in order to survive in New Orleans. She joined one of the smaller gangs shortly after landing in New Orleans. Because she had very little money, she took a job working for a group that was called the New Orleans Railroad Terminal Gang.

She worked as a cab driver. Because she was pretty, customers did not have a problem with her picking them up at railroad terminals. Once in the cab, she would pull out her gun and rob them. She earned 50 percent of everything she made each night. As time went on, she was rewarded for her good work and dedication. With her help, the gang's activities expanded to include illegal gambling, political intimidation, and narcotics.

Eddie was working for Rocco who wanted all the gangs to work under him. Eddie met Ella and they fell in love. He convinced Ella to help him get all the gangs together and convince them to work with Rocco, the Czar. Ella and Eddie were very successful in their efforts to help Rocco form his Mafia, the Brotherhood.

Rocco felt that James Harrison needed a professional enforcer so he sent Eddie to size up the situation. Eddie made the decision that the MacBride family must be eliminated. Rocco wanted Camden County to be his little New Orleans. The MacBride family was making it difficult for the organization and as a result would have to be dealt with.

"Do you have a plan to take out the MacBride family?" asked Ella.

"Yes, but it won't be easy," explained Eddie.

"Okay, what is the plan?" asked Ella with a half-smile on her face.

"Don't unpack your bag because we will not be here long. The ship leaves at 9:00 a.m., and we will be on it. The MacBride family functions like a real honest family. They pulled some strings and were able to get out on bail. We don't have much time because they will reorganize and go after James Harrison. They have dinner at 5:00 p.m. every day. I will show up at five and invite myself to dinner. I will make an excuse to go into the kitchen to get a glass of water. At that time, I will unlock the kitchen door for you and the soldiers.

The MacBride family never brings guns to the dinner table. They will be helpless. Kill the father and all his sons. Don't kill the women and children. I will duck under the table but don't kill me," said Eddie with a grin on his face.

That evening Eddie showed up for dinner. They were glad to see him. They wanted to hear what James Harrison was planning.

"Well my friends, they don't tell me much because I am the new guy on the team. I can tell you that they are planning on killing all of you," stated Eddie.

"If they try to come after us, we will be ready. You see this mean machine it is a Tommy Gun. I just got it a few days ago. It is ready for action," stated Harry MacBride with pride.

"My throat is dry. I need some water. I will get it," stated Eddie shaking all the way into the kitchen.

I don't want my baby doll to get hurt. I don't know what to do. If they come charging in, the MacBride's might have enough time to start firing that Tommy Gun. I know, I will leave a note, telling them to split up. Some in the back door and the rest in front door because they have a machine gun. It is ready to be used. Shoot everything that is moving, even women and children. They are the cost of going to war, thought Eddie.

Eddie sat back down at the table and was trying to eat so that the family could be taken by surprise. He dropped his napkin on the floor and bent down to appear to be picking it up and that is when all hell broke out.

Ella came in first and was followed by the other soldiers. She was on top of her game. Yelling and firing at the same time. Eddie stayed under the table because he knew when Ella got started, she would not stop until she came out victorious.

Ella and the soldiers were so quick that the MacBride's never saw it coming and were totally unprepared for Ella. Ella was being Ella and the whole MacBride family died at 5:00 p.m. There was a little note in the diary that said, everyone has a beginning and an ending. This is the MacBride Family ending.

Without any expression on her face, Ella stood straight up with her chest poked out and was walked out, stating, "You can come out now baby. It's time to go home."

The next day, James thanked Eddie and Ella as they boarded the ship to go back to New Orleans.

Everything was going as planned for James. Redd his son was becoming a young man. He was a chip off the old block. James, his father would give him small chores every day. His mother was always sick with something. Therefore, James and Redd took care of everything and her most of the time.

The mayor of the county who was part the Brotherhood died.

Therefore, a special election was held to finish out the mayor's term. James backed a candidate that would support his dominating criminal organization but his candidate lost by a slim margin. The new mayor ran on putting a stop to organized crime. The mayor was committed to stopping all moonshiners and illegal activities in his county.

The day after the election James went into hiding with his wife and son. The new mayor sent the sheriff's office out to search for stills. James's liquor making corn farms were first to go. The sheriff's officers were told to burn all stills down to the ground. The smell of corn liquor was so strong it was burning the officer's eyes.

All the corn farms were vacant and everyone was gone. James, Zoe and his son Redd were on their way to America. They had made plans to go to New Orleans to meet up with Rocco. Rocco had big plans for James.

CHAPTER 23

"DOES THE DIARY tell what James did for Rocco in New Orleans?" asked Allie.

"Yes, and he was a big time player," responded Tom.

James was in charge of managing the dock workers and the docks. With the help of a produce merchant and political organizer, James was able to get winning contracts to provide dock labor to fruit companies in New Orleans. The stevedore contracts brought quick wealth and influence to the Brotherhood, which was the mafia. This underworld organization gave Rocco the street name as the Czar. The Brotherhood became the dominant criminal organization.

"James, you are doing a great job. New Orleans has not been the same since you and Zoe moved here. We now control everything but I need you to relocate to North Carolina. We are having trouble getting corn liquor into New Orleans. There are two hijackers that need some attending to. One is an ex-cop name Blake that we need to stop. He has a partner named Manny. Both of them have become big names as the leading hijackers in New Orleans. They hijacked my shipment of rum last week.

"These two are from Chicago and they came here a few months ago. I turned my head and ignored them as long as they were not stealing from me. Last week they hijacked my rum. I want my rum back. I also, want them to work for me. If they can be hijackers for me, then all the liquor they steal will cost me nothing. If they don't want to work for me, kill them both," stated the Czar.

James decided the best way to get these two guys was to set them up. James put out a message in the underworld that the Czar was bringing in a large shipment of rum. The time and location was also given. The shipment was coming in by boat from Canada. It was well known that Canada made the best rum and corn liquor. Around 1:00 a.m., the shipment arrived. The Czar's men were ready for Blake and Manny but the hijackers were not ready for James's men.

After all the liquor was placed on the dock, out of nowhere Blake and Manny appeared. They had machine guns and were prepared to use them. Within seconds, James and his army of soldiers stepped out and surrounded the two hijackers.

"Drop your weapons! If you don't you will die right here!" exclaimed James.

"We are Prohibition agents," stated the men.

James recognized Blake and Manny and was 100 percent certain they were lying. Without any warning, the two hijackers started firing their pistols. After the gunfight, the only men standing without any wounds were James and a few of his soldiers. Off they went with their liquor. James's mission was accomplished. He took both hijackers out and that was the end of robberies and holdups.

"James, you are a survivor and someone up above is looking out for you. In fact, you are special. You are a special survivor but I need to send you to North Carolina to grow and make corn liquor. The demand for our liquor is off the hook. Mainly because women are drinking liquor more than men. I need you to leave tomorrow. A farm has been purchased in your name. It will be a great place to raise your son, Redd. He can grow up to be an honest adult, doing honest work," stated the Czar.

"Tom, there is a big package that is labeled the Brotherhood," said Allie.

Allie was curious as to what she was going to discover in the package.

She knew that Jesse Donovan was in New Orleans, working with the Czar (Rocco) in security. Security could be anything when dealing with the Mafia. Tom's father Jesse, died while still working as the sheriff of Harrisonville. His death was a shock to everyone in his county. Allie slowly opened the package and flipped through the papers. In between the papers were pictures with names and dates on the back.

The first picture was James Harrison and Jesse Donovan. Next, was a picture of the Czar (Rocco). Allie picked up a picture that was faded but was labeled, Eddie and Ella, James and Zoe, and, Sally and Jesse. This was a family of criminals who were good friends, thought Allie.

"James, let's read the diary together, out loud," stated Allie.

"Okay, do we have to start now. Can we wait until tomorrow morning after breakfast?" asked Tom.

"Yes, dear!" said Allie.

As the sun was coming up and Tom was not quite awake, he started recalling what his father told him about his experiences and good times in New Orleans.

Sitting at the bar, the most popular club in New Orleans for gangsters, were Jesse and James together again. The gangsters loved the Hi Hat Club. It was the closest thing to being in New York City and Chicago without the drama of those two big cities.

New Orleans was becoming a stronghold for the mafia's underground criminal activities. Anything is possible in the Big Easy.

"James, I would like to get married one day but with my occupation and life style, it will be hard to find the right young lady. You are very lucky to have found Zoe. Your son, Redd is very smart and if necessary, I will always have his back," stated Jesse in a sincere tone.

"Jesse, friends like us only come around once in a lifetime. We were both born on the same day and almost at the same time. I believe I am 5 minutes older than you. Therefore, I am your older brother," explained James.

"This club has the best jazz music and singers in the area. Jazz started in New Orleans. It goes back as far as the early 1895s. I love this music. The jazz performers are mostly Creole. New Orleans is much different than the rest of America, mainly because here the liberal outlook life prevails.

The people in New Orleans appreciate good food, wine, corn liquor, bourbon, rum, and drugs. It has often been stated that this city is ungovernable because of their preoccupation with dancing," explained Jesse.

"Oh my goodness, look at that young girl. She is the prettiest gal in all of New Orleans! Who is she?" asked James.

"She is the new manager of The Hi Hat Club and all the speakeasies in New Orleans. I was told that she also sings and dances," responded James.

"What is her name? I need to meet her now," stated Jesse.

"Rita Picone is her name and she is an Italian piece of work," responded James.

"It looks like she is headed for the stage," said Jesse.

Just as she was going up the steps, a man yelled out, "Shake it but don't break baby because it took your mama nine months to make."

Rita turned around and gave him her middle finger.

Rita's hair was dark black. It was a perfect match for her milky white skin. Her small waist with her nice round hips made her look like a doll baby. She was everything a man could want in a woman. She was wearing a red strapless dress that was form fitting. Her diamond earrings were large and dangled from her ears. Rita was picture perfect.

Rita grabbed the mic and said, "Hello, suckers!" The Flappers were dancing behind her. She took one look at the Flappers and said, "Any bootlegger here is surely a pal of mine." Without music, she started singing the song "Me and My Gin." The whole place stood up as if it was the first time they had heard this song. But it was the first time they heard it the way Rita was singing. Without saying anything, the jazz band started improvising and the crowd went crazy.

The band played one more song, "Knockin' a Jug," and the tables were full of men and women dancing on top of them. What a sight to see. Everyone was having a good time. James jumped up on a table and took out his pistol and fired a flare of gun shots, yelling, "let the good times roll, baby" and the "ratty" music played on.

"James, I got to meet Rita. She is the woman of my dreams! She will fit right into my life style," said Jesse in a loud excited tone.

"God must have answered your request because here she comes," responded James.

"Hi, guys, my name is Rita. I saw you two looking at me. Take a picture, it will last longer than looking," said Rita in a smooth sexy voice.

"Rita, is there a special man in your life?" asked Jesse.

"No, but there could be soon," responded Rita.

"How about now! I am the special guy and you are my special lady. I wasn't going to come to the club tonight, but God wanted me to meet you. I was just telling James that any woman that I got involved with would have to understand me and my occupation. After I saw you give that customer your middle finger, I knew you were the one," explained Jesse with a humble tone.

"Stick around and when the club closes we can work on this made in heaven bonding," stated Rita.

Rita, being the new manager of all the clubs and speakeasies, forgot to pay off the governor and the local police. Without any warning, the police stormed into the club and fired several rounds of bullets to get everyone's attention. They asked the customers to leave or go to jail. James with his hands raised high said, "Why are you here?"

The sheriff in an angry yelling voice said, "Ask that bitch, Rita. She hasn't paid us for a whole month. I want my money now. The governor wants me to collect his money. In fact, the governor told us to pay you a visit. He wants his now or all the clubs will be closed, until you bill is current."

"You embarrassed me in front of all those people and they laughed at me when you turned around and gave me the finger," stated the sheriff's deputy with anger in his voice.

"Get over it, you MF, and here is my finger again. What do you plan to do about?" stated Rita laughing.

To calm things down, Jesse and James took the sheriff, the deputy, and Rita to the office. Jesse asked Rita to pay them off. Rita paid the sheriff off. The deputy still feeling hotter that the Fourth of July, said, "This is what I am going to do about it, bitch!" He pulled out his pistol and shot Rita in the head. Jesse yelled over and over again until James pulled him away.

The sheriff put a gun in Rita's hand, and his report stated that Rita was resisting being arrested. The officer feared for his life and others when he saw her gun. He had no other choice but shoot to kill. Case closed and everyone moved on.

James left the next day for North Carolina and Jesse felt lost. For a short period of time he and his best buddy were together again. Jesse stayed drunk off corn liquor for two weeks. The Czar would come by every day to check on him. Finally, the Czar said, "I had enough of your sorry ass. Sober up and I am sending you to North Carolina to be with James. I have a job lined up for you. You will be the new sheriff. The old one was killed trying to arrest a drug dealer. The sheriff lost his life and the drug dealer got away. Together, the two of you can control the whole county," stated the Czar.

James welcomed Jesse to North Carolina. He introduced him to all his farm workers. Jesse felt that the corn fields never looked this good in Ireland. Everything was well organized. Even the stills were lined up and looking like toy soldiers waiting to their next assignment.

As James was showing Jesse around the farm, they ran into Redd. He was glad to see Jesse. Redd understood, with Jesse being the new sheriff, the county would be under their control. Buddy, Redd's best and only friend, was working with him. Redd introduced Buddy to the new sheriff.

Taking one good look at the two boys, the new sheriff knew that these two boys were born to be criminals. It was in their blood. They would be friends until the end.

That night, Jesse thought about how he wanted the county to grow and what part he would play in its growth. He pulled out his gun and started cleaning it. As he was cleaning his gun, he took a long look at the bottle of corn liquor that James had given him. He started thinking, is this all I have to live for. A glass of corn liquor and criminals.

Just before he took his first taste of the corn liquor, there was a knock at the door. Jesse opened the door and it was pretty young girl. She was looking for work. She explained that James Harrison told her he might need a housekeeper.

Her name was Sally. Jesse hired her on the spot. She was born and raised in that county. She had never even left the county for any reason. She was smart but had very little education.

Sally worked long hours making sure everything was just right for Jesse. When Jesse got home late from work, Sally would help him take off his boots. His dinner was always excellent.

After working for Jesse a few months, Sally decided she was going to marry Jesse. Her plan was to get him drunk and crawl into bed with him. Jesse had sex with Sally but he thought he was making love to Rita. Rita was all he dreamed about every night. That night his dream came true, Rita was with him once again.

That morning, Jesse woke up early and found Sally by his side. Seeing her in bed with him made him sick to his stomach. He was sick because he though Rita had returned and she was not dead. Jesse slipped out of the bed and took a shower. Sally got up and went into the kitchen and cooked breakfast.

The smell of the food cooking made Jesse sick to his stomach again. James's only chance to make love to Rita was in his mind. He had visions of how wonderful it would have been. The girl of his dreams had finally come along.

Jesse got himself together and ate breakfast with Sally. At that moment, he decided that Sally would be a good replacement for Rita.

Whenever he was making love to her, he would pretend it was Rita.

It was Sally's birthday and they had been together for over a year. Jesse decided to take Sally to one of James's nicest clubs for her birthday dinner. Jesse loved Sally because when he looked at her, he saw Rita. After dinner Jesse took Sally by the hand and said, "Rita will you marry me."

"Who is Rita?" asked Sally.

"She was a childhood friend that I mixed your name up with hers. She was murdered on this day and I was thinking of how tragic it was for her to die so young," explained James as the lying words just rolled out of his mouth.

Sally believed Jesse and did not ask any more questions. "Mrs. Jesse Donovan," those words consumed all her thoughts. She did not tell Jesse right away but she was pregnant at the time she said, "I do."

The happy couple had their little baby boy in the month of September and they named him Thomas Donovan.

"How old were you when your mother passed away?" asked Allie with a curious look on her face.

"She passed away in my first year in college. I was almost nineteen," responded Tom.

"Oh my, the diary has many details about James and Jesse's involvement with organized crime in New Orleans and North Carolina," stated Allie.

"I can tell you a lot more about those two criminals than what's in the diary," explained Tom with disgust in his voice.

Most of the time my mother sat around crying. Her heart had been broken. My father became the town playboy. He would leave early in the morning and come home late at night every day even on the weekends," said Tom.

"Tom, your father wrote the following," stated Allie.

Moving to North Carolina made a big difference for James and his family. Redd was getting older and needed a home he could call his own. Zoe was getting sicker and sicker every day. James sent word to the Czar about Zoe being sick and asked if he knew of any good doctors that could examine Zoe.

When the Czar got the letter, he sent the best doctor in New Orleans to look after Zoe. The doctor gave her a complete and excellent physical exam. After the exam was over, the doctor went into the living room with a larger glass of corn liquor. As he sipped on the liquor he closed his eyes. He was trying to find a way to break the news to James about Zoe's condition.

Zoe was dying. She did not have long to live. The doctor's exam revealed that she was suffering from a bad case of whooping cough. If it had been treated sooner, the doctor felt she would have been able to recover. Her condition was too far gone for any type of treatment.

Zoe died within a few days after the doctor left. The obituary had a beautiful picture of Zoe and a few pictures of James and Red. Sally got the obituary ready for the Harrisons. It was a sad day for the Harrison family. James and Red recovered quickly from Zoe's death. The three of them were a great team. That is, James, Redd, and Buddy were a strong criminal force. They controlled the whole county. With the sheriff on their side, they were the town and the county.

Out of the blue, Jesse stopped by to see James and Redd. He wanted to tell them the good news. The town council passed a resolution renaming the town, Harrisonville. The town was dying and the Harrison family put new life into the town. They created jobs, opportunity, and a hope for the future of the town and county.

One night Jesse decided to go to The Palace instead of staying home and arguing with Sally. She was crying because Jesse when he got totally plastered would call her Rita while they were making love. She asked him to tell her the truth about Rita and he did. She was upset because he was in love with a woman he just met and never had any romantic contact with her. Sally felt he was in love with what could have been and his love for Rita was not real.

That was the night James met Laura. Laura had a slight French accent which made her sound very sexy. "Hello, gorgeous," said Jesse with a player's voice.

"Did I hear you right? You called me gorgeous," responded Laura.

"Yes, I called you gorgeous. What's wrong with that! You are gorgeous," stated Jesse with hopes for more conversation.

"Well, that's a good answer. Are you ready to order but gorgeous is not on the menu?" asked Laura with a smooth sliding tone in her voice.

"By the way, my name is Jesse Donovan. What is your name?" asked Jesse.

"My name is Laura Basset. I know all about you, Jesse. Don't mess with me unless you can handle me. I come from a pedigree of hardcore criminals. It's in my blood. I am a survivor—in my opinion, a special survivor," explained Laura with a tone that did not sound French.

CHAPTER 24

LAURA TOOK JESSE'S order, which was bourbon on the rocks. She wrote her address and phone number on a napkin with a big red lipstick kiss that was below her information. Laura was new at the club. She knew who Jesse was because she lived in New Orleans and worked for the Czar.

She had to leave New Orleans in a hurry because she was part of a small gangster group that were bank robbers. Laura would take a job working for the bank. She always applied for janitorial positions. In this position she was able to roam around the banks without being noticed. Her job was to locate the bank vault, determine the security system, and how much money was on hand every day. She would work as a janitor for about three months before her information could be verified.

The Czar wanted all of the gangs to come under one group. His mafia was known as the Brotherhood. Laura's gang was called the South Side Creoles. They played music at night and robbed banks during the daytime. With a lot of encouragement, they joined the Brotherhood.

The Czar gave the South Side Creoles a territory and set them up in business. They were to play their Jazz at night and sell drugs to the customers. Robbing banks was off limits. The Czar said it was a risky business. If things went wrong during a robbery, you could lose your life or go to jail for a long time. Therefore, the Czar did not want any of his people in that business.

Malachi Wallace was the leader of the South Side Creoles. He was not ready to give up robbing banks. He wanted to do one more big heist. He gathered up his gang and planned on implementing the plans that were confirmed by Laura but not executed. Laura was not completely comfortable with the plan to rob the First National Bank of New Orleans. Laura had reported back that security was tight. Malachi was aware of the security but this bank kept on hand large sums of money.

It was the largest bank in New Orleans, and its biggest customer was the mafia. Laura did not know that it was a mafia bank. The Czar and only a few close associates were aware of the bank's relationship with the Brotherhood. Malachi was determined to score it big with this last job. He felt that this would be his ticket to being an independent black business man. His dream was to leave New Orleans and start a legitimate business in New York City.

Laura was very concerned about this last bank job and decided to tell the Czar about the plans to rob the First National Bank of New Orleans. The Czar was shocked and took a hard long look at Laura for he was delighted that she told him about the plans to rob the bank.

That evening the Czar had Malachi, Laura, and the rest of the South Side Creoles meet at the Dreamland restaurant for dinner. After dinner, the Czar said the following to his gang members.

"I have worked long and hard as the ultimate leader of the Brotherhood. I will never let any of you destroy what I have taken many years to create. If I tell you not to do something, I expect you to follow my orders.

"It has come to my attention that this gang is planning on one more big heist. Drop your plans or I will drop you right now. If you want out of this business, let me know now. I will let you go with my blessings.

"I do have a few announcements to make. Malachi is going to be my number one lieutenant. Laura will be leaving for North

Carolina tomorrow. Malachi and Laura do you have a problem with my announcement? If you do let me know right now. If not, continue to enjoy your meal, and I will see all of you soon."

The Czar walked out the restaurant with steam coming out of his ears. He was extremely upset over the whole situation. He knew that Malachi's plan to rob the bank was doomed from the start because the bank's security was the best in the nation. Malachi and Laura would have not walked out of the bank alive.

The Czar told Laura to take a job as a waitress at the Palace. If everything worked out, he would move her up to management. The first night Jesse and Laura met was the beginning of a relationship that was made in heaven. Laura worked hard and after a few months the Czar moved her up to management. She was the head cashier.

Jesse wanted to ask Sally for a divorce but decided it was not worth taking the chance that she would do something crazy. After all, she was the mother of his child, Tom. He loved Tom and did not want to do anything that would hurt him now or in the future. Therefore, he decided to love both women. One as the mother of his child and the other as the woman of his dreams. He felt blessed by God to have both women.

Laura became pregnant and Jesse was very happy that he was going to have another little baby. He hoped the baby would look just like Laura if it was a girl. She was 5 years younger than Tom and they named her Joni. Sally knew about Laura but did not care. Jesse did not know Sally was aware of his relationship with Laura. Laura felt that she was Mrs. Jesse Donovan and no one was ever going to take that away from her. She was right. Jesse acted like a great husband without having sex with his wife. He felt that if he had sex with Sally it would be cheating on Laura.

Laura understood the situation and was willing to live as the mistress.

After all, most of the men in Harrisonville had something on the side. They named the baby Joni Basset.

Before the baby was born Laura was feeling concerned that Jesse should know more about her. So she cooked a great dinner and purchased Jesse's favorite wine. Laura got dressed in her prettiest, sexiest dress and set the table with beautiful candles and her best china. She was ready to do a tell all about her heritage.

"Jesse, I want you to listen to me. I have black ancestors. I have a twin sister who lives in New Orleans. Her name is Ella [Basset] Acosta," explained Laura in a serious voice.

"Wow, that's your twin sister! I know her. She had blonde hair and you have black hair. She is very tall and you are shorter," responded Jesse.

"We are not identical. We are fraternal twins. She is an enforcer under the Czar. He thinks very highly of her. She is one of the best in the business," explained Laura.

"They came to Ireland and were hired to take out a whole family of criminals for the Czar. She married Eddie Acosta and together they became the best in the business. They are next in line to take over after the Czar," said Laura in a tone that had verifiable information. "What do you think about me having black ancestors?" asked Laura.

"Who cares, you are my lady and that is all that counts to me. The hell with the ancestors. May they rest in peace and resides heaven," responded Jesse with joy in his voice.

The Czar sent word to Jesse that he was coming to Harrisonville for James's funeral. James's brother-in-law who was the town drunk was considered by James as a worthless piece of shit. Sammy the brother-in-law went to James's house to ask for a loan. James refused and Sammy shot and killed James. Redd was home and heard the noise. He saw what had happened and Redd with his gun Sue in his hand, fired several shots until Sammy was surely dead.

Jesse took care of everything and reported the shooting as self-defense. The next day, Jesse informed the Czar of what had happened. The Czar was upset but he knew this was the cost of being a criminal. Things happen and every day is a new day.

Redd called Buddy and together they continued to run all the juke joints and clubs. James funeral was on a beautiful, cloudless, warm day. It was a day fitting for a man like James who was dedicated, loyal, and dependable.

The Czar said he would be in Harrisonville around noon. The church clock struck 12:00. Every from New Orleans must have come with the Czar. The cars rolled into Harrisonville like a 4th of July parade. The Czar was in the first car. It was a white Rolls Royce Phantom Limousine. Eddie and Ella were in the next car which was a bright red convertible Ford Model Deluxe Roadster. Malachi and Lucille Wallace were behind Eddie and Ella, in a Falcon Knight Roadster.

The parade of cars consisted of thirty cars. The residents were lined up on both sides of the street. The fourth car had a black man dressed in an all-white tux who got out of his car. He stood in the middle of the street. The band flooded the street with their instruments. Next the Flappers, singers and the people on the sides of the street joined the entertainers. The band played the sounds of New Orleans Jazz.

It was a sight to see. James would have been pleased to see so many people enjoying themselves. James was gone and he was not coming back but Redd and Buddy together were good replacements.

When everyone arrived at the church, there was complete silence. Laura conducted the service. Jesse informed the attendees of how he and James were born on the same day and in the same hospital. Jesse read the obituary. The minister's eulogy was full of positive excerpts from the bible. The funeral service was extremely wonderful. It was conducted with full honors. James got a homecoming that was fit for a king.

After the service, everyone was invited to join the family at the Palace. The Palace was a few blocks down from the church. The commentary was just before the Palace. The band, dancers, singers and the attendees followed behind the band as they played "When the Saints Go Marching in." The dancers were doing the Ghanian Coffin Dance; it was to help the deceased to pass on in style. It was a sight to see. The towns people had never seen anything like this before.

They enjoyed the service, the atmosphere, and everything that came with it.

The Palace was jammed but everyone was having a good time. The band started playing ratty music because several guests with their instruments jumped up on the stage and started play with the band. The improvised music made the band sound even better. The Czar was very pleased with how well things turned out for James's funeral.

The Czar was staying at Jesse's home and planned to leave in the morning. "Jesse, do you think Redd is ready to be a leader of this county?" asked the Czar.

"Boss, he was born ready. He was born into a family of criminals on both sides. James raised him right. He did not cut corners when it came to showing Redd the ropes. James had Redd working with him, side by side.

"Redd has a friend named Buddy. I don't know much about his background but Redd and Buddy are joined together at the hips. I know they will be good for the county and Harrisonville," responded Jesse with complete confidence.

"Okay, then they belong to you. Keep them out of jail and alive," stated the Czar with a half smile on his face.

The next day Jesse did not waste any time. He had Redd and Buddy meet him that evening in his office. "Boys, I got your back. Don't do anything that I can't justify. I will look the other way as long as you don't get caught. I hope you understand what I am telling you," said Jesse with his sheriff tone of voice.

That night Redd and Buddy sat drinking moonshine on Redd's porch. "Buddy, you know our sheriff has issues of his own. That pretty little girl name Joni is his baby by that black woman Laura, he is seeing. I know Laura is black because I saw her and Ella talking. Later I asked Ella how did she know Laura. She said she is my twin sister," stated Redd.

"Who cares, it is his business. We have enough to think about then worrying about some one's woman!" shouted Buddy.

CHAPTER 25

"I DON'T SEE ANYTHING so far that will help me locate my half sister Joni," stated Tom with doubt in his voice.

"If we keep looking in those boxes, maybe you will find a picture of her. With a picture, I can show it to a few friends and they might know her," responded Allie.

"Look in the next box. It might have more pictures," stated Tom.

Allie slowly opened the next box. To her surprise it contained a well preserved police uniform, a security guard uniform with several plaques, letters of accommodations, thank you letters and letters from Laura.

In the bottom of the box were three thick notebooks. The notebooks contained detailed information about Jesse's career as the sheriff of Harrisonville with more information about the criminal activities in New Orleans.

Allie opened up a thank you letter from Joni. She was thanking the sheriff for his generous high school graduation gift of such a large sum of money. Joni went on to say that it would be used to pay for her first year in college. This gift will help me to fulfill my dreams of becoming a lawyer. Maybe one day I'll run for political office or some position to help residents or citizens of our country. I will be ready to serve if that is where God leads me. God bless Joni Basset.

"Allie, let me see the notebooks. I think I would like to read them by myself. My father asked me to be careful as to whom I shared the information he left me. If I feel that there is something that will help you bring down the Brotherhood, I will tell you," stated Tom in a serious tone.

"Tom the weather is very nice and it is time that we have some fun. Let's go to the beach for a few days. The Otter Banks Resort is only a few hours from here. No one will see us. When we return, I will leave and go back to New Orleans. It might be possible for me to ask Leroy for help in finding out where Joni might be working or hiding out," stated Allie in a concerned voice.

"Okay, let's leave tonight," responded Tom.

That night Tom not only took a few clothes but he packed the notebooks in his bag. Allie saw the notebooks and said, "No work or reading on this trip. It's to be a vacation."

Allie was determined to tell Tom the rest of her life story. She never had anyone to tell it to. She felt it was the right time and Tom was the right person. "Leroy was not only my boss but I was in love with him. I was inexperienced and thought that he was a normal person. It turns out he was the opposite of normal," explained Allie sounding like a person in a confession booth.

Allie put her head back and went to sleep. However, she was dreaming about her dangerous life with Leroy and if she should tell Tom everything.

Allie started thinking about poor Lynn Morton. I remember Lynn as if it was yesterday, thought Allie. While working for Leroy in his drug operation center, without anyone knowing it, one of the female money counters was an undercover cop. Her name was Karen but her real name was Officer Lynn Morton. Karen was very quiet and nice. She was also a good worker. Allie found out later that Karen got the job because of Leroy's mother who was Lucille Wallace.

Lucille was the local community organizer but was a front for the Brotherhood. Her job was to keep her ward under control and finding good workers for she was the Black Queen of New Orleans.

One day Karen was eating lunch at Allie's table. After the rest of the girls went back to work, Karen said to Allie, "You are not alone. You are very bright and need to better yourself. We all make poor decisions. If you ever feel that you want to get more out of life; I have some friends that can help you. Please don't tell Leroy about our conversation. If you do he will kill me," whispered Karen.

On a few occasions Allie and Karen would eat together. Sometimes Leroy would join them. Leroy had babies by at least three of the girls that worked for him. None of them worked doing the same job. The girls knew about each other but never made a big deal about Leroy being the father of their babies.

Leroy felt that Karen was getting too friendly with Allie. He thought they were planning on stealing some of his product or money. So he had Maxine, who was a money counter and one of his baby's mamas, to carefully listen to Allie and Karen's conversations. He wanted to know what they were up to. It was a few days before Mardi Gras and all the workers were getting excited about the holiday. This was the time that many visitors would be coming to New Orleans looking to do drugs and to have a good time.

The workers bagging the products were working long hours to fill the demand for drugs during Mardi Gras. Leroy did not know exactly what was going on with Karen but felt it was time to eliminate her. That was the way his mind functioned, thought Allie.

The first day of Mardi Gras Leroy demanded that everyone work the crowd. As Karen mixed in with the crowd, Leroy came up to her and stabbed her in the back. He was dressed like a clown and Allie saw him.

She turned her head away quickly so that Leroy did not see her looking. That love she had for Leroy was gone and she knew at that point he was not normal.

The thought of what happened to Karen, woke Allie up screaming. Tom pulled over and grabbed and hugged her. "You don't need to be scared about anything. I won't let the past seal your future," stated Tom sincerely. Hearing Tom's calm, understanding voice made Allie's body relax and she fell back to asleep. Allie woke up as they were pulling into the hotel. As Tom was helping Allie out of the car. Allie stated, "Tom, I need to tell you about my life as a young adult. I won't feel comfortable around you unless I explain how I got to be an FBI agent," stated Allie in very low tone.

"Let's just relax in the Jacuzzi with a glass of wine and you can me the whole truth and nothing but the truth," explained Tom as he smiled.

"I guess the truth will set me free," responded Allie with a big grin on her face.

While in the Jacuzzi, Allie had a few glasses of wine. She needed the wine for her to face the past. With the help of a lawyer who worked for the FBI, she became a survivor from the life as a professional criminal.

Allie told Tom that while she was working for Leroy, an undercover FBI agent was murdered by Leroy Wallace. She knew this to be true because she witnessed the killing. At the time she didn't know that the FBI agent was working undercover. The FBI agent told me, Karen was one of their agents at the time who was trying to recruit me.

"Does the name Sue Morton sound familiar?" asked Allie in a matter-of-fact tone.

"Yes, she was one of our best and was murdered just before she was able to provide information to the FBI on the top leadership of the Brotherhood," explained Tom.

"Do you know FBI agent Mr. Stevenson. He worked as a lawyer in New Orleans and was my guardian angel. He saved me," said Allie while letting out a deep breath of air.

"If I recall, Stevenson was connected to Harrisonville. I think his father name was Frank. Frank married a woman named Candee and they moved to California. Wow! I like to hear this story for sure," responded Tom with a curious look on his face.

"With the information that was turned over to the FBI by Karen, Agent Stevenson was able to locate the drug house and keep it under surveillance. In the middle of the day when most of the workers were busy working with the drugs and counting the money, Agent Stevenson grabbed me as I was getting into my car.

He took me to his law office and showed me pictures of people that the Brotherhood had murdered. One of the pictures was a picture of Lynn. That is when I learned she was an undercover FBI agent. Besides the pictures he had my complete history of my childhood years.

At that time, he did not tell me that my real mother was my aunt who gave birth to me while serving a nine-year prison sentence for a multitude of crimes. What happened next saved my life," explained Allie looking like a little school girl.

"Young lady, I believe you need a second chance in life. You are a criminal but I will defend you in court. Your defense will be; you are a criminal by genetic defect. It has been used before by one criminal in this state and all charges were dropped.

"This is the plan. I am going to turn you over to the FBI. You will be charged with several Federal crimes dealing with the distribution of drugs. If convicted, you could get life. I will ask my good friend Mr. Harrison to take your case. You don't need to pay him any money because he does most of his cases pro bono as long as he believes in you," stated Mr. Stevenson with a concerned look on his face.

"What do you want from me? asked Allie.

"You are a smart young lady, and I feel that you are worth saving. I want you to become an FBI agent. Your job after you graduate from the academy is to go undercover with the Brotherhood. Leroy knows you and he is your boyfriend. Most of your training will have to be done at night because you will be working with the Brotherhood during the day," explained Mr. Stevenson, sounding like a teacher.

"How do you know I have what it takes to be in the FBI?" responded Allie.

"We did a profile on you. To begin with, you are a criminal by genetic defect. Your birth mother, gave birth to you while she was incarcerated. Your mother was a career criminal. She started out at twelve, selling drugs for the Brotherhood on the streets of New

Orleans. Your father was a gangster from New York City. His name was Franklin Todaro. He was second in command with the New Orleans Mafia.

"Your grandparents on your mother's side were small-time con artists. They would go to race tracks and wait for a better to win big. Before a better cashed his ticket, they would approach them and offer to cash in the ticket. This type of person is call a ten percenter.

"The better would agree to give them ten percent. By doing this, the bettor did not have to pay any taxes because all the paper work was in your grandparent's names. After cashing the winning ticket, they would disappear and the better would lose everything. You see, it is not your fault that you were born into a family of criminals. Today you can fight the gene and become a better person," stated Mr. Stevenson with a voice that was speaking the truth.

"Can I have a few days to think things over?" asked Allie.

"Yes, this is a big commitment. It will take time, maybe years to get to the top people in charge of the Brotherhood," explained Mr. Stevenson.

"That night I thought long and hard about my relationship with Leroy and the Brotherhood. Leroy was all I had in the world. The Brotherhood was my family but I remembered seeing Leroy kill poor Sue. Leroy killing Sue was the reason I took Mr. Stevenson up on his offer," stated Allie with tears in her eyes.

"What happened when you went to court?" asked Tom.

"Oh boy, I felt like finding a large rock and crawling under it. They made my family and me sound like awful monsters. To make their point with the judge. The defense had my mother and father be present in court. Connie and Franklin, they were my parents. They were both serving life sentences for murder. At first I did not know who they were but my lawyer leaned over and said, "they're your parents and you are not going to end up like them," stated Mr. Harrison.

"My mother appeared to have been a pretty lady years ago. Drugs, jail, and neglect took a toll on her body and looks. My father appeared to be enjoying himself. He was glad to be anywhere as long as it wasn't his jail cell," stated Allie sounding very depressed.

"What happened next?" asked Tom.

"It took two months before my trial. I made it plain as day to Leroy that I was not going to implement anyone for a lighter sentence. I told him about Mr. Harrison and what my defense would be. That is, not guilty because of a genetic defect. If I was found not guilty, I would take classes at night as part of my rehabilitation. Rehabilitation would be conducted by a federal agency," responded Allie with some joy in her voice.

"What was Leroy's response?" asked Tom.

"Harrison will get you off. I was involved it a girl named Lola. They got her off. In fact, all charges were dropped. Allie, you know we go way back and you know what to do," stated Leroy in a strong tone in his voice.

The day before I went to court, Mr. Harrison said, "Tomorrow will be the biggest day in your short adult life. Therefore, I need to review your testimony and the witnesses that will follow. To begin with, your mother and father have agreed to testify on your behalf. They want you to have a chance at a fresh start. They don't know about your involvement with the FBI. It is a secret. Corruption goes very deep here in Louisiana. New Orleans is the worst. If we can bring down the Brotherhood, it will send a message that the FBI is alive and ready for action. By the way, I decided not to have a jury. The judge will decide the case. This judge is crooked. He is on the mafia's payroll. We want to get him and the Brotherhood. Never tell anyone about the FBI. If you do, they will find a way to kill you," stated Mr. Harrison in a stern tone.

Court started sharply a 9:00 a.m. Leroy was there along with a few of his gang members. The prosecutor saw Leroy and his gang and was happy they came.

"My mother and her sorry ass walked quickly up to the standing and she was sworn in. Mr. Harrison looked directly into her eyes and said, 'Are you a criminal?'"

"Yes, and I am proud of it. I was born into a family of criminals. My parents did not raise me. I raised myself. All by myself. I put clothes on my back, food in my belly and got an education from the streets. I was just thirteen when I became a responsible adult. Every time I got locked up, I pleaded guilty. I knew I would have a roof over my head, food, medical, and an education if I wanted one. These are things parents are supposed to provide for their kids. Well, my parents did nothing for me. Please God, send them to hell," stated Connie in tone that was scary.

The courtroom was packed. Standing room only. Everyone stood up and clapped. The judge had a hard time getting everyone to calm down. The judge kept yelling out, "Order in the court!" The noise from the crowd was getting heavier and heavier. Finally, the judge said, "Court dismissed until 9:00 a.m. tomorrow."

Court started on time, and the room was packed once again. Leroy and his thugs dominated the court room. People waited intensely to hear more about Allie's life and family. The judge sat down and asked Mr. Harrison if he was ready to proceed. "Judge, we rest our case," stated Mr. Harrison sounding very confident.

"Okay, is the state ready to present their witnesses?" asked the judge.

"Judge, we submitted about four-hundred-page report on Ms. Scarlett. If you had a chance to read the information, I know you would agree that she is the victim. Society did nothing to help her during her teenage years. She had no one in her corner. Therefore, we want to drop all charges and provide therapy and job training for her. She can be saved. It is the government's job now to correct the injustice that has caused her to be here in court today," explained the state's prosecutor.

The judge was stunned by what he had just heard and understood the total problem. "Yesterday, I read all the background information on Allie Scarlett. I have determined that she is the victim in this case. She had a mother whose parents were bad apples. They were so bad that their pretty little girl was left to take care of herself. Connie, Allie's mother is rotten to the core. The father is even worse.

If someone would have helped Connie, maybe her life would have been very different. It turns out that no one did. Connie gave a very moving testimony about her feelings. She had given up on herself but this mother does not want us to give up on her child. As a mother, she only wants the very best for her daughter. After hearing Connie, I have decided to send Allie to therapy, provide job training, and probation for two years. After the two years, if she stays out of trouble, her probation will be dismissed. May God bless Allie and Connie. Courts adjourned!" yelled the judge.

CHAPTER 26

"WELL, LET'S GET dressed and get a juicy steak. It feels like steak time with a nice green salad, and a baked potato. Your story is unbelievable but I know it is true. I would like to know if you were able to discover who are the top leaders of the Brotherhood," asked Tom.

"I believe it is now a female. After the Czar died, the leadership was up for grabs. There were all kinds of internal fighting. After a few years, things settled down for the Brotherhood. Maybe your father's notebooks might have more information about the Brotherhood reorganization," stated Allie as she rubbed her stomach to let Tom know she was hungry.

The next day, Allie and Tom sat on the beach soaking up the sun. The water was warm as bath tub water. It was good to get away from work, thought Allie. "Tom, after all my training with the FBI, I can feel the criminal is inside of me. It is very easy for me to work with the Brotherhood. Everything I did for the Brotherhood came very easy. I was born a criminal and with all my FBI training I had to work every day trying to be honest," explained Allie looking for reassurance from Tom.

"How long have you worked for the Brotherhood?" asked Tom.

"Too many years. I need to find a way to clear out. Leroy will never let me go. I believe, if we can find your half sister, that might be the key for me getting out of this business. If I can get out, maybe we can have a future together," stated Allie with hope in her eyes.

"Telling me about your life is almost the same as having a therapist. I am a very good listener and will not judge you. Everything you have done is about survival. I had to learn to survive also. It appears that my grandparents and father were career criminals and lived as if this was a way of life.

"My father was faithful to his job as the sheriff and provided law and order in Harrisonville. He understood the people of Harrisonville and loved being in charge. Remembering the stories my father shared with me, I have come to realize that the Brotherhood did not die with my father and James. It is alive and well even today. Just like any business, it had to make changes in order to continue as a force to be conquered by law enforcement," explained Tom as if he was still working as a prosecutor.

"There is a lot more to tell. To start with, Leroy's mother wanted all the workers replaced. The workers that were removed from the inside are on the streets selling drugs. I was the only one left that Leroy kept around. The new crew are hardcore criminals that would do anything to move up in the organization. It is a tough situation. Leroy is suspicious of everyone but he does trust me. Most likely because of where and how we met.

"I am anxious to see what's in those notebooks. I hope there is something that I can use to lockup Leroy and his mother. Both of them are dangerous people," stated Allie as if her life would be improved with both of them off the streets.

After two days of enjoying the beach, it was time to head back to Harrisonville. Allie and Tom were both well rested. They were totally committed in their quest to find Joni and bring down the Brotherhood. These are their goals and after the short vacation, they were also ready to seek justice for all the people the Wallaces had harmed or killed.

Tom packed up all his father's boxes along with the notebooks and put them in the car. He decided to go back to New Orleans with

Allie. He felt that they should be close to their suspects. This way Allie would be able to keep spying on Leroy and the Brotherhood.

Sitting at his kitchen table, Tom started flipping through the pages in his father's notebook. The pages were all numbered, and Tom started on page one.

The notebook was very detailed, and it started off saying the following:

Living in Harrisonville would have been a living hell without Laura. She was all that a man could dream of. She was smart, nice, pretty, and all woman. She knew how to please a man. The Czar had sent her to Harrisonville because of her situation in New Orleans. Her twin sister remained in New Orleans with her husband Eddie Acosta.

The Acosta's were in line to take over the New Orleans mafia after the Czar died but they both died first. I, Jesse Donovan, am the next mafia boss. I have kept my mafia life separated from my life here in Harrisonville. I didn't want my son to be part of the mafia, so I sent him away to college and encouraged him not to return.

We kept in touch and after his mother died we drifted apart. I was very upset to learn at his college graduation that he majored in criminal justice. But I was happy to read in the college brochure that he was number one in his class. After college he went straight to law school. I was proud of him but I had many sleepless nights wondering if he would be the law enforcement officer that would lock me up and throw away the key.

When the Czar took over the Brotherhood, he gave it a real kick in the ass. The organization now has many layers of leadership. I am the top man in charge. To begin with, many small gangs will operate under the name of the Brotherhood.

These gangs have their own organization. The gangs have a lieutenant, a leader, and soldiers. The gangs are specialists in different areas. The most important gangs in each territory are the drug gangs.

The soldiers recruited young boys and girls who live in poor neighborhoods to run the streets selling drugs. The drug sellers report back to their local soldier. The local soldiers report to their lieutenants.

The lieutenant is responsible for a designated territory. If there is a problem in that territory, the leader informs the lieutenant about the situation. All situations are dealt with and if the problem goes up the chain of command, the leader will be considered unreliable and removed.

In each territory there are houses of prostitution, call girls, illegal gaming, number writing, speakeasies, unions run mafia bosses, contracted law enforcement officers, the mayor, and governor. The lieutenant in each territory is a high ranking member of the mafia which is known as the Brotherhood.

Distribution of all merchandise is shipped to the mafia's warehouses. They are located all over New Orleans. Many of the local law enforcement employees work for the mafia during their spare time. Their job is to keep the street soldiers under control.

There are ten territories in New Orleans. The black neighborhoods are the hardest to control but bring in the most money from drugs. After Lucille Wallace murdered her husband

Malachi Wallace, she was given control over the black territory. Lucille is my best lieutenant.

The months that have five weeks, the lieutenants meet with me, Jesse Donovan, to give a report on their territory. All drug money is collected by the lieutenants on a weekly basis. That money is then turned into my lieutenant.

Everyone is under surveillance. Based on the merchandise that is on the streets, I know how much should be coming in each month. The lieutenants take 40 percent of everything coming into their territory and pay out 25 percent to it leaders and officers. The officers pay the soldiers.

My lieutenants pay off law enforcement each month. All transactions are made in cash. Our bank launders the money for us. It comes to the organization as clean money. Clair Bondurant, who is my accountant, keeps track of all transactions and how much we paid each politician. My street name is King James. King James allows me to remember my good friend, James Harrison. The Brotherhood belonged to us. Two kids who only wanted protection from other kids in our neighborhood.

Malachi Wallace was stealing from me but it was a very tricky situation. If I took him out, who could I trust to take over his territory? One night as Laura and I were having fun at Pearls Celebrity Bar and Grill in New Orleans, Lucille Wallace came up to me crying. She wanted help with her cheating husband.

I told her that her problem was personal and that she should find a way to handle her husband. I told Laura about Malachi stealing my products and money, but I did not know exactly how to handle him. Malachi was a big man and well respected in his black territory. If I took him out, it could start a war with the blacks. Malachi's territory was a money maker and he knew it.

The next day Laura told me that Malachi tried to talk to her. She refused his advances. He called her a black bitch. Laura could not understand how Malachi found out that she has black ancestors. James must have told the Czar that Ella had a black grandmother. The Czar always considered Ella the best in the business. As the Czar's number one enforcer, he made it his business to know everything about his top people.

James Harrison knew the twins were black. Therefore, he most likely told the Czar. Somehow, Malachi knew that the twins were black. Laura told me that I could set Malachi up to be killed by his wife.

The plan was to have one of the call girls chase after Malachi. James was to make sure when Malachi was at Pearls Celebrity Bar, Sonya would be working. Sonya's job was to serve drinks and if a client wanted more than drinks she was to for fill that want. At first Malachi resisted Sonya's advances but finally gave in. He had a thing going on with her for several months.

"Wow! Jesse's notebook is very detailed. Continue reading it Tom. I like to know more about how Jesse was able to remain in power for so many years without being arrested or killed," stated Allie with curiosity in her tone and on her face.

I called a meeting with Lucille and told her about her cheating husband. If Sonya had not been white, I believe Lucille would have just roughed her up a little. Lucille was furious about her husband and that white bitch. Her reward for killing Malachi and making it look like a woman's scorn, would be Malachi's territory.

It was Christmas Eve and Malachi met up with Sonya at the Acorn Inn. This was a local bar that most gangsters patronized. Lucille had got herself totally plastered by drinking bourbon all day. Without much encouragement she picked up her husband's Colt M1911A1 and dashed out the door. She was on a mission.

She planned only to kill Malachi but fire was coming out of her from all over. She couldn't help herself. She fired the gun two times. She fired once at Malachi's head and the second at Sonya's head. Then she dropped the gun and walked out as if nothing had happened.

Lucille has been a very loyal community leader and lieutenant for the mafia. Her territory is better run than it was under her husband. She was responsible for the upgraded system for selling all kinds of drugs in the juvenile detention centers in New Orleans. Her son Leroy is a chip off the old block. He works with her. Everything goes through Leroy. Leroy has a great criminal mind. He was born a criminal and that makes him an authentic criminal.

"Leroy is your boyfriend, right?" asked Tom.

"Only on paper. I'd like to nail all of them. My biggest accomplishment will be to bring down the Brotherhood and put Lucille and Leroy in jail for life," stated Allie with hope in her voice.

"Oh, here is a page on the Czar," stated Tom with excitement in his voice.

My good friend the Czar passed away in his sleep. Two days before he died, he had informed all his lieutenants that I, Jesse Donovan would be the new leader of the Brotherhood upon his death. I was young but understood the business. I was thirty-nine years old when I became known as King James.

The Czar was suffering from severe headaches, slurred speech, and blood was running down his nose. The doctor said there was nothing they could do for him. Within two days he died. All my decisions as King James were made as if the Czar had approved them. I copied his style of doing business. Which was do under others before they do under you. Always stay a step ahead of competition or the law.

With the Czar gone, I still had to show strength in all the territories because the leaders were trying to get complete control of their territories and cut out the Brotherhood.

It was a struggle for several years but I came out on top. To begin with, I started with the longshoremen's union bosses. Their stevedores were mostly hard core thugs and goons. This was the toughest group to keep in line, mainly because the leaders were changing often. It was changing because some goon was too inpatient and wanted to get to the top quickly.

I sent a clear message to the longshoremen and union leaders one night. The message was, the Brotherhood and King James control this union and not some self-imposed goon. I had Theresa and Vonda act like hookers and go down to the docks. The new union leaders were on the dock waiting for a shipment of meat, fruit, and vegetables to arrive. After the men unloaded the shipment and the trucks drove off, Theresa and Vonda open fired on the union bosses and all their goons. After that night, the longshoremen never questioned any of my orders.

Remember, the Brotherhood belongs to me. I was one of the originators and was not going to let anyone water it down to nothing. Shortly after the longshore night massacre, I called a meeting with only the territory leaders. None of their goons were invited. I wore a mask so my identity would be protected. I did not serve any food or liquor. I wanted to send a message that business comes first and you can party on your own time. After everyone was checked for weapons and were seated, Theresa and Vonda stood by the door. My orders were to shoot anyone who looks agitated or acts confrontational. I wanted complete loyalty and control. This is an underground criminal business and loyalty and control are the cornerstones of the mafia.

Theresa and Vonda worked as a team. They were recruited by Leroy when he was a resident at the juvenile detention center for males. They kept law and order in the female juvenile detention center. They were very good at their jobs. Even Leroy and his goons knew that if King James ordered them to do a job it was completed with no loose ends. At my meeting, I did all the talking. I said the following:

1. For us to make money, we need to function like a family. A family will always stick together and support each other.

2. My real name has never been used. Therefore, King James is my street name and that is the name you use in any situation.
3. New Orleans is not my home but my heart lives here.
4. The Brotherhood was started by me and a friend and it will continue to exist as long as we stick together and don't fight among ourselves.
5. Big bonuses will be given out every six months to the territory leaders who manage their territory efficiently with very little law enforcement involvement.
6. If I have to take over a situation dealing with the law, I can guarantee you the situation will not have a pleasant ending.
7. If a territory leader needs some assistance, provide help.
8. All money is to be sent to my accountant and if any problems occur, inform my accountant as soon as possible. The accountant has the ability to handle every situation that might interfere with your daily operations.
9. Do not try to reach me under any circumstances.
10. I love New Orleans and plan never to be a resident in one of their jails. With this message have a great day, goodbye.

"Wow! I can see why your father said, 'be careful with whom you share this information with.' There isn't enough to shut down the mafia, but it is a beginning," stated Allie.

CHAPTER 27

ALLIE AND TOM went back to New Orleans together. Tom put his father's notebooks in a large brown paper bag. Tom decided to store the books in Allie's dishwasher. She used her dishwasher as a file cabinet and the two of them agreed that was a safe hiding spot. Allie suggested to Tom that he stay in the house and not call anyone. She knew if Vonda found out that Tom was in New Orleans then she would surely try to kill him. If that happened Allie would have to kill or find a way to have Vonda locked up.

Allie looked at Tom and felt that she was so lucky to have met a guy as nice as Tom. She realized he could never be like his father, a born criminal. "Tom, I am going to visit Lucille Wallace. She might have some information about your half-sister. Is there any information other than her age that might be helpful in finding Joni?" asked Allie with a concerned look on her face.

"Let's see if she ever received a driver's license, if so, there will be a picture of her," stated Tom with a confident look on his face.

"I can use my computer with my FBI code to get into the motor vehicle system to search for her. If she has a license her picture will pop up," stated Allie as she reached for her computer.

Allie typed in Joni Basset, but a picture of a dark black girl with dreadlocks popped up. All the information about Joni was right but the picture was not Joni. It was obvious that Joni had someone use her information but the photo was of a black girl. "Your half-sister does not want to be found. The picture on the license is not her, but I know this girl. I have seen her before. She works for Leroy. I can use this picture to find out who she really is," explained Allie in a professional voice.

As Allie was opening up the facial recognition software, Tom was getting very anxious and started to sweat. First, his sweat was making him moist around his chest. As the program was loading his forehead was starting to drip sweat into his eyes. Tom kept wiping his face but the sweat returned.

"Bingo, we got a hit. Oh my! Her name is Tina Wallace. It states, she was killed in a police raid a few years ago. The raid took place at a bar owned by Laura's sister Ella and her husband Eddie Acosta. We now know the real name of the girl whose picture is on the driver's license. The license was issued around the same time as the raid that killed Tina," explained Allie with a puzzled look on her face.

"I remembered that raid," responded Tom.

"So do I, and it was a big story on the front page of the *New Orleans Times*. Tina was considered one of the top gangsters for the mafia. Her Uncle was Malachi Wallace. This whole situation is getting stranger by the day. In the note that Joni sent to my father, thanking him for his generous gift, she stated she like to go into law enforcement in some form. Maybe we are looking in the wrong places.

I remembered an undercover officer not only changed his name but had plastic surgery to change his looks. Maybe that is what has happened in Joni's case," stated Tom looking as if he had found the answer.

"Let's check the records for people who partitioned the court for a name change in New Orleans in past ten years. We will be looking for a white female age thirty to thirty-five, college graduate, single, born in Harrisonville, NC, and last name, Basset," explained Allie.

Using a special system created by the FBI, Allie was able to access court records. Because she wanted to go back ten years, the system was only set-up to allow her to retrieve up to eight years of court records. If she wanted to see older years she would have to get permission from her boss.

Allie felt that her boss was not to be trusted in this situation because he did not know she was an undercover with the Brotherhood. The upper level of the FBI wanted just a few people to know about her assignment with the Brotherhood and her mission. Her mission was to gather enough information to bring down the Brotherhood.

Allie and Tom decided it was time to call the director of the FBI. He had explained to Allie at the very beginning of her mission, he wanted to be kept updated on all information about the Brotherhood. Both Allie and Tom believed his half-sister was the key to bringing down the mafia in New Orleans and the ending of the Brotherhood reign of terror.

"Director, we know that Tom's half sister is known by the Brotherhood because while we were in Harrisonville, Vonda the enforcer for the Brotherhood paid us a visit. She told Tom to stop looking for Joni and if he continued, he would be killed," Allie's voice was full of hope and concern.

"My sister's driver's license has a photo of Malachi Wallace's niece Tina Wallace. Tina was killed in a drug raid a few years ago. We believe Joni has changed her name and maybe had cosmetic surgery to change her looks. We need you to give the court permission to allow us to research the records to see if Joni changed her name," explained Tom with hope in his eyes.

"Let me make a few phone calls to see if it is legal for me to ask the court to open up their records to the FBI. I will get back to you in a few days," stated the director.

"I don't think he will allow us to see the records unless we can give him more information. I will ask Leroy if he knows Joni. Leroy makes it his business to know everyone in the organization," explained Allie.

The next day Tom dressed up in a disguise and went to the mafia club. He needed to relax and just let his hair down. The club was one of the mafia's most popular spots. After a few drinks, he started talking to the barmaid and who was also the singer for the band.

He grew up in a small hick town in North Carolina called Harrisonville. The barmaid told him her best friend was born in that town. At that point she had his undivided attention.

"What is your friend's name. I know almost every family from that town. Even the family that the town was named after," asked Tom trying to not sound nosey.

"I don't know you and I have said too much as it is. She would be upset if she knew I told you that she was born in Harrisonville," explained the barmaid with fear in her voice.

"Okay, I understand," responded Tom.

The barmaid looked around the room and saw the manager staring at her. By the look on the barmaid's face. The manager could tell she was talking too much to the customer. The manager gave her a look that was designed to tell her to shut up.

Tom got home before Allie. When Allie got home, Tom was sitting in the kitchen reading his father's notebook. He was hoping he would discover something that would help him find Joni. He also wanted to know who was the top dog running the mafia in New Orleans.

Allie did not recognize Tom in his street disguise, and she pulled out her gun and was about to shoot when Tom turned around smiling at her.

"Hello, hotshot. I have some new information to tell you. I went to the club and had a few drinks. The barmaid started talking to me and I found out that her best friend was born in Harrisonville. She refused to tell me any other information. After she told me about her friend, she looked like a scared kitten. I decided not to pressure her and I changed the conversation and left," explained Tom as he took off his disguise.

The next day Allie went to the club. She was looking for the barmaid, but she was not there. Everyone knew Allie but they were ordered not to talk about the barmaid. That night the barmaid's body was discovered shot in the head in an alley a few blocks from the club. Tom and Allie knew they were closing in on finding Joni and the Brotherhood.

The next day, Allie got a call from the FBI director. He told her, he needed her to get more information on the Brotherhood. With more information he would open up all information systems to her. Allie was disappointed but understood his decision.

Tom and Allie were sitting in the living room reading Jesse's notebook when he saw a note on the side of page labeled "my little girl."

> My little girl is so sweet. Her black wavy hair makes her look like a porcelain doll baby.
>
> Today is her birthday, September 21, and she turns sixteen.
>
> A sweet sixteenth birthday party had been planned for her in New Orleans.
>
> It will be held at the most beautiful club that New Orleans has to offer. All my friends and their children are invited. A special band will perform with Joni's favorite singers and songs. A photographer will be hired to take lots of pictures. This will be Joni's day. I hope this day brings back good memories as she moves into adulthood.
>
> "Well, now I know Joni has black wavy hair and photos of her are somewhere around here in Harrisonville. My father didn't want the town to know that Joni was his daughter, therefore he didn't display Joni's picture in the house. I believe her pictures might be in his safety deposit box in Harrisonville or in New Orleans, somewhere," stated Tom as he continued to read the notebook.
>
> "It appears that my father asked Mickey Coonan and Jake Hutches to come to New Orleans to help run the organization. Mickey is the one who shot his father in the head because

he refused to work with James Donovan. Jake Hutches is Zoe's cousin. My father told me that he is smart and a very good business man," with his eyes wide open, Tom spoke like a good son.

For me to hold the organization together, I have decided to bring Mickey Coonan and Jake Hutches to New Orleans. With their skills, the family organization will withstand any attempt by other small gangs to try to take the Brotherhood down.

I own a house in New Orleans and that is where Mickey and Jake can live. It will also be their headquarters. Mickey and Jake arrived together and were very eager to start work. They had many big ideas that would fit nicely into the New Orleans organization.

I call all the territory leaders together. That also included Lucille Wallace. At this meeting, Lucille felt she and Leroy had worked very hard for the organization and wanted to have more power over their territory. In fact, they wanted to be independent.

Leroy told the group, that he was branching out into the college market and this market was reliable and had plenty of money to spend on drugs. Drugs were the Wallace's main product.

Mickey was a good looking big guy. He was 6'4" and weighed around 210 lbs. I looked at Mickey and without saying anything, he stood up. He was also good with words.

"Ms. Lucille, what you are asking is not possible. We are a family. If we allow you to branch off on your own, the family unit will start falling apart. I am here to let all of you know that the family that works together, stays together. No one will be allowed to leave," stated Mickey in a deep convincing tone.

Lucille got up and started cursing. "You white MFs, you don't control me! I am a grown ass woman. I will do my own thing anytime I want. God damn all of you," she stated as she started walking out.

Tina was standing in the front like a good soldier next to Mickey and Jake. With one wink of Mickey's right eye, Tina shot Lucille straight in her heart. Leroy looked up at Tina and she asked, "Do you want to go with your bad ass mother? He shook his head no and ran out the door.

I knew down the road Leroy would be bad news but for now, I needed him to run his territory without any interruptions. We were reorganizing and did not need any extra stress.

Within a few days, Mickey and Jake paid a visit to the longshoremen and teamster union bosses. The meeting went very well. Everyone was in full agreement as to who was in charge. King James was just a name to them. No one in the organization had ever met the King but the King knew them all. Mickey and Jake decided that a council would be a good idea and it would give each territory leader and union bosses more power. The council would decide what type and what quantity of drugs to buy, how the nightclubs would be run, who would be in charge of gentlemen's clubs, how and where they laundered the money, and all administrative decisions. King James would vote in case of a tied decision. No one except Mickey, and Jake would know my true identity.

Whenever I visited New Orleans, I came as an ordinary tourist or visitor.

I never tried to interfere with the business only if it was necessary. Most of the time I was with Laura. We always felt like newlyweds. It was a great time and feeling to be with her. She was always fun to be around.

The loss of Laura was devastating to Joni and me. Joni was in her first year of college when her mother died. Her cousin Zola was living in New Orleans when her mother passed away. Zola convinced Joni to go to school in New Orleans. Without any family in Harrisonville, she moved to New Orleans. At first Joni would stay in touch with me but as time when on she stopped communicating. I often believed she found out that I was her father or that she was a person of color.

Sally, Tom's mother, knew about Laura but she was willing to take a back seat to Laura. Her biggest fear was that I would leave her for Laura. Laura always had a plan. She hired a private investigator to look into Laura Basset's past and family. Without any warning, Sally looking like a lioness ready to protect her cubs, presented me with the following information.

"Your precious bitch is nothing more than a thoroughbred MF criminal. She and her bastard baby are both black. Her sister, Ella Acosta was a major player with the mafia in New Orleans. Her grandmother was French but lived in Ireland. Her name was Vera Donovan. She had a son by the name of Jerry Basset who married a black entertainer. The black entertainer was Josephine White. They had a set of twin girls named Ella and Laura Basset. Vera who was your mother, was the grandmother of Ella and Laura Basset.

"Vera was not your mother, but Conor was your father. The Basset twins do not have any Donovan blood. Vera and Conor were major players with the Brotherhood, which was created in Ireland. How the Brotherhood came about, I do not know. I want you to break it off with Laura. If you don't, I will expose her color to the town. This town will not like a white man having a baby by a woman passing for white. You are the sheriff and having a black baby is unacceptable to me and the town!" yelled Sally with anger and hatred consuming her.

Tom looked at Allie and Allie could not take her eyes off Tom. Sally had just verified what Jesse, Tom's father, had told him while sitting around the dinner table. Now Tom knew he had to find Joni. Not only to share the inheritance but to let her know she has a brother.

"Tom, put the notebook down. I think we have had enough of Jesse for now. Tomorrow we can concentrate on our mission. That is, to find Joni and to bring down the Brotherhood," said Allie as she leaned over and gave Tom a sweet kiss on the forehead.

That night as Tom lay resting in bed, he started thinking about his father. His father was the mafia boss in New Orleans. He was a very smart man to be able to wear multiple hats and function very good at his job as the sheriff of Harrisonville and the mob boss of New Orleans. With Mickey and Jake as his go to guys, things in New Orleans were being run very smoothly, thought Tom as he closed his eyes and went to sleep.

As soon as the sun came up, Tom pulled out the notebooks and started reading with his coffee in one hand. Mickey and Jake are great leaders. They have regular council meetings and most of the time things proceed with very little disagreements. They are special loyal comrades. The two of them are loyal to the bone. They would die, protecting me and the Brotherhood and I would die protecting them.

Leroy was very angry about Mickey killing his mother and wanted to get revenge. As Mickey and Jake were leaving the headquarters to go to breakfast, a car full of Leroy's thugs pulled up and started firing on them. Mickey was hit in the shoulder and Jake's leg received two bullets.

My two loyal comrades were almost eliminated. It was pre-planning on their part that saved their lives. Both of them were wearing bullet proof vests. Without the vests, they would have been killed. Tina heard the flaring of shots and came out of the headquarters firing like a crazy woman. She was good at leveling the playing field. That is just what she did. When it was over, all the thugs were dead. I know it was a sight to see.

Mickey and Jake recovered from their injuries. Leroy went underground because the council voted to put a contract out on him. Vonda was given control of Leroy's territory. She was a good fit for his territory because she was Hispanic/black. Most of the gang members knew her and felt very highly of her. She was very fair and a good listener. She dealt out punishment just like a parent with a child that was naughty.

It was almost noon when Allie got up. She looked around but did not see Tom. Her heart started beating real fast. Finally, she saw him sitting in the kitchen. She didn't want anything to happen to Tom. He was the best thing in her life at this point.

"Tom, I see you started reading without me. Your father was very detailed and his notebook tells a story that he wanted told. Is there anything so far that would help us convince the director to let us continue to search for Joni?" asked Allie.

"Allie, we could hunt down the photographer who took pictures at Joni's birthday party that was held at the hotel in New Orleans," stated Tom with a pleasant smile on his face.

"For now, put your disguise on and let's go to that bar you went to a few days ago and see if we can find out some more information," responded Allie grinning from ear to ear.

CHAPTER 28

WHEN TOM AND Allie got to the bar, they ran into Vonda. She was beautiful and looked perfect in her jeans with a very revealing top. Tom believed if she had parents that wanted only the best for her, she could have been a different person. He also felt that it was not too late for her.

Vonda insisted that they sit at her table. Tom was reluctant at first, thinking she might recognize him. Allie and Vonda were good friends. They were both locked up in the detention center as teenagers together many years ago. Tom didn't say much, he just listened to the two girls talk about old times.

"Allie, I got an early release from my twenty-year jail sentence because my appeal was accepted by the court. A lawyer by the name of Mr. Harrison heard about me and put an appeal in at no cost. He said what I did was evil but if I was under the influence of drugs at the time I killed my parents, he believed that I should have been given a second chance at becoming a better person.

"I learned to use drugs because my parents were drug dealers. They were low level players with the Brotherhood. Both parents were high school drop outs and were involved with the mafia and drugs as young kids. My mother often bragged about being the youngest kid on the block selling drugs. I never knew how it would feel living a so called normal life.

"I was twenty-five when Mr. Harrison took my case. He told me that my defense would be. I was a criminal because of a genetic defect. Being a criminal is in my genes. My parents had a few opportunities to do better but chose not to cooperate with the Feds to take down the Brotherhood. They were very loyal to the Brotherhood. The only thing I learned from them was loyalty. That is why I do my job and work hard at being the best, even if I am a loyal criminal," stated Vonda with pride.

"What happened when you went to court on your appeal?" asked Tom.

"Mr. Harrison told me that he had use this defense several times in the past. I gave him the names of grandparents and great-grandparents because he wanted to do some research to find out more about their lives. Just before we were to go to court, Mr. Harrison showed me a picture and a newspaper article about my father's grand-father. He was a bank robber. He and his gang had robbed over fifteen banks in the Boston area before they were all killed in a shoot-out with the police.

"My mother's father was in the moonshine business. He was killed by a man named Rocco who later became the mafia boss here in New Orleans. This was told to me by Mr. Harrison. He outlined my family tree of criminals, from my great-grandparents, grandparents, parents, and me. Most of my ancestors were criminals. I can't help myself. I am a born criminal," explained Vonda with tears flowing from her beautiful eyes.

"Vonda, I know how you feel. I was born into a family of criminals. It is not easy to stay the course because it is in our genes. Maybe one day we will be able to find peace and forgiveness," responded Allie.

"It was very embarrassing to have the judge read into the court records my criminal record and that of my ancestors. When it was all over the judge suspended my sentence to time served. I was released and put on probation for a year. I did the probationary year just like an honor student. I even had a job as a hostess in a bar and restaurant," explained Vonda sounding very proud of her only good accomplishment.

"Is that when you hooked-up again with Leroy?" asked Allie.

"I met his mother and she got me back into the business by telling me that the money I was making as a hostess was just chump change. I should come and work for her. She also stated that I was a born killer, for it was in my blood," stated Vonda with tears flowing down her face.

Tom looked at Vonda and felt nothing but pity for her. Here was a baby girl who came into this world without any knowledge of anything. Everything that she learned was taught to her by others. Even learning how to be a criminal and how to kill without feeling anything.

"Vonda do you know anyone from North Carolina?" asked Tom, talking like an investigator.

"North Carolina, no, but I believe I heard of a girl years ago who went to the University of Louisiana and became a top mafia member," responded Vonda.

Allie was very concerned about Vonda but felt that her life had already been determined years ago. Between the youth detention center and spending many years locked up as an adult, there was no returning to a normal life for her. Life for Vonda was as good now as it would ever be.

Vonda had adjusted to living a life as a criminal and over the years learned to love it. It was the only thing that she had that no one could take away from her. Even going back to jail could not destroy her love for the criminal life.

Allie turned around and saw Mickey standing behind her. "Who is this beautiful creature, Allie?" asked Mickey.

"This is Vonda, she has Leroy's old territory," stated Allie.

"I heard that the council had put a woman in charge of that territory but they did not say she was gorgeous," responded Mickey as if he had found love.

The dance floor of the club was completely empty and a lovely slow song was being played by the band. The singer had a voice that was blessed by God. Her voice was so great it would have made anyone fall in love just by hearing her sing.

"Vonda would you dance with me," asked Mickey with a voice tone that strictly meant for a man in love.

"Yes"! replied Vonda as if she had been waiting all her life to say the word "yes."

Allie and Tom sat close to each other enjoying the music. Tom looked at Allie and knew she was going to be Mrs. Thomas Donovan one day. Mickey was holding Vonda very tight as they danced as if he did not want to ever let her go.

When Mickey and Vonda returned to the table, Mickey shouted, "I found love."

Vonda was shocked to hear him say those words. Everyone in the room heard him. An old man slowly stood up and started clapping. Without any prompting, everyone was on their feet clapping. They were clapping because love had found its way into the room and landed on the two of them. The old man yelled out, "congratulations to the two of you for finding love. You are an inspiration to all of us."

Tom looked at Vonda and Mickey and was happy for them. Feeling loved, even if it is only for a short time is well worth it, thought Tom. "I believe it is time to order food. I going to have a medium rare steak," said Allie.

"Make that two medium rare steaks and a bottle of your best champagne. We want to always remember this day," stated Tom with joy in his voice.

"We will have your seafood platter for two," responded Vonda as happiness consumed her whole body.

Mickey did not tell Vonda that he was allergic to seafood. He felt that he would take an allergy pill later and that would solve his problem. After a day of fun and love, Vonda took Mickey home with her and they made love until they fell asleep.

The next morning, Allie got up and made breakfast for the two of them. Vonda kept calling out to Mickey to rise and shine but there was no answer. Finally, she went into bedroom and started shaking him. He did not move. She turned him over and by the look on his face, she knew he was dead. He forgot to take his allergy medication and died in his sleep. Vonda just sat at the bottom of the bed without a tear coming from her eyes.

God gave me joy for a short period of time. He is in control. Maybe I should give up my love for crime and find a new way to live, thought Vonda.

The council had a funeral for Mickey. He was a good soldier. At his funeral, Vonda got up and talked about Mickey as if she had known him all her life.

"Mickey lived the life he was born into. It was not his choice to be a criminal. It was in his genes. We can only live the hand that we are dealt. God will forgive him because he is a forgiving God. Before he crossed over, he told me that he believed in God. God brought Mickey and me together and he did not let Mickey die alone. Even though I only knew him for a few hours, we found love.

As of now, I'm going to turn my life around. I'm going to fix up what I messed up. I'm going to work on starting over again. To begin with I am going to call on God to help. With Mickey's short time of loving me, I now know that there is a better life waiting for me in heaven and on earth," explained Vonda with big tears falling from her cheeks.

Vonda stood straight up and held that position for several minutes and then walked out the door. For weeks, the council tried to find Vonda but she was missing in action. Some thought she had committed suicide but there was no evidence of committing suicide. After a few months went by everyone stopped thinking about her and continued work with the organization to keep it running smoothly.

Vonda's territory was split up into smaller units that were included in with the bigger territories. On Allie's birthday she got a letter from Vonda. She was wishing her happy birthday. Allie was so happy to know that Vonda was alive and well. She could not wait to tell Tom about the letter. The letter was mailed from Harrisonville, North Carolina. To Allie, that was a strange place for Vonda to live.

Why would she want to live in that town? She is a big town gal, thought Allie.

"I feel that we are getting closer to finding your half-sister and the leadership of the Brotherhood. I'd like to continue on reading your father's notebooks. It's providing us with some good information about daily operation of the New Orleans mafia," explained Allie with a confident look on her face.

Vonda never told anyone much about her family. She just let people think she did not have any family. Harrisonville was where her uncle and his wife lived. He was the minister of a big Baptist church in town. Most of the residents of the county attended his church. Vonda arrived in Harrisonville on a Saturday night and went straight to one of the bars. She got extremely drunk and ended up in bed with a male stranger.

She jumped out of bed but she was still drunk. The first thing she did was to guzzle down a large glass of bourbon. She took one look at herself in the mirror and decided it was time to go to church and ask God to save her. When she got to the church, the choir was singing "Oh How I Love Jesus." Vonda dropped to the floor and started crawling down the aisle towards the altar. Her uncle did not recognize her at first. She looked up at him and he knew her.

"My God is a mighty God. It took time but my niece has come home. God has defended her and now she is with the church!" shouted her uncle.

"I'd like to join the church and start my life over. I always wanted to be part of the church but did not know how. Therefore, I made up my mind and I just crawled in. I have nothing to offer but my sinful self," responded Vonda with tears flowing from her eyes and flooding her lips with water from the tears.

The letter that Allie received from Vonda was very warm and loving. She began by wishing her a happy birthday. The two girls were born in the same month but different days.

> I have found God. My Uncle and his wife are
> a blessing for me. They took me in and I have

found love for the second time. The love of God and my family is all I need. It is a challenge every day not to think like a criminal. I am not going to let my criminal genes determine my life anymore. Only God will determine my life. Hope you will visit soon. I will always be glad to see you.

With love,
Vonda

PS, I am using my real name, Rea Orejuela.

"It is a miracle that she wants to change her life. I like her new name. Rea Orejuela sounds like the name of a famous person. Maybe she will be famous one day for something great. Oh, I just got a text message from the council leader, telling me the council wants to see me right away. I wonder what's this all about," stated Allie in a concerned tone.

"Do you want me to come with you?" asked Tom.

"No, they might recognize you even in your disguise. You were a bad ass prosecutor and they would love to see you go six feet under. So let's be careful," stated Allie with a smile on her face.

The council leader called a meeting because there was a serious problem that needed to be discussed. It turns out that Leroy got locked up for multiple charges based on what Allie had given the director about him. To save himself, he volunteered to give up information on the Brotherhood if they agreed to drop the most serious charge, which was murder in the 1st degree.

Also, Leroy had reported back to the council before his mother was killed, with verified information that there is a mole deeply embedded in the organization. This mole is a high level member. Leroy did not know if it was a male or female but he was 100 percent certain that this information was true.

When Allie arrived at the headquarters, everyone was already seated. She felt that she was the focus of the meeting. As the Leader began to speak, Allie was shaking so badly that her knees were making banging noises. In the room was a bar with alcohol. Allie went straight over to the bar and poured herself a big glass of bourbon on the rocks. Before she sat down the bourbon glass was empty and she was totally relaxed.

The council leader was talking but Allie did not hear anything he was saying until he shouted out her name. "Allie is a loyal soldier. She has been with us since she was a teenager. Any information about the mole will be passed on to Allie. She will have the responsibility to find the mole," explained the council leader.

"Does Leroy know who is the current boss?" asked Allie.

"No, he only knows the council members and that is too much. We need him taken out. They are keeping him in their safe house. The night guard at the house, works for us. He is going to put rat poison in his food tonight. He is supposed to give a deposition tomorrow around 1:00 p.m. If things go as planned, he will be dead by morning.

The morning guard found Leroy unresponsive. An ambulance was called but he died in the emergency room. The Brotherhood is still alive and well.

"Tom, who do you think is the new mafia boss after your father died?" ask Allie.

"That's a good question. I often wonder who would be next in line to take over the organization. Jake is well qualified to run anything. He is educated and smart. Jake understands the business because he started out in Ireland. I believe we should concentrate on Jake. At the council meetings, he does not say much, he just listens," responded Tom.

"Let's have a glass of bourbon. This has been a day that should be written in someone's books. To begin with, Vonda is now Rea and has found God. She has destroyed a great number of people but God will be her judge. Next, Leroy was murdered because he was going to tell all he knew about the Brotherhood. The biggest problem for me was that the council knows that the organization has a mole among its ranks. I was so nervous that I had to guzzle down a glass of bourbon in order to calm my nerves," explained Allie looking relieved that this day was ending.

"If we continue to read my father's notebook, maybe we will find the person he wanted to take over. I like reading his notebook because it makes me feel closer to him even though he is no longer alive," stated Tom in a cool calm tone.

"There are a few things we can do in order to find Joni. First we can ask Rea for more information about the Brotherhood and the girl she told us about. Next, I can look for the photographer who took the pictures at her birthday that was held in New Orleans.

First thing tomorrow morning, I have a meeting with the director, and he is requesting that I give him a complete update on everything that has happened so far. I plan to start with your father and explain how the Brotherhood was formed. Is that okay with you?" asked Allie.

Allie and Tom checked in with the director. The director was pleased to see both of them. Allie asked Tom to tell the director about the origin of the Brotherhood. Tom had a flow chart to show the Brotherhood organization system.

"To begin with, my grandfather [Conor Donovan], grandmother [Vera Donovan], father [Jesse Donovan], and his best friend [James Harrison] were the Irish Brotherhood. The Irish Brotherhood was created by Jesse and James [two kids] in order to protect themselves from other kids that were giving then trouble. JD who was a member of the Irish Brotherhood was killed by Rocco who later became the mafia boss in New Orleans. He took the Irish Brotherhood to New Orleans but dropped the Irish part. All this happened in Ireland before I was born.

"Rocco, James, Jesse all relocated to New Orleans. In New Orleans, Rocco's street name was the Czar. His Identity was only known by a few members of the organization. When he died, Jesse Donovan became the mafia boss. He was known as King James. Jesse needed help in order to keep the organization together, so he invited

Mickey Coonan and Jake Hutches to come to New Orleans to help keep the organization from falling apart.

The Wallace family who are all dead, played a major part in the functioning of the Brotherhood. The Wallace's had the black territory which was given to one of the enforcers. We don't know where she is. She gave up the business and left town. We do know how many territories are under the Brotherhood control and who is in charge.

All this information is true because my father the sheriff of Harrisonville and mafia boss of New Orleans kept a notebook that noted all the major events of his mafia organization. Allie as the undercover agent was a witness to many actions of the Brotherhood.

"We are still trying to find out who is the current boss. I have a plan that involves a scheme that will take down the mafia territories one at a time. A secret task force will be needed. We need a name for the task force. What about the Gangster Enforcers?" explained Tom with excitement in his voice.

CHAPTER 29

AFTER A FEW minutes, Director Wheeler responded, "A task force was just what the FBI needs. Tom will be on board as a special consultant working with the task force. Allie will be the leader. The members of the task force can be retired FBI specialists and people who you find reliable and possess the skills needed to meet our objectives.

Allie must be protected; we know she is the mole. We can't have the leader killed and dropped on the FBI's front step. The task force must be a small group of specialists that are the best at what they do. Five members sounds like a good number.

The rules will be plain and simple. This is a secret force. If the task force is exposed, I will not back you up. If you need supplies or money it will come through me only. Take the gangs and the mafia out by any means necessary. Even if you have to bend the law a little or maybe a lot.

The task force should have a plan. The members should be ready on day one to go into action. I'd like to see the top leaders go to jail for life. This will send a message to any replacements that the FBI means business. The mafia is like a weed. If you don't pull it up by the roots, it will come back stronger, and bigger, and harder to get rid of. Good luck to you two and the Gangster Enforcers," said the director, feeling ten feet tall.

"Let's go get drunk. When we take out the mafia here in New Orleans, replacements will come. The mafia is like an octopus. It has three hearts, nine brains with smaller brains in each of its eight arms. Our plan must include law enforcement. The judges are the small brains within the arms of the octopus. The arms are the prosecutors who control the police.

The three hearts are gang enforcers like Rea. The nine brains are the territory leaders with their soldiers. It's going to take a long time to take down the mafia. The mafia has been around a long time and they know how the game is played. I would suggest that we get drunk, make love, and plan tomorrow," stated Allie with a twinkle in her eyes.

Allie woke up with a hangover but Tom was ready for action. He loved how Allie related the mafia to an octopus. Knowing how the mafia organization functions, to Tom, that would be the key to taking down the organization.

"Allie, you know we have to start at the top of the organizational chain. That means going to see the governor. I know him from his early days as a young upcoming politician. He was very ambitious and ready to tackle an issue if it was going to help him move up politically. I will not tell him about the task force, but I will come up with a story that will strike his curiosity. I will make him feel he is in the loop. If I mention the FBI director's name, he will surely want in on our plans to bring down the Brotherhood. He will feel important when I tell him that I report directly to the director.

"I did not have a chance to tell you that my father's second notebook went in to more details about all the politicians, prosecutors, police chiefs, police officers that were being paid off monthly by the Brotherhood. It also lists the nine territories and their leaders. My father kept good records. His records show the dates and amount that paid out to the governor, prosecutors, politicians, police chiefs, and police officers. He developed a code for each title. (Dog = Governor, Monkey = Politicians, Cow = Prosecutors, Hog = Police Chief, Pig = Police Officer.)

"Instead of using the governor's real name, he called him Shorty. He got the right name because he is short, about 5'2". Maybe a little shorter," stated Tom, feeling good because he felt he could handle the governor.

"Can you tell how long the governor was working with the mafia?" asked Allie.

"Yes, the records date back to when the Czar was living. There is a note on the side of the page that states, "The Czar was Shorty's major contributor to his first run as a state senator," explained Tom with a slight smile on his face.

"How are you going to handle him? May I give you a few suggestions? I would call and get a face to face meeting with the busy governor. At the meeting, talk about the good old days when everyone was honest. Explain to him how the system is full of swamp dogs and if he is interested, you have a way for him to climb out.

If he acts like he doesn't understand what you are talking about, then show him the notebook copies. If he still tries to act dumb threaten him with legal action by turning the originals over to the state attorney general's office to investigate him and his office. Offer him full legal immunity in exchange for his testimony and information leading up the conviction of the mafia leadership.

If he is the person you knew years ago, he will go for it. Don't give him any time to think it over. If the mafia finds out about any of this, they will kill him before we get what we need. Tell him, if he wants to stay alive, keep his mouth shut," stated Allie as if she had control over the governor's life.

"As a safety net, if he agrees, I will video tape everything he gives up on the mafia. He knows who the top people are and the law enforcement crooks. They all work together to hold on to the money and to stay alive. We will follow the money and that is how we can bring down the judges and the police department," explained Tom feeling great to get back at work and lock up the bad guys.

That evening, Tom called the governor and told him that it was urgent and in his best interest that they meet tomorrow. The governor agreed and asked Tom to meet him at this summer home in New Orleans instead of coming to Baton Rouge. He also told the governor the meeting should consist of just the two of them because what he wanted to share with him was very sensitive.

Allie wanted to go with Tom, but it was too dangerous for her. The governor might recognize her and to save himself, report her as the mole. Therefore, Allie contacted one of her most trusted technology friends and had him to equip Tom with a small camera and recording device. This device allowed her to hear, see, and record the meeting. Allie was very excited and hoping this would be the first step in ending of the Brotherhood. She felt that the two boys from Ireland who created the Brotherhood were long gone and it was time for New Orleans to say good bye to the Brotherhood.

Getting rid of the mafia would not be the end of organized crime in New Orleans but it would break up the big monopoly. Organized crime would look and function very differently. The crime leaders would no longer have influence over law enforcement or high ranking elected officials.

To Allie this would be a great day for her. Ending the Brotherhood would feel like closing the door on her ancestors who died as criminals and loved that way of like. She often prayed that she could find a way to manage her defective criminal genes and live a normal life. Finding Tom was God's small way of lending a helping hand for she discovered love and forgiveness for all the things she had endured during her early years. Now for the first time, hope and help was on its way.

Tom arrived early at the governor's summer home which was the home he grew up in. He looked around as he waited for the governor. Tom remembered Earl as an ambitious but honest person.

How did become a bad politician happen to him? It must have been the money and influence that cause him to sell his soul to the devil. I am glad I did not give my soul to the devil. It would have been easy to take the money and look the other way. With my father living a double life as the good sheriff of Harrisonville and the mafia boss of New Orleans, I could have easily become a crime boss.

The boxes my father left me were very revealing. I now think he wanted me to end the Brotherhood. He could have given his information to the FBI but he left it to me. The statement he said in his letter—"Be careful as to whom you share this information with"—has been in the back of my head for several months. I believe he knew that corruption was deeply rooted in New Orleans society and that was the reason for that statement. I now believe he wanted me to be the one to bring the Brotherhood to an end, thought Tom.

"Hello, my old friend Tom Donovan. It's been years since we ran around in Law school drinking and chasing after college girls wearing miniskirts. Glad to see you. Heard about the passing of your father. He was a good man. He will be missed," stated the governor with a big grin on his face.

"Thank you but I am here on official business from the director's office of the FBI. Therefore, I'd like to get right down to business. I know you are a dirty politician and I can prove it. My father had a notebook that he used as a ledger. The ledger listed everyone who was a dirty politician or law enforcement officer. They were paid off by the New Orleans mafia known as the Brotherhood. As you already know, my father was the mafia boss.

"I can offer you a way out but I first like to know how you got to be so corrupt. In law school you were so gung ho about bring criminals to justice. I was born into a family of criminals. Remaining honest was always an uphill battle for me. My only defense was that I possessed the criminal gene and had to deal with my dirty father who was the sheriff of Harrisonville. I did not know until he died that he was the mob boss of New Orleans. So tell me your story," stated Tom in a sarcastic tone.

"You are not the only one who came from a family of criminals. I had the criminal gene also. My family were poor people. My grandfather who owned a little juke joint in Harrisonville, NC, made moonshine and sold drugs in order to feed his family. He was killed in cold blood by Redd Harrison. Your father covered it up. Sheriff Donovan felt badly about the family and helped us for many years. He paid for me to attend college and law school. He hired my father as one of his deputies. He did most of your father's dirty work. My father would travel to New Orleans with your father to handle serious problems. He was a reliable enforcer.

"Our fathers tried very hard to make sure we did not become criminals. Having money was never an issue with me, it was about power. For you it was living and earning an honest career. You stayed away from your father and mother. I loved the power that your father had over others and wanted to be just like him. He was my idol. I should have been your father's son but he was blessed with you. A sorry piece of meat.

"Whatever you are offering, keep it to yourself. I am not interested. I am the mafia boss. I will remain the boss. I love my power. If you tried to use that ledger against me. I will kill you. So, I give you a choice. Stay alive and die of natural causes or die today. It is up to you," with a stern look on his face, the governor said goodbye Tom.

"Oh Tom, before you leave, I'd like to invite you to my grand-daughter's first birthday party. My son married a very pretty and nice gal from NC, I like her a lot. She has criminal genes and that is just what this family needs in order to keep the power in the family. I hope when I cross over my son and daughter-in-law will be ready to take over," stated the governor with a smile on his face.

Tom walked out of the governor's office with his head held up high. He realized that he had to change his plans. He left the governor as soon as possible. He needed to warn Allie about the governor. Allie needed to be protected and he had to come up with a plan to protect her.

That night he poured himself a large glass of corn liquor over ice with a small amount of orange juice. Sitting on the sofa, he fell asleep and started dreaming. In his dream he became the governor's chief of staff. In that position he would be able to advise the governor and spy on his other profession as the mafia boss.

Allie was already part of the Brotherhood and she was now upgraded as the governor's communication's director. Moving to Baton Rouge would not be a problem. Becoming the chief of staff for the governor would take some careful planning.

First, I needed to start thinking like a criminal. Thinking like a criminal would be easy since I spent my whole career working to put criminals behind bars. Next, I need to find a way to get rid of his chief of staff and the communication director without killing them myself. If Allie and I are placed in these positions, we will be able to get records on all illegal activities in New Orleans.

To get rid of the chief of staff and the communications director, I have to make it look like they are planning a coup. One of our task force members is a computer engineer. He can create pictures of the chief of staff and the communication director planning a coup, which the two of them would overthrow the governor as the Boss and take control of the Brotherhood.

The governor most likely would have them killed but the director of the FBI can offer them protection. They can be protected if they give a deposition as to what they know about the governor being the mafia boss. The two of them would have to leave Baton Rouge before the coup evidence is presented to the governor.

I would let the governor know that I have given into my criminal genes and with my experience I would be a valuable asset to his underworld organization and to his governorship. I would like to be considered as his new chief of staff. Then I would be able to move Allie up in the organization as the communication director.

To ensure that we get the jobs, I will give him the ledger but not before we put a copy in a safe deposit box. The notebook will guarantee our safety and keep us alive.

Tom started sweating and a cold chill went through his body as he woke up. At that point he knew just what to do to bring down, the governor and the Brotherhood all at the same time.

"Tom, you look strange. Are you okay?" asked Allie with her voice sounding concerned.

"Yes, I am okay. I need to tell you about my visit with the governor. You won't believe this man. He has a long history of being a criminal which includes his ancestors.

To begin with, he is from Harrisonville, NC. His father worked for my father as his deputy and mob enforcer. He claims that being a criminal is in his genes. I believe he is right but he needs to be brought under control. If he is removed as the boss, a new boss would emerge. Then nothing will have changed, just names. If we are working in his administration, we can keep on top of all his illegal actions. We will become the mob advisers," explained Tom with a defensive attitude.

"Did you tell him about the notebook?" asked Allie.

"Yes, but he didn't care. He stated that if I tried to use it, he would kill me. I believed him. The mob has many ways to get to a person and I want to marry you one day. I like to grow old with you. Dying early is not what I want," explained Tom with love in his voice.

Tom explained to Allie about his dream. She believed his dream was the right thing to do. She was all in. She thought it would not be hard being criminals and spies, after all it was in their genes.

Early the next morning, Allie and Tom decided to pay the FBI director a visit and explained the details of their plan. He was okay with it as long as if they had to kill someone, they were deemed criminals. The director told them not to come or call anymore. Their mission has changed. Stop as many criminal actions of the governor as possible and keep a record for illegal proceedings one day. Everyone agreed and Tom and Allie went home to get ready to move to Baton Rouge.

CHAPTER 30

ALLIE AND TOM did not waste any time getting together with the "Gangster Enforcers." Allie was in charge. Tom was the consultant. Jake was the communication expert. Lucky was the explosive and sharp shooter professional. Lynn was the investigator.

Tom called the enforcer members together and proceeded to bring everyone up-to-date. He informed them that their objectives had slightly changed. The objective was to disrupt the flow of drugs of all types that were entering New Orleans. Second, limit the amount of corruption within the longshoremen's union. Third, recruit informants to help with the drug traffic, sex slaves, and watch over the governor for he is the mafia boss.

"The governor is a smart and powerful man. Therefore, we need to make sure our information is credible. Does anyone have any suggestions as to how we proceed with the plan?" asked Tom.

"Tom, we don't need a coup plan. The governor's wife is about seventeen years younger than him, and she has had multiple affairs with other men. Some are older and some are young. She slept with some of the governor's millionaire donors, in order to secure their support for his first term as governor. She is now in love with his chief of staff. All we have to do is to show pictures of the two of them. They met at the Hilton every Thursday afternoon. She tells the governor she is going to the club to play tennis," Jake explained with a smile on his face.

"How do you know about her affair?" asked Tom.

"The head maid is the sister to the First Lady of Louisiana's limousine driver. They are my cousins. At family dinners, they tell us all the dirt that goes on with the governor's wife. She is a real tramp. The only thing she has going for her is that she is gorgeous. He is a fool. He thought he was marrying a virgin. He will have her killed if the pictures surface. I have pictures of her and the chief of staff and other men. I had planned to use them to get rich by selling the pictures to the First Lady," explained Jake feeling proud.

"Let's see the pictures. You can still get rich by selling them to the governor. He will pay you to keep from having to deal with a big scandal. The governor is up for re-election in November and will do anything to win," explained Tom feeling confident.

"Maybe we should show them to the First Lady and have her to get the chief of staff to resign. The chief of staff can dismiss the communications director which will become Allie's new job. By trying this first, we will have saved two lives and have complete control over the First Lady," stated Allie with a cocky look on her face.

Jake took the pictures of the First Lady, chief of staff, and a few other men and passed them around the table. All the pictures were so graphic they would have been rated XXX. The pictures were taken by the First Lady's limousine driver who was Jake's cousin David. David had planned to retire rich, also.

"Lynn, you are the communications expert for the task force. I believe you should present the pictures to the First Lady and let her know her options. Her options are: for her to show the pictures to her boyfriend and have him to resign and pay you for your understanding of this sensitive situation. Or you will sell them to the governor and he will have both of you killed. Any money collected will go to Jake and David," stated Tom without caring which option would be selected.

"I don't have any problems with the plan but I would like to offer a few suggestions. My meeting with the Frist Lady should be recorded. I can braid my hair and put a tiny recording devise in my hair. This device will record and video the meeting. Selina, the First Lady is no dummy. She has her own circle of killers. She will order them to kill me by the time I get home. Therefore, I should meet with her at a coffee house and ask her which option is she going to take.

"I will ask for $1,000,000. She has the money because her family are millionaires. She was born rich. I will give her five days to pay or her husband will see the pictures. At least I will be alive for five days. I will inform her that a set of pictures with her boyfriend and other men are ready to be mailed to the newspapers and her husband if she even thinks about having me eliminated," explained Lynn in a cold tone.

"I will be on top of the building across the street watching everything during the meeting. If Selina tries anything, I will take her out," stated Lucky with anger in his voice.

"Everyone knows their jobs. After we get control of the governor's office, we will have to do some targeted planning in order to disrupt the mafia operation at every level," explained Tom sounding like a man ready to engage the enemy.

"Let's go to the governor's favorite club and act like we own the place. The bill for food and drinks will be on our governor. Long live the governor. Tomorrow we will put our plan into action," shouted Allie.

Tom dressed up in his normal disguise to conceal his identity until he and Allie were placed in their new jobs in the governor's office. Allie was dressed in black jeans with a black silk shirt, looking like a bad ass gangster, Lynn wore a beautiful black dress that appeared to be made just for her, and both Jake and Lucky wore black suits with white shirts and a black tie. All of them had a concealed hand gun somewhere on their bodies. They looked good and they felt good. Good enough to take down the mafia all by themselves.

The club owner recognized Allie right away. He knew where she wanted to sit. She always sat in the same area. Never having her back to anyone so she could eyeball the whole room. This was

CRIMINAL DEFENSE: REDEMPTION

part of her training from law enforcement and the mafia. As the Gangster Enforcers proceeded to their table, everyone in the club turned around and stared as they proudly walked through the crowd to their table.

The band played on and the music sounded like it was made for the gangster enforcers. The music was great and Allie grabbed Tom and said, "let's dance. I will not take no for an answer. I am the boss," demanded Allie as she held her head up high as she approached the dance floor. Jake asked Lynn to dance and Lucky saw a pretty little gal looking like she was desperate and wanted to dance. It was obvious she did not care who her partner was, as long as she was on the floor. So, Lucky asked her to dance. She now was his dance partner for the rest of the night.

When the waiter came to the table, Allie told the waiter to bring a bottle of their best cognac. The waiter responded by telling her, "The best is Hennessy Paradise. It is an extrarare cognac. One 750 ml bottle cost $1,500."

"Sir, get it now and charge the cognac and our dinner to the governor," stated Allie in a demanding tone.

Allie and her task force drank and ate well. It was a celebration of the beginning of a new day for New Orleans. They all danced to the good sounds of New Orleans and did not leave until the club closed down.

The next morning, Allie was the last to get up. The task force were sitting around her kitchen table. "We have some bad news," said Tom in a low voice.

"What is it?" asked Allie.

"The governor's wife committed suicide last night while we were having a great time at the club," responded Lynn with disappointment in her voice.

"How did she die?" asked Allie with sadness in her voice.

"She was drunk and fell asleep in the garage with the car running. They said she died of carbon monoxide poison. The maid found her unresponsive early this morning," explained Tom.

"We believe the governor found out about her boyfriend who is his chief of staff and he killed Selina," said Jake.

Just then there was a loud knock at Allie's front door. It was Henry, Selina's driver. He was shaking from head to toe. Allie didn't want Henry to see the members of the task force so she stayed outside with Henry.

"Henry, what is going on? Why are you so upset?" asked Allie.

"I was taking the governor to the airport when he saw a picture of his wife under my seat. Along with that one picture were many pictures. I had planned to give them to my sister the maid but forgot they were in the car. My other cousin had planned to sell them to Selina. This was going to be our retirement fund," said Henry as if he was down and out forever.

"What do you want from me?" asked Allie.

"I know you are a high ranking member of the Brotherhood. I need you to protect me. The governor respects you and your opinion counts with him. Please help me," said Henry with watery eyes.

"How did Selina die?" responded Allie.

"My sister, who is the housekeeper, said that she looked at the cameras throughout the house last night. The governor and Selina were drinking bourbon in their bedroom and it appeared that Selina was given a folder. Upon looking at the contents, she started crying. Shortly after that, she fell to the floor.

"The governor picked her up and put her in her car. He started the car and made sure the garage door was closed. He told my sister if anyone asked. He would be at the New Orleans Sports Club. As the sun was coming up, the governor returned home and started looking for Selina. After a few minutes, my sister found her in her car with the motor still running. The ambulance was called but she was already dead. She died of carbon monoxide poisoning.

"My sister is very dedicated to the governor and knows he has ties to the Mafia. She would never rat him out. He has always rewarded her for her loyalty. The governor doesn't know about the cameras that Jake installed last year. If he did, my sister, Jake, and me would have been eliminated," explained Henry looking scared.

"So they ruled it a suicide, right?" asked Allie.

"No, they are saying it was an accident. She was drunk and passed out with the car running. My sister confirmed to the authorities that she was drinking all day and appeared to be drunk when she got in her car.

"I took the cameras out this morning while the governor was at the hospital. I need to become part of the Brotherhood to stay alive. I will do anything for the Brotherhood. Please tell the governor you knew of the pictures and was planning on giving them to him. He will believe you," explained Henry with a face full of hope.

"Does Lou, the governor's chief of staff, know about the picture?" asked Tom.

Before Henry could respond, his phone rang, and it was his sister. She was crying so loudly that Henry could not understand anything she was saying. Finally, Henry was able to hear her say, Lou was dead.

Henry's sister went on to explain that Lou was on his way to the hospital for he was concerned about Selina. Lou was speeding and the car went out of control and hit a tree. He was thrown out the car, and the car turned over on him. The state trooper said that he died instantly.

"Allie, are you going to help save me?" asked Henry.

"Yes, we have a plan. Go home and get some rest. If the governor wanted you dead, you would be dead," responded Allie feeling concern.

The task force while sitting at the kitchen table, came up with a plan that would break up the mafia and at the same time put most of its control in the hands of Tom. The plan was to have Tom become the chief of staff for the governor. The governor was aware of Tom's abilities and his connections to law enforcement. Tom would be his go-to man.

At first Tom was not sure if it was a good idea because he knew of his struggles with his criminal genes. Taking this position and pretending to be a crime boss's number one person would not be difficult. Sitting with his head hanging low, Tom raised his head and with a large smile on his face, quietly said, "Okay."

Tom got up and went into the living room. As he sat with his eyes closed he began thinking about his father and how corrupt he was as the sheriff of Harrisonville and the mafia boss of New Orleans. He thought so hard that it gave him a headache. He knew that as chief of staff to the governor, he had to play his part without any hiccups, or he would surely end up dead in a ditch.

Tom felt that the director of the FBI should be informed about the task force's plan but he did not want to give him too many details. All the details were to remain within the task force. Tom got up, poked his chest out, and held his head up high as he walked back into the kitchen.

Allie was ready to take her position as communications director for the governor without thinking about it twice. All she needed was for the governor to give her that job. Allie's background made her an excellent candidate for the slot. Allie was the leader of the task force but Tom was the true leader. With Tom the unspoken leader, Allie felt the job as communications director was waiting for her.

Late that afternoon, Tom set up a meeting with the governor. The governor covered his tracks and did not believe the meeting would reveal that he killed his wife and his chief of staff over their affair. Little did the governor know, Tom knew everything. Tom was very confident that he had the upper hand and the governor would have no other choice but to make him the new chief of staff.

Tom arrived a few minutes early for his meeting with the governor. As he sat in the foyer waiting his turn to meet with the governor, Tom started tossing around ideas how to approach the governor about wanting to be his chief of staff. Remembering their last meeting and how he left the meeting like a dog with his tail between his legs was not the outcome he wanted this time.

Thinking to himself, Tom, decided to start with small talk about his father and their relationship as students in college. They both belonged to the same fraternity and how drinking all weekend was normal for them. Tom, at that point, felt that he was born with a defective gene. The gene laid dormant for many years but now he could not control it no longer. Suddenly a big smile came across his face. It was the smile of a person who finally discovered his true calling in life. For Tom, it was to become the boss. Not just any boss but the mafia boss of New Orleans.

Tom, looked up and the governor was standing in front of him. "Hello, my friend. Come into my office, and let's talk. I am glad you called me. I was planning on calling you today. But as fate has it, you called me. I have something very important to ask you. I like to offer you a position on my staff. Not just any position but my chief of staff. You know all about me and I know all about you.

"I recalled how you made money by writing term papers for students and charged them big money. Also, had fake IDs made up so that you could take the finals for dumb rich students. I envied you. You were a true entrepreneur. Talents, like yours should not be wasted on trying to be honest. We were both born with the criminal gene and that is our defense. How about it, are you with me?" said the governor with a big smile on his face.

Tom cocked his head to one side and said, "Only if you make my girlfriend Allie as your communications director. She also was born a criminal. I believe you know her. She has worked for the organization for many years and now it's time for her to move up," explained Tom.

"My friend Allie has been a loyal soldier and in this business. Loyalty is the best thing a person can offer. Yes, bring in the girlfriend. When can the two of you start?" yelled the governor with joy in his voice.

"Now!" responded Tom in an upbeat tone.

As Tom was leaving, the phone rang, and the governor answered the phone. "Thanks for all your service, case closed," stated the governor.

"What was that about?" asked Tom.

"I had a small problem with my chauffeur, and it has been taken care of," explained the governor, looking very pleased.

Oh my, what have I gotten myself into. He kills people without blinking an eye. If he found out about the task force, all of us would be killed. I must never allow that to happen. I will help the task force. They will take down the governor and a replacement will step in. That replacement will be me. I will keep the mafia under control. That is the only way to handle this criminal organization, thought Tom as he exited the governor's house.

When Tom got home, he went straight to the bourbon. Feeling good about not having to say much to the governor but at the same time upset over the governor bringing up his college days as a cheater. He felt just like his grandfather who started the Brotherhood as an honest way to protect himself. The Brotherhood turned into New Orleans mafia.

Tom's cheating scam was the only way he could make big money without asking his father for anything. He was torn between being honest or being a criminal. *At the end, I guess the criminal gene won out, and that is my criminal defense,* thought Tom.

CHAPTER 31

I T WAS ABOUT 5:00 a.m., and Allie was having a hard time sleeping. After experiencing a sleepless night, she slipped out of bed. She could not believe that her clothes were soaking wet. When she looked at herself in the mirror, all she could see was the look of her mother when she saw her in court. In court years ago, her mother saved Allie from going to jail. After throwing cold water on her face, Allie went outside in the back of the house and sat down in her favorite chase lounge chair. After a few minutes, she was dreaming.

"Daughter, you are the love of my life. Your father and I had hoped you would follow a different path then us. It appears that you need a little help. I like to tell you a secret. I worked for Malachi Wallace as a young person and he is your father not Franklin Todaro. Franklin knew I was six months pregnant when he fell in love with me.

"We got married, and shortly after that, I was locked up. Yes, you were born in jail, but Malachi, the leader of the South Side Creoles, is your father. You need to take out the new leadership of the South Side Creoles before they find out about you. The new leadership, has always worked against Malachi, trying for years to take over. If they found out about you, they would cut you up in small pieces and throw you to the hogs.

"You must take them out first. I know you can do it. You have good genes. Much better than mine. Once you take them out, you can control the streets of New Orleans. They will belong to you. Being black will one day be an asset not a liability. Work hard for the position you want and not the position you are in," explained Allie's mother.

"Allie, Allie, why are you sitting out here in wet clothes. Are you okay?" asked Tom with a strange look on his face.

"No, I am not okay. I need to go the FBI's crime lab to check out something. I need to know if Malachi Wallace was my father. They have blood samples of his on file. I like to see if we are related. If so, Leroy was my half-brother," said Allie with watery eyes.

"I will go with you. But first, you need to clean yourself up. You look like a druggie looking for her next fix," said Tom with a big smile on his face.

The governor felt very relieved about Tom and Allie working under him instead of against him. What the governor didn't know was that they were working for the FBI with an undercover task force to minimize the Mafia so that their influence in the underworld of New Orleans would be ineffective.

The governor was not a dummy. He knew Tom, and Tom knew him.

Therefore, being a little paranoid about his two new recruits was always going to be part of his actions.

Feeling good about himself and very confident, the governor decided to throw a big party at his family home in New Orleans. He told his secretary to get in touch with his new communications director. Let her know to be in my office by noon today.

Allie and Tom stopped by the FBI director's office before going to the lab. They wanted to let him know they were part of the governor's team with very high ranking positions.

"Allie, I am very proud of Tom and you. In just a short time you were able to infiltrate the corrupt governor's inter circle. How did you do it?" asked the director.

"If we told you, the governor might find out and have you killed. Therefore, you are better off just knowing the outcome and not the details," explained Tom with a stern look on his face.

The supervisor of the crime lab was Allie's best friend. Allie asked her to run a test on her and Malachi Wallace to see if he was her father. She also asked Linda, the supervisor not to share the information with anyone but her. If she was Malachi's daughter, the new leadership of the South Side Creoles would put a contract out on Allie.

Allie got word that the governor wanted her in his office NOW! Once again, Allie was getting moist, and as she approached and by the time she entered his office, she was totally wet. Many things crossed her mind, but none of them was putting on a party for the governor.

"My young lady, I like to have a New Year's Eve Party. You have two months for planning. I only want the best of everything. I want important people to be invited. My daughter-in-law can work with you. Her name is Bella. She is a pretty little thing who has given me a beautiful granddaughter. My first wife was a real wife and lady. Not like that slut, Selina. God took her from me years ago. She died of brain cancer. May God bless her soul," stated the governor with sorrowful looking eyes.

Allie just stood motionless staring at the governor. Thinking to herself, she called him a real bastard. He just had his wife, chief of staff, and wife's driver wiped out and all he can think of right now is a damn party! What a sorry piece of shit.

"Allie, are you listening to me?" asked the governor.

"Yes, you want me to plan a New Year's party with the help of Bella, your daughter-in-law, right?" responded Allie.

"Okay, my secretary will give you my list of guests. You can add more names as long as they are people that I will feel good having around me," explained the governor as he turned his back to Allie and sat down in his chair.

When Allie returned home, the Gangster Enforcers were all sitting at her kitchen table. "We have a big problem Allie," said Tom in a concerned tone.

"So what is the problem?" asked Allie.

"Jake's informant sent word to Jake that the president of the Longshoremen's Union was working to get on the ballot for County Commissioner. He is a vicious corrupt union leader. Over the years, he has wiped out several top leaders in his organization. If he wins, he will kill the governor and his brother who is the lieutenant governor will take over. This means, he would bring in all his people and we would be sitting on the outside, looking in," explained Tom.

"Would he have any real power as a county commissioner?" asked Lynn.

"Yes, he would be in charge of commerce, which would cover all businesses, large or small. No one would be able to get operating permits, building permits or be allowed to do business in New Orleans without his approval. His next step would be to control the governor's office, the mafia, and become the future governor. This man will stop at nothing to get what he wants.

"Well, what should we do?" asked Lucky.

"There is only one thing we can do. That is, take him out. A few of his lieutenants will have to go with him. We can make it look like the South Side Creoles did the hit," explained Tom, feeling stronger than ever.

"This calls for a nice cold beer with a corn beef sandwich loaded with coleslaw. How's that sound team?" yelled Allie.

"Sounds good to me, but I will pass on the cold beer and settle for ice tea instead," responded Lynn.

"We need to take a break. If we take him out, there will be no turning back. We will be just like the mafia, heartless," stated Lucky.

"Let's go get some food. With a full stomach we will be able to think better," explained Tom with a blank look on his face.

Allie needed some air and went outside to get her mail. In the mail box was a letter from grandmother. She had not heard from her since she was put in foster care. In fact, Allie had cancelled the grandparents out of her life years ago. Without thinking she crumbled the letter up and shoved it into her pocket. She was planning on throwing it in the trash can when she got back inside but, she got side tracked because the task force was ready to go eat and drink.

While waiting for their food and drinks, Allie started talking about how crazy the governor acted and his plans for a stupid party. At one point she started crying. Her crying was uncontrollable. Tom had never seen Allie so out of control. It must have been more going on than the situation with the paternity test.

Suddenly, Allie pulled out the crumbled up letter that she received from her grandmother. "Tom, you read this out loud to all of us. This bitch of a grandmother is writing me after all these years. She must want something from me. I am not going to give her a damn thing!" with tears flowing from her eyes like a water fountain.

Dear granddaughter,

I love you. I am so sorry for all the pain I had caused you throughout the years. Your grandfather passed away last year, and he was the one who forced me to act the way I did towards you. He never wanted any children, but I did. He abused me verbally and physically for many years. I should have done better by my children and my only granddaughter.

Your mother died last week and her body is still at the prison. The cause of her death was myelofibrosis. I asked them not to cremate the body until you had a chance to say goodbye.

It is up to you if you want to say goodbye. They will hold the body for thirty days. After that, she will be cremated. Your mother did one good thing before she died. That was to help give you a second chance in life.

I don't expect you to reach out to me but that is okay. In my heart, I have always loved you and so did your mother. Life always takes strange turns but hopefully you have turned out to be a good and honest person. Let peace and God into your life and all turns will lead you in the right direction.

With love,
Your grandmother

"Wow, what a letter. Your mother was locked up in a Federal prison," responded Lynn in a surprised, squeaky voice.

"Tear up the letter, Tom. There is more to this story. Last night I had a vision. My mother came to me and revealed that my real father was Malachi Wallace. But first I need to relax with a big glass of bourbon.

"Early in the morning, I woke up wet from head to toe. I looked at myself in the mirror and I looked just like my mother. I went outside and fell back to sleep. At that point I started dreaming. My mother was in my dream. She told me that Franklin Todaro was not my father. My father was Malachi Wallace. If it is true; I'm in big trouble. The South Side Creoles will put a contract on me. They have killed all Malachi's family members to secure all of their territory.

"I had the FBI's crime lab to run a test for me to see if Malachi was my father. So far the test has not come back. If he is my father, we will have to wipe out the leadership of the South Side Creoles," said Allie in a stern-sounding voice.

"Let's take all the MFs out!" yelled Jake.

"Allie, you think you are the only one who has a sad story to tell. I have one even better than yours. As you can see, I am a black man and well educated just like my father. My father graduated from Shaw College in North Carolina. He was number one in his class.

He could not find a job in the white world so he moved to New Orleans to find work. A friend got him hired as a stevedore at the docks loading and unloading cargo from ships. He loved his job. Every day he would come to work wearing a suit jacket, white shirt and tie, with a large wide brim hat. Everyone knew he was well educated. They nicknamed him the Professor.

As time went on he became the supervisor for several crews. He was a very honest leader and wanted the leadership to stop participating in questionable activities with the mafia. The governor, who was a young union leader, became the vice president of the Longshoremen's Union.

"My father decided to run for president. Most of the worker were black and were happy to have an educated black person running for the top position in their Longshoremen's Union.

"My father won and the next day he was reported missing. The governor was next in line to be the president. My father's body has never been found. I was just a little kid at the time but had to hear my mother cry herself to sleep every night.

"I have devoted my life to getting even with the governor for killing my father. Now you see why I agreed to be part of the Gangster Enforcers. I want justice for my mother and father. I want to out the bastard governor. Not later but now!" yelled Jake with anger in his voice.

"Lucky and Lynn, do you have anything you need to share with us?" asked Tom with a smile on his face.

"Yes, Lynn and I were juvenile delinquents. We are cut from the same mold. We were in and out of detention centers for most of our teenage years. The last time we were locked up for selling drugs. A man named Mr. Stevenson represented us in court and asked the judge to release us under him. He became our legal guardian. He treated us like we were his biological children. He sent us to a private school in which we had tutors to help us catch up to our grade level. He paid for us to go to college. He helped us join the FBI. I know he is in heaven looking down at us and guiding our every step.

"Unlike most of you, our story has a happy ending. Both of us would like to see the end of the Brotherhood but done the right way, without killing anyone. We want the governor and all his followers brought to justice. I want them locked up for life.

"Mr. Stevenson died recently and left all his assets to the two of us. We are not related by blood but we are sister and brother because of our wonderful guardian, Mr. Stevenson," stated Lucky with a joyful feeling inside of himself.

"So after all this truth telling let's say a prayer. Lynn would you like to do the honors?" asked Tom.

"God bless our coming and going for the days ahead of us will be troubling. Keep us from falling into a hole that has no bottom. We need your blessings and all of us have been saved by you for a reason. We have been criminals in the past but now we are working to make things right. That is our criminal defense," stated Lynn speaking like a spiritual leader.

The next day felt like a new day for the Gangster Enforcers. Allie decided to go to the FBI's crime lab by herself. If she was the daughter of this dangerous mobster. What difference would it make? She believed and felt she was in control of her life.

Thinking to herself as she drove down the busy highway, her vision was blurred by tears rushing down her face. Traffic was heavy and within a short flash of bright light, her car hit the concrete barrier and rolled over. Heavy black smoke had engulfed the crushed car. It would not be long before the car would blow up. Tom had decided to follow Allie to the FBI crime lab for support even through Allie insisted on going by herself. He jumped out of his car and without knowing how strong he was, turned the car over and pulled Allie out.

While sitting in the hospital waiting room, Tom decided it was time for him and Allie to get married. Tom had never been married before and neither had Allie. Now Tom, for the first time, understood how his father must have felt about Laura. Many things were running through his mind and Allie was the main thought at this time. Next was finding his half sister. Tom saw a doctor approaching him and he started sweating like a mad man. Tom was setting himself up for some bad news.

"Tom, I am Allie's doctor. She is awake and a little confused. She thinks she is Mrs. Franklin Todaro. Do you know who that is?" asked the doctor.

"Yes, her mother. She just died a few days ago. She is having a hard time dealing with the loss of her mother and a few other family matters," explained Tom with a concerned look on his face.

"My advice to you is to just go along with it. She is not going to know who you are. Before she leaves the hospital, I will have the hospital psychiatrist explain the current situation to her. It will be troubling to her but over time she will have a full recovery," stated the doctor sounding very confident.

When Tom walked into Allie's hospital room she gave him a big smile. "When can I leave the hospital doctor?" asked Allie.

Looking like he lost his best friend, he stated, "In about a week."

"Doc, where is my husband? Is he in the waiting room? How did I end up here? Oh, I know, I just had my baby. I am glad I did not deliver the baby in jail. That is not a good place to have a baby," stated Allie as if she knew all the answers to her questions.

Without any warning, Allie's eyes sailed back in her head and she was having a seizure. The doctor was call in. After stopping the seizure, Allie saw Tom and was grinning from ear to ear. "Hello, good-looking. I am glad you are here. Tom, can you tell me what happened," stated Allie feeling happy to be alive.

"You must have blacked out for a few seconds and crashed your car into the concrete barrier on the busy highway. I was behind you. I wanted to be with you for support at the FBI crime lab. I know you could handle things, even if the outcome was not good," explained Tom.

"Tom, I want to ask you something. You might need to have a few days to think it over," said Allie with tears of joy in her eyes.

"What is it, my love? Anything you want, I want it too," responded Tom as if he knew what she was about to say.

"I like to get married. I like to marry you as soon as possible," stated Allie with love all over her face.

"We were meant to be together. God's plan for us started with a flat tire on a lonely highway and a highway once again opened our eyes to the truth. We love each other. Yes, I will marry you. Get well and we will get married the day you leave the hospital. Thank you God for all your blessings," stated Tom for Allie was his first real love.

CHAPTER 32

LYNN HAD ANOTHER secret that she did not share with the task force. In her career as a FBI agent her cousin was also a FBI agent working undercover with the Brotherhood. Sue Morton was her cousin and was murdered by Leroy Wallace. Even through Leroy was dead, she wanted to eliminate the Brotherhood, for it was this underworld organization that killed her cousin. Not just Leroy Wallace.

Lynn felt guilty about joining the task force mainly to get even with the Brotherhood. Therefore, she decided to tell Allie and let her to decide if the members of the task force should know about her cousin. As she entered Allie's hospital room all the task force members were stationed around Allie's bed.

"We called you several times, Lynn, but could not reach you. Allie and Tom are getting married right now. We are her family and there is no reason for them to wait any longer," stated Jake with joy in his voice.

"Who is the minister?" asked Lynn.

Just then the minister walked in. "I am," said the tall, slender older man.

Lynn took one look at the minister and knew who he was, the killer minister. Sue often showed Lynn pictures of the top underworld figures and this minister's picture was stamped "important player." All the mafia territories reported directly to him.

"Rev, the family would like to talk to Allie in private. Would you please step out in the hall for a few minutes?" said Lynn in an unkind tone. "What is going on with you Lynn?" asked Allie.

"Allie, postpone getting hitched until you can find a real minister. This man works with the mafia. He is number two in the organization. Tell him you decided to wait until you leave the hospital," stated Lynn.

"Okay," responded Allie.

The minister was known as the mafia killer minister. He took his orders directly from the governor. Late afternoon, the previous day, the killer minister introduced himself to Allie. The two of them decided he would perform the wedding from her hospital bed.

Allie could not understand why this minister had convinced her to get married right away. The only thing she could come up with was that the governor believed he was better off with the two of them (Allie and Tom) as a married couple. Therefore, if any criminal charges were ever filed against one of them, the other one could not be forced to testify because of the spousal clause in the law.

No, thought Allie. *That is too simple. It's got to be something else.* After several minutes, Allie gave up. *I love Tom, and if the governor feels we should be together for once he is on the side of love.*

With the task force all in Allie's hospital room, Tom wanted to have a meeting. He felt that they needed to start taking action against the underworld organization as soon as possible. Tom had been thinking about what to do first. In his pocket was some loose change. As he tossed the change around and around in his pocket, finally it hit him like lightening.

"We must go after the money!" shouted Tom.

Without soliciting a response, the whole team as one unit yelled, "YES!"

"Money, money, money! If we take the money, that will undo their power and influence. Without money, power or influence the governor will go down. When he goes down we can take him out along with the rest of the trashy MFs," stated Jake with joy.

"I think we first need to help Allie plan her wedding. After all, it will be the first for both of them. I know a great person of faith who I could ask to perform the service. His name is Father Kevin Harrison. He often tells his story at AA meetings and during his sermons. Whenever I know he is going to deliver the word that Sunday, I always attend. Father Harrison is young but grew up quickly in a family that was born with the criminal gene.

"I was told that he is from a small town in North Carolina that was named after his family, called Harrisonville. Tom, I believe you are from Harrisonville, right. If so, you must know his family or him," stated Lynn with a curious look on her face.

"Yes, I know the family, but that is all I know. I went on to college and never really returned to Harrisonville. That family was my father's best of friends," responded Tom looking slightly annoyed.

"Father Harrison, at an AA meeting said that he is an alcoholic. He shared his stories about drinking moon shine at an early age. The moonshine controlled his life. But God saved him. He was in a few serious accidents but God lifted him up and did not allow him to reach hell's bottom. He said, when he accepted God as his savior, everything changed. He stopped stealing, cheating, drinking, having his way with women, and loving money. Now he is only in love with God!" shouted Lynn, sounding like a spokesperson for God.

"Well, what a testimony. I feel like I want to stop drinking. But that is not going to happen anytime soon," said Lucky with a big grin.

"Okay, let the girls plan the wedding. Us guys will develop a plan to stop the flow of underworld money. They love money and if it starts drying up, they will turn on each other. Like the old saying goes, 'money talks and BS walks,'" stated Tom as if he was an expert on money issues.

In a few days, Allie was released from the hospital. She was happy to had made it home after totaling her two seater sports car. She was grateful to be alive but she could not let it go that she might be Malachi Wallace's daughter. For two days she was very quiet around the taskforce. The taskforce saw her quietness as something connected with the accident. Allie made a decision to tell the task-force about her dilemma. Which was, should she ask for the results of the test or just move on. Without saying anything to Tom or the taskforce, she decided to get the results.

Lynn was busy making plans for the wedding. She wanted it to be nice. She had hoped to have gotten married but the right man never showed up. Allie and Tom had decided on Christmas day. This was a tough time of the year to have a wedding but it could be done. Lynn thinking to herself, that the governor's New Year's Eve party would take place just a short week later. Maybe, they should select a new date for the wedding, thought Lynn.

Allie called Lynn and expressed her concerns about a Christmas wedding. After a short conversation about the wedding it was decided that a June wedding would be nicer. This way the plans did not have to be rushed. By the sound of Allie's tone and voice, Lynn was aware that something was not right with Allie.

"Allie, what's going on with you?" asked Lynn.

"I went to the FBI crime lab to get the results of the paternity test. My mother was right. I am the daughter of Malachi Wallace. Both Malachi and my mother were criminals. They had criminal genes and they have been passed down to me. I am glad I am not planning on having children. It would be an awful thing to pass on to a child," explained Allie with watery eyes.

Allie did not know at the time that she was pregnant. She was three weeks but had not shown or felt any symptoms. Lynn tried to convince Allie that she should not feel as if she was damaged goods. Being the daughter of a scum bag like her father did not mean her destiny was determined at birth.

Allie knew she needed to tell Tom about the test results but she feared that he might have second thoughts about her and their upcoming marriage.

"Allie, Tom loves you and he is not going to drop you like a hot potato. That man is not crazy. He has waited all these years for the right woman and letting you go is not in his plans. His father was a criminal and your father was a criminal. See it all balances out. Let it go or it will eat you up, and Malachi will win," stated Lynn as she looked straight into Allie's bright blue eyes.

"Lynn, I am not only Malachi's daughter but I am black," responded Allie.

"Allie, what difference does it make. You once told me that he is looking for his half-sister and she is black, right. Therefore, he will be just adding to his inter-racial family. It sounds good to me," stated Lynn with a smile on her face.

Allie felt better after talking to Lynn. Sitting in her living room she could hear the door knob turning. It was Tom. Without any warning, she began to shake. She was having another seizure. Fortunately, Tom had just arrived home. He quickly laid her down on the floor and called 911. After a few seconds she stopped shaking but was unconscious. Allie made it to the hospital alive, and the emergency doctor started work on her right away. Tom called Lynn and the two of them sat in the waiting room together.

"Mr. Donovan, Allie is stabilized but she lost the baby. She was about three weeks," stated the doctor with sadness covering his face.

"Baby, she was pregnant?" shouted Tom.

"Tom, she did not know she was pregnant," explained Lynn in a sorrowful tone of voice.

"Doctor, don't tell her about the baby. That might put more stress on her. She is dealing with some family issues and this might be more than she can handle right now," said Tom, pleading with the doctor.

"Okay, but you need to tell her at some point. It is not fair to keep it from her," explained the doctor.

Tom and Lynn looked down at Allie and saw this beautiful lady lying helpless in her hospital bed. Allie realized that she must come clean with Tom about her real father. The doctor explained to Tom, Allie, and Lynn that something was causing her seizures and she must start taking medication to control the problem.

"Tom, Allie has something she needs to tell you. I will wait in the hall so that you two can talk," explained Lynn as if she was a referee.

Allie started crying. Her crying was uncontrollable. Tom held her close and reassured her that whatever it was he needed to know, they would work it out together. This made Allie feel good about their relationship and she was now ready to tell the man of her dreams, who she really was.

"Tom, before I met you I was in love with you. I would see you from time to time in my boss's office. You never noticed me. The timing was not right for us to meet until you had the flat on the highway. I could not believe that the man I loved finally crossed my path and needed my help. What a day of joy that was for me. What I am about to tell will change our lives forever. Remember, I love you today, tomorrow, and forever," said Allie with nothing but love on her face.

"Allie, I have a confession to make of my own. Watching you eat at that diner while my flat was being fixed made me realiz that you were a blessing from heaven. Just looking at you, I felt that I had finally met the right gal. So whatever you want to tell me. Just keep it to yourself for I am not interested in hearing it. Like you said, I love you today, tomorrow, and forever," said Tom with love all over his face.

"Tom, you look like you want to tell me something. I know that boyish look you get when you to need to tell me something that is very important. I can handle whatever it is. Please release the stress and tell what is going on. Is it something the doctor told you about me? If so, tell me now!" said Allie with stern look on her face.

Tom took a deep breath and bent over and kissed Allie on her forehead. Without anything more said, he started talking. He told Allie that she was a few weeks pregnant and she had a miscarriage. She looked up at Tom and began to cry.

"A baby!" said Allie.

Tom walked out of the room for he was fighting back tears. Lynn ran into the room and starting hugging Allie. Tom called for the nurse for Allie was having another seizure. The nurse within seconds, put a tongue presser into Allie's mouth to keep her from biting her tongue. When Allie came out of the seizure, she looked up and saw Tom, Lynn, Jake, and Lucky. Without any warning, Allie shouted out, "I am the daughter of a lifetime criminal and a family of criminals on both side. Malachi Wallace is my father and I have his genes. That is my defense!"

"Defense. This is not a court of law. We are not the judges. All of us have a past. We came together for a common cause. That is, to bring down the mafia. We will never be able to stop the mafia but can eliminate its powerful influence over the legal system, and cut into their sources of income. Maybe if we don't kill all of them, we can put a few in jail for life. That will send a message that the Gangster Enforcers are open for action and are ready to take them out," said Lynn like a forceful leader.

Lucky responded to Lynn's speech, "Lynn is right. We feel your pain, but life goes on. We all love you, so stop having seizures. Let's all be stress free and honest. We are family. Allie, let's go home."

As Allie laid in her nice comfortable bed she started thinking about all the juveniles she helped to become drug addicts while working as a distributor of drugs in the detention center.

Then she remembered, she had sex with Leroy who was her half brother. At that point, she started sweating and felt like a seizure was coming on. Immediately, she started taking deep breaths to help calm down. It worked and she fell back to sleep.

Tom woke up first and started looking at Allie while she was still sleeping. He could not forget all that this outstanding person had endured at such a young age. He believed it was God's intervention that saved her. Even though her road going forward was not easy, she was a survivor. If she was ever held accountable for past criminal offenses against society, it would be expected that her defense would be, "I became a criminal because I was born with the criminal genes. Both my mother and father were born criminals. ancestors passed down to her half-brother and her the criminal genes," thought Tom as he looked at Allie with total love in his heart.

Tom had something he needed to share with Allie before he said anything to the task force members. He wanted to move the task force members into Allie's house. Her home was big enough for all of them. As they worked on plans to take out the mob, they also needed to include working together to stay safe. The best way to ensure everyone's safety was to live together.

Tom called the task force members and asked them to come over to Allie's house, for he had some important business to discuss with them. Allie was the last to come to the kitchen table. Tom had already gotten her approval about having the task force to move into her home. She agreed and believed it would help to keep all of them safe from the mob.

Tom realized that Allie did not look happy and decided to drill Allie about her health. She did not want to keep secrets from the task force so she decided to tell them about her relationship with Leroy Wallace.

"My new family is this task force. When Tom and I get married, we will still be family. Therefore, I want to share a few things about me with you. First, I recently found out that the man I thought was my father who was born a criminal was not my father. As you know, my father was Malachi Wallace. He was a criminal all the way to his bones. My seizures are caused mainly by anxiety over my discovery about my father.

"I am undercover with the Brotherhood. As a top leader of the Brotherhood, I worked my way up to the top. I met Leroy while I was incarcerated in a juvenile detention center here in New Orleans. I worked for Leroy as his bag lady, collecting drug money. After getting out, I ran away from the halfway house that I was living in and went to work for Leroy. This time I handled all the collecting, counting, and managing, the money laundering process. One day we all got caught.

"Mr. Harrison a local lawyer represented me in court. After reviewing my history, he presented my case to the judge. My defense was, I was a descendant of hard core criminals on both sides of my family. He convinced the court that I was a criminal because of an inherited criminal gene. Mr. Harrison was a very good lawyer. The judge and court believed him and I was placed under Mr. Stevenson's supervision.

"Mr. Stevenson was an FBI agent who specialized in weeding out corruption and the underworld organizations in New Orleans. He recruited me for the FBI. After my training was over, I was placed inside of the Brotherhood organization, that's where I started," stated Allie sounding proud.

"Allie, I think you should go to a therapist. Your problems are deep and long-term. A therapist can help you sort your life out. I have a lady who is very good. She helped me and many others in the past. Here is her name and number. Just tell her, Jake Who Ate No Cake recommended you to her. Tell her that and she will see you right away. Most people have to wait three months to get a visit. She is also my cousin," explained Jake, looking very honest.

The task force started moving in the next morning. Everyone had a housekeeping chore. Just before dinner was served, the phone rang. It was for Allie. It was the governor's daughter-in-law, wanting to set up a meeting to discuss the Christmas party.

CHAPTER 33

A LLIE HAD AGREED to meet with Bella, the governor's daughter-in-law to lay down plans for the New Year's Eve party of the century. That was the way the governor would have expressed his feelings about the party. As Allie sat waiting for Bella, she started thinking about who to invite when Bella appeared.

She was nothing like Allie had pictured her. Bella was a tall slim girl with pretty long black curly hair, accented with bright blue eyes. She looked so young and innocent to be a criminal. But criminals come in all shapes, sizes, colors, and age thought Allie.

"Hi, I'm Bella. I have heard many good things about you from some of my father-in-laws associates. I understand, you have been with the organization for many years. I was told you started as a teenager. Wow, you must have done something right to still be vertical and healthy. Most young people in our organization never reach thirty," said Bella with great respect for Allie in her voice.

"Where should we have the party? The governor talked about having it at his home in New Orleans but I think it would be easier to have it at the country club. The club has everything we need. They have a caterer, waiters, bar, and can provide live music. I was also thinking there should be a theme, maybe something to do with New Orleans food and jazz," explained Allie feeling good about her suggestion.

"How about calling it classy jazz?" We could ask the guests to wear outfits that represent the spirit of jazz dating back to prohibition. The music would start with the prohibition music era and continue to present day. Every hour a new band with a singer would start up. The MC will encourage the guests to dance, drink, eat, and have fun," responded Bella feeling happy to be working with Allie.

The governor's secretary gave Allie a list of the guests that he wanted to invite. His list was made up of thirty-nine state senators, 105 state house of representatives, a few relatives, and many friends and associates from New Orleans. Allie looked at the list and felt that the majority of them were criminals. Therefore, since she was allowed to invite people, the first on her list was the task force. Next she wanted the leadership of all the New Orleans wards, local union leaders, and top-level drug dealers to be on her list.

Allie gave Bella a copy of the guest list for her to add or subtract names. Bella saw a few names that made her break out in a moist sweat. She recognized names that were associated with the drug cartels. For many years the two most powerful cartels survived territory wars and learned to get along even though they didn't trust or like each other. Having the South Side Creoles and the West Side Brothers together in one big room was going to make it a very interesting party. Both groups had a few things in common. They worshiped Malachi Wallace until new leadership took over after the Czar passed away, who was the leader of the Brotherhood and the mob boss.

The governor was the leader and controlled the underworld organization at all levels. Both cartels feared the governor. He was known for getting rid of problems before a problem would get rid of you. Jesse Donavan was one of the original Brotherhood leaders and was hand-picked by the Czar to take over when he died.

Jesse was respected by all his people. The governor is feared by all his people. Allie understood how the governor functioned and she was planning on 350 guests. All of them would be at the party. Allie quickly jotted down on her note pad gift tables. The governor expected a monitory gift from every guest. That was their way of showing loyalty and respect. The governor's way to show appreciation for loyalty and respect was by having a great New Year's Eve with only the best of everything.

Bella was concerned about inviting the South Side Creoles and the West Side Brothers to the governor's party. She felt that it was a bad idea. The two cartels hated each other. Having them in the same room was a definite no, no. But Allie insisted it would be okay because she was going to talk to both sides.

The invitations went out and the governor was given a copy of the guest list. As he looked it over, a smile came over his face. He knew this would be the first time his two top gangs ever met in a social setting. Therefore, he asked Allie to beef up security in case these two gangs decided to cause a disturbance.

Allie asked Bella to go with her to meet with the South Side Creoles and the West Side Brothers. Bella did not know how much Allie knew about her but she did not want to take a chance that her old identity would be exposed by some of the older members in these two groups. When it came time to meet up with the groups Bella informed Allie that she was not coming because the baby was sick.

Allie was glad Bella did not come because she would be able to cut the BS with the two groups and lay it all on the line with them. Allie told the gangs that no weapons were allowed at the party. The security would be ready to handle any problems. Whatever you feel about each other let it go for a few hours and just have fun and enjoy your self. Both sides knew Allie, trusted and respected her. She had been with many of them since her years in the juvenile detention center. Because of her history with them, the two gangs wanted to respect her and honor her request. Everyone shook hands and walked out with big grins on their faces.

The governor purchased a house in Baton Rouge near the governor's mansion for Allie, Tom, and their staff. Allie got the governor to accept Lynn as his new secretary, Lucky was to be the communication specialist, and Jake the head of security. This house was to be the offsite headquarters for t Allie's hand-picked staff. The governor had plans for Allie and her staff because he knew her background and her long history with the Brotherhood. He believed her to be a loyal soldier, just like her mother and father, Malachi Wallace.

The governor knew from the very beginning that Malachi Wallace was Allie's father. He didn't care that she had black blood running through her veins as long as she did her job. Being Black and looking white was a plus in his book as long as she was not a blood line family member.

As Allie and her task force staff were setting up their office space in the offsite headquarters a man came to the door. He informed Allie that he had orders from the governor to put this truck load of boxes in the basement. Tom stopped in on the guy and peeked into his box. It was neatly packed with blocks of marijuana. Allie stopped a guy because his box was a different color. She opened it up and it was loaded with Heroin. The task force was shocked.

Without much delay, drug paraphernalia was pouring in and a tall, good looking man walked in last. He was in charge of the basement underworld operation. Tom and Allie both recognized him. He was on the FBI's most wanted list. He was a native of the country Colombia and the head of the North/West Brotherhood Cartel. The task force was shocked and decided to go to lunch.

The governor was always one step ahead of the task force for he was very smart, measured and a wise mob boss. At this point, the task force knew that they had to make plans that were irreversible or they would end up dead in a ditch.

During lunch, Jake pulled out a list of possible strategies that were easy to implement. These strategies would go undetected until it was too late for the mob to do anything to counter attack.

Jake's plans started with him using his influence with the governor's office to take over the security of all the mob's territories. Next, having Lucky handle the procurements of all merchandise whether the purchases were legal or criminal. Lynn as the governor's secretary and would know when shipments of drugs from Colombia were scheduled to arrive at the Louisiana docks.

Lucky added that they could have their FBI informants by way of the task force notify the FBI about any criminal activities that were going to go down. Allie was concerned about the basement operation at the offsite headquarters and what they could do about it.

"Allie, if we cut their supplies off at the point to entry than the basement will dry up. As the basement dries up, they will turn on each other. They will begin not trusting anyone. The governor will start making stupid decisions. When things start going downhill, we will step in and take him down. He will not know what hit him," explained Tom looking as cool as a cucumber.

"Let's call all the leaders together tomorrow at our headquarters. We will introduce everyone to the governor's new staff. At that time, we will hand them their invites to the party. Also, explain once again that they will not be able to bring any guns. This will be a happy celebration to bring in the new year," said Lynn with a big smile on her face.

Allie decided she was going to pay Juan Orejuela, who is the head of the North/West Colombian Cartel a visit. As she was walking down to the basement, she heard voices coming from the kitchen. It was the governor, talking to Tom. Tom was asking the governor why he allowed Juan to come and set up business in Baton Rouge.

"Well, Tom, it's like this: keep your enemies close. If you follow this simple rule, you will live to retire a second time," stated the governor as he started laughing.

Allie heard what the governor said and began thinking, *Maybe that is why he had all of Tom's and her handpicked staff at the same location.* As she continued to walk down the steps, something told her to just let it go. For what the governor said goes both ways.

"Hello, Allie, good to see you again. It's been a long time. If it had not been for your boyfriend, that Wallace guy, we could have become the modern day Bonny and Clyde," said Juan with a smart, silly look on his face.

"Knock it off, Juan. Our relationship is strictly business. I have a fiancé. Tom and I are engaged to be married in a few months," explained Allie without showing any emotions.

"There is something about you that has been very troublesome for many years. After you hooked up with Wallace and his operation, something changed. You have always appeared to be all in with the business but I can tell you are hiding something. Every once in a while, I think about you and your dedication to the organization and how you have survived many years without a scratch. Most of us have been shot and left for dead but not you. Well, God much be your best friend," stated Juan smiling.

Juan stood for a few minutes just looking at Allie. Thinking to himself, he knew he'd better keep an eye on her for she could be a cop, informant, or worse, the FBI.

"Hey, Juan, I see you have met Allie and Tom. Tom and I go way back and he is the chief of staff for the governor's office. He will keep us all out of jail. Allie is the communication's director for my office, and she will respond to all forms of requests or communications connected to everything we do. The three of you are to work together like one happy family," stated the governor with a deep down business look on his face.

All the Cartel leadership in New Orleans attended the next day's meeting. Allie was to conduct the meeting, but the governor showed up and took over. Allie did not care but was concerned about what he might say. Most of the participants were people of color. It was common knowledge that he only put up with them because he needed them and they needed him. It all worked out because no one ever brought up the race card at any meetings or get togethers. It was considered off limits.

The governor introduced Tom, Allie, Lynn, Lucky, and Jake to the attendees. Many of them knew Allie but Tom and the rest of the staff were new to them. Because of Allie, everyone was accepted as the leaders in their positions. The governor reinforced the rules, be nice to each other and no guns. The invites were given out and the group appeared to be very happy. Juan had something he needed to tell Allie but wanted to wait until the right time.

Morning came early and the Gangster Enforcers were so proud of themselves. They had infiltrated the biggest underground operation in Louisiana with very little effort. Mainly because of the governor. Now their next step would be harder. To compile a list or record of all the mob's operations. The easiest way to do this was to go through the governor's records. From his records, break everything down into smaller units.

"Let's get through the New Year's Eve party, which will happen in less than thirty days from now. Lynn, we need you to secretly take pictures of everyone who attends. It doesn't matter if they are straight or crooked, we need all pictures. After the party we will identify and label the pictures.

"I will get all the governor's information off his personal computer. I can slip away during the party, go to his office, and download his files on his personal computer. Tom, Lucky, and Jake can keep the governor occupied with interesting stories. Hopefully everything will go as planned. If not, we all might be dead by morning," explained Allie like a desperate boss.

Without any notice, Juan walked into the meeting room. "I'd like to talk to Allie alone," said Juan with a demanding tone.

"Okay, let's talk," responded Allie.

The two of them went outside and sat in Juan's car. Juan did not want any of his conversation over heard by anyone. Even Allie's fiancé was to be left out of the loop. "In this business, you can't rely on or trust anyone. In the end, we will lose. I just want to set the record straight. I know all about you. My sister, who was born in America, is of Colombian heritage. I was born in Colombia. Our parents ran the biggest Columbian cartel here in America and in Columbia for many years. They were partners with the mafia boss called the Czar here in New Orleans. The cartel was passed down to me.

I am telling you this so that we understand each other. My sister who went by the name of Vonda whose real name is Rea Orejuela was a big part of the family business. She is hiding out in North Carolina acting like a born again Christian. I know for a fact, there is only one defense for being a criminal who was born into that world. That is, we are criminal by blood. It is in our genes. Rea will return one day and claim her seat next to me. She is good at what she does. You know that for a fact. She is just on a little vacation right now," explained Juan sounding positive about Rea.

"Do you have any other concerns?" asked Allie.

"Yes, Tom as you know, was a law enforcer for many years until he retired. He knows how we operate. I don't trust him, you, or the governor. Tom has the criminal gene also. He wants power and will do whatever it takes to get it. Keep your eyes on him.

"I believe something big is going to happen at the New Year's Eve Party. I am planning on protecting myself and my people. I hope you do the same for your staff. Oh, by the way, Bella has the criminal gene. She is black and if the governor knew that, he would freak out. He hates blacks but they are part of the business. It is ironic that his granddaughter has black blood. Bella is a quiet and a behind the scene gangster. She knows how to take care of business if necessary," explained Juan as if he was providing cute little updates on members of the organization.

When Allie walked back into the meeting with her staff, she had a strange look on her face. She was concerned about what Juan had just told her. That is, he did not trust Tom, the governor, or her. It appeared that he was privileged to information that was not known by many people.

"Okay Allie, what's wrong?" asked Lucky.

"Juan is a very dangerous person. We should keep a good eye on him most of the time. Did any of you know he is Vonda's brother?" asked Allie.

"I did, and I was planning on telling the task force at this meeting that they were related," said Tom.

"I have some information that was supplied to me by one of our informants. A big shipment of cocaine and marijuana is coming in by a meat shipment from Colombia. The drugs will be packed inside of the pigs, chickens, and cows. The Longshoremen who are connected to the mafia will be unloading the shipments. The meat inspectors will come in after the meat with the drugs are loaded onto the freezer truck.

"We can dress up like police officers and take the truck. If they try to shoot at us, we can take them out. The truck can be taken to a wooded area and set on fire. This will cause a big loss of money for the cartels. If the drugs are destroyed, Juan's cartel will think it was done by South Side Creoles. They will start pointing fingers at each other. By the time they figure it out, we will be well on our way and the money supply will start drying up.

"The governor will be upset and will have Juan investigate to see who was involved. This will start a drug war and the Gangster Enforcers will be ready to take on all of them," said Lucky with a wide smile on his face.

"I feel good about Lucky's plan. How about the rest of you?" asked Jake.

"Let's go for it!" yelled Lynn.

"I have had enough of everything today. Let's go back home and go to the governor's favorite club and walk in like big time gangsters. After all that's what we are," responded Tom.

"Can we order that expensive bourbon again?" asked Lynn.

"Why not," responded Allie laughing so hard that tears were rolling down her face.

CHAPTER 34

T HE GANGSTER ENFORCERS walked into the club and the waitress knew who they were and led them to the reserved area for VIP customers. The music sounded good but loud. The band was playing smooth jazz that was made famous by jazz legends. Allie looked up at the stage and was shocked to see Bella singing and dancing with in a very provocative dress. It was obvious she was a professional and her talent was in her genes. At that point Allie felt that what Juan told her about Bella was most likely true. Even though Bella personally appeared to be that of a sweet young lady, without any criminal genes and was certainly in doubt now by Allie.

Bella left the stage and the crowd went wild. You could hear the crowd yelling for more. She was fantastic and the air was full of left-over excitement. The way she danced and sang was like nothing the audience had ever seen. They wanted more of her. Bella came back out on stage and they clapped. She was their hero and they loved her.

"Well, Bella has some hidden talents, that she forgot to tell me about when we were discussing the music for the New Year's Eve party. I am going to let her handle the music. I will do the rest," stated Allie feeling somewhat left out.

As Bella was walking out of the club she eyed Tom and came over to his table. She was surprised to see Allie's staff. "You are great.

Maybe great is not the word for you. How about out of this world!" said Tom with his eyes wide open with joy.

"The governor never told us about your talent. He only talked about and praised his pretty granddaughter," said Allie with a wide smile on her face.

"He loves my singing. He is the one who introduced me to his son. I was working for the organization and one night the lead singer for the band was found dead about a few blocks from here. I told him I could sing and dance to anything the band played. So he gave me the floor. I only sing on Friday night, now that I have a baby," responded Bella feeling proud.

As the task force was eating dinner, Tom started thinking back to the barmaid that he was talking to in this club, who was found murdered. Tom got out of his seat and ran over to Bella before she exited the club.

"Bella, did that barmaid that died have long blonde hair and very slim?" asked Tom.

"Yes, I was the manager at the time and after getting pregnant, I didn't need to work at all. Singing and dancing is in my genes and with her passing, gave me an opportunity to for once do what I loved," explained Bella.

"Well, I met her once but never ran into you here," responded Tom with complete certainty.

"Okay, you ran into me tonight. A night that I was at my best. I love singing all types of music. Especially the songs our clients identify as their music," explained Bella looking a little concerned.

"Gang, tomorrow I am going to the FBI's office to look up information on the barmaid's murder. I think we might be on to something," stated Allie feeling hopeful.

After an evening of drinking the best bourbon and food, the task force somehow made it home safely. Tom and Allie laid in bed, talking about the barmaid who was found dead and started wondering if Bella had anything to do with it.

Allie decided to get Bella's DNA and fingerprints to see if there might be a match with any evidence that might have been collected at the crime scene.

It was hard for Allie to fall asleep because she could not stop thinking about what Juan had said about Tom and Bella. Tom has criminal genes but in his private and professional life he has always been honest, thought Allie.

Allie did not know about Tom's college and law school days in which he had a small lucrative illegal test taking and term paper writing business. Her love for Tom would have made it almost impossible for her to believe Tom's criminal genes had gotten the best of him.

As the sun was coming up, Jake started ringing his bell. "Rise and shine, and let's go get the degenerate governor and his cronies. That shipment of drugs is coming in tomorrow and we need to plan down to the very last detail," stated Jake with excitement consuming his voice.

Lynn and Lucky made breakfast for the group. Everyone was excited because tomorrow would be their first action against the mob.

Destroying the drugs would be the first step to disrupt the cash and drugs flowing into Louisiana. Little did they know that destroying the drugs would set off events that would affect all of them.

"All of us have the criminal gene. We must hold back from doing more tomorrow than is necessary in order to destroy the shipment of drugs. I know that Lynn and Lucky have their reasons for joining the task force because they want to take out the Brotherhood for all the pain they caused them as teenagers and other kids selling drugs for the Brotherhood. It is no excuse for wanting to kill everyone connected to the Brotherhood. Remember, the FBI director would like to see them all locked up for life.

"The governor killed my father because he was running for the President of the Longshoremen's union. He also did away with my cousin his limousine driver. He needs to die. I will take care of him myself," explained Jake, looking like an angry black man.

"I understand what Jake is saying as I learned years ago, 'do unto others before they do under you,' keep that as your motto as we take on the mob tomorrow night at 10:00 p.m.," responded Tom with a grin on his very white face.

Allie, Tom, Lynn, Jake, and Lucky were all anxious to get going on the plans to highjack the drugs coming from Colombia. Because Jake was the security person and understood what was needed to highjack the drugs, he was given the job to get weapons that were necessary for the task to survive, and take the drugs, and destroy them.

Tom did not want the girls with the guys because it might be a bloody mess. Allie and Lynn insisted that they were in this all the way. To keep from being recognized, they all dressed up as superhero characters. They all looked so good that even their parents would not know who they were.

The task force had everything they needed and the time of arrival of the shipment was verified through the informant. Lynn and Allie were loaded down with guns strapped across both shoulders. Lucky was issued a Barrett M107, which he knew it was reliable and consistent if he needed to take out the drug dealers from a distance. Jake used his own gun which was a Winchester Model 21. Tom decided his father's handgun that his father wore with pride was to be his weapon of choice.

"Before we leave out for our first mission to take out the mob, I want to make it perfectly clear to the Gangster Enforcers that we are better trained, better equipped, and smarted than any of the people we will be going up against tonight. They only know how to follow orders; we know how to follow our years of training to take them down.

"If possible, don't kill any of them. We want them to report back to Juan explaining how they were outnumbered. They will exaggerate as to how many of us were involved. This gang of thugs will let the drugs go or we will have to take them out. If we do have to take them out, let one go so that he can report back to Juan.

"Juan and the Governor will blame it on the South Side Creoles because they don't like the Governor. He feels that the blacks are only good enough to cook, clean, and buy and sell drugs. Oh, I forgot, sing and play music," explained Tom with some concern on his face.

"I agree with everything Tom has said. Just remember, Juan also does not like the governor but he is necessary for his underworld organization to continue without too many interruptions. At some point we might be able to use him later on," stated Allie, looking serious.

"Let's pray that we will accomplish our goal tonight and be able to continue to achieve our mission. That is, to bring down the Brotherhood and limit the mobs influence in New Orleans," said Lynn.

No one knew how to pray so everyone accepted Lynn's words as their prayer. The group left well before 10:00 p.m. to secure the best positions and hijack the drug trailer and destroy it's contents.

Lynn said to Allie, "I had a strange dream last night that was very scary and upsetting. I tried to block it out but couldn't. Therefore, I looked it up in my dream book. I looked up knocking and yelling at my door. It stated, Danger is trying to come in and take over. Do not engage in any actions for the next few days that are dangerous. If you do the result will not be good."

Allie being a product of New Orleans started slightly shaking. She grew up believing in dreams and voodoo and decided to tell Jake to stop the van and pull over. "I have a strange feeling that this is not the right time for us to take any actions against the mob. Let's just hide out down at the docks and see how they operate. There will be more shipments coming in for Thanksgiving, Christmas, and New Year's Eve holidays that we can steal and destroy. If we take the next shipment, it will really hit them hard. Their supply of drugs will dry up and customers will have to get high off of bourbon," stated Allie with a slight giggle.

Jake parked the van about a mile from the docks. As they were walking to a secluded area that had a good view of the pier, it started pouring down large rain drops. Thunder and lightning came without any warning. The conditions made it feel very cold and uncomfortable. Just as Allie was about to say let's go, Juan appeared with Vonda and the governor. "I think this ship is about more than just drugs," stated Lucky.

Within seconds, young girls started exiting the ship. They were escorted to a large old looking van that was being driven by the task force's informant. The informant kept looking around as if he wanted to be rescued. It was all Allie could do to hold Tom and the guys back. These girls were very young. Maybe about thirteen to twenty-one years old.

Hiding out in the bushes, the task force felt helpless and wanted to save the girls. Allie made the decision to wait and see what was going on. After all, the cargo was placed in the trailer it took off, the van with the girls was next. The governor's limo followed the van. The task force rushed back to their van and followed the van. The road was dark and slippery, but the van was moving fast. The driver did not have any respect for the road or the weather. Within seconds, the van started slipping and sliding and ended up slamming into a telephone pole.

The task force slammed on their brakes and headed over to the old van that was now upside down. Before Allie and the task force could reach the old van it blew up. The governor's limo did not stop, it just sped off. Allie and Lynn started crying and screaming. It was all the guys could do to keep them from getting hurt trying to save the girls. The van driver was thrown out of the car and he only had minor injuries.

"It is awful what just happened here but this is my ticket out of this business. The governor will think I died in the crash. I have money tucked away and can start over. If you guys ever need me for anything, call me. Jake has my number. Good luck!" said Louis the informant.

Allie and Tom arrived at the office early, so that they could survey the basement to see if the drugs were there. Sure enough, they were packed nice and neat inside a false wall. It was a large shipment and Allie and Tom just kept looking and shaking their heads. In all their years working with drugs they had never seen a shipment this large.

"Wow! This is money. The governor and Juan must be getting very comfortable with their underworld operation and will slip up soon. When they do, we will be there to take them both out."

Allie was sitting at her desk trying to catch up on the governor's correspondence with her eyes, head, and mind focused on the mail when Vonda walked in.

"Hello, girlfriend!" shouted Vonda.

"Hello! Hello! Hello to you also!" responded Allie.

"You have moved up from the Outhouse to White House. This a vast improvement from working for the Brotherhood in the juvenile detention center to being the governor's communications director. I knew from the very beginning; you were born to be a leader. So here you are working for the governor. I am happy for you," stated Vonda with a half smile on her face.

"Why are you here? Your new life was not enough for you?" asked Allie, trying very hard not to let on about last night's disaster.

"Well, by now, you know Juan is my brother, and he needed help with a special type of merchandise that was coming in. He believed that I had the expertise and experience to help with an important job. But last night it went up in flames. Therefore, I plan to just stick around doing odd jobs for him. I feel very comfortable here back in my place of birth," explained Vonda, smiling from ear to ear.

"Do you want me to call you Rea or Vonda?" asked Allie.

"You can call which ever one you like as long as you don't call me too late for dinner," responded Vonda laughing out of control.

Bella rushed into Allie's office and was surprised to see Vonda. She never liked Vonda. As Vonda was leaving she bumped into Bella and stated, "Stay out of my way or next time it will be more than a bump," said Vonda with a look on her face that would have scared the devil.

"Allie, I just want to update you on the party. I have all the music lined up. I will perform the last hour of the party. I have some good old songs my mother would listen to over and over again. I often wondered why she loved that ragtime music. It appeared to make her feel good.

"The menu looks great! The governor will be pleased. What is the count for the number of guests?" asked Bella.

"It is about five hundred or more. There will be guests from all walks of life including many politicians, all the territory bosses, family, and few close friends," responded Allie.

"My husband, Marc, is nothing like us. In fact, he doesn't know anything about his father's involvement with the mob. He has a good job working as the head of the science department for Louisiana State University. He got that position by working hard. His father had nothing to do with it. I love him and want him to stay clean. If he knew what is really going on, he would turn all of us in," explained Bella with a look of concern on her face.

So Allie seized the opportunity to get Bella's fingerprints, to see if they matched anything that was recovered from the crime scene of the waitress/barmaid who was murdered.

"Bella, I have some good Bourbon. Would you like to have a midmorning drink with me?" asked Allie.

"Why not. I'm on my way home," stated Bella.

Allie quickly bagged up Bella's glass and tucked it down into her handbag. She was hoping the FBI lab would be able to tell her something about Bella.

All guests would be in costumes for it was a costume New Year's Eve party. A picture of every guest would be taken. Everyone would be checked for weapons. The only people with concealed weapons would be security. This was Juan's update. Juan was concerned about the "South Side Creoles" because they knew how to get what they wanted. That is, to take out the governor and put one of their people in charge.

The South Side Creoles believed that the business was hijacked by an outsider who took control by force. He was not elected by the underworld. Plus, he had never paid his dues in the form of hard work for the mob. Juan's concerns were real and he decided to have his own plan in case the party turned into a bloody bath party.

Allie knew that the governor was home for the day. He wanted to spend the day with his granddaughter. He adored her. She was a very pretty baby. Therefore, this was her opportunity to check out his computer for all the law enforcers, politicians, and others who were being paid by the governor to do his dirty work. It didn't take long for Allie to get into his system. His password was his granddaughter's name, Gina.

To Allie's surprise, she found the dates of future drug shipments coming in from Columbia and was everything she needed to stop the flow of drugs into New Orleans. She printed out everything and left. She went home and waited for the task force to arrive.

"Guess what, the Gangster Enforcers are alive and well, and we will take all the mob down. Not just one at a time but all at the same time. With our criminal genes and our system, we are a criminal's worst nightmare. We understand how they think. Their money talks and without it they are nothing. Let's get it together and take them out," stated Allie, sounding like a military commander.

CHAPTER 35

ALLIE ONCE AGAIN had a hard time sleeping, therefore she got up and went into the kitchen. To her surprise, Lynn was in the kitchen sipping on a glass of wine. Lynn was totally involved in her own thoughts that she did not hear Allie until Allie said, "Boo!"

"Why are you drinking this early in the morning?" asked Allie.

"It's my motivation for wanting to be part of the Gangster Enforcers. It scares me and at the same time motives me. I want to get back at the Brotherhood. The only person that I could call a friend, died in the Juvenile Detention Center of an overdose of cocaine. She was only fifteen years old. Losing her made me want to work hard to get back on the right track and fight for justice for all who were or have been victims of the actions of the Brotherhood. I hate all of them! I fear what I might do at the New Year's Eve party," sobbed Lynn with tears rolling down her pink cheeks.

"I understand your fears and pain. We have a job to do. If it means taking them all out, then that is God's plan. That wine looks good. It's five o'clock somewhere so let's drink and hope we come out on top," stated Allie with her eyes wide open.

Allie never told Lynn why she could not sleep but she did tell Tom. Allie told Tom she has a great aunt name Aunt Maggie. She lives in New Orleans near a swamp because she doesn't like people. The last time Allie saw her Aunt Maggie was about twenty years ago.

Aunt Maggie never got married or had children. She devoted her life to voodoo and psychic readings.

Customers would come from all over the world for her services. My grandmother told me her sister was born with a light covering over her face that was called a vail. It was removed and because of the vail my great aunt had the power to see the future. On her own she studied voodoo and could place spells on people.

Allie had a dream about her aunt and decided it was time to pay her a visit. Allie wanted to know what the future had in store for her, Tom, and the Gangster Enforcers.

After telling Tom about her great aunt, he told Allie he didn't believe in such stuff as voodoo or fortune telling. But he explained to her that if it made her feel better then she should go see her great aunt. Visiting her great aunt might answer some other questions she wanted to know about her family. One question would be, why was her mother a criminal?

The next day, Tom went with Allie to visit her great aunt. It took a long time to get to her place but they found it. Allie knocked on the door and an old sweet voice said, "Come in, Tom." Tom looked at Allie and was shocked and surprised that the old lady knew his name without seeing him.

"I have been waiting for you Tom, a long time. It took my great niece to get you here. I have some very important information to tell both of you. First, let's have some bourbon. It will relax you and take the edge off of what I am about to tell you," explained Aunt Maggie with a large smile on her extremely wrinkled face.

"I might be *old*, but I am not cold. I have very good eyesight, good hearing, and my sense of smell has gotten better with age. I am approaching one hundred and hope to live a little longer. Who knows what might happen during the night. That is why I entered my great nice's dreams to guide her here to me.

"Tom, your father left you a few boxes with his personal belongings.

"There is one box left that you didn't open. You need to go back to Harrisonville and finish the job of looking into the last box. The last box has a 20 oz. bottle of special oil that I made for him over thirty-five-plus years ago. This bottle of oil was dipped into holy water to cast out evil.

"Your father came into this world with criminal genes. I told him to rub his hands with this oil before noon and before midnight for nine days to keep him from living the life of a criminal. Jesse Donavan did not believe in my gifts that I was born with. He did not even open the bottle until it was too late. At the end of his life he became a believer. He sent word to me to please help his son remain an honest person.

"Your meeting Allie on that lonely highway was made possible through God. Your willingness to come meet me was because of God. My longevity is God's doing. Do you believe in me?" asked Aunt Maggie.

"Aunt Maggie, yes! Yes!" responded Tom who was completely tuned in on the old lady.

"If you do what I told your father to do, then you will come out on top in every situation. Allie should do the same thing with you. After the nine days, take that bottle of oil and put the names of all the top mob leader's names into the leftover oil. Even the governor, Juan, and Wanda should be included. They will never be able to harm any of Allie's or your blood family members. All their actions will fall short when it comes to harming the two of you," stated Aunt Maggie.

"I'd like to ask you a few questions. Will I ever find my half sister? Allie and I would like to get married. Is marriage part of God's plan for us?" asked Tom.

"First of all, you have already found your sister. She is around you almost every day. She doesn't know you and you don't know her but you will. She will save your life soon. Don't tell her she has black blood until everyone is out of danger.

Also, you will become the next elected governor of the state of Louisiana. Your lieutenant governor will be a lawyer in New Orleans who is known for defending juveniles and low income innocent clients for many years. His last name is Harrison. You will meet him at the governor's New Year's Eve party. The two of you will instantly become good friends.

"Beginning of next year, Allie and you will be married. She is two weeks pregnant with twins. They are fraternal twins. One good looking boy who looks white with hazel eyes and one beautiful girl with golden light brown skin. She will have black wavy hair with sky blue eyes. When she enters a room all heads will turn. Her beauty will be something that most people will envy," stated Aunt Maggie.

"Is there anything else we need to know?" asked Allie.

"Be sure you do exactly what I told you to do. If you do, every day you will come out on top. This is the last time we will meet. My time on earth is almost up. I stayed around waiting for the two of you. Now I can lay down and go away in peace. Oh, I forgot to tell you to wear your cowboy hat whenever you among criminals. The hat will provide extra protection," explained Aunt Maggie.

"Allie and Tom were so excited that they decided to drive straight to Harrisonville, NC, without stopping. They wanted to call the governor to let him know they would be out of town for a few days but decided against it. They were anxious to get their hands on the oil.

"Allie this time, we will have a family and they will be raised in an honest environment. We have the criminal gene and the oil is our defense. It will keep us and our family honest forever," explained Tom with joy on his face.

"Tom went into the basement to get the last box but could not find the box. He started sweating from head to toe. Allie saw what was happening and solved the problem.

"Tom, I put all the boxes in the attic. I did not realize the unopened box would be that important," responded Allie. Without any hesitation the two of them rushed to the attic.

"I got it!" shouted Tom.

The box was about the size of a shoebox. The bottle was wrapped in layers of newspapers that made the bottle look larger than life. If fact Tom thought, it was their life stored in this powerful bottle of oil. He was right, the oil held their future. A future full of joy and peace.

"I think we should say a prayer before we rub the oil on our hands. We are both blessed to have found each other with God's help. I will say the prayer," Tom said, looking relieved.

"Dear God, only once in a life time does a hero come along. My hero is Tom. You have blessed us both and we will work every day to help make others' lives better. We will raise our children to be adults that will continue our good deeds and love God.

"We both have always believed in you God. We are very blessed to have survived for many years of uncertainty. Once again, thank you, God. Amen," said Allie with tears of joy rolling down her rosy cheeks.

Tom poured a few drops of the oil into Allie's hands and waited for her to do the same things to his hands. The oil appeared to disappear quickly from the hands after it was rubbed into their skin.

"Remember, it is now before midnight and tomorrow before noon for nine days," said Tom like a dedicated believer.

Allie and Tom got up early and were eager to go back to New Orleans for this day was the first day of their new life. Tom looked in his closet and picked out his best and favorite cowboy hat. He put it on with pride. He felt that nothing could stop him now. He was right, nothing could stop him from accomplishing all his goals. He liked the idea of his becoming the governor of Louisiana. His father took care of Harrisonville with perfection and he would take care of Louisiana the same way.

Allie still had the glass that Bella used for her bourbon in her handbag. She dropped Tom off at the office and she went to the FBI headquarters. The head of the FBI lab was a good friend of Allie's and did not require any formal request for running the prints to see if there was a match. It only took a few minutes but the results were negative.

"Well, Bella is not a known criminal. I guess that is good thought Allie as she drove back to the office. As she was getting out of the car, Juan appeared out of nowhere.

"Where have you been? The governor has been trying to locate you since yesterday," stated Juan looking a little agitated.

"I went to visit my hundred-year-old great-aunt who doesn't have long to live," responded Allie.

"Did you know that someone has connected me to the van that killed all those illegal young immigrant girls. I want you to find out who this person is and have Juan to take care of it," stated the governor.

Allie called Tom and told him the situation. Tom was the governor's chief of staff, and it was his duty to find out who was the whistleblower. Tom put his hat on and went to the governor's office. As he entered the governor's office the lieutenant governor was standing by the governor. They knew it was not Tom or his staff because they were never informed about the delivery of drugs or the girls.

"This whistleblower, I was told by an insider, has pictures of me and Juan, and Vonda sitting at the docks in my car the same time this shipment of drugs and girls arrived. The FBI has a sworn affidavit from the whistle-blower as to what took place that night," said the lieutenant governor.

"Everyone in the van died that night. We have a mole among us. Let's set a trap for the mole. I have a shipment of drugs coming in the Sunday before New Year's Eve. We will only tell Juan and Allie. If anything happens to that shipment, we can follow up on their connections to other people," stated the governor.

"By the way, that hat looks good on you. You should wear that one more often," stated the lieutenant governor.

When Tom got back to his office, Allie was on the phone with the director of the FBI. The director wanted to see her and Tom in his office as soon as possible. After telling the Gangster Enforcers about the governor's situation, she ordered all of them to wear an ankle gun for protection.

Allie and Tom while on their way to New Orleans stopped at the same diner that they had their first meal together. Tom wanted to talk about their dangerous governor. Allie was all ears.

"The governor's family is from Harrisonville, NC. His father, Jumbo, was killed by Redd Harrison. Redd killed his father over a dispute about stealing his corn liquor customers. My father was the custodian and sheriff of Harrisonville. He gave money to Jumbo's wife to help the family out. He also paid for the governor's education for both undergrad and law school.

"His aunt Rita killed Redd, and my father covered it up for he did not want the town to have to deal with Rita's murdering Redd. He told the Harrison twins to burn down the house and make it look like a house fire killed Rita and Redd.

"So you see, the governor was born with criminal genes. He has never used his criminal genes as a defense or excuse to kill. He is a born outright killer. We must stop him before he kills again," stated Tom.

After eating, Allie poured a few drops of the oil into Tom's hands and then into hers, stating, "Day two, Tom."

"I checked out the calendar and our ninth day of this ritual is on New Year's Eve. We need to remember to rub our hands with the oil before midnight," stated Tom.

The FBI director was waiting for Tom and Allie. He appeared to be pleased but had a concerned look on his face. In his hands was a thick binder. He opened up the binder and started reading off money figures. These figures were the expenses for the task force operation. The director was not pleased with the amount of funding spent to support the task force, but after reviewing Allie's report, he was pleased with the results so far.

"Tom we need to bring the governor in for questioning about the accident that killed fifteen young girls. As you know by now, we have an informant who was present at the time everything went down. He had a camera that we gave him. He has used it on many occasions. When do you two think we should bring him in?" asked the director.

"Let's do it at his New Year's Eve Party. All the crooks will be attending. This will be a good time to get them all. Jake, who is on our task force, is the head of security and his people will be FBI personnel," stated Allie, smiling as if it was an ace in a hole.

"One more thing. Bella is an FBI agent. I don't want her husband, baby or her injured at any point. Do whatever you can to protect her. Don't tell her I told you. She might give in and tell her husband. He is an honest guy and I want to keep him out of all this mess," explained the director.

That night the task force sat around the dining room table eating Chinese food and drinking wine. No one said anything. It was very quiet. Suddenly the door was being pounded. It was Louis, the informant.

"I need a place to stay. The Governor had the pathologist to make a special report for him. Juan told the Governor that two males were in the van with the girls. In his report, only one male body was found in the van. This male is black and I am white. The Governor sent his men out to the crash sight to see if they could find me. Juan knows me. I have worked years and years for him. My body was not found. They are looking for me. They know I am the whistle-blower. If they find me, they will kill me. I need a place to hide out. They will never think I am here," explained Louis as his lips, hands, and legs could not stop shaking.

"Okay, you can stay in the basement. Only come out when we are here. The basement has a full bathroom, radio, and TV, that should be enough for a self-imposed captive," stated Allie with a wide smile on her face.

The day's events took a toll on the Gangster Enforcers, which caused all of them to go to bed with a bottle of wine in their hands. Lynn, Jake, Lucky, Tom. and Allie all just wanted to finish the job and get back to living a square person's lifestyle.

Lucky wanted to be back on his house boat in Florida fishing. Jake wanted to be in Vegas betting on the ponies. Lynn wanted to find a man and cook for him. Allie and Tom wanted to get married and raise their two children that were on their way. Anything can happen during the night and that's what scares Allie the most.

CHAPTER 36

T HE NEXT MORNING, the gang got up early. Lynn cooked a great breakfast. Everyone was still hungover from yesterday's events. Jake grabbed his gun and strapped it to his ankle. The rest of the gang did the same thing. They realized, danger was lurking around the corner.

"Hello, everyone! I had a great peaceful night's sleep. It has been a long time since I slept that well," said Louis with a smile on his face like a kid who had just found money from the tooth fairy.

"All of us are going to be leaving and going to work. Remember, you are to stay in the basement while we are gone. Here is a gun. Keep it with you in case you need it. We will be home very late. Take food with you to the basement. Remember to follow order, *stay alive*," stated Allie with a concerned look on her face.

Allie was sitting at her desk when she started hearing a lot of noise coming from the basement. She asked Tom and Jake to go to the basement to find out where it was coming from.

To Tom and Jake's surprise, the basement was full of equipment and girls cutting and bagging up the drugs. All the girls were dressed in two-piece swim suits. On one side of the room was used for counting and wrapping the money. The drug supply side had an armed guard with a rifle walking around the room. His job was to make sure the girls were not stealing and continued to work until the whistle blew for them to take a break.

Vonda was in the adjacent room. She had a camera in which everything that was going on was within her eye sight. Without any warning, Vonda entered the drug/money room. She went up to the guard, looked into his eyes and quickly pulled out her pistol and shot him in the head.

"That will send a message to all of you. Don't steal anything, not even a dollar or an ounce of drugs. If you do, you will end up at the bottom of the ocean. Tom and Jake, clean up this shit!" yelled Vonda and she walked back to her desk as if everything that just happened was all in a day's work.

Tom and Jake found a large rug upstairs and rolled the guard up in the rug. They put him in the trunk of Jake's car but took pictures of the guard to send to Allie. The picture had a note with the date and time, stating Vonda's handy work.

When Allie saw what Vonda had done, she called Juan and told him she believed Vonda was losing control and he needed to do something about it. Juan said he would take care of it.

Late that evening Juan met with Allie and her team. He wanted to go over the final arrangements for the New Year's Eve party. Bella heard about the meeting and surprised everyone when she walked in unannounced.

"Hello, everyone! You can't have a party without me. I am the party. My singing will bring everyone to their feet. My food selection will be the best that money can buy. So just continue and I will join in when I am needed," stated Bella looking very happy.

"I have the security under control. As guests enter the foyer with their invitation, Lynn will take a picture of them holding their invitations up to their chests and without their mask on. She will collect the invitation and they will put their gifts on the gift table. If it is an envelope with money, it will be dropped into a locked box.

No weapons will be allowed. Everyone will be searched for guns or weapons. The security guards have been handpicked by me. My job is under control," stated Jake with a confident spirit surrounding him.

"It will be Christmas in a few days, and I'd like to do something that is fun. Let's have a small Christmas party with just us and maybe a girlfriend or boyfriend, and close friends. I'd like to invite the governor. We can have a small room at the club reserved for us. Bella's band can play and she can sing. This will get us in the holiday spirit. Maybe for one night we can forget about killing someone. Otherwise, a moratorium on any activity involving criminals," said Allie with hope all over her face.

Everyone agreed and Tom and Allie looked pleased because they felt that the oil was protecting her and Tom from all evil. Allie also remembered she was pregnant with twins and did not want to be caught up in any situations that would stress her out.

When Allie got home, the first thing she did was to look for Louis. He was the only person that could unravel the governor's power. Without Louis's testimony, the governor would not be convicted of anything unless there were others who would come forward and help to convict the governor.

To Allie's surprise, Louis had left the basement. The task force looked inside and outside the house and could not find Louis. The task force decided to go looking for him. He was not driving so he could not have gone far. As they were looking for Louis, it was getting close to midnight and Allie was getting nervous because her and Tom needed to rub the oil on their hands.

Tom looked at Allie and knew exactly what she was thinking. "Don't worry, sweetheart, I got some oil with me. I carry a small amount with me all the time. It is our life line. I would not leave home without it," stated Tom with a smile on his face.

New Orleans was full of bars and finding the right one that Louis might be at was almost impossible. Jake remembered the bar that he first recruited Louis years ago to work as an informant was located in the South Side Creoles territory. Louis had family in that neighborhood and most likely was with them. As Allie and Tom was walking past a bar, one of the customers saw Allie and yelled out to her.

"The word is out that you are black. Welcome to the family. I am Malachi Wallace's nephew, Pee Wee. Come in and have a drink with your family member. Miss wannabe white gal. I know this man you are with. He locked me up several time. I understand he now works for the governor. So, you see a criminal lies in all of us. Even big shot Mr. Donovan," stated Pee Wee, feeling proud of himself.

Allie and Tom stepped inside the bar. It looked okay on the outside but inside had a dirt floor that was covered with cigarette butts. Most of the customers were black with a few white women hanging onto the black guys. The jukebox was playing some great R&B songs. Allie and Tom decided to stay and let their hair down for one night. Tom's hat and the oil would protect them from any danger.

Allie ordered cranberry juice and Tom ordered Bourbon. The bar was very smoky and very hard to see people. As Allie was sipping on her cranberry juice, she felt a light tap on her shoulder. She looked around it was Louis.

"Louis, we told you not to leave the basement. The governor has his people looking for you," stated Allie, looking upset over the situation.

"I needed a break. After all I that have gone through, I just want to get high and relax. The FBI has my statement on video tape. If anything happens to me, the governor will still go down. Order me a double hit of bourbon and I will be right back. I have to go take a bathroom break," explained Louis as he slurred his words.

"Oh no! Vonda and Juan just walked in," said Lynn.

Allie got up and rushed back to the men's room. "Louis, climb through the window and go home. Don't stop until you get there! Juan and Vonda are here and they are searching for you. You should have stayed in one of the FBI's safe houses. Please do as I say and go home.

"Allie, there are no windows in this bathroom. What should I do?" responded Louis.

"Stay put, and I will get Lynn. Lock the door, and stay quiet," stated Allie as she returned to the table and grabbed Lynn.

"Lynn we have a problem. Louis is in the bathroom and he needs to get out now. The bathroom doesn't have any windows. Can you go in the back and see if any of the girls are wearing a wig? If so, give her big money for the wig and some female clothes," responded Allie with a rushed look on her face.

Lynn came back with everything, and Louis put on the wig and clothes. He walked right past Juan and winked at him and said in a deep, sexy voice, "Hello, good-looking. Hope to see you around sometime."

Tom, Allie, Lynn, Lucky, and Jake were having such a great evening that they forgot about Louis and his situation. Allie wanted to tell the gang she was pregnant but decided to wait until the Christmas Party to break the good news.

The task force was walking around the corner, heading toward a dark alley when Pee Wee jumped out in front of them. "Tomorrow I am going to be rich. The governor's contract on a sorry ass informant was enforced by me. I was standing outside smoking a joint when he took off his wig and I recognized him without even thinking about it. It was Louis the rat. I killed him, and I got his head in this sack to prove he is dead. This will make the governor's day. Thank you, thank you, Governor, for this is my big payday. $100,000, and I don't have to split it with anyone," stated Pee Wee bursting with joy.

"I will go see the FBI director first thing in the morning and tell him about what happened. We need to leave Pee Wee alone until we get the governor. We can make him testify against Governor for ordering the hit on Louis," stated Allie with warm tears flowing down her face.

Allie was sitting at her desk and Tom walked in. "We need to talk. Things are getting out of hand and we need to take the governor out as soon as possible," stated Tom, sounding like a gangster.

Before Allie could respond, Bella was standing at the door. "Hello, lovebirds. Can I come in? I have come up with a great idea for the entertainment for the party. I heard Tom singing in his office and Allie told me she loves to sing. Therefore, the three of us can be the entertainment during the last hour of the New Year's Eve party. What do you two think?" asked Bella.

Both Allie and Tom agreed it was a good idea. They could practice with the band the day before and Tom had some of his original songs that he was eager to sing. His songs were love songs that focused on his love for Allie. Allie did not know about Tom's songs and he wanted to surprise her New Year's Eve with a ring and a formal marriage proposal.

The governor was feeling great. His legal battles he felt were over, and the Christmas party was a great way to start enjoying the holiday and his granddaughter. The next few days were very quiet, until Bella over heard the governor talking to his lieutenant.

"I am very blessed. My bloodline is of pure-white blood. My granddaughter is white all the way to the bone. We are descendants of Vikings. They never mingled with blacks," stated the governor with pride.

After hearing the governor, Bella was upset. She believed she was white, but she never questioned her mother about her ancestors. She didn't even know that her mother was a twin. Laura never wanted to talk about her sister or her family. Ella was nothing like Laura. She worked for the underworld organization as an enforcer. Another name for an enforcer is killer.

Bella had some old papers of her mother's and decided after what she heard the governor say about black people, it was time to look into her family's background. The first group of papers were just old paid bills. Next she saw a picture of her mother and another girl who looked just like her standing together with their arms around each other. On the back was a dated and a note stating twin sisters, Laura and Ella Basset.

"Why didn't my mother tell me she had a twin sister? All these years I lived without any family, thought Bella.

"Oh my, here is a picture of my grandparents. My grandmother was a black woman," said Bella quietly to herself.

On the back of the picture, their names were noted, and they were identified as grandparents.

As Bella looked closely through the papers she found her birth certificate. The name of her father was left blank. Bella was upset but started crying when she remembered what she heard the governor say about his bloodline being solid white. All she could think about was protecting her baby.

The only person Bella wanted to tell about her discovery was her husband. She felt he loved her and it would not matter that she had black ancestors.

As she ran into the kitchen, her husband was playing with the baby. They looked so good together but she knew, she needed to tell him what she had just discovered.

Without thinking, Bella just shouted out, "I am black!" At that point she fainted. Marc rushed to catch her before she hit the floor. He caught her and as she was coming to, he stated with a big grin on his face, "You are the love of my life. I married for love. If it makes you feel better, I was told you had a black grandmother. Your grandmother was a famous singer and dancer in France. I was told this shortly after I met you, by a girl from Harrisonville who was trying to hit on me. Your talent is in your genes. Sorry baby, I love you today more than the day I married you."

As Bella and Marc sat talking, she was still concerned about the governor and his feelings about black people. Bella and Marc decided that it would be better to keep their secret and the baby would be told about the family history when she was old enough to understand.

Allie, Lynn, and Bella wanted to look dressed to impress at the Christmas party. The three of them went shopping together. All three of them had secrets and did not plan to share anything with each other.

Bella looked a little off but she did her best to hide her feelings from the ladies. It was a great shopping day. They all purchased dresses that made them look stunning and beautiful. The Christmas party was tomorrow night, and the ladies wanted it to be a great night for everyone, even the governor.

This would be the governor's last Christmas as a free man. New Year's Day he was going to be locked up on a long list of charges.

Only Allie knew that this was going to happen. The FBI wanted it to be kept quiet so that they could round up other key players of the underworld organization at the same time. This operation was labeled Operation Turning Point.

The hall at the club was decorated like a Christmas fairy tale. As the three girls entered the hall, all eyes turned to them. Tom was talking to the governor, Jake was looking at one of the waitresses, Lucky was at the bar, Juan was sitting at the table with Vonda eating barbecue ribs. Vonda felt left out because Allie, Lynn, and Bella seem to have found a new friendship that she was missing out of.

Bella saw that Vonda was not very happy and decided to start the entertainment early. The room was full with family and friends. Bella was dressed as if she was her grandmother. Her dress was a red silk strapless dress. It appeared to be made just for her. Her dress left nothing to your imagination. She wore a flapper's headband in her hair. It was definitely a throwback look. Marc was a proud husband. He knew the Christmas party guests were in for a real treat. Bella turned to the band gave them a signal to start playing.

"I always wanted to write my own songs so tonight you will be the first to hear my originals. Feel free to shout, dance, or just chair dance. Whatever makes you feel good tonight," stated Bella with her body gearing up to let it all out.

The beat from the band was just right.

Bella bellowed out, "Came home early from work and my so called friends were trying to put a speakeasy in my house. Cigarettes butts and beer cans all over the floor. I had to stumble over two people to get through the front door. These so call friends of mine were trying to put speakeasy in my house. Yes, these so call friends of mine were trying to put a speakeasy in my house.

"I started to the bedroom, but it would have been too much for me to bear. Pour me a glass of bourbon. If I can't beat them, then I will join them. These so called friends of mine are trying to put a speakeasy in my house."

Bella and the band's musicians got down with this song and the party was up and running. Bella danced and sang for a long time.

Everyone was on the floor dancing. Without any warning, Marc jumped up on the stage with Bella and grabbed the mic. He was a little tipsy but so was everyone in the room. Only Bella knew he had a great voice and was happy he was going to show off his talent.

With his other hand, he grabbed Bella.

"Baby let me rock you with this good old sexy stuff, until you can't get enough. Baby let me rock you with this good old sexy stuff, until you can't get enough," sang Marc until his face was bright red.

Bella looked around and Tom was on the stage. He took the mic and started singing.

"A man makes his music but the love of his woman keeps him alive," sang Tom with a golden voice. His song was nice and slow. Jake was slow dancing with Lynn and Lucky took control of Vonda. Juan found a partner and everyone enjoyed Tom's song and the band's music.

Just before the party was over, the governor thanked Allie and Bella for putting together a great party. As the governor was leaving the stage, Juan pulled him aside and said, "we need to talk."

"The FBI are going to arrest you on New Year's Day. They have a long list of criminal charges against you. Even sex trafficking of those young girls that were be transported in our van. This all came from my contact with the FBI.

I am leaving with Vonda to go back home to Colombia. We will return someday when the heat dies down. All the cash belongs to me. I will leave you the drugs. You can sell the drugs to the territory leaders at a reduced price," explained Juan looking very determined to get his way. "Oh no, half of the money belongs to me. You will not leave here with that money, over my dead body. I took all the risk and you walked around like a big shot, you and that crazy sister!" yelled the governor.

"You can't stop me. The money left an hour ago. We will be leaving now. My private jet is waiting for us. Hasta luego, my good friend," said Juan will a wide smile on his face.

CHAPTER 37

BELLA DECIDED TO tell Marc everything about herself and her situation. She didn't know that Tom was her half-brother who had been looking for her. Knowing he was her half-brother would be joyful news for her. In fact, it would be a wonderful Christmas gift. The gift of having a loving family.

"Marc, my name is not Bella. It is Joni Basset. I was born in Harrisonville, NC. I do not know who my father is but whoever he is, my mother loved him, even on her death bed.

"I was recruited by Mr. Stevenson an FBI officer who recruited honor roll college seniors. He told me that Harrisonville was the hub for organized crime. As we sat, he convinced me to join him in the fight to stop or slow down the underworld organization in New Orleans.

"He knew we were dating and that your father was a crooked politician. We both agreed that he needed to be stopped. I love you and I am not willing to give you up. Therefore, the FBI protected us all the way. You are the only one who knows I am an agent. Now you are married to a black agent.

"They changed my name so that I couldn't be traced back to Harrisonville. I loved my name, and hopefully one day, I will be Joni Basset Dumont again," explained Bella, looking as if the world was closing in on her.

"Bella, the governor is my stepfather. He loved my mother and her two-month old baby boy, me. I do not have his criminal genes. He gave me the love of a father and was a great provider. My mother's passing, broke his heart. That is when he turned into a criminal. He felt he had nothing to live for. I have known for a long time what he had become but overlooked his business dealings. He has gone too far. It is stated time to reel him in," stated Marc.

"You do know that he is the head of the mob here in Louisiana. He controls everything. He has ordered people killed and in some cases killed them himself. He is a very bad person. We need to leave now before all hell breaks loose. He is going to be arrested in a few days. If he finds out our baby has black blood. Who knows what he might do. The FBI has a safe house that we can use. I will call the director and let him know we are heading to the safe house," explained Bella.

As Bella was packing some clothes, Allie and Tom were at her front door. Tom wanted some answers from Bella. He was convinced that she knew his half-sister was Joni. The thing that gave her away was her talent. Plus, Allie's great-aunt told Tom he had already found Joni.

"Bella are you Joni Basset from Harrisonville, NC?" asked Tom.

"Yes, why do you want to know?" replied Bella.

"I am your half brother. Jesse Donovan was our father," responded Tom.

"You and Allie must go. We are getting out while we are still vertical. You are criminals and I need to get away from all of this because my baby might be in danger," explained Bella.

"We are here to protect you. We are FBI agents. We know you are also but we were not allowed to tell you. The director feared it might blow your cover. We need to stay put and let the FBI do their job," explained Allie with a concerned look on her face.

"I just told Marc about my background and how I became an FBI agent.

"There is more to my story. I met Marc in college and was dating him. The FBI wanted me to infiltrate his father's network of crimi-

360

nal activities. The FBI didn't know at the time the governor was the mob leader. They were looking to take down the Brotherhood. The Brotherhood was mainly the top dog in New Orleans. Just before I married Marc, I found out the governor was next in line to take over all of Louisiana when Jesse Donovan passed away.

"Jesse Donovan was not a killer. He found ways to keep things going without having to kill someone himself. In a few cases, he had to have a person eliminated," explained Bella, feeling relieved.

"Sorry to tell you, but Jesse Donovan was your father. That is why he paid for all your education. He loved Laura, even though he was married to my mother," stated Tom, relieved that he found Joni.

Tom took out his wallet and pulled out a folded up letter and handed the letter to Bella. "The letter explains everything and our father loved both of us and wanted me to find you. I hope we can be good friends when the governor and the Brotherhood no long are functioning." stated Tom.

Bella took the letter and before she could finish, tears started rolling down her pretty light pink cheeks. Tom told her to sit down and he would read the letter out loud to everyone. When he finished, the room was extremely quiet. Everyone was lost for words. Finally, Marc broke the ice by saying, "This has been a day full of surprises. Some good and some not so good but we have to accept the bad with the good," explained Marc as if he was in control.

Lucky looked at the group and felt that it was time for him to step up to the plate. "I like to say something. During the New Year's Eve party, the Brotherhood will be put out of business. If they go, so does all the territory mob leaders. They all answer to the Brotherhood. When the guest pictures are taken, the FBI lab division will be in a room across from the foyer. If that guest's picture shows up on the FBI's most wanted list, they will be arrested on the spot. If anyone has an outstanding warrant or anything criminal, they will also be arrested.

"We have concluded that all the territory leaders and their soldiers will go down at the party. We will not make a big deal out of it. The FBI will quietly remove them. The governor will not notice that they were removed. We will give a few of them a lesser sentence if they give names and other information that will lead to the arrest of police officers, politicians, and other elected officials that have participated in criminal misconduct. Allie has already turned in a list of names who are working with the governor's underworld operation.

If a guest is on that list, they will be arrested during the party. We will have busses ready to take them to a processing center. This will be the biggest mob round up that ever hit New Orleans. We will be sending a message that the FBI is open for business," stated Lucky with a wide grin on his partially wrinkled face with a few gray hairs protruding from his chin.

"Is there anyone keeping an eye on the governor?" asked Bella.

"Yes, all the hired help is now working with the FBI. We know everything he is doing. Even when he is using the bathroom. He is not going to get away from us. By the way, Juan and Vonda have gone to Colombia. We let them go. They will be dealt with later," explained Lucky.

Little did the group know that Lucky had his own plans for the governor. He wanted to kill him the same way he killed his father. Cut his throat and let him bleed out. That is what the governor did to his father who was running for longshoremen's union leader.

Vonda was definitely out of control and going back to Colombia was the best ending for the Orejuelas, whom the director planned to deal with later.

"Vonda and I go way back. She knew me before I changed my name. We were good friends. She was the first female I met when I started dating Marc. She was already working big time for the mob as an enforcer. She once told me she got most of her training in the Juvenile Detention Center while working for the Brotherhood. The Wallace family found out that she was related to the Orejuela Cartel in Colombia and used her influence with her family to start shipping drugs of all kind to New Orleans.

"When I changed my name, I told her that I was on the run from the FBI and needed a new identity. She believed me and didn't question any part of my story. She protected me from everyone. She told me how Tom was looking for me. She didn't know why, but Tom being in law enforcement left a bad taste in her mouth. That is why she went to Harrisonville to scare Tom off. If she knew I was FBI, she would have killed me."

CHAPTER 38

"WELL, THAT'S MY story. Oh, I asked the owner of Harrison Paradise Club to give us a smaller room for the New Year's Eve Party. A smaller room will make up for the fact that we plan to take down many of the mob leaders. The smaller room will make everything look normal.

"I also, invited the Harrison family to the party. They are a very nice family. Nick and Eva work very hard trying to make New Orleans a better place to live for all its residents and at the same time, provide quality legal service for the needy. They are Lola's aunt and uncle. Nate and Zola work with all the churches and non-profit organizations in the community to help the poor. They are the parents of Lola and Father Kevin. Ted, Lola's husband, works with Nick and Eva at their law firm. Father Kevin is a devoted priest in our community, who tries to introduce God to all who are seeking help and redemption," explained Bella feeling proud.

"Bella, can we now call you Joni?" asked Marc with a silly look on his face.

"Marc, whatever makes you happy. I am happy to know I have a family and our baby will grow up knowing she is part of a loving, caring, and honest family," responded Bella, looking extremely over joyed.

"Everyone, listen up. Tom and I decided to get married after the party. We have asked Father Kevin to perform the service. One more thing, I am pregnant with twins, a girl and a boy. I am only a few weeks along but some of you might say, how do I know all of this. That part is a secret," explained Allie with watery eyes of joy.

Tom sat back in his chair and was trying to remember what was in his father's notebook. After a short period, he got up and went into the bedroom and retrieved the notebook that was tucked under the mattress. As he was flipping through the pages, he found what he was looking for. It was a chart of several family trees of people who lived in Harrisonville and some of them, later moved to New Orleans.

The notebook had several pages devoted to Ellen Laura Basset who was Joni's mother. He listed Joni Basset as the daughter of Jesse Donovan and Ellen Laura Basset. The next names were Ellen Laura Basset and Ella Lynn Basset twin daughters of Jerry Basset and Josephine White Basset. Grandparents were listed as Conor Donovan and Vera Donovan.

Ella Lynn Basset married the gangster from Chicago Eddie Esposito and they had a daughter named Zola. Zola married one of the Harrison twins (Nate Harrison, both of them, were criminals until they were saved by God).

Nate and Zola were the parents of twins. Father Kevin Harrison and his twin sister Lola. Lola married Ted Woodson.

The notebook had a special message for Joni.

Dear Joni,

You are not alone. Your cousins will welcome you with open arms.

Father Kevin Harrison and Lola Esposito Harrison are your first cousins. Even though they do not know you very well. They have always known about you. Your mother over the years kept them informed about you. Your mother didn't want them to visit, in fear that the town's people would find out that you have black blood.

I feared that if it was known, your mother would have been forced to leave Harrisonville and she wanted to be near me. Yes, my daughter you do have friends and family. May God bless you and keep you safe.

Love,
Father

After reading the notebook pages, Tom called Joni into the bedroom. "Joni, this is for you. The information on these pages, should have been shared with you years ago. But like the old saying goes, "better late than never," said Tom with a nice comforting smile on his face.

When Joni finished reading, she dropped to her knees with tears flowing down her beautiful pink cheeks. "I should be mad as hell but I am not. Things happen for a reason and only God knows the beginning, middle, and the end. I am proud and glad to have a family. Not just any kind of family but one that thinks highly of each other and are loving people.

With the new babies coming. My little girl will grow up with cousins, and an aunt and uncle who will love her always," stated Joni with tears of joy flowing down her face.

After sharing Joni's information with the rest of the group, Allie said, "Let's get back to business."

The lieutenant governor informed the governor about his criminal dilemma with the FBI and his options on how to proceed. What the both of them did not know was that the FBI had a recording of Louis's testimony about the governor's involvement with all areas of underworld criminal activities which included murder.

"I don't know what they have on you, Governor, but it must be big stuff. The word is out that you are going to be arrested on New Year's Day. Don't worry, I will be a good replacement. I will run the Brotherhood with a professional touch. It appears that they don't have anything on me. I hope I don't have anything to worry about," said Robert, the lieutenant governor.

"Everyone has something to worry about. Believe me, the FBI knows about you. They know you are second in command of the Brotherhood. You were with me the night those whores died. If they get me, they will surely bring you down with me. I hope you understand what I am telling you," explained the governor looking calm and cool.

The governor felt he needed a plan. Spending time in jail would never be part of any plan of his. He felt that he would rather die first, then to spend any time in jail. The governor sat in his favorite chair with a glass of bourbon in his hand. After a short period of time he fell asleep. Without trying, he started dreaming. In his dream he was in court, defending himself against crimes against humanity.

The prosecutor stood up and said, "We are charging Governor Nicolas with crimes against humanity, which are murder, sex offenses, kidnapping/abduction, bribery, burglary, gambling, prostitution, drug trafficking, human trafficking, weapon law violations, liquor law violations, and more will be added later. How do you plead?" asked the prosecutor.

"Not guilty, because of a genetic defect. I am a criminal because my ancestors were criminals with the criminal gene. That gene was passed down to me. The criminal gene comes from both sides of the family," explained the governor.

"So that is your defense. Not guilty by genetic defect. Okay, enter it into the records," said the judge.

The governor woke up and was wet all over. The thought of even being charged with anything was scary. The governor took a few more sips of the bourbon that he was holding on to very tightly and fell back to sleep.

In his dream, a man they called Lucky held a knife up to the governor's throat. I'm going to kill you. It won't be now but it will happen. You will bleed out like a pig the way you killed my father. My father was a good man and would have made an outstanding president of the Longshoremen's Union.

"Killing you will be payback for my father and all the lives you have destroyed through the Brotherhood. Your hatred of black people has made you wealthy. Their lives are miserable without any hope, because of you selling them drugs," stated Lucky with anger in his voice.

"Wake up, Governor, you are having a nightmare. It is a big one. You are shaking all over. Man, you are sweating like a pig. Whatever you were dreaming it has you all shook up. Have a few slips of your bourbon. It will help to relax you. You need something maybe a little stronger than bourbon. I have some weed. Let me light you up a joint," said Robert, his lieutenant governor.

"Thanks, Robert, it was an awful dream. I was in court for multiple criminal charges and felt that I was going to be convicted on all of the charges. Jail is not in my vocabulary," responded the governor.

"The New Year's Eve party is tomorrow, and I need to get ready for my guests. It is going to be a party that will be remembered for many years to come. During the party, a helicopter will take me out the country, to Columbia. Juan and Vonda will pick me up," responded the governor with a quivering, trembling tone of voice.

Jake, the communications specialist for the Gangster Enforcers, without anyone knowing it, put a surveillance system in the governor's office and all the rooms of his house. When Jake heard that the governor planned to leave the country to keep from being arrested, Jake decided to kill the governor before the party started.

Joni, Lynn, and Allie were excited about the New Year's Eve party. Joni's costume was a copy of Josephine White's most famous performance outfit. The dress was very provocative and left nothing to your imagination. She looked just like her great-grandmother and she felt good.

Lynn was of Irish heritage and her costume was a mystic renaissance medieval Irish dress. Allie dress like a slave, for she wanted everyone to know she was proud of her being who she was. After all, she didn't choose her parents but was glad to have been born. Becoming Mrs. Thomas Donovan would be one of the most joyful days of her life. It was now time to put on their costumes and get to the club.

Tom, was suited up like a Western outlaw. In his holster was a real gun. Tom knew that with this large group of criminals, it was better to be prepared. He was also wearing his nicest cowboy hat. He felt untouchable and walked around the ballroom with a big smile on his face from cheek to cheek.

Lucky and Jake were dressed up like medieval soldiers. They walked around the ballroom with a small gun tucked in their shoe, just in case they needed to react to a situation quickly.

At 10:00 p.m., New Year's Eve, most of the guests had arrived. The FBI had all their people in place. As the guests arrived, Lynn took a picture of each and they were searched for weapons. The FBI was in a separate room with a surveillance camera, observing each guest as they entered the ballroom. If they were on the FBI's list of wanted suspects, they were taken to a special room and arrested. Just about every fifth person was arrested. Everything was going very smoothly until the governor arrived.

The governor was high off of alcohol and drugs. The band was playing some great songs. Dancing and having fun was surely on display at the party. The food was displayed with a touch of New Orleans. On a table by itself was a barbecued whole pig. Around the pig were colorful decorations made from veggies that were typical of New Orleans.

The governor jumped up on stage to welcome everyone to his party and to thank them for their gifts and for coming.

"This evening, I want all of you to eat and be merry. This is a day that will go into the books. The food is great and my daughter-in-law will be the last performer and you are in for a real treat. She performs like a black person but she is white all way to the bone. So let's hear it for Bella," said the governor as he jumped off the stage.

Allie was sitting at the bar drinking cranberry juice. The governor's speech and the sound of his voice made her go ballistic. His negative statement about blacks gave her the courage to charge the stage and tell the governor off or put him in his place.

Tom looked up and his beautiful woman, the love of his life was on the stage. He knew whatever she was going to say would shock the governor and the guests. Tom took a deep breath, and Allie began.

"The governor is right. Bella whose name is really Joni Basset Nicolas is the great grand-daughter of the famous Josephine White Basset who was a black entertainer living in France and married a Frenchmen. She is black and inherited her great grand-mother's musical skills. So, Mister Governor, she is only partially black, all the way to the bone.

"I just want to add one more thing. I am also partially black and proud of it. It is a person's character that defines them and not the color of their skin or their parents," said Allie with watery eyes.

Within seconds, Joni and her husband were on the stage with Allie hugging her. "To all of you who want to hear Joni, let's give it up for her. The guests started clapping and the band lit the room up with loud great rocking music. Joni, do your thing!" yelled Marc.

The governor was so embarrassed that he left the ballroom. Jake was keeping eye on the governor for he was going to kill him for murdering his father. Jake had consumed several glasses of bourbon and was totally smashed. Even though he was drunk, he still understood what he wanted to do.

"Governor, Governor, I need to talk to you," said Jake.

"Oh, another nigger hanging on to me," responded the governor.

"Can we go outside. I have something very important to tell you," said Jake.

As they were going outside, Jake was considering how he was going to kill the governor. Without much thought, he grabbed governor around his neck with a full nelson hold. Then he took his pocket knife and cut his throat. The blood was going everywhere. Jake dropped the governor, and he fell to the ground.

"This is for all your crimes committed against humanity. You are surely going to hell!" stated Jake.

Jake did not go back into the party. He just walked down the street until he got home.

Tom was very proud of Allie for her courage and honesty. After Joni finished entertaining the guests the band continued to play great music. It was almost midnight and Tom needed to find Allie. She needed to take her last drop of the oil before twelve o'clock. Allie and Joni both saw Tom and ran over to him. Tom put the bottle up to her mouth and then to his, just as the clock struck twelve o'clock.

Joni saw Pee Wee coming towards Tom, looking like a monster. She pulled out her small pistol from under her dress and was ready to shoot Pee Wee. As Pee Wee got closer, Joni saw a knife in his hand. It was aimed directly at Tom. Just before he could stab Tom in the stomach, Joni shot Pee Wee in the heart, and he was dead before he hit the floor.

Tom was shocked over what had just happened. Allie's great-aunt was right. Joni, his half sister, did save his life. The band was now playing "Auld Lang Syne." Everyone stopped what they were doing and started singing.

"I guess the hat and oil also saved me," stated Tom with a big smile on his face.

All the members of the Gangster Enforcers were still in the ballroom except Jake when the FBI director walked in. Jake went home.

"I am very proud to let you know that the top leaders of the Brotherhood have been booked. Hopefully, we can get the governor tomorrow," said the FBI director with joy.

Just then an agent burst into the room and yelled out, "The governor is dead. Someone killed him!"

Allie and Tom looked at each other for they knew it was Jake who took out the governor. Killing the governor was first on Jake's list. Plus, he was missing from the meeting.

"Well, that is one more criminal that the taxpayers won't have to spend money on for room and board. I believe he is from Harrisonville, NC. Tom, that is also your hometown, right? Harrisonville can be very proud of producing an outstanding law enforcer like you.

"To begin with, I'd like to thank the Gangster Enforcers for their fine work and leadership. The big cheese is also gone, the governor.

"At the party, we arrested ninety-four criminals and one lieutenant governor. To keep from going to jail for life, he has agreed to testify against all ninety-four criminals. We also know the locations of each territory leader's warehouse that stores the drugs and money. Everything will dry up for a while. But just like weeds, the leaders, drugs, and criminals will come back. Therefore, we must stay active and do our part to keep shutting them down.

"Tom, I like for you to think about running for governor of Louisiana. There will have to be a special election within a few months to replace the governor and his lieutenant. We need you and law enforcement will back you 100 percent," said the director.

"Yes, I would be honored to run and I already have a suitable lieutenant governor in mine. We all know him. He is working for people of this state without asking for anything in return. His name is Nick Harrison. I will ask him to be my running mate. Allie and I are getting married. It will be tomorrow.

"Father Kevin Harrison has agreed to marry us. He is a blessing from God. The weather is going to be very nice tomorrow and at noon we will tie the knot. Everything will take place right here, in the club house garden. All of you are invited," stated Tom with joy all over his face.

When the taskforce got home, the front door was wide open. Jake was sitting at the kitchen table with patches of blood all over his face and clothes. No one said a word. Tom and Lucky walked over to him and took him by the arm and led him to his room. There they took off his clothes and put him in the shower. Lucky destroyed his clothes and tucked him into his bed.

No one said a word. But they all knew what had occurred. "My mother always said don't say anything about the dead unless it is good. Good, the governor is dead," stated Lynn with smile on her face.

That was the end of that conversation.

CHAPTER 39

DRUGS AND CASH were still in the taskforce office basement, but the FBI arrived early to pick up the money and drugs. The director was with them and he explained to Allie and Tom that this was the first stop. They had a list of all the other warehouses, and would be working hard for a few days retrieving and logging all the evidence. Once again, he thanked them for their service. He also told Allie that he was putting in a recommendation that she be promoted to crew leader for organized crime.

Allie and Tom's day finally had come. It was a day made in heaven. The sun was brighter than it had been in weeks. The air had a warm breeze to it. The guests were dressed to impress. The Harrison family arrived early with Father Kevin. Tom was walking around greeting their guests. He saw Joni and grabbed her hand.

"I have some family members that I want you to meet," stated Tom, feeling really good. As he approached the Harrisons, Father Kevin said, "Hello Joni. We were hoping to meet you before the ceremony started. I'd like to introduce you to your family. To start with, Lola and I are twins and we are your cousins. Zola is our mother, and your mother's niece. Nate is our father, and his twin brother is Nick. So there you go, family that was brought together today by the Holy Father," stated Father Kevin with the holy spirit pouring out of him.

It was now time for the big event. Allie was dressed in a beautiful white silk long wedding gown with pink flowers around the waist. She looked like she just stepped out of a magazine. Tom was in a white tuxedo with a pink band around his waist to match Allie's flowers.

Her bouquet of flowers was raised and arranged by Lola. The garden was full of seasonal plants. What a gorgeous sight to see. Father Kevin announced to the guests that he would like to say a few words before he started the wedding ceremony.

"What a great day. We all know where we been but only God knows where we are going. Today two people who met on a lonely highway are joining together as husband and wife. Tom and my family are from Harrisonville, NC, and our pasts have shaped our future. Many of you were born with the criminal gene but that is not a defense for how we should live.

"Our defense comes from God. He has delivered us from evil and his future plans for us are all good. So today we will celebrate this union between Tom and Allie. May all of you rise and say Amen," requested Father Kevin.

When the ceremony was over, Jake, Lucky, Tom, Lynn, and Allie gathered together and gave each other a big hug.

"It is all over. We can return home and live a normal life. I found my man. Lucky and I are a couple but we didn't want it to interfere with our work, therefore we didn't tell anyone. We plan to live on his houseboat in Florida and I will cook for the man of my dreams," stated Lynn with a smile on her face.

"I'm leaving for Vegas in the morning. The ponies are calling my name!" yelled Jake.

The FBI director approached the gang and once again thanked them for all their service. "May all of you go in peace but remember the work of the FBI is never done," stated the director.

"Let's toast to that. Amen!" yelled Allie.

ABOUT THE AUTHOR

ALICE J. HARRIS-WOOD is the founder of The Fisher House, a group home for seniors. She wanted a place they could call home which provided all services at an affordable price. As a high school teacher, local civic leader, and church music director, she excelled. She is well-known in her town and surrounding areas for many years of dedicated service. Her dedication and success came from having a strong family foundation.

www.ingramcontent.com/pod-product-compliance
Lightning Source LLC
Chambersburg PA
CBHW030355030726
47497CB00002B/350